Born and raisehas
drawn on her ow   *eys*,
her first novel f   ral
contemporary   le
Jones. Her home   , North Wales.

CATRIN MORGAN

Lily of the Valleys

Futura

A Futura Book

ISBN 0 7088 4307 7

Reproduced, printed and bound in Great Britain by
BPCC Hazell Books Ltd
Member of BPCC Ltd
Aylesbury, Bucks, England

Futura Publications
A Division of
Macdonald & Co (Publishers) Ltd
Orbit House
1 New Fetter Lane
London EC4A 1AR
A member of Maxwell Macmillan Pergamon Publishing Corporation

To the memory of my grandfather,
Evan Jones,
and of my father,
Vivian Jones,
whose lives wrote Lily's story

PART ONE
1887–1888

He brought me unto the banqueting house
and his banner over me was love.

Song of Songs
Ch. II, v.4

CHAPTER ONE

South Wales: 1887

B RIGHT SUNLIGHT FLOODED the small front bedroom
in the top end house on Rhyswg Road. A frothy
white gown was gloriously displayed against the dark
mahogany of the wardrobe door. Margaret Ann Jones
was preparing for the big social event of her year.

'Margaret Ann – Dada says we'll be late if we don't
leave in ten minutes. What are you doing up there?
You're never still doing your hair? Tell me when you
want hooking into your frock and be quick!' Her
mother regarded lateness as the first step on the road
to hell. The Jones family were never late for the Whitsun Marching.

Margaret Ann stopped playing with the fine tendrils
of curly red-gold hair which escaped so flatteringly to
frame her small face. 'All right, Mam, I'm ready now.
Come up whenever you like.'

She was delighted with the half-clad image that
looked back at her from the mirror panel in the
wardrobe door. At seventeen, this was the first time
she would appear for the Whitsun Marching dressed
as a woman instead of as a child. Her mass of unruly
curls had been disciplined into a plaited chignon, but
the silky tresses never stayed in place and now curled
bewitchingly round her face like exotic ivy. The face
was small and heart shaped, with dazzling blue eyes

and the clear fair skin of the rare redhead who escapes freckles. Margaret Ann was tiny – barely five feet tall, with high round breasts and a classic handspan waist, further neatened today by murderously tight stays. The fine cotton drawers which covered her shapely legs were concealed in turn by a cascade of petticoats, their frills trimmed with cutwork embroidery. Only her small feet, neat in glossy black boots, peeped from beneath the flounces of white cotton.

Traditionally, female children, unmarried girls and many married women dressed all in white for the Marching. Margaret Ann was no exception. The colour in her outfit was provided by yards of narrow blue satin ribbon slotted through the flounces of the skirt, echoed by a broad blue velvet cummerbund, and by a posy of brightly-coloured silk flowers on her big straw hat.

Her mother bustled into the room, wearing the neatly-patterned dark blue silk gown she had chosen to accentuate the freshness of her daughter's dress. 'You're a vain one, aren't you?' she said, but in pride, not disapproval. 'Twirling around admiring yourself in your petticoats, were you? Well, give us that frock and I'll show you something really worth looking at!'

She reached up to the wardrobe and unhooked the hanger. An old sheet had already been spread on the floor to permit Margaret Ann to step into her frock and pull it on without marking the delicate fabric.

'*Diawch*, I hope you're really this small, girl! Don't seem possible now it's made up, do it?' Mrs Jones held out the blue cummerbund, its seventeen-inch span making it look more like an armband than a belt.

'Well, you measured me, Mam. Of course it's right.' Margaret Ann stepped into the foaming pile of material and her mother helped her draw it up around her slender body. It fitted without a wrinkle and the little belt clinched smoothly over the waist seam.

'That'll show them how a pretty young lady do look.

I made a job of that worthy of a Cardiff tailoress!' Her
mother's tone dripped satisfaction. This might be officially a religious festival, but in Mrs Jones's mind she
was preparing the girl for her debut at Court. With a
final flourish she positioned the straw hat and secured
it with two silver pins.

'Grandma's hatpins, too. What if I lost one, Mam?'

'Don't talk! You'll know better than to come home
here if you do!' But Mrs Jones's tone made it clear that
such an event was unthinkable.

As they descended the steep stairs into the long passage which passed for a hall, Margaret Ann's father let
out an appreciative gasp. 'You'll be the prettiest girl
there today, *cariad*. Lovely – really lovely!'

He ushered both women out of the house in front
of him and they set off down the hill to the village. At
first there was no one to look at their finery. Everyone
not planning to walk in the procession had gone to
watch it. This was the one time each year when it
was permissible to stare openly at your neighbour's
new clothes and speculate on how much they had
cost.

Abercarn's entertainment facilities were divided
about equally between Jehovah and Bacchus, with
seven chapels and the same number of pubs. Then
newly-built corrugated iron structure in which the
village's few Anglicans worshipped gave God a slight
edge. Whit Monday was the day on which everyone
with a claim to respectability proclaimed it publicly by
forming up in procession outside their place of worship and marching together like a fashion-conscious
army to an open air service in the park. After the
service everyone processed back to their respective
tabernacles for a hearty tea. They marched behind
silk banners which portrayed biblical scenes in violent
aniline colours, borne aloft by chosen teams of the most
important worshippers, and sang hymns as they went.

The less reputable members of the community invariably trailed behind the believers, dirty and barefoot, chanting music hall songs or children's doggerel, but the well-rehearsed voices of the godly usually drowned their caterwauling.

The Salvation Army band provided music, but it was a mixed blessing, as each chapel sang its own repertoire, and the contingents immediately preceding and following the Army invariably found themselves belting out 'Onward Christian Soldiers' or 'Love Divine' against the musicians' version of the 'Battle Hymn of the Republic'.

The Jones family worshipped at the Garn, a Congregationalist chapel at the top of the High Street. As William Jones shepherded his womenfolk up the road towards their starting point, Margaret Ann was already drawing compliments from the spectators who lined the roadside.

'I wish you were marching with us, Louisa,' he told his wife. 'Margaret Ann will have her head turned by all this fuss without you there by her.'

But Mrs Jones was one of the volunteer tea-makers today, and he was to be Margaret Ann's only chaperon. Mother and daughter embraced briefly outside the Sunday schoolroom where the tea preparations were already under way.

'Now mind you stay well in the centre and no waving to people by the road. And don't go too heavy with the singing at the start. Remember there'll be all the hymns at the *gymanfa* as well.'

'Oh, go on, Mam – you'd think I'd never marched before! Look, there's Mair Edwards over by there with her brother. We can go with them. Her Mam's doing the tea as well.'

Satisfied that her daughter was with the right companions, Mrs Jones moved off into the schoolroom. Margaret Ann smiled secretly. Mair was well-dressed,

but she was big and angular and her sallow complexion
suffered in contrast to her white dress. Her physical
shortcomings only pointed up Margaret Ann's petite
prettiness. They formed a neat line, with a couple
of the small girls from the junior Sunday school in
the middle and Margaret Ann's father and Mair's
brother at each end to protect them from unwelcome
approaches by strangers. Mair pouted slightly when
she saw the arrangement and whispered her dissatis-
faction.

'Just like Dafydd and your dada to see we don't have
any adventures,' she said. 'What chance will we get to
mix with anybody nice with them at the ends of the
row?'

'Don't be daft, girl! You know what it's like, once we
start off, with the junior boys' class shy-iking those little
rodneys from the Ranks who tag on the back. Dada an'
Dafydd will be so busy going to get them back in line
that we could join the Baptists without them noticing.
Stop worrying.' The two girls smiled conspiratorially at
one another as they took their hymn sheets from the
minister's wife.

The two brawny bearers who took the main weight of
the Garn banner on ebony poles hefted their burden
into shoulder-slung leather pouches and a somewhat
milksop Pre-Raphaelite image of Jesus curing the man
sick of the palsy was unfurled upon the sunny afternoon. Supporters fore and aft moved forward with the
gold satin ropes which stabilized the great silk sail and
the Garn contingent moved off at a dignified amble
to join the other groups of worshippers. Tenors and
baritones led them into their first hymn:

'We're marching to Zion,
Beautiful, beautiful Zion,
We're marching up unto Zion,
The beautiful city of God!'

Raggedly at first, then with mounting confidence, the contraltos and sopranos joined in. Mr Barrington, Sunday school teacher of the senior boys, marched backwards alongside the procession, conducting with his forefinger. 'Once more, now, to get us into good voice. . . We're MAR-ching to ZI-on, BEW-tiful, BEW-tiful ZI-on. . .' Satisfied that they were singing in time he faced forward again and strode out, still conducting. At the rear of the procession a gaggle of barefoot, dirty urchins capered and mocked him, arms flailing, puny chests puffed out. Margaret Ann silently wished he would stop making a fool of the congregation before they got down to the centre of the village where most of the spectators had gathered.

'When I see him behaving like that I wish we were Church,' hissed Mair. 'If one of their lot carried on like that, the vicar would have 'im out straight away.'

'Yes, but they'll never beat Chapel singing,' said Margaret Ann. 'I know he's an awful show-off but we've got the best tenors this side of Nantyglo.'

Just the same, she wished Barrington would stop his capering. Without his antics, the whole procession would have been smart and military, a worthy backdrop for her first grown-up frock.

They passed Parfitt's butcher shop and the warm air wafted a trace of sweet blood-smell to their nostrils. The abattoir behind the shop had been busy before the holiday week-end.

Just beyond the butcher's, the new recreation hall built by the local tinplate workers gave the street a little more dignity, preparing it for the small market square. Now they were in the main part of the village and people crowded the pavement to inspect their neighbours. The south side of the market square comprised a whole row of public houses – the Market, the New Inn, a couple of nameless beerhouses and, on the corner, Abercarn's nearest claim to an hotel, the Commercial. The Commercial catered for all sorts, with a respectable saloon bar and off-sales counter looking out across the market square, and a rough, low-ceilinged bottom bar opening on to the High Street at a lower level. Once it had been the inn's cellars, but for twenty years or more the landlord had made extra profits by throwing it open to those who could not afford saloon bar prices. The bottom bar had been closed for a couple of hours to avoid the risk of drunken customers staggering out into the path of the respectable marchers, but the upper bars were doing a lively trade. Plenty of the village's miners and tinplate workers preferred beer to public piety and the closest they got to the religious procession was to come out, tankards in hand, and gawp as it wound past the square.

Mair and Margaret Ann ostentatiously looked away, seeking more respectable sights, as they passed the Commercial, only to glance back hurriedly when they thought no one was watching them. After all, most of the attractive young men were gathered outside the pub, and neither girl wanted to miss the attention of a potential admirer.

He was standing at the open window of the saloon bar and staring fixedly at Margaret Ann. She caught his look and expected him to glance away, but he continued to gaze at her. He was the best-looking man she had ever seen, unusually tall and broad-shouldered, and with flat, mesmeric, almost dangerous eyes. As she continued to stare at him, he closed one eye in an enormous wink, then began silently to mouth the words of the hymn, in rhythm with Idris Barrington's ridiculous rending:

'We're MAR-ching to ZI-on,
BEW-tiful, BEW-tiful ZI-on. . .'

Margaret Ann blushed furiously and looked away. When she judged he would no longer be mocking her, she whispered to Mair, 'Who's that in the window of the Commercial? I haven't seen him before.'

'Where – who d'you mean? Oh, yes, isn't he smashin' looking? But they do say he's really rough. You know old Mrs Walters in the top of the Ranks? Well, it's her grandson. She brought 'im up – his mam died having him and his father was killed down the Blackvein a good fifteen years ago, I think. He've been living over Ynysddu this long time, but old Mrs Walters is in a bad way and I think he've come back to keep an eye on 'er. You don't want to get interested in him, though, Margaret Ann. He've got an awful reputation.'

'Have he? What for?'

'Goodness knows, but when I asked Mam and Dad what they were saying about him they said it was none of my business except that nice girls shouldn't bother with 'im.' She lowered her voice – 'I think there was somethin' about him getting a girl into trouble. . .'

'Hush – if Dada hears you there'll be ructions. They don't even let me talk about things like that. . .'

'All right, then, but you did ask. Just you remember, he's a bad lot.'

She could tell that from the look in his eyes – but he was so handsome. . .

Suddenly the sun was sparkling on brass instruments and the Salvation Army band wheeled smartly into Bridge Street just ahead of them. Zion was killed stone dead by their triumphal marching music and after a grimace of alarm, Mr Barrington resumed his backward march, encouraging his pilgrims to new melodies.

'All right, everyone, let's join together to praise the Lord, follow the band's tune, one, two, three:

'ON-ward CHRIS-tian SO-WO-WO-LDIER-ERS
MAR-ching as to WAR,
With the cross of JEE-ZUZ
GO-wing on before!'

Singing lustily, the Garn contingent followed the band
into Bridge Street and Margaret Ann lost sight of
the young man with the strange eyes. But his image
remained in her memory long after she had returned
home that evening. *Silly girl*, she told herself. *You may as
well put him out of your head now, because there's no chance
of you and him ever even meeting one another.* Instead she
tried to concentrate on the flattering attentiveness of
the minister's younger brother at the schoolroom tea
that afternoon. Now there was a suitable young man!
Good prospects, nice manners, respectable family and
no ties. You couldn't expect him to be tall and good-
looking as well. . .

CHAPTER TWO

MARGARET ANN KNEW how to avoid fights. Any respectable girl who had spent her life in a mining valley learned the rules early. It helped to stay as far as possible from public houses, which was why she started to cross Abercarn High Street one September afternoon before she reached the Commercial Inn. But the brawl that had just started inside the bottom bar over an accusation of cheating was too sudden and savage for containment. As Margaret Ann moved into the street, two men tumbled headlong into her path from the open doorway.

The one on top had a firm grip on his opponent's throat. As Margaret Ann watched, horrified, he freed his right hand and attempted to jab two grimy fingers into the other man's eyes. Outrage overcame her aversion and she lunged forward to try and stop him.

'Leave him – leave him, please! You'll blind him!' She grasped the filthy coat sleeve and tugged ineffectually.

The fighter momentarily lost interest in his quarry and turned on her, murder in his eyes.

'Stay out of this, you whining bitch! That bugger 'uv tried his tricks once too often. I'm gonna make sure he can't see to do it again!' As he spoke he shook her off and raised his arm to strike her. A cold voice as threatening as an open razor prevented him from finishing the act.

'Touch 'er and you're dead.' It was a calm statement, not an angry threat, but Billy Stout knew better than to ignore it.

'Only mindin' my own business, wasn't I, Evan?' He adopted an ingratiating grin to accompany the wheedling tone. 'Just settlin' up – didn' want no interference, that's all.'

'Well, hop it, or you'll 'ave more interference from me than you know what to do with.' He still hadn't raised his voice but Stout, almost grovelling now, scrabbled for his cap which had fallen in the struggle, then scuttled backwards into the bottom bar. The newcomer turned his attention to the other fighter, who was fingering his throat and groaning melodramatically. 'You'd better get goin', an' all, Dai Two, and not back in the Commercial, neither. Try that old trick again and they'll be finding you in the canal one of these nights.'

Dai recovered abruptly, got up and moved off hurriedly towards the Bush, where the customers were less aggressive. Alone, Margaret Ann faced her rescuer.

She knew him by sight already and now was blushing furiously because her own impetuosity had put her in the position of having to recognize his existence. Eyes downcast, she thanked him in a voice that barely rose above a whisper. The ensuing silence lasted so long that she glanced up to see if he was still there.

'That's better, girl. I like people to look at me when they talk to me. Now, if you can't keep yourself from interfering with bad 'uns like that, I'd better walk you to where you're going.'

'I'm all right on my own, thank you. That was just unlucky. You go on your way, now.'

To her consternation, he grinned broadly, transforming his dangerous, cold expression to that of an amused schoolboy. 'Afraid someone will see me with you, are you, my flower? I don't suppose your mam would think much of that, or the ladies in the chapel.'

It was too close to the truth. Her blush intensified. 'No – no, of course not. It's very good of you to take the trouble. But I'm only going up to old Mrs Moses's house with these things. . .' She gestured lamely at the small basket of bread and cakes she carried.

'Give it here, then. Ma Moses is too far gone to tell anybody who you're with.' Seeing her further hesitation he grew impatient. 'Oh, come on, girl, it's two o'clock in the afternoon. I can't harm your good name by just carrying your basket, can I?'

She had no choice. Another refusal would have been churlish. And although her parents would disapprove strongly if they knew, she found this good-looking escort hard to resist. They crossed the street together and started in the direction of Mrs Moses's cottage at the top end of the village. Margaret Ann tried to look anywhere except at her rescuer, but she managed numerous quick, darting glances which confirmed her many previous impressions of his magnetic good looks.

Evan Walters was over six foot tall in an age when childhood malnutrition kept most working men under five foot six. He had huge shoulders and a deep chest, but his long, muscular legs prevented him from looking brutish. He had a fine head, with thick, straight hair of such a dark brown it appeared black, a straight, almost aristocratic nose and a beautifully sculpted mouth. His eyes were the feature that made him look dangerous. Large, wide-set and fringed by black lashes, they were such a pale grey they seemed made of quicksilver. His clear white skin, almost too fine for a man, accentuated the mesmeric quality of the eyes. Margaret Ann found a multitude of intensely sensual images crowding her mind, all of them connected with Evan Walters and none fit to tell her mother. She was relieved when he broke the silence – except that the deep, deadly voice intensified his allure.

'Had a good look, have you? There's no charge for staring, so stop being so careful about it.'

'I wasn't. . . that is. . .I hardly know you, Mr Walters . . . and – '

He cut in with a laugh. 'You know me well enough to remember my surname. That'll do for a start. Now look, I don' mind telling you I'm glad Billy finally took a poke at Dai Two. The little bugger deserved all he'd 'ave got if you hadn't been there, but that apart it gave me a chance to talk to you.'

Instantly she was on guard. 'And why would you want to do that? My friends usually get to know me by meeting me in chapel or with the family, all tidy, not like that!' She gestured contemptuously back towards the Commercial.

'You don' really need me to answer that, do you, Margaret Ann?' She tried to remind him it was Miss Jones, but couldn't bring herself to do so. 'I been look-ing at you this long time – and you've been looking at me. But I 'aven't been in chapel for twenty-odd years and seeing that I'm not twenty-seven yet, that sets me with the heathens that your lot don' talk to. I could 'ave gone on looking without getting anywhere from now till doomsday if it hadn't been for that fight.'

'How dare you say I've been looking at you?' It was true enough to make Margaret Ann thoroughly flus-tered and she put on a show of indignation to cover her confusion.

He laughed again. 'Remember las' Whitsun March-ing? Now when I was little and still going to chapel, they said you went marching Whit Monday to praise the Lord. You know – ' he broke into song:

'We're marching to Zion,
Beautiful, beautiful Zion,
We're marching up unto Zion
The beautiful city of God!

'Well, I come out of the Commercial to watch as the holy pilgrims went by, singing their heads off. You went on singing, but you stopped looking at your hymn sheet and there was nothing religious about the way you looked at me then. Hoping to convert me, were you girl?'

She feigned fury. He was too close for comfort. She had dreamed about him for three nights after the marching. That thought was all that prevented her from storming away from him now. 'You're a lout, Evan Walters, and I'm ashamed to be with you! Give me back that basket and leave me alone. I'm grateful you saved me but I don't have to put up with this!' She reached for the bread basket.

Unconcerned, Evan merely swung it beyond her reach. 'Not so fast, my lovely. I'm not asking you to do anything you'll be ashamed of after. And I'm glad you looked at me like that. Shows you must 'ave seen some of the looks I'd been givin' you!'

She had, on several occasions since Whitsun, and the flattering memory prevented her from acting too rashly. As she hesitated he spoke again.

'Look, I don't want to be anything but respectable with you. I want to meet you proper, not like that back there, but I'd never get a chance any other way. Now you're talking to me, I don' want to let you go. When we get to Ma Moses's house, I'll even wait outside, if you like, then walk you home,' – he raised an enormous hand to silence her protest – 'strictly respectable, and ask to see your Mam or Dad and tell them what happened. Whatever they think of me, they wouldn' want you going home by yourself after somethin' like that. God – that Dai Two could be waitin' to pay you back for gettin' him into trouble with me, did you think of that?'

Margaret Ann gave in gracefully. When she thought about the whole incident, she realized it provided the chance she had dreamed of to introduce this strange, dangerous young man into her circle. There was no other respectable way of getting acquainted.

'All right, then, Evan, but you've got to behave properly. . .and mind you don't say God or – or something even worse in front of either Mam or Dada.'

'I promise. Your mam do speak Welsh, don' she?'

'Yes, but Dada doesn't. He went to the National School and they stopped him. Why?'

'Poor lady. She can't 'ave much chance of speaking it, then, what with that and the chapel being English Congregationalist.'

'No. She sings in the ladies' choir but that's the only time. . .'

'Not any more it isn't, *cariad*. Better in Welsh than English, me. My grandmother brought me up and she couldn't speak a word of English. I'll give your mam a chance to talk a proper language for a change. That'll stop 'er getting funny with me.'

It might, too, thought Margaret Ann. Her mother read the Bible in Welsh because she preferred it to the English version. If a new acquaintance spoke the language of her fathers, she might be persuaded to ignore his rough clothes and dubious reputation. And the possibility of being accosted by Dai Two if she returned home alone was unpleasant.

'All right, then, but mind you stay outside the front door until Mam decides whether you can come in. She's very particular about who she lets over the doorstep.'

'So I do hear.' Margaret Ann knew her mother was regarded as something of a snob by many of the villagers. She sought for a tone of mockery in his response, but could find none.

They arrived at old Mrs Moses's house and he surprised her once more. 'Afternoon, Sal. 'Ow you been keepin' this long time?' It seemed Evan knew the woman better than she did.

'Evan, *bach* – come on in! There's lovely to see you!' The rosy-faced old woman raised a crippled hand in greeting and he took it as gently as a nurse handling a new-born child.

'*Bach*? It's a long time since anyone called me that, girl. I been six foot one for the last seven or eight years!'

'You'll always be little to me, Evan. Remember 'ow you used to get in over the wall when we was living up the farm, and steal my apples? You was little enough then, little enough for an 'iding!'

'I probably still got the marks, Sal, but don't tell nobody you made me cry, eh? Them colliers think I'm a real 'ard man.'

She beamed at him. 'Oh, I know you'm the roughest one of them all. Ashamed, you should be, 'specially when you're with a young lady like Margaret Ann. What are you doin' with him, Margaret Ann? He's a proper rodney!'

Evan gave her no chance to answer for herself. 'I'm her knight in armour today, Sal. Just been rescuin' her from the dragon, you know me.'

'Aye, I know you, Evan. I thought you *was* the dragon!'

'Now, now, don' give away all my secrets. I'm trying to impress this one here.' He gestured exaggeratedly at Margaret Ann, who was listening in mounting confusion. She gave Sal Moses the bread and cakes from her mother and firmly led the small-talk away from how she had acquired her escort.

But Sal was not to be distracted for long. Any possibility of a romance between Margaret Ann and Evan was better gossip than she had heard for months. There'd be blood on the moon when her mam heard about it, for sure. But somehow they looked so right together that Sal hoped it would be a long time before Mrs Jones found out.

'You two seem to be old friends,' said Margaret Ann. 'I thought you didn't get many visitors, Mrs Moses?'

'That's right, girl. It's ever such a long time since I saw Evan, but that don't mean he's a stranger. When he was little, he was in and out of our 'ouse all the time, till he got big enough to rob the orchard, that is. Then our George told 'im to bugger off, but 'e was a good boy after George died, an' all. First one to come round an' ask what I needed. Come to think of it, you got me into this little 'ouse when the farm got too much for me, didn' you, Evan?'

'Oh, I wouldn' say that, love. Just told the coal company agent that the farm would make a good house for a manager if he found you somewhere else to go.'

'Yes, but you know as well as I do that they'd 'ave 'ad me out in ten minutes when I stopped bein' able to earn enough on my own to pay the rent.'

'He didn't realize it though, did he, Sal? Got you in here and all settled and thought he 'ad a real bargain – and he did. I was just in the right place when you lost George and got a chance to see you kept a roof over your head.'

'Just the same, I'll always remember it, mun. I been wonderin' why I don' see you much these days.'

'Well, you know. . .a lot of things 'ave 'appened in the last three or four years. . .' He became confused, then seized on a good excuse. '. . .and settin' up on my own was a bit of a business, remember. I'm only just gettin' on top o' that.'

Sal smiled and nodded. She knew very well that Evan had also been obsessed with a wild young Irish girl from the Sirhowy Valley and that their liaison had absorbed his spare energy for four years until she went off eighteen months ago. Since then, gossip said, Evan had thrown himself into work, drink and fighting. But if Margaret Ann knew none of this, Sal wasn't going to

be the one who destroyed Evan's chances by telling her.
Instead she turned to his work.

'Going well now, is it? You seem to 'ave a bit more
time these days, if that's anything to go by.'

'Aye, Sal, it's easing up now. But I got to keep my eye
on the buggers just the same. They all think they know
better than the boss.'

Margaret Ann was curious. 'I thought you worked
down the pit, Evan.'

''Course I do. But I'm no coal hewer any longer. Last
year I managed to get enough put by to put a gang together and get a contract on a couple of new headings.
We 'aven' done bad and I took a couple more this spring.
There's a decent living for all of us the way I do it.'

That made a lot of difference. Margaret Ann
digested the information and decided that her mother
would be less likely to reject Evan out of hand when
she knew about this. Heading contractors were the
aristocracy of the colliers. They were the men who
managed to prove their skill and strength, to accu-
mulate a financial stake which enabled them to open
up and mine sections of collieries as sub-contracting
freelances to the coal companies. The contractors
employed their own colliers – usually gangs of six.
The company paid by the weight of coal cut according
to a pre-arranged price list. A contractor with keen,
skilled coal hewers in his gang could do very well for
himself. It was a big step up from being a mere collier

Her mother was putty in Evan's hands. After they
had chatted to one another for almost half an hour,
Mrs Jones included her daughter in the conversation
for the first time by speaking English.

'But how rude of me, Mr Walters! I never thought to
offer you tea, and after you being so kind, too! Have
you got time to stay for a cup?'

'Not today, Mrs Jones, but thank you all the same. P'raps I could come another day?' Margaret Ann held her breath.

'Of course, of course! The sooner the better. That's the first good conversation I've had in a really comfortable language since my mother passed away! Next Sunday, perhaps? Mr Jones will be here then and I'm sure he'd like to meet you.'

They said their farewells and Margaret Ann watched the tall figure march jauntily off down the hillside. How had he managed it? She had hoped to win her mother over with a little embroidery of his prospects as a self-employed man, but it had been quite unnecessary. Mrs Jones enlightened her.

'Just goes to show you never can tell by looking at someone, doesn't it? I've always thought that Walters boy was a really rough sort. But do you know, Margaret Ann, he speaks the purest, most beautiful Welsh I've ever heard?'

'Now how would I know, Mam, seeing as I don't talk the language myself and you and he 'ave been clattering on like a couple of Swansea cockle women?'

'Watch your tongue, my girl. Just because you were nosy about what he had to say for himself. . . All very complimentary it was, anyway. He knows very well what a good family you come from and he's making sure not to push himself. It was good of him to bring you all the way home in case that awful man was waiting to accost you. Mind you, he was only too willing, from the way he was looking at you. . . Good prospects, too, from what he was saying about the headings he've got down Risca. If he do go on like that for a few years, he'll have enough put by to get right out of the pit and start a proper business.'

It was hard to believe they were discussing the dangerously handsome street fighter whom she had dreaded introducing such a short time ago. Margaret

Ann was young and unworldly. It never entered her head that her mother was only eight years older than Evan and every bit as susceptible as she to his quicksilver eyes and air of menace.

CHAPTER THREE

OCTOBER WAS SUCKING up the last juice of summer and pouring it out in a golden stream to celebrate a bountiful year. Evan sat high on the mountainside above Abercarn and stared blankly down over the glowing reds and golds of the natural landscape to where the mining operations had violated the valley bottom. He sighed. The days were much shorter, now. Soon it would be back to never seeing the sun at all: down the pit before dawn, up after sunset. He lashed out savagely at the grass that swayed gracefully beside his heavy boots. What a bloody life! Slave away your best years for pennies and then lose everything that made it worth the effort! It made him wish he had never been born.

Abruptly, his mood lightened, as he noticed a familiar figure approaching up the hillside. Ellen Rourke's hair was like a brilliant flame, against which the bronze of the autumn bracken became dull. She was tall and graceful, and now her swinging, long-limbed walk ate up the distance between them as she strode up the track to meet him. Evan stood up, suddenly gauche, rendered inarticulate by his choking need for a rebellious Irish tinker girl. He crumpled his thick workman's cap in his effort to seem calm, casting about desperately for some self-assured greeting which might conceal his passion.

As she drew level with him, he managed to say, 'Got my message then, did you?'

Ellen twinkled at him. 'Did you ever know me to go out walking just to enjoy the beauties of nature? You choose some awkward places, Evan, I'll give you that.'

He mumbled something unintelligible. There was no real reason why he should not have seen her in the market square, or at his house. No reason, except that Margaret Ann Jones might have found out. . . Evan wondered why that should be so important. Margaret Ann was not in the running if Ellen was around, so why was he being so secretive?

But already, Ellen was giving him the answer. It was far from certain that she *would* be around for long. 'What brought this on, anyway?' she asked. 'Did you hear I might be moving on?'

'Christ, no!' Such immediate evidence of departure alarmed Evan. 'I only just heard you was back in the valley. You can't be going already!'

'Well, I might and I might not. There's precious little to hold me here, isn't there?'

'Could I hold you?'

The lazy, brilliant smile suddenly made her face beautiful. 'Depends on what you're offering, me darling.'

There was no doubt in Evan's mind now. 'Everything I've got, girl. Me. My bed. My board. A proper place for you. Marry me.'

Her smile was fading, but she moved closer, standing only inches in front of him. Instinctively, Evan put his arms around her and enveloped her in a suffocating embrace. He buried his face in the glorious hair, murmuring, 'Oh, God, I love you, Ellen!'

She drew back. The smile was quite gone now, replaced by something like pity. She shook her head. 'You don't understand, do you? I don't want none o' that. I've not spent more than a dozen nights

under a roof in me whole life. Why should I start
now?'

Evan was perplexed. 'But isn't that what you do
want? You can't like it, living in that wagon with the
whole family, cooking by the road side, out in all
weathers.'

'I like it a damned sight better than I would belonging to some man – even you, Evan – for the price of
a feather bed and an oven for me bread. Look at me,
Evan – really look at me. I'm twenty. I aim to look as
good as this when I'm thirty. What chance'd I have if I
was slaving away to bring up a family, with a new baby
every year? I'd be old in three years, and then you'd be
looking at some fresh young kid and leaving me to the
pots and pans.'

'You'll never get old, and I'll always worship you.'

Tears trembled in her slate-grey eyes, making them
seem bigger than ever. 'Thank you for that, my darling. I know you mean it now. But I'd never hold you
to it.' Ellen shook herself angrily, as though shrugging
off a vain dream. 'But it's more than that. I've got plans
for meself, and I'll never get started if I settle down in
a mining village.'

Evan's hopes were ebbing fast, but he strove to control his bitterness in case there was a chance to salvage
something. 'Sit down by here and tell me,' he said.

They were standing beside a great rugged boulder
above the Pant-yr-Esg road. All the local children called
it the Rock of Ages. Now he drew her into its lee
and they sat down together. Ellen turned towards
him, her face suddenly radiant with enthusiasm. 'I'm
going to be someone, Evan – go somewhere outside
these dirty old valleys. Guess where I been all the
summer!'

'If I'd known that, you wouldn't have been there
long. I'd have found you and brought you back,' he
growled.

'Don't be grouchy. You wouldn't hold me against me will, would you?'

'Sometimes I think I could commit murder to hold on to you.'

She shivered, suddenly frightened. There was something in the big man's tone which went beyond idle boasting. Ellen forced the cheerfulness back into her voice.

'I been touring around with a travelling thee-ayter!'

He was impressed in spite of himself. 'How? Where?'

'Mmm, here and there. Mainly the Rhondda Valley, but right down past Cowbridge and Bridgend in August. Then back up around the farming country along the Usk when they was finishing off the harvest. The farm folk had more time to enjoy themselves then, and sometimes we got a share of the harvest suppers if we arrived at the right time.'

His face was darkening. 'Who's the "we"? I thought you liked to travel alone.'

Ellen laughed, all good-natured now she was sharing happy memories.

'Nothing to worry a man like you. . . A nice crazy man and his wife and pack of little kids. Fellow called Haggar. He used to run a puppet show, but his missus was an actress before they teamed up and she wanted to tread the boards again. I happened along the very moment they was short of another female.'

'So you just left? Not only me, but your father and brothers, too? You always said you wouldn't move in with me over Ynysddu because you had to look after them.'

'Ah, well, our Liam came home with a pretty little girl who'd been kicked off a farm because she wouldn't go with the gaffer. She's been tagging along since the spring and she's much better at cooking and washing than I'll ever be. So I thought, come on, Ellen, here's your chance, it's now or never.'

He was glaring at her. 'That must have been some
time after Easter, when you went off and left me,
too, pretending you had to look after them. It nearly
killed me, losing you like that. I couldn't even stay
over Ynysddu – I had to get away. That's why I'm
back here.'

Ellen grasped his arm, genuinely contrite. 'I'm sorry,
Evan, I really am. But don't you see? I couldn't have
gone if you'd kept on at me, too. It was bad enough
with Pa. . . I didn't really lie to you. I just didn't come
to let you know I was off.'

'No, and I went looking for you at half the hiring
fairs between here and Chepstow, thinking you was
going into service to try and raise some money for your
family.'

She pressed her fingers against his lips. 'Hush, now,
darling – please. Can't you see, this is just why I
couldn't tell you the truth? You'd have stopped me
from going.'

'Well, would that have been so bad? You're as pretty
as ever, but you don't look no richer that I can see.'

'There won't be much money for a long time yet, but
Mrs Haggar says I have a natural stage presence and a
grand memory for lines. She thinks I could go a long
way.'

'Aye, a long way from me. . .' Evan spoke so quietly
she could hardly catch the words. He clambered to his
feet. 'This was a waste of time for us both, really, wasn't
it? I come here all ready to give you everything I had,
and you come to tell me you were throwing yourself
away to join a travelling circus.'

In an instant, she was up beside him, furious. 'I'll
have you know it's no travelling circus! It's a proper
theatre, with scenery, and costumes, and music,
and. . .and. . .'

'And other shows like Scarrott and his wild beasts
and bare-knuckle fighters to keep you company when

you get to your pitch! Theatre? Don't make me laugh –
I been going to them travelling shows since I was little.
You'll be joining up with a freak show along with all the
other gippos and diddicois!'

'You bastard – don't you ever call me that!' and Ellen
drew back her arm to strike him.

He caught both her hands and shook her hard
enough to still her fury. His tone was piteous when
he spoke again. 'Ellen, don't. I love you. I need you. . .'

'Oh, Christ, who'd be a woman?' she murmured, as
his arms went around her again and she yielded to his
embrace.

Half an hour later, dusk was on them, and Ellen was
determined to go. Their lovemaking had been stormy
and wildly exciting, as it had been often in the old days,
and afterwards she had looked at his handsome face,
quiescent now, and wondered if he was really what she
wanted after all. But in her heart she knew he was not,
and now she must make the break. She stood up, shaking the grass and bracken from her skirt, straightening
her blouse and looking for the shawl she had worn over
it.

Evan knew he was beaten. His face was blank with
pain, but he sounded normal enough. 'Come on, I'll
walk you into the village,' he said. 'Where are you going
tonight?'

'The van is down in Risca. If you take me to the
station, there should be a train soon. I've got a bit o'
money for once, so I won't need to walk.'

'Pay from your stage act, I suppose.' The bitterness
oozed from his voice.

'Some, yes. I earned it just as honest as if it was for
mending pots or doing laundry, so don't you pretend I
didn't. I just want to better meself, Evan, that's all. I'd
be an awful wife for a collier.'

'So you do keep saying. All right. I'm not deaf or daft. I believe you.'

He did not speak again during the two-mile walk back to the station. Ellen made a couple of efforts at light chatter, but she might as well have been alone. He set a killing pace and a couple of times she stumbled on the unmade road. He reached out instinctively to prevent her from falling, but remained silent. Eventually they arrived at Abercarn station and Ellen bought her ticket. A train was approaching as they came out of the booking hall. Evan handed her aboard, still saying nothing, but did not turn away when she closed the door. Ellen let down the window and leaned out towards him.

He looked at her for the first time since they had started walking, then reached out and touched her cheek briefly. 'You'll get tired of it one day, *cariad*,' he said. 'When you do, I'll still be here, even if you'm fifty with snow white hair. Come and find me when you need me.'

Somewhere a whistle blew, and the engine began to pull away from the little platform. Ellen was crying. Evan's last memory of her was a fluttering hand and her weeping face, thrown into stark relief by the gas lamps which hung from the booking hall canopy. He stood there alone long after the noise of the train's departure had faded, then uttered one despairing sigh before turning away towards his barren terraced cottage.

An abyss had opened at Margaret Ann's feet, unremarked by anyone except herself. Face to face with Evan Walters, she let her everyday good sense slip away and drowned in romantic dreams of being possessed by him for ever. Once they had parted, though, she soon became painfully aware of the terrible problem posed

by her obsession with him. The smallest things set her
worrying about it. Today it was the fine worsted winter
dress which her mother had made for her. Margaret
Ann went to her room to try it on and was regard-
ing her reflection with complete satisfaction when she
remembered Evan and her pleasure froze.

What good was a new gown like this when she could
not go anywhere wearing it, accompanied by Evan? It
was hardly informal enough for a short stroll in the
High Street with him, or for sitting in the parlour
with him as her mother poured tea for them. It was
a dress for chapel, for choir practice, for young people's guild, or for a smart shopping trip to Newport on
the train. . .all the numberless social occasions which
revolved around her place of worship or middle-class
aspirations. Evan Walters was determinedly pagan and
working class in equal measure and in his cynicism had
swept away all the legitimate social events at which
they might otherwise have been seen together. For a
while Margaret Ann had tried to pretend it was of no
importance. After all, he seemed serious enough about
her. . . Once they were married, she could attend such
functions on her own, if necessary, and go home to her
Evan afterwards.

Home! That provoked her even further. The nature
of their future home was the real root of her dissatis-
faction, and she knew it. Evan's grandmother had died
and he had taken over her tenancy of the cottage in the
Ranks. It was clean enough – Granny Walters had seen
to that and had drummed her example into Evan – but
the four cramped rows of coal company houses had a
grim reputation as the roughest dwellings in the Western Valley. Margaret Ann had always pictured herself
returning from her wedding to a graceful detached
villa, or at the very least a comfortable house like her
parents' home on Rhyswg Road. What a come-down it
would be to live in the Ranks! She had almost wished

her mother would intervene and say it was out of the
question, but Louisa was quite besotted by Evan, with
his handsome face and beautiful Welsh.

When Margaret Ann expressed misgivings about the
Ranks house, her mother had dismissed it all as childish. 'A man like Evan won't be there more than five
minutes, girl! He've got prospects. You'll have your
own detached house over West End, or one of them
big semi-detached villas in Cae Gorlan Road, before
you've been married five years.'

Margaret Ann had been taken aback. 'B-but Mam, I
thought you'd be the first one to say I mustn't consider
the Ranks. . .'

'Of course I would, if it mattered tuppence. But it
doesn't. It would be a different thing if you was going
there for life, but I'd be surprised if you're still there
when your first child is born.'

Margaret Ann coloured. 'I should hope so, too! How
could you even think about that?'

Louisa was getting angry. 'That's enough! D'you
want the boy or not? If it do take him a little bit
longer to get enough put by to do better, you'll come
back here when you're having your first child, all right?
Anyhow, that's a bit previous now. So far as I do know,
he haven't even asked you to marry him yet.'

Margaret Ann was painfully aware of that. She
thought of little else, when she was not agonizing
about whether she could adjust to life as a miner's
wife. It was late January now, almost four months since
the day he had met her mother. Not long, perhaps,
for couples who were constantly thrown together by
shared family social activity, but for a pair in unusual
circumstances like their own, it was an age. There was
a rigid limit to what they might do together, and no
scope to broaden their contact. Unless Evan spoke to
her father soon, Margaret Ann knew she must end
the relationship. It could hardly continue indefinitely

as a series of teas with her mother and walks down the
High Street.

But Evan showed no inclination to change things. At
Christmas, Margaret Ann had entertained high hopes
of luring him into the chapel festivities, or of including
him in their family celebrations and prompting him to
a proposal, but she was doomed to disappointment.
When she invited him to come for Christmas dinner
and to spend both Christmas Day and Boxing Day with
them, he merely gestured dismissively.

'I won' be here for Christmas, thanks all the same.'

Her heart lurched. There had been much talk in the
village lately of a big demand in Canada for experienced miners. What if he had decided to emigrate?
She waited anxiously for an explanation, but none was
forthcoming. Eventually, she was forced to ask him. 'I
didn't know you were going away. . .where?'

Evan smiled. 'Oh, you don't get rid of me that easy,
girl. It's only for a few days. I'm going to my brother's,
down Cardiff. We've just worked out one heading up
the pit and we won't be opening the new one till January, so I thought I'd go and stay with Rhys for a bit
while the work was slack. It's a couple of years since
I've seen him.'

Her relief was visible, and she strove to conceal it
with small talk. 'I never knew you had a brother.'

'Not a man to boast about, our Rhys – not that I'm
ashamed of him, mind, we get on well – but your chapel
people wouldn't think much of him.'

'Why ever not?'

'He's what they would call a publican and a sinner –
especially a sinner!' said Evan with exaggerated relish.
'That's why he got away from Abercarn as soon as
he could. Always said he felt crowded here. He was
a seaman for years, and now he do run a pub down
the docks.'

Margaret Ann was scandalized. 'Don't tell our Mam,

whatever you do, Evan! She wouldn't let you in the house if she knew that!'

He laughed at her. 'Lips that touch liquor shall never touch mine, I s'pose?'

She nodded, round-eyed and apprehensive. 'Mam and Dad signed the Pledge when they was seventeen. Did it together at a mass meeting in Risca. They got me to sign when I was seven. You know we'm strict Temperance.'

'Amazing what your mam can ignore when she do set her mind to it, though, ennit' he said.

'I don't know what you're on about.'

'Oh, yes, you do! Your mam do know as well as anybody else that I like my pint a bit too much. She've never tried to make me sign the Pledge, though, or said I mustn't come to the house.'

That had surprised Margaret Ann, too. A lot of things surprised her about the way her mother had taken to Evan Walters. She was still too naïve to take into account the effect of his build, looks and physical magnetism. Louisa Jones had never been so close to that much maleness in the whole of her virtuous life, and she was not going to let a little thing like his drinking habits deprive her of his company.

Her daughter might not understand that, but she knew instinctively that a publican brother who lived in the dockland underworld would be too much even for Louisa's new-found moral mellowness. 'If Mam do ask, just say you're staying in Cardiff with family, all right?'

After he had gone, she scolded herself crossly for being so worried that her mother would cease to approve of him. It might be for the best... Albert Williams, the minister's younger brother, had been making eyes at her again. He had just started work as a schoolmaster in Birmingham and was likely to do very well for himself. His skinny shoulders and prominent Adam's Apple seemed less serious drawbacks when

they came wrapped up in a white collar job and a sub-
urban house with a garden. If only Mam would start
pushing them together, the way she had before Evan
came along, Margaret Ann knew she wouldn't hesitate
for long. But no such support was forthcoming. Louisa
merely lamented Evan's absence from their Christmas
celebrations, and grudgingly invited Albert to high tea
on Boxing Day, along with half a dozen other friends
and acquaintances. She made it clear that in her view,
her daughter was committed to Evan Walters.

But when the year turned, Evan came back from
Cardiff and resumed work at the colliery, never
mentioning marriage, or even engagement. By the
time she tried on her new dark blue worsted gown
at the end of January, Margaret Ann was almost sure
she would prefer to wear it in the company of Albert
Williams than to await the dubious blessing of a proposal from Evan.

Until February, it was a moist, mild winter, but then the
weather changed suddenly and freezing winds howled
along the valleys, bringing heavy snow and swiftly putting an end to the old and infirm. This much was not
unusual; but after a couple of weeks, sickness began to
spread among the younger, healthier population, too.

Will Jones had never been robust. He had been lucky
to be the only son of a family of some slight gentility,
who could afford to let him stay at school until he was
fourteen and then to start work as a messenger boy in
the pit manager's office. At first the pay was dismal,
but it was light work and later, when he graduated to
clerical tasks and then to basic accounting, the financial rewards improved, too. Working underground, he
would have succumbed to pneumoconiosis early on. As
it was, he survived, with nothing worse than winter
bronchitis attacks, until the influenza outbreak of 1888.

He was sent home from the coal company area office shortly after noon on 10 February. Louisa was unwell herself and he had got himself off to work that morning. Had she seen his condition then, she would never have let him go. Now she was aghast as he stood at the open front door, swaying, sweating, half delirious.

'*Iesu mawr*, Will! You've never walked up that road in the snow in this state?' His attempt at a reply was choked off by a spasm of coughing. 'Come on, quick, let's get you by the fire and out of them wet clothes and boots. Margaret Ann – come here and help your father! Bring us one of them thick blankets and a towel!'

She knelt and unlaced his sodden boots, then removed them, along with the thick socks. She began to rub his feet briskly to restore the circulation. Although Will was sweating hard, his feet and hands were freezing. Margaret Ann arrived with blanket and towel, and Louisa began undressing her husband.

'Out and make some strong tea, girl, quick,' she ordered, 'and plenty of sugar, an' all. Then you can boil more water for the bottles. I want his bed as warm as this room.'

After Margaret Ann had warmed the bed, she lit a fire in the tiny bedroom grate – something she could never remember seeing since she herself had been put in the room as a small child to recuperate from pneumonia. One look at her father today had told her he needed all the warmth they could give him.

By the time she returned to the kitchen, Will was so bad it required the strength of both women to steer him upstairs. Once in bed, in spite of bottles, feather quilts and fire, he still shivered so hard that the bedsprings rattled. As afternoon turned to evening, his condition worsened. By eight o'clock he was delirious.

Louisa Jones passed her hand across her face in an exhausted gesture. 'It's no use,' she said, 'we'll have to

have the doctor.' She went and parted the bedroom
curtains, gazing grimly at the snow which still hurried
down in freezing drifts. 'I'll go. I'm not having you out
in this.'

Margaret Ann was horrified. 'Of course you won't!
You'm nearly as bad as Dada – it's only him being ill
that's kept you on your feet. I'll fetch him.'

Louisa shook her head mulishly. 'No daughter of
mine is walking to the Swan and back in weather like
this. I'll wrap up warm and I'll be back before you do
know I'm gone.' But her voice shook as she uttered the
last words. Rhyswg Road was on the bare, west-facing
mountainside, overlooking the village hundreds of feet
below. It could be blustery on a summer afternoon.
Tonight it was arctic. The doctor's house was less than
a mile away, but it was at the foot of the mountain and
anyone going there would be travelling into the teeth
of the storm. Fortunately, before either of them had
to set off, Dafydd Parry, their next door neighbour's
twelve-year-old son, arrived.

'Our Dad said Mr Jones was sent home dinner time
looking bad, and Mam sent me in to see if there was
anything we could do to help,' he explained.

'Oh, yes, love – bless her for her kindness, and you!
Will you go for Dr Morgan?'

The boy was round-eyed. 'Is it that bad, Mrs Jones?'
House calls from the doctor were invariably matters of
life and death for people in their circumstances.

Louisa nodded, grim-faced again. 'I've never seen
him so poorly, and he've had some terrible bronchitis
in his time.' She gave Dafydd a hastily-scribbled note
for the doctor and he left. Louisa returned to her husband's bedside.

Will's breathing was harsh now, as noisy as an animal's. As she entered the room he was seized by a
spasm of coughing which seemed set to tear him apart.
Louisa rushed forward and held him up in a sitting

position to help him draw breath. For a couple of minutes, she took his full weight, before the attack eased and he slumped back against the pillows. She started to straighten up, then stumbled. Margaret Ann, at the fireside, gave a sharp cry and moved to steady her.

'Mam, what is it? Are you all right?'

'Yes, just give me a minute. . . Oh, *Duw*, no, maybe not. . .' and as Louisa reached out for her daughter, she collapsed across the foot of the bed.

Margaret Ann was frantic. Her mother looked much like her father, shivering, sweating and breathing erratically. The girl hardly knew where to start. She knew how to nurse the sick, but the effect of seeing both her parents collapse drove out any practical considerations. She stifled a sob of pure panic, glancing up at her father. For the moment, he seemed to present less of a problem than Louisa. The coughing bout had exhausted him and he appeared to be asleep. Her mother, on the other hand, was groaning and tossing about, trying to recover her wits and her strength.

At a loss, Margaret Ann sat down beside her and attempted to raise her into a sitting position. Louisa was a small woman, but inertia made her heavy and she slumped down again as quickly as Margaret Ann managed to get her up. Fighting a desire to run from the house and leave them to it, Margaret Ann forced herself to start thinking. The chair. . .the Windsor chair by the fire. That was good and solid. If she could move it over here before Mam slid right off the bed, there might be a chance of levering her into it. The high back and arms would support her then while Margaret Ann got blankets and pillows to warm her until the doctor arrived. She let go of her mother for a moment and made a dash for the chair, forcing it into the narrow gap at the bedside to get it as close as possible. Even in that brief moment, Louisa had started to slide down again, and only the ornate brass bedstead prevented her from falling to the floor.

Somehow, Margaret Ann got her into the chair, then fled to her own room to fetch blankets and pillows. Eventually, her mother was warmly wrapped and wedged in firmly enough to stay in position. Calmer now, Margaret Ann risked leaving her parents for long enough to prepare another hot water bottle. She could hardly put her mother in the same bed as her father. Both were too sick for that. Louisa must take her room and she would sleep in a chair... Sleep! Suddenly it occurred to her that if she was nursing two people who were incapable even of sitting up unaided, there would be precious little sleep for her in the immediate future.

As the big iron kettle boiled on its trivet over the kitchen range, she heard her father coughing again. The bedsprings jangled, then there was a loud thump. Margaret Ann uttered a cry and dashed back upstairs. As she had feared, her father had fallen out of bed. He lay beside it, groaning weakly and trying to raise himself. Louisa was still oblivious of her surroundings.

Sheer desperation enabled Margaret Ann to lever him back into the bed, first propping him against the spindly side chair which normally stood by the bedroom window. By the time she had finished, she was sweating as hard as her father. She had twisted her back and she was sobbing with a mixture of pain and terror. All this, and it couldn't be an hour since Dafydd had gone for the doctor! How would she manage for a week, or a fortnight? Margaret Ann shut her eyes and willed herself not to be sick.

Someone was rapping on the door. Thank God – maybe Dr Morgan could get her some help! She flew to answer, but as she did so her father started slipping sideways again. 'Oh God, please help, please! I can't leave him...the doctor'll go... Please God, please

God. . .' Helpless, despairing, she crouched beside
her father, weeping uncontrollably. That was the way
Evan Walters found her minutes later when he rushed
round to the back door and came upstairs looking for
her.

One glance told him all he needed to know. Without
explaining his presence, he pushed Margaret Ann aside
and heaved her father right into the bed, buttressing
him with a pillow to prevent him falling again. Then,
saying only, 'You stay by there,' to the terrified girl,
he picked up Louisa out of the chair and carried her
off to the other room. Moments later, he called out, 'I
seen another bottle down in the kitchen. Get it up here,
there's a good girl.'

Margaret Ann obeyed him almost mechanically, conscious only of intense relief at the temporary removal
of responsibility. Down in the kitchen, the stone hot
water bottle still stood where she had left it. She filled
it, rammed home the stopper and rushed back upstairs.
As she entered her own bedroom, she was shocked
back to reality by the sight of Evan removing the last of
her mother's clothing and slipping a flannel nightgown
over her head.

'What are you doing, mun? It – it's not decent. . .'

Evan raised his head and stared at her for a moment.
One glance at his expression silenced her. 'I'll pretend
I didn't hear that,' was all he said. Then he gave
the nightgown a final tug before hoisting Louisa into
the bed and gesturing to Margaret Ann to pass the
hot water bottle. He tucked the bedclothes in, then
turned back to the girl. 'No spirits in the house, I
s'pose?'

She knew better than to look scandalized again.
'N-no. . . Mam wouldn't have none in here. But old
Mrs Roberts next door but one do like a drop of brandy
now and again.'

'Right then. Get round there now and make sure she

hands it over. Here. . .' He reached into his pocket.
'She's a stingy old bugger. Better give 'er this to buy
some more. . .' He passed over half a crown.

'But that would buy three bottles!'

'Do you want to help your parents or just discuss the
price of strong drink? Get going while there's still a
chance it'll do some good!'

This time she heeded him, and sped off without
bothering to put on a coat.

By the time Margaret Ann got back, Evan had taken
complete charge. Extra blankets were heaped on the
bed her mother occupied. A fresh bucket of coal stood
in the hearth in the other bedroom and the fire had
been made up. Downstairs, the kettle had been refilled
and set to boil again. Dry tea leaves awaited the hot
water in a warmed pot on the hob. Neither of her
parents seemed to have stirred while all this activity
took place.

'How did you manage it?' she asked, bewildered,
remembering her own panic.

He smiled. 'Brute strength do have its points. You
just weren't big enough to be in three places at once.
Now, before I take that brandy up to your mam, pour
us a bit to go with the tea.'

Margaret Ann recoiled, shocked. 'But you can't –
you're tending the sick!' Immediately the words were
out, she bit her lip, waiting for him to snap at her and
then leave. Instead, he laughed.

'You can have me well-oiled and here or sober and
gone, girl. Take your pick.' Silently, she broke the seal
on the brandy bottle and poured a good quarter-pint
into an empty milk jug. Then she handed over the
bottle and he turned to take it upstairs.

Five minutes later he was back. 'They'm both sleeping all right,' he said. 'There's nothing we can do now
until the doctor have seen them. Let's sort ourselves
out.'

Evan moved over to the hearth, took up the tea-pot and poured them both a cup of tea, adding a hefty measure of brandy from the jug to each cup. 'You'll thank me for it before the night is out,' he said, handing her the cup.

Now that someone else had taken on at least temporary responsibility for her parents, Margaret Ann bzbegan to think clearly again. Suddenly she realized it was far too long since Dafydd had departed to find the doctor.

'Evan, I don't understand. . . When you come, I was expecting Dr Morgan. How did you know you were needed?'

'I was down the doctor's myself. Mrs Ellis the Commercial collapsed while I was in there and I went for the doctor because Alf couldn't leave the bar. Dafydd and me got there at the same time – and we got the same answer. Dr Morgan was out on a list of calls as long as your arm and no hope of getting here before tomorrow morning. It's turning into a proper epidemic. I told Mrs Morgan about Siân Ellis, then when Dafydd told me you was managing on your own, I thought I'd better come.'

The tension caught up with Margaret Ann as he spoke. At first, she tried to control herself, but before he had finished, shock, fear and gratitude combined to make her burst into tears. 'Oh, Evan,' she said between sobs, 'I can't tell you how glad I was to see you. I was so frightened. . .still am, for that matter. What shall I do? I don't know where to start.'

Then she was in his arms and he stroked her hair and made small, comforting, inarticulate sounds to soothe her. 'Hush, hush, now, *cariad*, don't worry. You got me, haven't you, and the doctor will be here in the morning. See if Dafydd's mother will come in and help you. If she can't, I'll stay. . .'

That made her glance up, as scandalized as she had

been to find him undressing her sick mother. But one
look at his face told her that moral protests would
be as out of place now as they had been then. She
held her peace, silently thankful she was no longer
alone.

CHAPTER FOUR

MARGARET ANN'S FATHER survived for three days after his collapse. Her mother hung on for a week. They were buried together on 20 February. By then the influenza epidemic had taken hold and their deaths were only the first of many. About thirty people died in the villages of Abercarn and Cwmcarn, most of them young children or old people. Will and Louisa Jones were remarkable only in being middle-aged fatalities. Dr Morgan told Margaret Ann it was because her father had always suffered from a chest weakness, and her mother had been ill for some weeks with an embarrassing female complaint about which she had never told them.

'This flu caught her at the worst time,' he said. 'She just didn't have the strength to fight it.'

The funeral service took place at the Garn chapel, then the all-male procession of mourners followed the two horse-drawn hearses up the long gradient to the new public cemetery at Chapel of Ease. 'Just as well they've opened it, an' all,' Evan told one of his colliers. 'Walking five miles up that mountain to Mynyddislwyn in this weather would have finished off a few more, I reckon.'

As it was, illness thinned the ranks of mourners. Back at the Rhyswg Road house, Margaret Ann kept her grief and fear at bay by talking to the women, who never attended the cemetery at Valleys funerals, and making tea and ham sandwiches for the inevitable male callers who would arrive after the burial.

Those who consoled her were largely other villagers and friends of her parents from the chapel. There was no close family apart from her great-aunt, her mother's unmarried kinswoman who had worked as a governess for a rich family in Cardiff until they bought her an annuity and she retired a few months previously. Auntie Mattie had arrived at Rhyswg Road the day Louisa died, summoned by the minister who had guessed Margaret Ann was too distressed to think of sending for her.

Until then, Evan Walters had stayed with the girl, silently challenging neighbours to think ill of his unchaperoned presence at all hours of the day and night. It was this as much as concern for Margaret Ann's physical welfare that had moved Pastor Williams to send for Mattie Richards. The morning after Louisa's death, in the kitchen with Margaret Ann, Mattie approached the question of her great-niece's future.

'Have you given any thought to what you'll do now?' she asked.

Margaret Ann looked up at her great-aunt, an expression of naked fear on her face. 'I – I don't dare. I can't think of an answer.'

Mattie embraced the girl, full of pity and understanding. She herself had not been far from such a state once, but a better than average education for a girl of her class had saved her. Margaret Ann had no such advantages. After a while, Mattie nerved herself to say what must be said. Finally, she told the girl, 'There isn't any choice, really. It will have to be domestic service. I can suggest a couple of places, and Pastor Williams can give you a character reference. Perhaps I can find someone willing to train a nanny or a cook. That would be much better than starting as a maid.'

Margaret Ann started back in horror. 'What are you saying, Auntie? I couldn't work in somebody's kitchen all the time, be at their beck and call at all hours! I've never been used to nothing like that!'

Mattie sighed. 'Neither had I, love, but when Dada died there wasn't any choice. I had to go away.'

'Yes, but you was a governess. I could get used to that, I think. That would be nearly like belonging to the family.'

Her great-aunt shook her head. 'I'm afraid that opportunity wouldn't be open to you, Margaret Ann. They have. . .er. . .greater demands for those posts.'

'I don't understand.'

'My father was a schoolmaster. Oh, nothing grand, mind you – just a little village school over Machen way – but he was a learned man and he taught all of us well. Louisa's mother, our brother George and myself, we all had first class handwriting, knew our arithmetic and history and geography – and above all, we spoke very well. He was most particular about that – always said, "Matilda, never mind about the Welsh accent. That's charming in small doses. But mind you enunciate each word properly, and watch those aspirates!" I never forgot that for a moment.'

Margaret Ann was gaping at her, deeply impressed. 'What's an aspirate, then?'

'You see? You wouldn't know where to start, my dear. You must have noticed the difference between your speech and mine.'

'Well, yes, but I thought that came from you living away with gentry and picking it up off them.'

'Quite the reverse. If I hadn't sounded like this from the beginning, they'd never have let me near their children. It's all right for a nanny or a groom to use the speech of the Valleys, but if you're to teach the children

of the rich, sounding right is everything. I'm afraid you
don't, my dear.'

'But surely you could teach me?'

Mattie shook her head. 'Nothing would please me
more. But it's not something you can pick up in a few
days, or even a few weeks. It would take a year or more.
And even if I did manage it, what would you teach your
charges? When did you leave school?'

'When I was thirteen.' She brightened at the memory. 'None of the other girls stayed that long. They all
come from big families and they had to go off to work
or look after their little brothers and sisters. I stayed as
long as there was anything to learn.'

'Oh, dear, I wish that was true, but I very much
doubt it. I'm sure you know your Bible backwards, but
apart from that, how much else d'you know?'

Margaret Ann shrugged, perplexed. 'I'm a very good
seamstress. I do lovely embroidery. I do sing like a bird
– and play the piano. That must count for something.'

'Of course it does, but not without history and geography and so on. If only you were a little more pol-
ished, I might persuade someone to take you as a
lady's companion. . .' Then Mattie shook her head
dismissively. 'But no. In the wrong situation, that can
be worse than maid of all work. A companion with a
domineering mistress is the unhappiest of girls. No,
I'm afraid it will have to be nanny or assistant cook.'

Margaret Ann was close to tears. 'What about sewing?' she said, in mounting desperation.

Mattie pondered that for a moment. 'Now I wonder. . .you must be good if Lousia trained you, because
she was a wonderful needlewoman. I wonder if there'd
be enough work from the better families around here
to keep you going. . .'

They had still been trying to decide on that when
they were caught up in preparations for the funeral, and it had not been discussed since. Now it was

almost over, Margaret Ann was pondering the question again. She knew there would be insufficient work among the professional people of the area to keep her going. The ordinary families did their own handwork. Dressmaking and general domestic sewing were usually undertaken as extra jobs by widows who had other means of support. She shuddered as the prospect of domestic servitude loomed closer. In an effort to banish the thought a little longer, she began bustling about the kitchen, moving the plates of sandwiches to a table by the door ready to be taken into the parlour; straightening the ranks of best bone china cups and saucers which had apparently spent a whole lifetime on display behind glass in the dresser, waiting for a moment such as this.

Minutes later there was a flurry of activity outside. Footsteps crunched on the footpath and someone hammered the iron door knocker. 'I'll go, love,' Auntie Mattie called. 'It'll be the men coming back. You wet the tea.'

Margaret Ann moved to warm the teapot, hearing the murmur of newcomers' voices in the small hall as she did so. Then the half-glazed door from the passage clicked shut and she turned sharply. Evan Walters had just come in and closed it behind him. The misery of the past few days and the bleak uncertainty of her future overwhelmed her. Margaret Ann ran to him and flung herself against his big body. Evan's arms came up and around her and she felt safe again for the first time since he had helped her with her sick parents.

For a few moments he did nothing beyond holding her and letting her cry. Then, very gently, he stood away from her and raised one hand to brush the tears from her face. 'Hey, come on, now, girl. . .a few tears is all right, ennit, but you can't go in there looking as if you've drowned.' He fumbled and pulled out a

creased but clean handkerchief from his pocket, and
dabbed at her wet cheeks with it. But as he did so,
fresh tears flowed. He sighed. 'Look, this ent getting
us nowhere. Now what's the matter? You wasn't crying
like this about your mam and dad a couple of days ago.'

'I know, Evan. . . it's not just that. . . It – it's everything! Oh, I'm so frightened about what will become of
me. The very thought of being somebody's maid. . .'

'You, a skivvy? You wouldn't last five minutes!'

That made her cry even more. Skivvy! What an awful
word, the lowest of the low. But that's really what she
would be, whatever Auntie Mattie said to dress it up. . .
Then Evan's next words put a stop to all other thought.

'Any rate,' he said, 'it's not worth thinking about.
You'm going to marry me, and I can keep my own
wife with what I earn.'

Margaret Ann's tears evaporated and she gaped at
him. 'What did you say?'

'Grief turned you deaf, have it? I said you was marrying me. Or don't you want to?'

'I – oh – that is. . .well, I didn't expect. . .'

That provoked his big booming laugh and she almost
reached up to try and muffle it with her little hand
unless it shocked the mourners next door.

'Margaret Ann Jones – for the last three months
you've been doing nothing but ask me to ask you,
in a roundabout sort of way, and now you're pretending it's a big surprise. Try it on them in there!
Anyhow, what's it to be? Me, or some Lady Muck's
back kitchen?'

'Oh, Evan, you! You, with all my heart.' She went to
his arms again.

He kissed her, very gently, then said, 'It won't be
easy, mind, for either of us. We'm too different. I do
love you, though, you remember that.'

'And I love you, Evan! Oh, it won't be so difficult.
Love is what matters!'

Evan looked very sad. 'You're still ever so young, really, aren't you, Margaret Ann?'

Before she could reply, a noise in the passage outside made them separate, and moments later Mattie and one of the other women were in the room, taking the plates of sandwiches and demanding to know if the tea was brewed yet. Spirits soaring, Margaret Ann hurried to help them.

Mattie Richards was delighted at the news that her great-niece was to be married. 'Oh, what a relief!' she said. 'He seems a bit of a rough diamond, but it's always better to have a man to protect you than trying to look after yourself.'

Margaret Ann was surprised. She certainly held that view, but she had not expected her educated great-aunt, with a lifetime's independence behind her, to agree. 'Would you rather have spent your life raising children and taking in washing down the Ranks than doing what you did?' she asked.

Mattie smiled and said, 'I don't have to give it a second thought. Of course I would! What do you think my life has been? Elegant tea parties? Flirting with the curate at church suppers? Going to orchestral concerts in Cardiff? Not a bit of it!

'It's been putting up with other people's spoiled brats because if you discipline them too much they tell lies about you to their parents. It's a scrappy tray of supper in your bedroom because the servants all think you're stuck-up and the family have guests for dinner. It's getting Sunday afternoon off, when a walk in the park is about all there is to do, and then only when the weather's fine. And what do you get at the end of it? I'm one of the lucky ones. My last family were generous and the annuity will at least keep me housed and fed for the rest of my days. But I've known old governesses

end up in the workhouse because they were thrown
out when they were past working. No, my love, when
you're a working woman, you start with nothing and
you end with nothing. I know there's a lot of unhappy
wives about, but not half as many as there are unhappy
spinsters!'

There was no one else whose approval she needed.
Margaret Ann felt odd – a combination of complete
freedom and a sense of being abandoned. Evan's proposal had made life bearable again, but she was deeply
conscious that it did no more that hold off the gaping
void left by her parents' deaths. She would have to face
that some time; it was her good fortune that she need
not do it alone.

Now, though, there were practical difficulties. In
normal circumstances it would have been unthinkable in so straitlaced a community for a girl to marry
immediately after her parents' funeral. But Margaret
Ann was in a unique position. She had no means of
financial support. There had been half a week's pay
owing to Will Jones and the coal company had made
it up to a week in deference to his daughter's predica-
ment. The rent was paid on the Rhyswg Road house
until the end of the quarter, still some weeks away, and
there was more than half a ton of coal in the shed at
the back. But where could Margaret Ann look for food
once the few shillings of coal company money ran out?
The ten sovereigns in a decorative biscuit tin in the
parlour represented her mother's life savings. That
must be her dowry and her source of income until her
marriage, for she had no means of earning more.

Then there was the matter of her unchaperoned
state. Auntie Mattie departed the day after the funeral. From now until they married, when Evan visited
her they would be alone under the same roof, and
this time with no excuse of her sick parents to keep
things respectable. The first time he called on her after

the funeral must be the last until they were married, Margaret Ann told him.

Evan eyed her sceptically. 'And when is that going to be?' he asked.

'That's the trouble. It really shouldn't be till Easter – even then it's hardly respectable – but I don't know how I can live until then.'

'You'm bloody daft if you do think I'm waiting that long, girl.' He did not seem unduly put out; it was merely as if he were stating an obvious fact. 'I've never waited that long for nobody in my life, and I ent starting now.' There was one you'd wait for till doomsday, a still voice inside told him, but he hurriedly turned his thoughts elsewhere.

'Well, what do you think we should do?' said Margaret Ann.

'It do stand to reason, don't it? We'll go and talk to your Reverend Williams and ask him to marry us as quick as he can. That don't seem such a big thing to arrange.'

'But I told you, Evan, it wouldn't be respectful to the dead! What would the neighbours think?'

He laughed at that. 'Unless you'm thinking about tramping back up here every day to ask them, I don't expect you'll ever find out,' he said.

That threw her into further confusion. 'But this house. . .surely you don't expect me to leave it?'

The smile died on his face. 'Why not? What was you thinking of doing? I live down the Ranks, you do know that.'

'Of course – but this is such a lovely place, and it's all furnished, tidy, ready for us to move in. All you'd have to find would be the rent.'

'Aye, and that's nothing, of course! Let's see, the last I heard, it was just about double what the Ranks house do cost me.'

'B-but I thought you was earning good money.'

'I am, Margaret Ann, but there's good money and good money. This is a boss's house. Your father got it a bit cheaper because he was on the staff, but even then he could never have afforded it if you'd had any brothers or sisters. I'm an independent contractor. Even if they let a working man take over the place, they'd charge me the full amount, not the employee rate.' He brooded for a moment, then went on, 'Anyway, the last place I'd want to live would be up here.'

'Why not? It's lovely!'

'Oh, yes, of course it is, if you don't have to get up at four o'clock of a January morning and walk the extra mile and a half to the pit, then work eight hours underground and walk back the extra at the end of it. The Ranks is far closer, and it's all on the flat.'

Cracks were beginning to appear in Margaret Ann's dream. 'But I'd be so much happier here!'

'So to hell with how happy I'd be, eh? Look, Margaret Ann, if you do marry me, you take the Ranks along with me – and we get married in a couple of weeks, right? If that don't suit you, you'd better find someone else.'

Fighting back tears, she shook her head. After a while, in a very small voice, she said, 'All right; the Ranks it is.'

'There's a good girl!' He softened slightly. 'Best to start fresh, anyway. This place would keep reminding you of the past. And you can take as much furniture and stuff as you do like – there's nothing much there now.'

That made her realize she had never seen the inside of his house. She had supposed it was like Sal Moses's cottage, but then remembered Sal's was furnished with the remains of her farmhouse goods and chattels, a far cry from what most Ranks dwellers could run to.

She gulped, forcing herself to face another unpleasant prospect. 'P'raps we should go and have a look at your house so I can see exactly what I'll want to take.'

'Good idea! I'll come and fetch you tomorrow after work and we'll spend the afternoon there.'

'Not unless we do see Pastor Williams in the morning and get that side of things sorted out. I don't care what you do say, Evan, it's just not right for me to be going in and out of houses with you and nobody else there.'

He gave an exasperated snort. 'Your bloody mother and her airs and graces! She might not have had two brass farthings, but she knew how to give you big ideas! That's not for the likes of us, Margaret Ann, that's for the bosses. Nobody'd care two hoots if you spent the whole day in my house with the curtains drawn and the doors locked. They might have a giggle about it, but they wouldn't care.'

'Well I care – and I'm going to be true to myself. One of us must have some standards and it do look as if it will have to be me!'

Evan's temper was rising now. What was so wonderful about this priggish little virgin that he was letting her carry on so? If he had any sense he'd walk out now, while there was still time. . .but he had given his word, and she was all alone, and he had never seen such perfect skin or such a tiny waist. . .

He got up to go. 'Now you listen to me, Margaret Ann. I'm only working until one o'clock tomorrow, because it's Saturday. I'll get bathed after, then come up and fetch you, and we'll go and see your minister. Once he have said when he'll marry us, you can tell him I want you to come and look at the house and leave it up to him. If he do say it's all right, maybe that will be good enough. If it ent, then you'll come into a bloody bare place on your wedding day, because I'm not doing nothing to it before you do see it.'

He crammed on his soft workman's cap and turned to leave, not even bidding her goodnight. Margaret

Ann was so miserable about the whole business that she sat down and sobbed for half an hour after he had left.

Evan's hobnail boots crunched on the frosty road as he headed downhill towards the village. The decisiveness he had shown in handling Margaret Ann was dissipated now and his mind was boiling with doubts about the future. As he walked, the conflicting ideas seemed to swoop in tightening circles like great sinister birds. Evan's mouth worked as he mentally argued out the matter with himself.

At one point he said aloud, 'You must be mad, mun. She do want you body and soul. . .' but that did not settle his tension and he continued to wonder why he was so set on marrying Margaret Ann.

Who could be further from Ellen Rourke? And who could be more his type than Ellen? That meant it was madness to take Margaret Ann. And yet, when he looked at her enchanting little face, or watched her pert, graceful walk as she moved along the village street, he felt a lot more for her than a passing warmth. He even derived pleasure from the passionate way she pursued her ideals of respectability and self-improvement. In his heart, he knew it was a mistake to marry her, and that was what had made him hold off for so long. But he had a big man's weakness for small, helpless things and the tragedy of her double bereavement had swept aside all his caution.

Was that enough for him to change his whole life? It depended how much he'd be losing. Just now, that seemed precious little. He was growing tired of working hard, earning his pay and then drinking and brawling it away. He was weary of rising alone in the cold predawn and coming home to an even colder hearth at night. He was capable of looking after himself; his cottage was clean and he ate properly. But it was

bleak and unlovely. Evan wanted a woman's warmth,
and he wanted children. Ellen, it seemed, would give
him neither. Apart from her, the only woman he had
seen in years who stirred him was Margaret Ann Jones.
And she was available.

He was still grappling with the question when he
reached Abercarn High Street. He had planned to
go straight home – company was the last thing he
wanted in his present mood – but as he passed the
main door of the Commercial, his resolve weakened.
A couple of pints would send him off to sleep a lot
better than the memory of that row with Margaret
Ann. . .then again, he didn't want to be bleary-eyed
and bad tempered when they went to see the preacher
tomorrow. . . He was swept by a desolate vision of
chapels and preachers, the telescoped memory of a
childhood that had seemed all deaths and funerals and
hellfire sermons.

'Oh, bugger the preacher – and you and all, Margaret
Ann! You can have me as I am or not at all,' he muttered, and pushed open the pub door.

CHAPTER FIVE

N O ONE COULD have called it a perfect day for a wedding. Still, Evan reflected, looking out through the back bedroom window at the lowering grey sky, it wasn't snowing or raining, and that was something. The grey, iron-bound cold March day matched his mood. He wanted this marriage, he kept telling himself, so why did he feel so imprisoned? His spirit knew why. The answer was roaming along a country road somewhere, free as the tinkers she had sprung from, tagging along behind some third-rate travelling players. Evan sighed and sluiced cold water from the china basin over his face and shoulders. No point in might-have-beens. Margaret Ann was here and now and she would make him a good wife.

Good was the word... Even now, she was staying with the minister's family over in Cae Gorlan Road, because she and Pastor Williams had decided it was not quite proper for a young unmarried woman to live alone in a house where her husband-to-be could come calling without a chaperon. It seemed much wickedness could happen in two weeks. *Never mind, Evan,* he thought. *After today, she's all yours, and none of them will be able to say anything about how you do behave with her. Except Margaret Ann herself,* the insistent little warning voice whispered. . .

'That'll be the day!' he snorted aloud. 'There's one person do wear the trousers in this house – me! It'll take more than Margaret Ann to make it any different.'

Perhaps, but she had already made a lot of difference to the house itself. Two weeks ago, it had been a whitewashed cottage, with stone flagged floors and a few sticks of minimal furniture. Now there were rag rugs on the floors, the walls had been papered in the parlour and main bedroom, and the whole place was bursting with the ornate mahogany furniture which Margaret Ann had moved down from the Rhyswg Road house. For the first time ever, the cupboards were crammed with china and glass, and there were neat piles of bed and table linen in the big press under the stairs. Now and then, Evan felt he was choking under the mountain of household goods.

Even now, he was eyeing one of them suspiciously. It was a wood and glass clock, the glazed sections showing off the pendulum and weights, the wood, stained black to counterfeit ebony, forming barley-sugar columns and finishing the whole thing with an absurd classical pediment topped by an imperial eagle. It was almost unnecessary to look at the face to learn the timepiece was made in Germany. It was Margaret Ann's prize possession, and had always hung in the passage at the Rhyswg Road house. Now it occupied a similar position in Evan's cramped cottage. The trouble was that here the passage was so narrow it was almost impossible to stand back far enough to see the time.

He managed it now, and discovered that nervousness had wakened him far too early. The wedding was at noon; he was ready to go and it was still barely eight o'clock.

Evan was wearing a new suit – only the second he had ever owned. He had hoped to get away with the other one – the one Gran had bought for his father's funeral. But he had been only seventeen when she got

him that, and though she had bought it loose and long,
he had grown three inches in height and filled out a
couple of stone in the intervening decade. It still went
on him, but the sleeves stopped two inches short of
his big knobby wrists and the trousers hung clear of
his ankles. He looked ridiculously like an overgrown
version of the boy urchins whose portraits appeared
on advertising hoardings. Over the years, it had been
worn only for funerals and a couple of weddings, but
even so the cheap material was shiny and threadbare.

A week ago, he had reluctantly spent a little money
on a three-piece suit of the cheapest grey tweed he
could find. It was as stiff as board and the hairy surface scratched like barbed wire, but it fitted him like
a glove and his magnificent physique and swaggering
walk made it look acceptable. With it he wore the only
decent possession his father had passed on to him, a
gold half-hunter watch and chain. 'Wouldn't call the
king my uncle!' he told his reflection in the watery old
parlour mirror.

Evan moved into the back kitchen. He had lit the
range on waking that morning, and the banked-down
fire had warmed the small room. Lamplight brightened the grim morning and he started to feel more
cheerful. Maybe a bit of breakfast would help. . .

But when he opened the food cupboard and contemplated the piece of cold cooked bacon and the half-loaf
of bread, his appetite disappeared. Plenty of time for
eating after. There was a hamper of fresh food he
had bought yesterday, sitting snug on the slate slab in
the larder. That was for Margaret Ann to unpack. He
sliced a hunk of bread off the loaf and spread dripping
on it, then went to make tea. That would do him well
enough until dinner time.

The snack was finished and the teapot washed and
put away within minutes. Evan stalked around the
small room like a tiger in a zoo, clasping and unclasping

his hands, continually wandering over to the window
to peer outside. After a while the warmth became stifling. God damn, it was only quarter past nine now! He
couldn't stand any more of this. A walk would do him
good. . .

Outside, the raw morning air made him move swiftly. He pulled on his soft cap and tied his white muffler
tightly around his neck. Wedding or no wedding, he
wasn't going to catch no pneumonia from walking
about in just his suit. Within minutes he was strid-
ing out of the village on the Gwyddon road, with no
particular destination in mind. It was quiet up there,
beyond the distillery pond. He could sit and watch the
water and have a think. . . Finally, the time began to
slide away. When he took the half-hunter from his
waistcoat pocket, it said half past ten. That was better!
He could take his time going back now, call for Arthur
Webb who was his best man, maybe have another cup
of tea, and it would be time.

As he strolled back through the market square, a
familiar, unwelcome voice hailed him. 'Evan, boy!
Where you been? Haven't seen you this long time!'

'I'd a' thought you'd be quite pleased about that,
Billy, considering what happened last time.' It was Billy
Stout, the thug Evan had driven away from Margaret
Ann. There had been further trouble since then, and
Evan had been provoked into fighting him. Stout was
adept with the boot and the broken beer glass, but Evan
had been a street fighter as long as he had – and Evan
also had huge fists and nimble feet. Stout had been
dragged away unconscious, minus two teeth and a lot
of self-importance. He would not lightly forgive such
treatment, and now Evan was wary of the man's apparent friendliness.

'Why should you want to see me now?'

'Oh, this and that, boy. Someone been looking for
you this morning.'

'When? Who was it? The minister, one of the Webb boys?'

Stout shook his head, his eyes shining secretively. 'What, for Evan the ladies' man? This visitor was female, all over.'

'I thought you'd have learned to lay off Margaret Ann Jones by now, Billy. Come on, spit it out. Who?'

But Billy had slid away, just beyond reach, and now he was moving off before Evan could catch him.

'That's for me to know and you to find out, mun. So long. See you down the Bush some time. I do like it better than the Commercial. . .less violent . . .' And his voice faded as he turned the corner up the High Street.

Evan's impulse was to run after Stout and shake the information out of him, but second thoughts told him that was probably what the man wanted – to stir him up and make him look like a bruiser in chapel later on. Better ignore it, keep his temper. It could only be someone like Sal Moses coming to wish him luck, anyway. Margaret Ann certainly wouldn't let him see her on their wedding day before the ceremony. As he speculated, he turned left almost automatically, to avoid following Billy. That meant that instead of heading for home or the chapel, he was approaching the Commercial. Evan glanced longingly at the open door. God, he could just do with a pint now . . .straight down, wash away the nerves and the cobwebs, make him ready for anything. . . And make you reek like a brewery in front of Margaret Ann and the minister, said the voice of his conscience, which was sounding more like Margaret Ann's with every moment that passed. Rebellion began to mount in Evan's breast. What was wrong with a man having a drink, just one drink, before he got married? There'd be precious little for the rest of the day! And anyhow, didn't Siân Ellis keep some mint humbugs under the bar for her more timid customers to suck on their way home? That was it! He could have a drink and still keep everybody happy.

Alf Ellis, the publican, pulled him a pint, and grinned as he handed over a couple of the mints Evan asked for. 'By damn, even the big ones do get caught in the end, eh, Evan?' he said, but it was friendly teasing, without the malice of Billy Stout. Evan smiled sheepishly and began to move over to the corner with his drink.

'How's your Siân, now, Alf? 'Ave she got over her flu yet?'

Alf nodded, solemn again. 'Oh, aye, just about, but she's still weak, mind. The doctor told her to get out for a walk in the mornings, to strengthen her up a bit, like, but she still ent strong enough to serve behind the bar. Won't be for another month, I don't reckon. She's out now, walking down as far as the Swan. I'll send her through when she do get in – she'll want to give you all the best for today.'

'I'm off in a minute, Alf. It's the bride who's allowed to be late, remember?'

'Hey up – here she is now. I'm glad she won't miss you – very fond of you, she is.'

But Siân Ellis looked confused rather than pleased to see Evan. Instead of coming straight into the front bar, she glanced at him and then hurried through to the back of the pub. Puzzled, her husband followed her. Evan vaguely heard them murmuring to each other, then Siân finally came in and took a seat beside him.

'Evan, love,' she said, 'you – you do know I wouldn't make trouble for you and Margaret Ann, don't you?'

'Course I do.' He grinned wickedly. 'Don't tell me you've heard something bad about her!'

Siân managed an answering smile, but she was uncomfortable. 'Hush, now. You know how much chance there is of that! No, it's something I hardly like to tell you. . .but – but I can't keep it secret. You'd never forgive me if you found out.'

Evan's merriment faded as she spoke. 'What's wrong?'

'When I was out walking, I thought I'd come back up the canal bank. I got just the other side of the lock and I could hear somebody crying. . .not loud, more like a child whimpering; desperate, like. At first I couldn't see nothing, and then – well, she was all curled up in a ball, sitting down on the stones at the foot of the lock, with a black shawl wrapped up tight around her.' Siân lost her nerve momentarily and her voice faded.

'Margaret Ann?' said Evan, misunderstanding. 'On her wedding day? What was she doing there?'

'No, love, not Margaret Ann – that's the trouble. That other lovely girl – the Irish one.'

'Ellen – Ellen Rourke?'

'Aye, that's it.'

He started to get up. 'Is she still down there?'

Siân reached up and pressed him back to his seat. 'Wait a minute, Evan, please, you must hear me out!'

She managed to make him listen to the rest of it. 'She didn't know about you and Margaret Ann, Evan. I think she've had some sort of setback – she looked really worn out, and sort of thin, no colour. She'd just come back to see you, she said. But she didn't like to come to the house, just in case it made things awkward for you. She got here early this morning – to tell the truth, I reckon she'd slept out somewhere – and she come into the village as soon as it got light. The first person she seen was Billy Stout. She don't know him, but she said he was wearing an old battered brown bowler hat, and that must be Billy. She gave him a message for you and he went off to deliver it, only instead of that he come back an hour later and said he couldn't because you was off getting married.'

Evan, ashen-faced, bowed his head, fighting for self-control. 'I'll kill that bastard when I do get hold of him,' he said through clenched teeth. 'I saw him only half an hour back and he just led me on. . .'

'Steady, now, Evan. Remember, you are getting married this morning. Nothing you can do to change that, is there?'

Evan stared at her. 'I don't know, Siân. I just don't know what to do. If Ellen do need me, I got to see her, at least.'

'And what about after? You know you won't just see her. Margaret Ann do need you even more. Look, *bach*, I like Ellen, what I do know of her, much more than Margaret Ann. But Ellen can shift for herself. She's born to it, and you don't need me to tell you that. But Margaret Ann. . .you'd destroy her if you left her now. How are you going to live with that?'

'But what shall I do about Ellen? I can't just leave her there like that.'

'I know, but she's a sensible girl. I told her how things are. You go and see her now. You've still got time, if you'm quick. Talk to her, but leave it at talk. If you don't, you'll regret it the rest of your life.'

'I'll regret it the rest of my life if I do, an' all, that's the trouble.'

Siân managed to smile at him. 'Go on now, mun. It's eleven o'clock. She's still down by the lock, but you'll have to shift if you'm going to get there and back by twelve. I'll send someone to tell Arthur Webb to meet you outside the Garn. Hurry up. You'll manage.'

He was out of the door almost before she had finished speaking.

The canal that passed through Abercarn had seen better days. Too soon, the railway line had come after it, efficiently mopping up the goods traffic which had floated along its brown waters to Newport. Now it had more the look of a country stream than a transport artery in an industrial area. It was still used for bulkier goods carriage, but sometimes a couple of hours would pass without a barge going by. As a result, the south side of the small stone bridge just beyond the base of the lock gates was a good place to hide from the world. Small boys played pirate games there in summer, and in the autumn, women sent their children to pick blackberries and cobnuts. Now it was a retreat for Ellen Rourke.

When Evan found her, she was getting up and brushing the dead grass from her skirt. Siân Ellis was right – she did look as though she had suffered a setback. The brilliant hair was as flamboyant as ever, but her formerly voluptuous body was thin as a rail. She was deathly pale and blue shadows deepened her eye sockets.

None of this worried Evan too much. He had lived with poverty and overwork all his life. The girl could have come to look like this after a couple of days without a good meal and two or three nights sleeping under hedges, and would recover equally fast with food and shelter. It was the despair on her face which concerned him more.

He saw her before she was aware of his presence. He stepped forward and said, very quietly, 'Ellen, my love,' then held out his arms.

She glanced up, gave a sob, then rushed up the bank and flung herself against him. 'Oh, Evan, me darling, what have I done? I sent you away and now it's too late!' And she began crying in earnest.

He let her weep undisturbed for a while, then said, 'Can you talk about it?'

'Oh, sure! It's no great thing – just me and me big ideas, that's all. The Haggars are off the road.'

He wanted to laugh out loud. He had feared, at the very least, that some stranger had made her pregnant and then abandoned her. He managed not to betray his emotion and merely said, 'For good?'

'Who knows? It was terrible, Evan – one of their little girls drowned in the river while we was camped there. Mrs Haggar went well near crazy, and after a bit Mr Haggar said he'd have to stop the show for a little while until he could get her back to being herself again.'

'So they had to send you packing, is that it?'

'Just about, yes. They're lovely people – they'd never make me leave. But they'd have run out of money and food soon enough without another useless mouth, so I said I'd make my own way till they was back in business.'

'They must have owed you some wages, though.'

She managed a watery smile. 'Sure, but little Miss Moneybags has to say, keep it for the little 'uns, they need it more. Now look at me!'

Evan's face was unreadable. He hardly knew how he felt – foolish, for having worried too much about this girl; relieved, that she was in no greater trouble than a lack of employment; certainly regretful that she had come back now, ready to accept him, when he was on the brink of marriage to someone else. Wait, though; did he really regret that? He knew he would have if she had flung herself into his arms saying she couldn't live without him. It was another matter when he was just the bolt-hole she ran to when her travelling show closed down. Margaret Ann worshipped him. This girl would never regard him as more than insurance for bad times. . .

Some of his doubts must have communicated themselves to Ellen, for now she looked up at him, suddenly aware he was not all passionate concern.

'What is it, Evan? Don't you want me any more? Am I really too late?'

Gently, he held her at arm's length. 'Aye, girl, I think you are. You know I'm getting married in half an hour?'

She nodded, eyes never leaving his face. 'I-I thought when you came, you might have. . .'

'. . . Changed my mind?' Evan shook his head. 'She's not so tough as you. It'd break her. Anyhow, I'm not playing second fiddle to a travelling showman.'

'You know you'd never be that!'

'What am I, then? If that kid had lived and the audiences had kept coming, you'd be flashing your petticoats at some tentful of miners without another thought for me. That's the truth, ennit?'

'You don't understand! I love you.'

'You only get one chance, and you had yours up Pant-yr-Esg four months ago.' Even as he said that, he knew it was untrue; knew that if she came to him freely, not in desperation, he would still be putty in her hands. Today, though, the decision was easy. He dipped a hand in his pocket. 'Look, *cariad*, I can't give you more than two pound. That's a lot more than I can afford, getting married an' all. But I won a bet the other night. I can manage it if I'm careful. Get yourself a good meal, then for God's sake go home to your father, and put the rest by. You'm safer there than with any Haggars and you'll have a few bob from me to keep you going until you find some work.'

She took the money, a shamed flush staining her face. 'I thought you'd be offering love, not money, Evan,' she said, softly.

His face was cold. 'Love won't keep you warm under a hedge on a March night,' he said.

'But a place in your bed and by your fire would, I see that now.'

'I told you, you should have seen it four months back. Somebody else have taken the offer now. I changed my mind, too. I couldn't wait for ever after all.'

'Four months is a long time shy of forever.'

'I'd been waiting years before that, girl, and well you know it. Now, come on, off down the station and get a

train as far as Crosskeys, at least. And if you're going
to walk from there to Ynysddu, get some food inside
you first.' He helped her up the bank and stood awkwardly beside her at the roadside. Ellen, silent, showed
no inclination to start her journey. Finally, Evan said,
'I've got to go, you know that. She's waiting. . .'

Jealousy flared in Ellen's eyes. 'Aye – and much joy
may it bring her! Goodbye, Evan. I still say you're mine
underneath. Just remember. . .'

All the way up the road to the Garn, Evan was
exulting. He was free of her, free at last! The spell
was broken just because she had wanted him at the
wrong time for the wrong reasons. Perhaps it was a
sign of a clean break, a new beginning. His doubts
about Margaret Ann were gone now. Of course they'd
be happy. All he needed was a girl who'd love him and
not be always looking elsewhere.

He took out his father's half-hunter. Nearly five to
twelve. Even the timing was perfect. As long as she was
just a little bit late, she'd never even suspect how close
he'd run it.

Arthur Webb was on the steps outside the chapel.
He uttered a huge sigh of relief when he saw Evan
approaching. 'Thank God you're here, mun! I was
beginning to wonder if you was coming. Thought I'd
have to marry her myself. . .' His self-confident laugh
belied the beads of sweat on his upper lip.

Evan slapped his friend's shoulder. 'Bit of unfinished
business to sort out, that's all. Everything all right here,
is it?'

'Oh, aye, lovely. Mrs Williams have done a smashing
display of daffs in there – I think she've made it special
to make up to Margaret Ann for her mam and dad not
being here.' He paused and dug around in his waistcoat
pocket. 'And here's the ring, safe and sound. No backing out now, Evan.'

The big man smiled. 'I've never been more sure of

anything than this. I been on my own too long, Arthur. Time I had somebody to keep me warm o' nights.'

'The way that one do look at you, there'll be no trouble keeping warm,' said Webb. 'Come on, the minister's in there already and I think he's getting nervous.'

As they went through the chapel porch, Evan grinned. 'Hey, you know who's giving her away, because her dad's dead, do you? Giggly Williams, the minister's brother!'

It meant nothing to Arthur. Evan dropped his voice, 'Margaret Ann was quite sweet on him when I met her. I think she had high hopes of a white doorstep and a bay window. It couldn't have been the width of his shoulders, I know that!' He fell silent, and the two men walked down the narrow aisle, suddenly made awkward by the unfamiliar sanctity of their surroundings.

As Margaret Ann and Albert Williams arrived in the chapel porch at five past twelve, the organist struck up Wagner's Lohengrin wedding march. Williams looked down at her and squeezed her arm fondly. 'He's a lucky man, Margaret Ann – he doesn't deserve you!'

She gave him a radiant smile. 'Thank you, Albert – but you'm wrong. He saved me.' And with that she faced forward and began her triumphal entry to a life of purgatory.

CHAPTER SIX

T HERE WAS A party for the newly-weds after the ceremony at the minister's house – more neighbourly kindness in memory of Margaret Ann's recent bereavement. By mid-afternoon, Evan would have sold his soul for a quart of bitter, but warm fruit punch or tea were the only drinks on offer. Finally, they set off in a borrowed pony and trap to do the rounds of friends like Sal Moses who were too infirm or old to get to the wedding.

By the time their courtesy calls were complete, the early spring dusk was deepening. Evan drove down the centre row of the Ranks, stopped and lifted his bride down from the trap. 'Now,' he said, 'just to get the neighbours talking, I'm going to carry you over the threshold and then leave you – no, don't be soft, not for long! I'm just letting you make yourself at home while I take the trap back to the manse. If it do stay here till the morning, they'll steal the pony's shoes!'

Margaret Ann laughed in spite of the implied reminder of the roughness of the neighbourhood. 'All right, love,' – she savoured this first use of the intimate term – 'I'll make us some tea in about an hour. Take care, now.'

He carried her inside the low front door, set her down in the narrow hall, then bent and kissed her, deeply and passionately, for the first time. Drowning in his embrace, Margaret Ann staggered and clutched his arms. Evan smiled wolfishly. 'P'raps I should let that old pony manage for himself for a bit after all. . .'

She giggled shakily and fended him off. 'Get away with you – we've got the rest of our lives. . .' the enormity of that thought silenced her immediately and she gazed at him, suddenly still, as he turned to leave.

Precisely an hour later, he was back. The passage was dark, but lamplight spilled from the open kitchen door. A great contentment lapped over Evan. It was the first time in more than six months that he had come into this house with the knowledge that someone was eagerly awaiting his arrival, and then it was only his granny. He walked quietly along the passage. *Take her by surprise*, he thought. . .*see what she do get up to by herself*. . .but when he got to the door, he found the room was empty. The teapot was standing, warmed and ready, on the stone hob beside the fire. Two fine china cups and saucers had been placed side by side on a white cloth over the dark red plush table cover. But there was no sign of Margaret Ann. Evan went in, took off his cap and jacket, and went to get his tea. As he started pouring it, Margaret Ann came into the room. He stopped in his tracks.

'*Duw*, there's lovely you do look!' They were the only words he could find. She was like a painting brought to life.

His bride might be inexperienced, but she was intelligent, and she knew she lacked the confidence to undress gracefully in front of him. Their new home was so small that after his return, there would have been little opportunity to do anything else. So while he was away she had taken off her boned corset and voluminous petticoats, and put on a white robe of fine cotton lawn, ornately bordered with blue satin

ribbon and lace. She had been secretly trimming it in
every spare moment during the week before the wedding. The original garment had been a chaste cover-up
designed by her mother to form a foundation for her
bottom drawer. It was still completely respectable, but
its luxurious look lent a subtly wayward quality to
her obvious virginity. She had let down her hair and
brushed it and now it hung in a glowing veil to her hips.

Evan was spellbound. The intensity of her new sexual allure and acute consciousness that they were alone
together, married, banished all rational thought. With
an almost imbecilic expression on his face, he gestured
at the table. 'Tea, Margaret Ann?'

He loved her then. She stared at him incredulously
for a moment, then burst out laughing. 'I was thinking
of something stronger, *cariad*.'

He moved across the room and swept her up in his
arms. 'Evan, put me down – you'll drop me on the
stairs!'

'Not a chance, girl!' and he dipped his head to avoid
the low arch at the bottom of the staircase.

Her parents' enormous brass bed dwarfed the cottage's main bedroom, the feather mattress and eider-
down billowing seductively in all directions. Margaret
Ann had already turned back the covers, and he laid
her down in the fresh sheets as tenderly as though
she were made of glass, spreading the glorious hair
out across the pillow.

She gazed up at him, shy but fascinated by the beauty
of his face in the soft golden lamplight. Evan returned
her look steadily, then said, very quietly, 'Until the day
break, until the shadows flee away, turn, my beloved,
and be thou like a roe or a young hart in the mountains
of Bether.'

'Evan, that's the Old Testament! I thought you said
you was a heathen.'

His laugh was soft and teasing. 'Yes, but wouldn't

you know the one book I do know by heart is the
indelicate one!'

Margaret Ann felt the blush staining her throat and
cheeks. The Song of Songs was the book their Sunday
school teacher always hastily passed over. When she
had peeped secretly at it in the family Bible at home,
she found it littered with coy marginal notes explaining that the graphic descriptions of male and female
beauty were really elaborate references to God and
His Church. It had not stopped her and her friends
reading the forbidden passages with much embarrassed giggling. Suddenly, though, she knew they had
been wrong; as wrong as the dried-up old theologians
who made the pompous notes about the Church and
God. The Song was a wonderful love poem, and now
someone was speaking it for her, the way it had been
intended.

He reached down and stroked her long red hair and
said,

'. . .the Rose of Sharon and the Lily of the Valleys.
As the lily among thorns, so is my love among the
daughters. . . My beloved spake and said unto me,
rise up, my love, my fair one, and come away. For lo,
the winter is past, the rain is over and gone; the time
of the singing of birds is come, and the voice of the
turtle is heard in our land. The fig tree putteth forth
her green figs, and the vines with tender grapes give
a good smell. Arise, my love, my fair one, and come
away.'

He sat down on the edge of the bed, the big, scarred
miner's hands now moving softly as a child's to unfas-
ten the ribbon which held together the neckline of her
nightgown. Margaret Ann felt no more nervousness,
no false shyness, either, about showing her body to a
man. The composer of that ancient love lyric and her

husband were one man, all men, and for this moment
she was all women. She had no idea what he intended
to do to her, and no fear about it. It could be nothing
bad.

As he slipped the fine cotton off her shoulders, he
began to recite again, his basso voice soft as black
velvet:

'Thy breasts are like two young roes that are twins,
which feed among the lilies. Until the day break,
and the shadows flee away, I will get me to the mountain of myrrh, and to the hill of frankincense. . .
Thou art fair, my love, there is no spot on thee. . .'

He bent, and began kissing her breasts, softly, but
with rising passion. Margaret Ann rapidly began to
forget who or where she was. He raised his face,
resting it against her body for a moment, and said,
'I do know a lot more of it, but I don't think we
want more now. . .' Then he reached over and turned
out the lamp. He even understood that too much
light would be wrong for this first, secret time of
intimacy.

When they eventually woke to broad daylight they were
woven together like one many-limbed being, wrapped
around with the tangle of her hair. Evan patiently
smoothed it back, then traced the line of her features with his finger. She smiled against his hand,
and said, 'I do know already what we'll call our first
daughters.'

'What if they'm sons?'

'There'll be daughters, too. Rose of Sharon, then Lily
of the Valleys.'

He had already bent his face to her body again
and his big laugh rumbled up, muffled against her

ribcage. 'Terrible mouthful, girl. Better call them Rose and Lily, don't you think? And if you'm that set on choosing names, p'raps we'd better see about getting babies to give them to. More fun than naming, any day. . .'

CHAPTER SEVEN

Evan's gang of colliers were soon singing Margaret Ann's praises. He had always been a harsh taskmaster, vicious with slackers and moody even with the best workers. But after he married, he seemed to mellow.

'I've never been much for chapel girls, myself,' said Tommy Watkins to his butty, 'but if that Margaret Ann can turn Evan soft, I might even think about finding a bit and trying it out.'

'And what would your Cati say to that, Tom? Holiest place she've ever been is the back bar down the Market Tavern! Sometimes I think you two must of got married in there.' Owen Price had known Watkins long enough to realize that Tommy's acquaintance with womanly virtue was minimal.

Tommy glared at him, the daydream shattered. 'Don't talk, mun! You should of seen her this morning, lying there flat on her back with her mouth open, snoring like a bloody great sow. When I do see her like that, I think I must have been a bit tipsy when I met her.'

Price hooted with mirth. 'Tipsy? You was stiff drunk. Mind, she must of been, an' all. There's times I think she got a worse bargain than you did. You got to look like Evan to land a catch like Margaret Ann.'

'You reckon?' Tommy's admiration had turned to malice as he contemplated his own unsatisfactory lot. 'Well you just watch how long it do last. They may be little lovebirds now, but the first time he do get drunk and knock her about a bit, it'll be another story.'

'No, you got him wrong.' Owen took a last swallow from his can of cold tea, then prepared to resume work. 'Evan do save his fists for men. He never laid a finger on that Irish piece all the time they was together, and she give him a hell of a time.'

'That shows how much you do know. She never pushed him.'

'Only 'cos she was too busy dodging him.'

'That's right. But this one don't want to dodge him, do she? He never knew where he was with Ellen Rourke. Had to mind his manners. He couldn't shake Margaret Ann off in a month of Sundays – and I bet he'll want to soon enough.'

Price glanced over Tommy's shoulder and signalled him to silence. A big shadow interrupted the dim glow from their lamps, which they had left beside the roadway. 'What's this,' Evan wanted to know, 'fancied a lie-in this morning, did you? Come on, I don't hire you to sit around after dinner.'

Watkins and Price picked up their mandrills and headed back towards their stint. 'You wait and see,' muttered Tommy. 'Give it six months and he'll be back to kicking us arse over tip if he do catch us like that.'

'Keep your voice down, mun,' warned Price. 'If he do hear you, he'll do it this minute.'

In fact it took little more than three months.

He only hit Margaret Ann once. It was the night he got drunk for the first time since their wedding, after they quarrelled because she would not make love now that she was pregnant.

It started trivially enough. When she told him the good news after he arrived home from the pit, he embraced her instinctively, delighted by the prospect of fatherhood. Then, inevitably, jubilation turned to desire and his hands began to stray over her breasts and hips.

'Come on, my lovely,' he murmured against her neck. 'Let's go upstairs for a bit, and celebrate.'

Margaret Ann stiffened and drew back. 'Wh-what d'you mean, celebrate? There'll be none of that until after I've had the baby.'

He was aghast. 'You don't know what you'm saying. You can't be more than six weeks – you've only missed your time of the month once, even I can work that out.'

She was tight-lipped. 'Decent men don't notice that sort of thing. That's private. . .intimate. . .'

'Don't be so bloody daft! What could be more intimate than the things we've done? It's part of being man and wife. I do know you'm still young, girl, but you can't really expect me to keep off you for eight or nine months. It'd be more than flesh and blood could stand.'

Margaret Ann was really angry, now. 'Not eight or nine months, Evan – a year, probably. The midwife do reckon it takes a good year from conception to get back to being all right again. It's keeping at it like animals and then starting again straight after that do make so many girls old before their time. Well, not me!'

'We'll see whether you will or not, my lady! I'm sick of all these false airs and graces. Rhyswg Road ent Buckingham Palace, you know.' Evan leaned towards her again and grabbed her around the waist, roughly this time. She tried to back away but he was too strong for her. 'You'm my wife, Margaret Ann, and you'll do what I say, in or out of bed. Come here.'

But instead she wrenched away from him. As she did, he grasped the fragile fabric of her dress and it tore apart from shoulder to waist. Suddenly her eyes were burning pools of hatred in a bloodless face. 'I might have expected that from you, you great brute!' she said. 'Now leave me be and get back to your sty!' And as he stood, blankly staring at the fragment of cloth in his hand, she whirled away up the stairs, slamming the door as she went.

Evan did not try to follow her. After a few moments, he flung the material aside and said, 'Well bugger you, then – I'm off.' He knew she would be upstairs, curled in their bed and watching the door as though expecting a barbarian army to pound across the threshold. Well, she'd be disappointed. He wasn't hanging around where he was not wanted.

Hours later, he staggered in from the Commercial, drunk and penniless. He was ready to make peace now, but only if his wife met him half way. But Margaret Ann's lifelong conditioning against drink ensured that no such tolerance lay ahead. The lamp was out in the back kitchen and the fire had burned low. He shook down the ashes and banked it for the night, cursing quietly as he staggered against the hot grate bars. Upstairs, the brass bed creaked. Well, one thing was certain. She wouldn't be opening her arms to welcome him. . .

Evan started up the stairs. Might as well get it over with as quick as possible. Then she'd forgive him and that would be that. A year without doing it, indeed! The news must have made her a bit crazy for a while, that was all. . . He reached out to push open the bedroom door, but it did not budge. He tried again, this time more forcefully.

'Margaret Ann? What's wrong with this door? I can't shift it. . .'

'No, and you won't, neither! The chair's under the latch, jammed solid. It'll take more than a drunken thug to get through that!'

'Will it, be buggered?' The words came out in a furious bellow. This was too much! Who the bloody hell did she think she was?

Evan stood back on the narrow landing and took a rush at the door, flinging his shoulder against its plank surface. There was a splintering noise inside, and abruptly he was in the bedroom, the shattered fragments of the chair scattered around him. 'Gone mad, have you?' he said. 'When I do want to get in somewhere, it takes more than an old chair to stop me. Now come here.'

'I will not – I ent afraid of you! Let me pass.' She was standing in front of him, barefoot and in her nightgown, dwarfed by his great bulk.

'Where d'you think you'm going?'

'In the other room, if you're staying in here. I will not share a bed with a drunken pig.'

'You'll do just what I bloody well tell you.'

Her stare was full of contempt. Perhaps it was that, more than her words, which moved him to violence. 'And how are you going to make me?' she asked.

'Just – like – this, you stuck-up bitch!' he roared, striking her back and forth across the face in time to the first three, strung-out words.

By his standards, he had not hit her hard. But he had never hit a woman before, only men, and Margaret Ann was small even for a female. The impact threw her back on to the bed, blood spurting from the corner of her mouth where her teeth had driven into her lower lip. Her hand flew to the wound and she stared up at him, face blank as an animal's. There was no plea for mercy, no cry of pain, merely that contemptuous look in her eyes again.

Evan could not help what he did next. It was her silent invulnerability that did it, he realized later. He could have beaten her to a pulp, and still she would have looked at him like that. Driven by a fury that was more despair than anything else, he threw himself on her, tearing at her nightgown, gritting out, 'You will have me...you will...you'm my wife, understand?' And to his eternal shame, he ripped the gown from her and took her by force, feeling her hatred pulsing out at him with every shuddering movement of his own body.

She lay absolutely still. It was soon over. Afterwards, he slumped on her, trying not to burst into sobs. Eventually she said, 'There. You've had what you wanted. Now get off me, you animal, and go in the other room. And don't you come near me again until after the baby have come.'

Alone in the other room, he wept for his lost love, for his lost dignity and for the loneliness which stretched ahead of him. Oh, God, save me from virtuous women... Ellen, love, I should have listened down there by the canal that morning. I should have listened and taken you instead. I wasn't made for no Sunday woman...

Margaret Ann stayed indoors until the bruises had disappeared from her cheeks. After that, she silently returned to her normal domestic routine, and even allowed him back into their bedroom. But he knew better than to lay hands on her again during her pregnancy. His colliers suffered for it, and the Commercial saw a lot more of his wages, but gradually Margaret Ann reverted to apparent normality. It was as if that terrible night had never happened...except that they both knew it had, and that their marriage would never be the same again.

The following February, their first son was born. He was a big, fair-haired, handsome baby. And he had a club foot.

PART TWO
1895–1901

I charge you, O ye daughters of Jerusalem,
by the roes, and by the hinds of the field,
that ye stir not up, nor awake my love,
till he please.

Song of Songs
Ch.II, v.7

CHAPTER EIGHT

1895

ABERCARN MARKET SQUARE was teeming with activity. For a few weeks after harvest, it was always like this, with extra farm produce to be bought up for bottling and preserving, and, for once, plenty of cheap meat available as the farmers slaughtered extra stock before the onset of winter. The modest boom attracted travelling entertainers, looking for quick pickings before life got harder with the onset of cold weather. Today the afternoon was brightened by a fire-eater, the perennially popular old man with his performing bear, and a Punch and Judy show. It seemed half the village was out to goggle at them.

Margaret Ann sighed, exasperated at her own ungainliness, and muttered, '*Duw* help, girl, you should be used to it by now – it have happened often enough!' Then she took a firmer grip on the stout willow basket beside her. She was strong in spite of her small stature, but she was also seven months pregnant with her sixth child.

'Here – let me! You shouldn't have to carry that in your condition.'

The woman who wrested away her basket was about the same age as Margaret Ann, whip-thin, tall and dark, with white skin that threw the hair into sharp contrast. Margaret Ann was vaguely aware of having

seen her before, but was at a loss to put a name to the
face.

'It's all right, you don't know me. I'm from up the
Gwyddon – farmer's wife. You do live in the Ranks,
don't you?' And her helper turned towards the terraces,
still carrying Margaret Ann's shopping.

Puffing along beside her, Margaret Ann tried to protest. 'You must be ever so busy, down here selling your
own produce. Don't put yourself out for me – I can
manage, really.'

'Aye, I know you can manage, but I don't see why
you should have to. Anyway, I'm here to buy, not sell.
We'm sheep farmers. Come on, now, you can repay me
with a nice cup of tea.'

Her name was Jennifer Job and she lived alone with
her husband on one of the most remote farms in the
parish. Over tea, she was very talkative. 'You must
think I'm a terrible chatterbox,' she said, 'but we'm
so cut off up the Trwyn that I never seem to talk to
anybody except Harry, and you do run out of new
things to say after a while.'

Jenny had started out as a domestic servant at
Abercarn House, but she was a country girl and was
unhappy in the heart of the mining valley. Her job as
kitchen maid and then as assistant cook gave her little
contact with life above stairs, and after a few years she
was convinced she faced a dreary future with no prospect of improvement. Then, one market day, she met
Harry Job, whose family had farmed the Trwyn, at the
remote top of the Gwyddon valley, for generations. His
cousin Emrys, an indoor servant at Abercarn House,
acted as matchmaker, and within a few months, Harry
had asked Jenny to marry him. She had not been madly
in love – he was shy and moody – but the thought of her
own home and family in a beautiful rural setting were
very attractive.

Jenny made a wry face. 'That was ten years ago. You

get tired of a lovely view when there's never any people about, and the family never did come along,' she said.

Rocking one toddler on her lap and hoping against hope that the two who played boisterously in front of the fire would not start fighting, Margaret Ann wondered momentarily if Jenny knew when she was well off.

'Haven't you got any friends at all?' she asked.

Jenny shook her head, suddenly tearful. 'Y-you must think I'm awful, coming on to you in the square like that and then babbling away about my troubles – but I was getting a bit desperate, to tell the truth.'

'I'm glad you did. I'm lonely for female company, too – and it do sound as if you need a friend. Why are you so worried?'

'Not worried, exactly. . .maybe frightened would be a better word.' The intensity of her tone chilled Margaret Ann. Jenny went on, 'Harry's brooding over things, I can tell. There've always been Jobs up the Trwyn, but it do look as if I'm barren and we'll be the last ones. . .'

Then she was crying, and Margaret Ann hurriedly put down the baby to go and comfort her new friend. 'Come on, now, it may be his fault, not yours. Have he said he blames you?'

'Not in so many words. . .but he don't talk to me much at all, now. We always used to come down to market together, but now he sends me on my own, often as not. . .oh, dear God, what am I going to do?'

The intensity of the woman's grief overcame the fact that she was almost a stranger. Margaret Ann was intensely moved by her hálf-told story, and a self-pitying voice told her that her own plight was little better, although apparently so different. She embraced Jenny Job and spoke with an authority she did not feel.

'You'll be my friend, that's what. There's no reason why you should live so cut off, just because you'm a few miles up the valley. And another thing – why are you giving up hope for children? You can't be any older than me.'

'I'm twenty-eight.'

'You do wear a lot better than me, then. I'm only twenty-six. But you've got years ahead of you for having babies yet.' She gave Jenny a long look. 'I suppose you are still. . .er. . .living as man and wife?'

Jenny's eyes were downcast. 'Not often, now. Not this long time. He do seem – well, far away from me, somehow. . .'

'Well, you better get him a bit closer, hadn't you, or you'm never going to be a mother. No wonder there's no sign of a family!' Margaret Ann, whose own sexual experience was confined to Evan's almost insatiable demands, found it all but incomprehensible that man and wife did not make love several times a week.

'I don't think I'd know how to suggest it, now.'

'How about flirting with him – you know, as if you was still courting?'

Jenny stared at her blankly for a moment. 'But I never did. Emrys introduced us, and we went walking and talked, and looked at the farm, and then he asked me to marry him.'

'Just like that?'

'Well, yes. He was the first man who ever made an approach. . .'

'But after – when you went back home after the wedding – what then?'

The other woman looked away again, blushing this time. 'I-it frightened me, the first few times. I didn't know, see, nobody had ever told me that was how. . . I got used to it later on, mind. I do miss it terrible, now, but I think he've made up his mind I don't want none of that.'

'We'll just have to change it for him, then, won't we?' *Duw*, she told herself, and I thought I was the innocent

when I got married! Time to put modesty aside and
explain that there's nothing wrong with enjoying it. . .

Jenny Job stayed for more than two hours, and by the
time they parted they were firm friends. At the door,
she squeezed Margaret Ann's hand and said, 'You've
been so kind to me. I really think I might manage,
now.'

And it seemed that matters improved between husband and wife. Jenny started coming in to market four
times a month instead of the one or two visits she had
been used to. She always stopped to see Margaret Ann
and on two occasions she brought Harry with her. He
was short and powerfully-built, quite handsome in a
brooding, dark way. His presence inhibited Margaret
Ann from asking whether Jenny had made any progress, and then she had other matters on her mind for
a while.

The first day she and Jenny were alone together
again, she had been feeling restless and light-headed
all day. After a while, she said, 'Funny, but I usually feel
like this when the baby's going to come. It isn't due for
another fortnight, so far as I can tell.'

As she spoke, a dull ache started at the base of her
spine. That confirmed her suspicions. 'Jenny, quick –
I think you'd better go down and see if the midwife is
in. I'm starting, and it don't seem right.'

The midwife was out on another confinement, but
one of the older women in the Ranks was almost as
competent and swiftly came to help. Jenny stayed with
her for the rest of the day and through the night, while
Evan sat in the back bar of the Commercial drinking
himself to a stupor. Margaret Ann gave birth to twins
just before dawn the next day, after a frightful labour.
The first was stillborn. The second, badly deformed,
survived for less than an hour.

'Just as well,' said Eluned Hughes, the helpful neighbour. 'It would have been a curse if that second one had lived, wouldn't it?' She and Jenny were outside in the wash-house, Eluned scrubbing her hands and arms clean of the blood and fluid that had spattered them. The two tiny corpses were wrapped together in a piece of worn-out linen on the plain deal table. The makeshift winding sheet drew Jenny's eyes irresistibly, and she trembled as she looked at it.

'Why are they together like that?' she asked eventually. 'Surely the stillborn one don't have to be given a funeral?'

Eluned gave her a wondering look. 'There wasn't no doctor or midwife here, was there? Neither of them do need a funeral.'

'But I didn't think that was allowed. . .'

That provoked a grim chuckle. 'Lots of things that's not allowed do still get done, my lovely, and most of them do a damn' sight more damage than this. Have you got any idea how much it do cost to raise five kids?'

Jenny shook her head, mute in the face of the other's friendly scorn.

Eluned went on, 'Well, let me tell you it's too much to leave any spare for burials. As far as the law is concerned — and that do include the midwife, the doctor and the Registrar — they was two stillbirths. The doctor won't be interested enough to examine them, anyhow. That way it'll cost Evan half an hour up the cemetery with a spade and that's the end of it.'

'But it — he — was alive for a little bit, anyway. Don't that earn him a decent burial?'

'Jesus loves the little children, kidda, and he do love them just as much even if the minister haven't said a few pious words over their poor dead flesh. We'm not Catholics. It's their souls that do count, not their bodies. These two was unsoiled, and I'm sure God will know that without no expensive funeral. Come on, now, back in the house, you. I'll go and get Evan from the Commercial. Sooner these two's gone, the better.'

'He can't still be down there at this hour?'

'Evan have got a lot of friends, Jenny. Siân will look after him. He'll still be there.'

She found them in the market square, Evan sitting on a low wall outside the dark, barred public house, Siân Ellis close beside him, the drunken weight of his head resting on her shoulder.

Siân looked up wearily as Eluned approached. 'Over, is it?'

'Aye. Twins. She'll be all right, but not the babies.'

Siân turned to her companion. 'Evan, love? Come on, now, time to go home. Margaret Ann do need you.'

He looked up, bleary-eyed. 'It went wrong, didn't it? The others was all quick. . .quicker than this, any-how. . .'

'Aye, it went wrong. That's why you've got to go home to her now. She's bad, Evan. Go on, quick. Oh – and have one of these before you go. . .' With a rue-ful grin she took one of her strong mint humbugs out of her apron pocket and offered it to him. 'That one would smell drink on a man while the last trump was sounding!'

White-faced, exhausted, Margaret Ann lay in the big bed in the tiny room which smelled of blood and sor-row. She held Jenny's hand with a strength born of exhaustion. It was easier to cling on than to let go. Then Evan came in and it all changed. Jenny felt as if the room had become charged with electricity. As the big, inarticulate man stumbled into the bedroom, Margaret Ann stiffened and opened her eyes. Jenny knew instantly that as far as they were concerned, they were alone. She backed away from the bed as Margaret Ann let go of her hand, but could not leave because Evan unintentionally barred the way. Not that it mattered to anyone but Jenny.

The pair consumed each other with their eyes, their underlying passion for each other communicating their emotions in a way that words never could. Evan sat gingerly on the edge of the bed and leaned forward to cradle his wife as gently as if she were a new-born child. Head pressed against her breast, voice muffled by sobs, he mumbled, 'I done that to you, *cariad*. Can you ever forgive me?'

'Hush, now. . .nothing to forgive. It do take two, don't it?' Her tone was passionate, tender, loving – why, thought Jenny, she sounds more as if she's just made love than gone through labour!

She caught sight of her friend's face as Evan eased Margaret Ann back on to the pillows. She even looked fulfilled. Jenny realized with a shock that to this woman, children were incidental. Her life made sense only in relation to her consuming passion for this big drunken miner who could never hope to make her happy. It was tragic. . .and marvellous.

Jenny's path to the door was clear. She left them together and went downstairs. Dawn had broken now, and thin grey light was seeping in through the kitchen windows.

'Come on, love, I think you and me could do with a bit of breakfast before you go home,' said Eluned. 'Cup of tea, anyway.'

Jenny shook her head. 'Thank you, but I got to get back. Harry will be worrying. . . They'm all right now, up there. Tell Margaret Ann I'm thinking about her. . .' Then she wrapped her knitted shawl tightly around her thin shoulders and started the long walk home.

CHAPTER NINE

T HE WOODLAND TRACK wound steeply upward, oaks and beeches gradually giving way to dark conifers which seemed to lean forward over the narrow road. It was getting silent, too. The birds and animals preferred the dappled sunlight of the mixed woodland to this gloomy place. Margaret Ann shuddered involuntarily. No wonder Jenny felt so cut off. Even on a mild, sunny afternoon, this place felt haunted. Poor Jenny...the sooner she had a few children to break this endless silence, the better.

The ordeal of her own stillbirth over and her recovery complete, Margaret Ann was fulfilling a promise to visit Jenny Job at home. She had walked four miles from the village and still had not arrived at Trwyn Farm, but until the track became so gloomy she had been enjoying the fresh air and the rare treat of getting away from her brood of children for a whole day.

She would never like her neighbours, but Mrs Smith, who lived next door, was trustworthy enough, and had raised seven children of her own. When she heard Margaret Ann was unable to visit Jenny until she found a child-minder, Edith Smith came to her back door and said, 'I may as well sit in your house as mine for the day, love. Can't do nothing much with my leg bad, so I'll keep an eye on your lot and you get off up the

Trwyn. Last time I saw that Jenny Job, she looked as if she could do with a bit of company.'

Margaret Ann demurred for a while, then blushed furiously as Edith grinned and added, 'Don't worry, I won't go rummaging through your nice things, my lady. I ent doing this for you – I'm doing it for Jenny, see.'

Margaret Ann was on the point of refusing the offer, but she desperately wanted to get away for a few hours, to be free and private for once. She swallowed her pride, managed a fixed smile, and thanked Edith for her kindness.

Now, approaching the farm, she wondered whether the outing had been such a good idea. No wonder Jenny was in such a state after ten years up here. She was nervous on her first visit. . . The track swung round a hairpin bend and Margaret Ann gasped in delight at the prospect in front of her, all disquiet temporarily forgotten. Ahead, the dark fir trees fell away. On a spur of rock, overlooking a precipitous drop into the valley, was a compact slate-roofed cottage, its rendered walls washed a soft shade of gold. A fat puff of smoke trickled from the chimney and an equally well-rounded tabby cat was sunning itself outside the oak plank front door. A riot of flowers spilled from the neglected garden plot around the house, running down to a low stone wall that bounded the drop. It must be possible to see ten miles across the mountains from any one of those front windows. If she had a view like that, she'd never miss Abercarn at all. . .

Then she was at the gate and Jenny was rushing to meet her from the front door, excited as a child at Christmas. 'Oh, Margaret Ann, I'm so glad you'm here. I was that worried. . . Thought I might have asked too much of you, to walk all the way up here after what you've just been through.'

'That was months ago, girl. Much less work to come

up here than to stay home picking up after five boys and a man, I can tell you.' As she uttered the words, Margaret Ann regretted them. Jenny's expression told her instantly that she would have given almost anything to spend her time looking after a houseful of her own children.

Watch what you say from now on, Margaret Ann told herself. Then she gave her friend a dazzling smile and embraced her. 'Come on, then, show me your house,' she said. 'It do look lovely from outside, anyway.'

It was many weeks since the women had seen each other – months since they had talked alone. They prattled happily about small matters while Jenny showed Margaret Ann around the farmhouse, but after a while Margaret Ann became more interested in the building than in their chatter.

'Funny, it do seem ever so much bigger in here than it looks outside,' she said, as they went through yet another small upstairs room, only half-lit by the tiny windows which peered blindly back into the hillside.

'That's because it do go back a long way – and of course it goes down another floor with the drop in front, so what would be cellars on the flat is good open rooms here.'

'It's much older than I expected, too.'

Jenny nodded, disquiet flickering across her face. 'Too old, I do think sometimes. There've always been Jobs here – hundreds of years, I mean, not three or four generations. They was always too stubborn to buy the freehold. Said the land was too poor for any farmer in his right mind to want to own it. But it have kept them snug enough. They do move on as sitting ten-ants every time the estate changes hands. Just pays the ground rent to a new freeholder every few generations. They do even think the ghost is theirs!'

'Ghost?' Margaret Ann's voice trembled. She was

superstitious in a way that only the fanatically religious can be. 'Is the house haunted, then?'

'Surely you haven't lived in Abercarn all your life without knowing about Pwka'r Trwyn?'

'Well, no – there was some nonsense when I was little with the boys daring each other to walk up around Ysgubor Wen barn on their own without the Pwka'r getting them – but here?'

Jenny tried to inject jauntiness into her voice and failed dismally. 'You don't realize, coming up this way, how close we are to Ysgubor Wen, do you?'

'It must be miles away!'

'No, girl – it's just up the back. Used to be leased to the Job family until they stopped arable farming and concentrated on the sheep.' She was almost whispering now: 'It used to wander up as far as the barn, but it really preferred the house.'

'This house, you mean?' Margaret Ann was shivering.

'Yes. Just over a hundred years ago, when Harry's great-grandfather farmed the place, it got really bad, throwing things about, causing an uproar – then it fastened on to one of the farm servants, seemed to take to him, like a friend, and everything went quiet. Harry reckons the Jobs have always said Pwka'r do need looking after, and if he ent fed regular, he do get angry after a few years.'

'Well, if he've been quiet since the 1790s, he must have lost his appetite for good!' Margaret Ann hoped she sounded more sceptical than she felt.

'I wish you could make Harry believe that. He've been getting awful funny about it lately. . . Says he's started hearing things again and there'll be trouble 'less we'm kind to Pwka'r. I caught him putting bread and milk out for him the other night.'

'*Duw*, d'you think he's all right?' Fear of the supernatural was banished from Margaret Ann's head

immediately on hearing this down-to-earth evidence
of mental disorder.

'I wish I could tell. One minute, he've nearly got me
believing I can hear the Pwka'r. The next, I think he's
losing his mind, and I start worrying about that an' all.'
She glanced around fearfully, as though half afraid
of being overheard. 'Look, sometimes what he do say
don't sound so daft. This is ever such a funny house.
Come over here a minute.'

They were still in the small, gloomy, back-facing
room. Jenny drew her across to the fireplace – really little more than a roughly-finished inroad into the great
chimney breast which thrust up the centre wall from
the kitchen below. 'There's an old, old story about the
Pwka'r,' she murmured, 'from way back before Harry's
great-grandfather. This was a very prosperous farm
then – almost a manor house. There was a couple
of girls working indoors, as well as the farm servants
outside. And for years and years, the story says, there
was a locked room upstairs. . .up here, that is. It wasn't
locked the usual way. They really must have had someone – or something – they wanted to keep hidden. This
locked room didn't have no door.'

Margaret Ann was goggling at her now, fearful of
what she would hear next but too fascinated to end the
conversation. 'What was in there, then?'

'The Pwka'r! He lived in this house for years, inside
the room where no one could go an' look at him.
And only the master and mistress – they was Jobs
even then – knew how the food and drink and clean
linen was taken in to him. Then, one day, the kitchen
maid was down below, there, admiring the dairymaid's
hands. Dairymaids do often have nice hands because
of having them in the milk all the time. Anyway, this
girl must have been a bit vain, 'cos she was preening
herself down there in the kitchen by the fire, and
saying, "I wonder if I have the fairest hands in the

Gwyddon, or if I haven't, who have?" And then, a
beautiful clear voice – they couldn't swear to it being
a man or a woman – said, "Pwka'r have got the fairest hands!" And, oh, Jesus, Margaret Ann, then this
perfect little white hand, hardly bigger than a child's,
slipped through the ceiling just by the chimney breast!'

Margaret Ann, gripped by the narrative, let out a
terrified gasp. 'Good God! What did they do then?'

'Ran like hell of course.' Margaret Ann was in no
state to correct Jenny's language. 'They was terrified.
I think I'd have dropped dead on the spot!'

'Me an' all,' said Margaret Ann. Then she got a grip
on her nerves. 'But surely that can't have happened? It
must be just an old story to frighten the little ones. . .'

'That was what I used to say when Harry tried to
scare me with it. But what d'you think of this?' She
bent at the point by the chimney breast where she had
led her friend moments before, and pulled back the
brightly-coloured rag hearth rug. Beneath it, installed
so perfectly flush with the wide ancient oak floorboards
as to be almost invisible, was a small trapdoor. Jenny
slipped her fingers into a notch in the wood, there was
a click and it opened, upwards, towards them. 'There
ent no way of opening it from underneath,' she said.
'I've got up on a ladder down there when Harry wasn't
about, and had a good look. Who ever used this, only
the person in the room could work it.'

'B-but there's a perfectly ordinary door over there.'

'Now there is, yes, but come and have a look at
it.'

They emerged on to the landing. Margaret Ann
studied the door. 'It don't look no different from dozens of others to me.'

'No, but it's different from the others in this house,
though. Look at the doors on either side – they'm dark
oak, and they've weathered black. They've got old iron
latches, too. This one's much newer oak and it have got

a push bar to shut it. What if it wasn't here when the
other doors was put in?'

Margaret Ann was clutching at straws. She did not
want to believe this uncomfortable old tale, particularly
with a solitary walk ahead of her that afternoon. 'It
must be coincidence, Jenny! That trapdoor can't have
been there for hundreds of years without nobody finding it. I know it isn't obvious, but if you was making a
fire in the grate, you'd spot it straight away.'

'Aye, if the boards was bare, you would. But they
wasn't. I don't think Harry knows about it. I don't think
anyone else have known for generations. If I hadn't
gone getting ideas about using this room, I wouldn't
know – and I'd rather it was that way, an' all! A couple
of years ago, I suddenly thought the room would be
good for dry storage in the winter – or even as a little
sewing room or something, you know, getting all the
warmth up from the kitchen range.

'It hadn't been used for God knows how long. Harry's father was a widower for years and the house was
neglected till I come. The floor wasn't bare when I
started poking around – it was covered in some sort
of rush matting, so old there was no colour in it, just
sackfuls of dust. I tried brushing it, but I could see I
was wasting my time and in the end I just pulled it up.
Then I brought a bucket and scrubbing brush up here
to give the floor a good going over before doing up the
rest of the room. I wasn't so keen on the idea by then;
started feeling edgy every time I turned my back on
the window – but I don't like leaving a job unfinished.
Of course, the minute I started scrubbing over by the
hearth, I found the door. Got it open nearly straight
away. . .'

'And Harry had already told you the story of the
Pwka'r's little white hand?'

'Aye – I'd been sharp with him about it, an' all, told
him off for frightening me with old wives' tales. I'd

have died rather than tell him what I'd found. The
next day I took a good look at the kitchen ceiling.
The door is tucked away far behind one of the beams
– you wouldn't notice it in a month of Sundays – and
I'm absolutely certain there's no way to open it from
down there.'

'What did you do then?'

'What could I do? I wasn't telling Harry, but I
couldn't just stop doing up the room, or he'd have
been suspicious. I got a big rag rug and put it down
so it would cover the door. Then I made some pretty
curtains and put in a table and a couple of hard chairs
– making some pretence of using it, at least. After that,
I just let the whole thing drop. There's so many rooms
in this place, that's easy enough to do. When he asked
me, months later, why I never used the little room for
sewing, I said it had turned out not to be so cosy after
all. He never asked about it again. I don't know why I
brought you in here today. . .shouldn't be frightening
you with it. . .but what with the way Harry's behaving,
I needed to talk about it.'

'Of course you did! Come on, let's go back down to
the kitchen and have a nice cup of tea.'

Jenny had left a mid-day meal laid out ready for
them before she took her friend around the house.
Now she drained the hot vegetables and served them
on to plates already laden with cold baked ham and
pickles. But neither of them did more than toy with the
food. Margaret Ann was disturbed, sensing that Jenny's preoccupation with the vivid old tales disguised the
true source of her distress: her husband's increasingly
strange behaviour. She was sharp enough to know the
real trouble lay between man and wife, but at a loss
to cut through all the eerie mumbo-jumbo that surrounded it. In the end she decided simply to try and
let Jenny explain matters as she saw them.

Eventually she said, 'I know it must have been

frightening, finding the room like that and connecting
it with the story. . .but that was a couple of years ago
and you seem to have lived with it all right till now. Why
have it come back on to your mind so much lately?'

Jenny made much of stirring her tea as she sought
words to describe her misgivings. 'I – I don't rightly
know. Things have got so jumbled up this past year.
Sometimes I've wondered whether I'm losing my
mind. . .' She raised her hand to silence Margaret
Ann's objection to that idea.

'No, it's all right, I know that I'm really nothing worse
than lonely. But I know it's not that with Harry. It's
something worse. . .much worse . . . Trouble is that
with him, it's all tangled up with this ghost nonsense.'
She fell silent again, pondered her feelings, then said,
'I think he would have got bad anyway – maybe even if
we'd had babies early on, like he wanted – what I really
mean is the ghost thing isn't what's turning him funny.
But if I'm going to help him at all, I've got to get the
Pwka'r out of his head.

'I thought at first that I could do it by showing him
the room. You think it over – there's an old story about
some strange thing hidden and scaring the servants.
I've found proof that someone – some *one*, mark you –
might have hidden there. It could have been an outlaw
– could even have been someone religious, a Catholic,
maybe. If the Jobs was hiding someone like that, they'd
never let on to the servants, would they? I thought,
if I tell Harry that, lead him through the puzzle and
explain it, he'll drop the whole nonsense. But Margaret
Ann, in the end I was afraid to. What if I explained
it all, and he accepted it, but didn't get better? He
might have started having funny ideas about me, and
what would I do then? Even now, he do frighten me
at times.'

'Have he been knocking you about?'

'Never. Sometimes I'd feel safer if he had. No, he do

sit there in the corner, muttering a bit to himself, looking around as if he can see the Pwka'r. Then suddenly
he seems to remember I'm here and he starts staring
at me, like as if I'm not really me at all but someone
strange who he don't trust.'

Margaret Ann was alarmed now. 'It don't sound to
me as if you'm safe up here on your own.'

Jenny could not meet her eyes. 'There's nothing we
can do about that, is there?'

'But there must be!'

'For better and for worse, in sickness and in health,
remember?'

'Aye – and I remember the other bit – Till death us
do part. I don't like it, Jenny.'

The other woman managed a nervous laugh. 'Oh, I
expect I've got a bit carried away. It's probably nothing. Poor old Harry! He's just feeling a bit off colour
and there I am blackening him to my friend. He'll be
all right.'

'But will *you* be?'

'I just said, it's probably only me getting carried
away, girl. Tell you what – Harry do have his dinner
about three o'clock at this time of year, so's he can go
back and get a really good long stint done through the
light evenings. You don't need to go for a couple of
hours, do you? Stay and see him for yourself. If you
think there's something to worry about, I'll give it a bit
more thought.'

'All right, then, Jenny, but just remember: it's a long
way to call for help if you find out we was both wrong
when you'm up here alone with him.'

The entire matter was so disturbing that neither
woman found it possible to continue the discussion.
They turned gratefully to small talk, only getting
back to serious matters more than an hour later
when Jenny hesitantly broached the old topic of her
unsatisfactory sexual relationship with her husband.

'Y-you know what you was telling me about flirting with Harry an' all? Well, I tried it, and it seemed to work. . .for a while, that is.'

Margaret Ann's flash of hope for her friend faded abruptly.

Jenny went on, 'It must have been during that couple of times I brought him with me when I come to see you – you know, before you was ill. I never got the chance to tell you about it because we was never by ourselves.'

'He seemed happy enough then, even if he was a bit shy.'

'Oh, he was, he was. . .but it didn't seem to last. At first it was just like you said. He only needed a little bit of encouragement. But after a couple of months he started saying he was getting terrible nightmares. That didn't stop him. . .us. . .straight away. I was ever so keen, because there wasn't any sign of a baby on the way, so I kept making a fuss of him and leading him on. But then he started losing interest. . .' – she blushed at an unwelcome memory – '. . .once he even pushed me away, said he was worn out. And then the nightmares got really terrible and he said he thought he should move to the bedroom next door, so he wouldn't disturb me, like. . . Both of us knew it wasn't that really.'

'And haven't he come back?'

Jenny shook her head. 'No, and I do hear him wandering about downstairs sometimes, muttering and crying to himself.' A tear trickled down her cheek. 'I just don't know what to do, Margaret Ann.'

'*Duw,* it have taken you long enough to get it out, girl! This is awful – telling me in dribs and drabs you made me think it wasn't all that serious. But he's dangerous! There must be some family or friend you can go to.'

'Nobody.' She sighed, apparently exhausted by contemplating her problems. 'That's why I've been trying to convince myself things are all right here. I'm alone, Margaret Ann.'

'If only you could come to me. . .but we've only got the two bedrooms and with the five boys. . .'

That managed to raise a laugh from Jenny. 'I wouldn't dream of it! You've got quite enough to worry about without having me on your plate, too. I told you – it'll work itself out.'

They drank more tea, then went out for a walk. Somehow the big sunny kitchen no longer held any appeal for either of them. Ten minutes after they returned, Harry arrived for his dinner.

Margaret Ann could see no sign of abnormality in his behaviour. He was shy, as usual, but polite, to Jenny as well as to her. He ate a hearty meal and then went outside to sit on the stone garden bench and smoke a pipe before returning to his work. He was even thoughtful enough to ask Margaret Ann if she wanted his company for part of the walk back.

When they were alone once more, Jenny said, 'Well, how did he seem to you?'

Margaret Ann shrugged. 'I wouldn't have noticed a thing, love. But he'd hardly be likely to let it show in front of me, would he?'

Jenny clutched her arm. 'Tell you what – accept his offer to walk down as far as the Little Trwyn with you. See how he do sound when you'm by yourself with him. Then you can tell me what you do think next time I'm down for market.'

Margaret Ann could not admit to her friend that she was reluctant to let Harry go with her. On balance, she preferred to face the gloomy pinewoods on her own than share them with a madman. *But Jenny's sharing her whole life with a madman*, she thought. *Come on, girl, it's only a half-hour walk.*

It was four o'clock by the time they set off, and Margaret Ann was beginning to wonder if Evan would

be angry at her long absence. One look at Jenny's
haunted face as she waved them off convinced her
that it was worth risking his wrath to have stayed as
long as possible. Now she was walking down the lonely
track with Harry Job. The golden farmhouse was out
of sight and thére was no sound except the crunch of
their boots on the dirt road.

It was some time before Harry spoke. Then he said,
'Sometimes I do wonder if Jenny is suited to such a
lonely place.'

The remark was so in tune with the women's earlier
conversation that Margaret Ann was momentarily at a
loss to respond. Then he added, 'You have to be bred
to it, really. When I was a boy, our Mam often wouldn't
see nobody but me and Dada for three months at a
time.'

'You remember your mother, then? I thought she
died very young.'

'Oh, aye, she did. But I was about fourteen when she
passed away.'

'And she liked it up here?'

'Well, Dada said not in the beginning. But she got
used to it, and in the end she really loved it.'

'What did she die of?'

He stopped and made great play of re-filling his
pipe. Then he looked up and fixed her with a flat stare
that challenged her to comment. 'Fell in the stream
– the deep bit where we dip the sheep in autumn.
Got caught between the iron holding bars at the weir
end. . .she couldn't swim, but it wouldn't have helped
if she could have. Her foot was trapped.'

Margaret Ann fought a hysterical impulse to run
back up the road and drag Jenny Job back to Abercarn
with her. When she finally managed to speak, her voice
sounded high and unnatural in her own ears. 'Wh-what
was she doing down there, Harry?'

'D'you know, that's what I kept asking our Dad?

Couldn't understand it. She never could stand sheep, and it was a terrible climb down from the house to the dip. Dada always said she was taking his dinner down for him wrapped in a cloth, because he'd gone off without it in the morning.'

'That seems reasonable enough. Why couldn't you understand it?'

'Oh, I don't know. It was just, well, she hadn't been noticing anything very much for weeks before that. . .she just drifted about all the time and left us to ourselves. She wasn't really cooking us many meals, let alone running after us with dinners in a cloth.' His face became dreamy.

'Sometimes I do think that she'd had enough of everything, and p'raps she went down and looked in that deep cool water and thought, "There's peaceful," and just slipped into it for a rest. . .' His mood changed. 'But I 'xpect I was wrong. I usually am.'

After that he was perfectly normal, telling her what he had been doing that morning, and going on to describe the small tree plantation he was thinning out for the rest of the day. Soon they had reached the confluence of the two Gwyddon streams at Little Trwyn, and he said goodbye.

In spite of their largely commonplace exchange, Margaret Ann was still chilled by his obvious belief that his mother had committed suicide, with its tacit statement that he saw nothing odd in the act – she just slipped into it for a rest – almost as if he sometimes got the same idea. Still, she reassured herself, if he do only try and do away with himself, Jenny should be safe. And with that thought she had to be content.

She left him standing beside the stream. She looked back once and he was still there, but now he had started wading across the little ford. He had stopped, and was gazing fixedly down at the fast-flowing clear water which chuckled over the insteps of his big work boots.

CHAPTER TEN

WHEN MARGARET ANN crossed the market square on her way home that evening, it was unusually busy. The flurry of activity was concentrated around a garish marquee which had been pitched at the east side of the square near the market hall. Two burly men in faded red flannel vests and rough work trousers were erecting a makeshift platform in front of the tent.

Margaret Ann tried to maintain a dignified indifference to the scene, but she was as interested as anyone else. Moments later she got the chance to satisfy her curiosity. Siân Ellis came out of the Commercial carrying a tray laden with covered dishes of hot food. A pot boy followed her, burdened with two half-gallon jugs of draught beer. 'Food for the troops,' she told Margaret Ann with a grin.

'Who are they, Mrs Ellis?'

'Travelling theatre – William Haggar's Players. There's classy, ennit? Haven't had them here since long before your time, but they do give a good turn. Staying till the end of the week, they do say.' She hefted the tray into a more manageable position and moved off towards the marquee.

Watching her go, Margaret Ann caught sight of a flash of flame-red hair as a young woman ducked out beneath the tent flap to receive the food from

Mrs Ellis. Bet she wasn't born with it that colour, she thought. It's probably not as red as mine if the truth's told. . . Reluctantly, she continued her journey home. If only there was some excuse to stay! The whole scene had a sort of raffish excitement about it that she had never experienced outside novels. . .except, perhaps, once or twice in Evan's arms. . . That sent her mind off at a tangent. Yes, she thought, and we all know where that excitement do lead! The prospect of the little house with its vast cargo of children filled her with weariness and banished the thrill of the newly-arrived show.

But she was not the only one who had seen the players. Edith, apparently unhindered by her bad leg, had taken Margaret Ann's brood out for a walk that afternoon, and they had passed the square just in time to catch the Haggars parading into the village.

John Daniel, her eldest son, limped to greet her, eyes shining with excitement. 'Oh, Mam, we got to go to the show!' he said. 'They've got a great big bass drum and two monkeys and a nacrobat that can juggle and they do plays. They'm singing tonight an' all!'

Margaret Ann looked questioningly at Edith, who appeared almost as excited as the children. 'It's true, Margaret Ann,' said the woman. '*Duw*, they looked grand! If it's a nice day, they'll act out on the platform, but Inside If Wet.' She enunciated the last words as if reading them from a poster. 'They'm doing *Maria Marten* tomorrow night. Our Alf's taking me if it's the last thing he do do!'

'*Maria Marten*?' Margaret Ann was horrified. 'But they can't put that on in front of children – it-it's not decent!'

''Course it is. The villain do get his just deserts, don't he? It'll help teach them the difference between right and wrong. Better than chapel, any day.'

'Not for my children, it isn't. I don't know what this

village is coming to. Band of Hope is on tomorrow
night. They can all come to that instead.'

One glance at the circle of small mutinous faces
which surrounded her was enough to convince her
she was to be disappointed. They were silent for a
while, then Haydn, the third boy, piped up, 'Our Dad
have said we can go. He said we'd all go together if you
wanted to.'

Margaret Ann looked sharply at Edith. 'Is that true?
Where is he now?'

Edith shrugged. 'I don't know, love, why should he
tell me? I give him the stew out of the oven, like you
asked me to, and the little 'uns had some an' all, then
he had his bath and went off out. I said I'd wait till you
come back. Don't worry – he knows what a long walk it
is down from the Trwyn. He wasn't off with you.'

Margaret Ann compressed her lips and stayed silent
with difficulty. She had no intention of letting this nosy
neighbour see how angry she was. How dared Evan
come in here and promise the boys such a spectacle
with never a by-your-leave, then go off out somewhere
again without even waiting to tell her? It was too much!

'I'll be off now, then, Margaret Ann. Think I might
take another turn up the square and see how far they've
got. They did promise they'd put on a bit of a turn
tonight, sort of appetizer, you know!'

'Oh, yes, I know all right!' said Margaret Ann, unable
to restrain herself any longer. 'That red-haired girl
they've got with them, showing all she've got, I'll be
bound. You can see she's no better than she should
be!'

Edith gave her a long, level look. 'You saw her then,
did you? She come from around here, years back. Did
you know that?'

Margaret Ann wondered what the older woman was
trying to say. Aloud, she only said, 'Well, I never saw
her.'

'You wouldn't, not up the Rhyswg. Main roads and markets was always her patch. She's tinker Irish from over Ynysddu way, but she had friends over here for a long time. Ellen Rourke, her name is. She can't have been back to Abercarn, ooh, let's see, this six or seven years.'

'I'm surprised anyone remembers her, then.'

'If you think that, you can't have got a very close look at her, Margaret Ann. She was a raving beauty a few years ago, and she've worn bloody well considering the sort of life she've been leading.'

'Please! Watch your language in front of the boys. They're not used to that sort of thing!'

Edith's eyebrows rose as she remembered some of Evan's choicer oaths, but she held her peace. 'All right, Margaret Ann, sorry. We'm not all so genteel as you, I know that. I'm off now, then.'

Belatedly, Margaret Ann remembered the woman had done her a favour. 'Oh – er – wait a bit, Edith. Thank you ever so much for staying here today. I brought these back from the Trwyn for you.'

She turned to her basket and carefully removed six of the two dozen eggs Jenny Job had given her. 'Thought you might like to boil a couple for your supper.'

'That's really good of you, girl. I'll say goodbye now, then.' Edith's eyes were on the other eighteen eggs which still nestled in the basket, but it was obvious that Margaret Ann's generosity had exhausted itself with the small gift. Edith borrowed a bowl to carry the eggs, then left the younger woman to await her husband's return.

Evan was not his usual self when he came in shortly afterwards. Watching him, Margaret Ann was perplexed by the change. What was it? Eventually she decided he seemed just like the young man she had met so long ago when she was scarcely more than a child with unrealistic hopes for the future. He was charged with energy and excitement, lighter on his feet, eager to see what was round the next corner. Lately he had often been morose with the boys, but not this evening.

'All ready to take your mam to the show, then, lads?' he said, bending and sweeping the youngest effortlessly up to shoulder height. Emrys giggled gleefully at him and kicked his little feet, absorbing his father's happiness.

'I – I don't know that we should go, Evan. . .' Even to her own ears, Margaret Ann's protest sounded petty and kill-joy.

He eyed her over the child's plump little body. 'Why not? Bit of a stroll and a laugh never hurt nobody on a fine evening that I heard. Or have the chapel decided to put a stop to that, now, an' all?'

'I didn't mean that. It's just that I'm not sure whether it will be a bit . . . well – you know. . .for the children.'

He threw back his fine head and laughed. 'They won't see nothing like as bad as they do see round the village every day of the week, you daft ha'porth! Where d'you think we'm living, Park Lane?'

She blushed. 'I like to think my children would make me proud of them wherever we lived.'

'Well, a little Valleys show ent going to harm them, 'specially when their dad's there to beat hell out of them if they get the wrong ideas.'

Maybe it's their dad you're really worried about. . .a secret inner voice murmured at her.

'Oh, all right. If I do say no, you'll only go on about me being a spoilsport.'

'That's a good girl. We better get out there soon, if we'm going to see anything. The square was filling up when I come through.'

'Oh, yes, where was you when I come in? Down the Commercial, I s'pose.'

He was busying himself with Haydn and Tom and

somehow the question was not answered. But she could smell neither beer nor Siân Ellis's mints on his breath when he brushed past her.

It was a fine summer evening, still light, and the excitement of the players' arrival had kept a good crowd from their beds. The Haggars had timed their arrival well: give the audience a tempter on Thursday night, when they had no money and plenty of time on their hands, then have them all panting for the main show on Friday when most of them had just got their wages. Those who escaped on Friday would still be flush and eager for two shows on Saturday, then the company could rest on Sunday before moving on to the next little community early the following week.

They offered a variety of skills – song, dance, juggling, even a puppet theatre for children – and for grown-ups, too, when human performers proved unreliable. But their main business was play-acting. Mrs Haggar came from a long line of travelling players. Her husband, the illegitimate son of an Essex housemaid, simply loved anything to do with entertainment and had taken to life on the open road as the route to his dream. Their warm-up routine was a series of short turns along music-hall lines, aimed at whetting people's appetites but with little relevance to the dramatic repertoire which would be unleashed next day. Depending on their mood and the number of actors at their disposal, that might be anything from *The Maid of Cefn Ydfa* to a drastically-trimmed *Macbeth*. Sometimes it was both.

Now, though, William Haggar had done a fast assessment of his clientele and decided on Ellen Rourke's Family Medley. He called it that because the choice of songs enabled him to dress Ellen up in a child's short frock that showed off her shapely legs and pert breasts,

the songs presumably pleasing the women while the
men contemplated more obvious attractions. He invariably made an arrangement with a tolerant landlord that
after the main show broke up, they would go into the
saloon bar and entertain on a rather more intimate level
for the all-male audience they found there.

The candle-powered footlights flared at the edge
of the platform, the dusty plush curtain swung aside
and out of the tent tripped the most unlikely child.
Ellen's hair was plaited into two long braids which
hung down in front and jiggled provocatively each
time her uncorsetted breasts moved. The blue and
white frilly lawn dress ballooned in the light evening
breeze, displaying lace-trimmed drawers and long legs
sheathed in white silk stockings.

It was a well-chosen medley. First came what Haggar
called the 'Aah' song, designed to disarm any of the
women who might question his motives for dressing the
girl singer thus. Tonight it was *Daddy Wouldn't Buy Me a
Bow-Wow*, sung with plenty of flouncing and strutting
and leading up to much vigorous self-hugging when
Ellen reached the lines, 'I've got a little cat, And I'm
very fond of that. . .'

Then it was time for a touch of old-fashioned moral-
ity, strengthened by its apparently childish source.
Here Ellen became serious almost to the point of
tragedy. Haggar spoke a rhyming introduction, casting
himself as the dissolute father of a neglected daughter,
whom he was about to leave to face domestic tragedy
without his support. But as he left, he said, touching
hand dramatically to eye, his girl's pure voice beseeched
him:

'Don't go out tonight, Dear Father
Don't, refuse this once, I pray;
Tell your comrades Mother's dying,
Soon her soul will pass away;

Tell them, too, of darling Willie,
Him we all so much do love,
How his little form is drooping,
Soon to bloom again above.

Don't go out tonight, Dear Father,
Think, oh think how sad 'twill be;
When the angels come to take her,
Papa won't be there to see!'

It always worked like a charm. Most of the moral battle-
axes in the square were Temperance, and nothing
stirred their emotions more than a raw appeal against
the evils of drink, with a little innocent death to spice
the awful tale. After that they were ready for almost
anything, and a brisk rendering of *Our Lodger's Such
a Nice Young Man* slipped through without any of the
hard-liners appearing to notice the salacity of Ellen's
delivery.

After that, Ellen went off and the troupe launched
into a juggling act and some mild acrobatics for the kids,
followed by a comic turn. A dramatic monologue ended
the brief show, designed to give them a foretaste of the
serious entertainment scheduled for the next day. It
seldom mattered that much what they ended with, because by then a couple of Haggar's planted men in the
audience would have circulated the news that the cast,
particularly Miss Rourke, would be refreshing themselves later at the Commercial. That was when men
started sliding away to lift the emergency money from
behind the parlour clock or the bottom of the Coro-
nation biscuit tin. It could be replaced tomorrow, and
tonight there was something worth spending it on. . .

On such a warm night, it was unthinkable to close
the pub windows, particularly when there was such

a crush. Well after midnight, a rich Irish coloratura voice floated on a cloud of blue tobacco smoke out of the saloon bar, across the market square and through the close-curtained windows of the Ranks:

'The bluebells were accepted by the maiden.
She said, "I'll keep them safely all my life;
But then, suppose you meet some other lady
And I should never be your darling wife?"
He shook his head and took another kiss,
Then once again he whispered this. . .'

The baritone voice which took up the refrain could only be Evan's. As Margaret Ann, undeceived at last, pressed the pillow to her ears, the reunited lovers sang together:

'I'll be your sweetheart
If you will be mine.
All my life
I'll be your Valentine.
Bluebells I've gathered,
Take them, and be true.
When I'm a man
My plan
Will be to marry you.'

CHAPTER ELEVEN

T HE REALIZATION THAT Evan and Ellen Rourke had been lovers and were lovers again drove all other thoughts from Margaret Ann's mind. Marriage and motherhood had taught her to be adaptable and over the years she had discovered survival skills she would never have dreamed she possessed during her pampered girlhood. But nothing had prepared her to deal with her husband taking a mistress.

She hardly knew which was worse – the thought that everyone else in Abercarn was aware of the liaison and was secretly mocking her, or the terrible hurt of losing her man to someone he loved better. Her only defence was to become more prim than ever, to distance herself still further from the coarse-mouthed, sharp-eyed neighbours and retreat within the fortress of her religion. At least the girl did not stay long in the village. The troupe packed up as planned the Monday after they arrived and moved up the valley to Nantyglo. But that was only a postponement. Everybody knew Haggar's watchword was 'Follow the Coal'. Except around harvest, his company stuck close to the villages of the mining valleys and it was only a matter of time before they were back in Newbridge or Crosskeys – quite near enough for a man in love to walk there and back after work on a long summer evening. And maybe one night he wouldn't bother to walk back, either. . .

Evan was curiously gentle with her. Nothing was said between them about the affair: Margaret Ann was too mortified to raise the subject, and Evan felt guilty, although he knew she had realized what was going on. Now he treated her like a delicate child, bringing small treats when he had a few pence to spare; staying off the beer; treating the children more affectionately. But his new kindness merely rubbed salt in Margaret Ann's wounded pride. She could not see his attentiveness as an effort to express regret and affection, but as the side effect of being made happy by another woman.

The other great change in their life together was worse: he stopped making love to her, and Margaret Ann was forced to admit to herself that she had not submitted reluctantly to him till now, but that their physical compatibility had been the core of all that mattered in their marriage. Every night he came up to bed after her, undressed in the dark and slid gingerly between the sheets, as if afraid he would damage her by touching her accidentally. His daily work was back-breaking, and ensured that he slid off to sleep swiftly in spite of the tension; but Margaret Ann did not. She lay in the darkness for hours, stiff and cold, her mind, unbidden, casting up fantasies of Evan and Ellen Rourke tangled together in the ecstasy which was now denied to her.

Summer dragged on, and somehow Margaret Ann came to terms with the new way of things. Gradually, her more rational self slid into the iron routine she had used to keep herself going while she was too miserable to think clearly. Almost unnoticed at first, normality began to return. It was painful, but at least it never degenerated to the scouring anguish she had experienced during those first enlightened days in mid-May. She was so preoccupied with her own survival that she quite forgot Jenny Jobs' problems. Determined to avoid gossipping tongues and knowing looks, she hurried up

to the market early in the morning and was back at
home, working herself beyond thought, by the time
the square filled up. When she thought of her friend,
she pushed the matter aside. At present she was unsure
whether she had strength to carry her own emotional
burden, let alone someone else's.

But eventually, guilt set in. By July, she realized she
could no longer neglect Jenny – poor Jenny, who didn't
even have children or close family to whom she could
turn. Margaret Ann began to wonder why her friend
had not sought her out at the house. At first her
own self-consciousness convinced her Jenny must have
heard about Ellen Rourke and was deliberately staying
away, but she knew that was unlikely. In the end, she
decided to resume her mid-morning trips to market,
instead of the dawn rush. But she went twice at the
busiest time of day, without catching sight of Jenny.
Then, on the third occasion, she saw the Jobs' pony
and trap outside an ironmonger's in the High Street.
She started towards the shop door, expecting to see
Jenny, but instead was almost knocked over by Harry
as he shouldered his way out.

He would have passed Margaret Ann without any
sign of recognition, but she reached out and tugged
his sleeve, saying, 'Harry – Harry, didn't you see me?
Where's Jenny? We haven't had a talk this long time.'

He seemed to return reluctantly from some remote
place. 'Aye. . .er. . .Jenny, you say. Of course. . . should
of come and seen you. . . She do send her love,
Margaret Ann, but she's ever so busy at the moment.
Lot of soft fruit in the garden. . . She's bottling it by
the ton,' – here he even managed a hollow laugh –
'says we might even have enough to sell down here
by September. She says not to bother coming all the
way up the Trwyn again. When she've finished with
the fruit, she'll be back down and you can have a good
old talk, all right?'

Margaret Ann nodded, wondering where this exten-
sive fruit garden could be. All she had seen when she
was at the Trwyn had been flowers and trees. Still, she
hadn't gone far from the house. . . She shook herself,
irritated at her own suspicious mind. Harry had probably cleared a fruit garden somewhere that got the full
sunlight, that was all. Where else would Jenny be? She'd
be thinking the Pwka'r had got her soon. . .

Abruptly, Margaret Ann wished that thought had
not crossed her mind. She made a determined effort to
be reasonable. 'You do look a bit tired yourself, Harry.
Why not come home with me for a cup of tea? The boys
do like playing with the pony.'

He backed away. 'N-not today, thank you, Margaret
Ann. . .got to get back, see. . .told Jenny I'd get her
another jelly bag for the blackcurrant jam. Next time,
p'raps. . .probably have her with me then. . .'

A group of boys dashed between them, shouting
and squabbling over a handful of marbles, and while
Margaret Ann's attention was distracted, Harry was up
on the trap and setting off towards Gwyddon Road.
'Wait – Harry . . .' she called. But if he heard her, he gave
no sign of it.

The Wednesday and Saturday markets came and went
the following week, with no sign of either Jenny or
Harry Job. Margaret Ann was getting really concerned
now. One of them always came down once a week. And
if Jenny really had been making jams and bottling fruit,
she'd be wanting more jars and sugar by now.

On Sunday afternoon, returning from Sunday
School with the children, she confided her worries
to Evan. He was so relieved to hear anything from
her beyond the minimal exchanges they had had since
May that he made much of the Jobs' recent absence.

'Aye, you're right girl, it is funny,' he said. 'You'm

wrong about Harry not being down this week though. I saw his pony and trap outside the Market Tavern about nine o'clock last night, and I thought, you'm leaving your wife on her own up there a bit late. . .then he come out and jumped up and drove off as if Old Nick was after him. P'raps he'd just realized what time it was.'

Margaret Ann was not comforted by his words. 'Old Nick, or Pwka'r Trwyn?' she said, half to herself.

Evan was puzzled. 'Pwka'r Trwyn? Where did you get hold of that? I haven't heard nobody mention that old tale for years.'

'Jenny do mention it quite a lot. She thinks Harry do believe the Pwka'r is at the farm.'

'*Duw*, I hope not!' Evan's laugh was uneasy, although he was usually sceptical about ghost stories. 'Pwka'r used to be a bit like the Irish banshee.'

'How d'you mean?'

He could not quite meet her eyes. 'Well, you know. . .only started turning up around the place when somebody in the house was going to die. Only Pwka'r seems to be the Jobs' own family banshee.'

Margaret Ann felt somewhat relieved. 'That's all right then. It was Jenny I was worried about.'

'What have that got to do with it?'

'If Pwka'r is just the family whipper-in for the Jobs, she's all right, ent she? She's only one by marriage.'

'I don't think it do work like that.' He just failed in his attempt at a light tone. 'Harry's mam was only a Job by marriage, but his dad was always going on about how the Pwka'r started coming round for his supper a few months before she went.'

'Oh, God, Evan – let's go up there, now! Edith will come and sit with the boys, I'm sure.'

The intrusion of everyday concerns like a child-minder jerked Evan back to normality. 'Don't be daft, love! We can't go tearing off on a five-mile journey without no invitation, nor any explanation why we'm there.' He assumed a babyish, whining voice: '"Hello, Harry. Just come to see if Pwka'r is giving you any trouble. . ." He'd be well within his rights to kick us down the mountain.'

'But I'm telling you, Evan, he do take it serious, even if nobody else do! What if he have gone mad and he's just hearing voices? If it's the Pwka'r that he do hear, don't you think that means Jenny's in danger? I do. If Harry thinks the Pwka'r come and took his mam, p'raps he's preparing the way for Jenny by believing the Pwka'r have come for her, and the next step will be for him to give it a helping hand.'

Evan shook his head, bewildered at her reasoning. 'You should be writing stories,' he told her. 'Things like that don't happen up here.'

'They happened all right when Harry Job was four-teen and his mother was found trapped in the old sheep dip, though, didn't they?'

'Love, his mother had been a bit funny for years. If she hadn't ended up in the sheep dip, she'd have died in the county asylum. That wasn't no Pwka'r.'

'There you are – his mother was mad! Harry prob-ably is, too. Please take me up there, Evan – please!'

The big man was thoroughly embarrassed now. He feared there was something in what his wife was saying, but the thought of invading another man's home with accusations of madness and even attempted murder was too much to contemplate. He drew Margaret Ann towards him and adopted a placating tone.

'Look, I tell you what. Go to market Wednesday morning and ask a couple of the stallholders if they've seen either of the Jobs yet. If they haven't, hang on until dinner time. They'm always down by then if they'm coming, ent they?' She nodded. 'Right. Well if they ent, ask the market men to keep an eye out for them, then pop back to check up just before I get home from work.

I'll bath straight away and come up there with you. How does that suit you?'

She was weakening. 'Well, it do sound sensible, I admit. . .all right, then, I'll leave it till Wednesday. But wouldn't it be better to go up now, today, when you'm rested, instead of having to drag off up there after working a shift?'

He looked away. 'I – er – I said I'd go down Crosskeys this evening and see Albert Short's pigeons. He've got a couple of new racers. . .fine birds. I sort of promised.'

Margaret Ann's attention veered away from Jenny Job as she remembered a tattered poster she had seen on the hoarding near the chapel that afternoon. 'WILLIAM HAGGAR'S PLAYERS,' it had said, 'LIMITED APPEARANCES, MONDAY TO THURSDAY, 27–30 JULY ONLY, CROSSKEYS, CWMFELINFACH, BLACKWOOD'.

Wednesday promised to be a hot, brazen day with a hard blue sky and the air already still and breathless early in the morning. By ten o'clock, Margaret Ann was doing the rounds of the market stalls. There was no sign of the Jobs' pony and trap, and none of the traders had seen the couple that day.

'Bit early for them yet, love,' said the egg woman, who sat beside a round table with a vast black umbrella shading herself and her produce. 'Try about twelve, that's usually their time.'

'But they haven't been coming at all, lately, have they?' asked Margaret Ann.

'Harry Job have, yes. But you know his missis have been ill this last five weeks?'

'It's news to me. I was talking to him week before last and he said she was busy with preserving fruit.'

The egg woman raised her eyes and made an irritated noise. 'That man do never know if he's coming

or going! Secretive sod, if you ask me. Always afraid
someone will pry into his business. You'm her friend,
ent you? Well, there you are. I 'xpect he thought you'd
be up there to see her if he let on. Never did like company, did Harry Job.'

Margaret Ann's anxiety was growing again. 'You
seem to know him quite well.'

'Wouldn't say that, but I used to know the family well
enough, after the mother died. My son and daughter-
in-law lodged up there for a year or two to help Harry's
father run the farm and look after the boy after she
went. But they never could get on with old man Job and
the boy seemed to be growing up just as bad. In the end
our Owen got a job as cowman down Abercarn House
and they left. I don't think there was another soul went
near the place till Harry got his hands on that Jenny.'

'Oh. I – I thought Harry had relatives down
Abercarn and Newbridge. Wasn't there a cousin working at Abercarn House?'

'Yes, there was plenty of family then – the one you'm
thinking of, Emrys, went off to Canada last year with
his wife and baby. But Harry would go to them, they
never went to him. The way I heard it, none of the
family wanted to set foot inside Trwyn Farm. They
was all scared stiff of it. By rights, the tenancy should
have been shared by Harry's father and the father's
elder brother. It was big enough in them days. But
the brother wouldn't have it as a present. Even Harry's
dad let the estate have Ysgubor Wen barn back. Always
having little fires and accidents and the like there, and
they got superstitious about it. Anyhow, that's all long
past, now. The brother died years ago, and after that it
was only Harry, Emrys, and Emrys's brother and sister.
The brother died young and the sister went over the
Rhondda to live when she got married.'

Margaret Ann had no need to ask the egg woman
what the Jobs had been frightened of. She already

knew. In fact she was beginning to accept Pwka'r Trwyn as a member of the family. It seemed he was so real in the minds of generations of Jobs that he had taken on some independent existence. Somehow there was nothing benign about it.

She moved on, doing as Evan had suggested and leaving messages in case Harry or Jenny arrived later. Just before noon, she was turning for home to get a meal for the children, and made a last call at the iron-monger's in case Harry went back there.

The ironmonger was puzzled. 'Surprised I haven't seen him before now,' he said. 'Last time he was in, he ordered a replacement blade for an old-fashioned saw he've got. Said he had to have it fast and how quick could I get it. I told him by last Saturday, and he said good because he needed it for work Monday morning, he'd be in here first thing. He never come, though.'

It was the last straw. Evan would not be home for two hours or more, and then he would need to bath, change and eat. They wouldn't set off much before four o'clock. Margaret Ann made up her mind. She was going alone.

She hurried back to the Ranks and called on Edith Smith. 'Edith, have you got time to look after the boys till this evening? I think Jenny Job's sick and I want to go up to her. I'd like Evan to come on after me, an'all, so it would have to be until this evening.'

Sensing that something was deeply wrong, Edith consented immediately.

'Give me half an hour to put Evan's dinner on and feed the boys, then I'll knock,' said Margaret Ann. 'And whatever you do, make sure he do come up after me as soon as he can.'

'D'you think it may be that bad then?' Edith was wide-eyed.

Margaret Ann made a quick decision. 'I tell you how bad I think it is, Edith. If your Alf ent busy when he do

come home, it'd be a good idea for him to come up with
Evan.' The other woman nodded. 'And if Evan do say it
ent necessary, don't listen. You make Alf or one of your
boys come.'

'Right you are, girl.' She dropped her voice to a whisper. 'It's that Harry Job, ennit? Always said there'd be
trouble there.'

Always, remembering afterwards, it seemed to
Margaret Ann that she had run the five miles to
Trwyn farm, although she knew she could not have
done. As she went, the hard blue sky gradually darkened with heavy storm clouds that nudged into the
steep hillsides. By the time she reached the conifer
plantation, the air was thick and breathless. Today it
seemed even more silent than before. The only sound
which penetrated the unearthly stillness was the sinister
gurgle of the Gwyddon stream deep in the valley below.
It was no comfort.

She breasted the final rise and turned the hairpin
bend which brought her within sight of the house. She
did not know what she had expected to see, but whatever it might have been, she was disappointed. The
house stood there as before, golden and somnolent. It
took more than a few thunderheads to make the place
look haunted. The colour wash was too soft, the flowers
too unruly, the dozing tabby too peaceful.

But today there was no plume of smoke escaping
from the chimney. And the broad-planked oak front
door yawned open, the sultry afternoon making the
interior seem dark and threatening.

Margaret Ann stopped by the garden gate. Now the
silence was too oppressive for any human voice to break
it. She made a couple of false starts, then managed a
high, cracked cry: 'Jenny? You in there, Jenny?'

The tabby gave her a disdainful glance and moved
off. A sudden bellow rent the air and Margaret Ann
let out a sob of panic before she realized the source of

the noise. It was Blodwen, the house cow, calling from her outhouse. She sounded as if milking time was long overdue.

Margaret Ann advanced up the garden path, trying to reassure herself. Of course there was a reasonable explanation for the silence... If Jenny was off-colour, she might be asleep, and the farm had to be run, whether or not the farmer's wife was sick, so Harry would be out with the sheep somewhere, or down in the plantation...

She reached the door and gave it a push. It yielded, groaning in protest as though no one had moved it for a long time. A ripe, mildewy smell hit Margaret Ann's nostrils and she recoiled momentarily. *Duw*, if that was the way Jenny preserved her fruit, someone should give her a few lessons! It smelled as if it had been fermenting in the jars...

The front door opened into a small stone-flagged hall, and thence into the big, comfortable kitchen. That seemed to be the source of the smell. Margaret Ann forced herself to move briskly into the room.

No wonder there's a stink! she thought. Someone had been bottling fruit, all right, but they seemed to have lost interest and gone away. One glass jar was lying on its side, a great gout of unidentifiable black ooze spilling from its wide neck on to the table top. It was a mass of green mould and blowflies, and seemed to be the source of the bad smell. The coal range had gone out, but not before a big steel preserving pan had burned on its trivet. Impossible, now, to see what it had contained. It was black and as hard as old toffee.

What on earth was Harry playing at? If Jenny had been taken ill while she was doing this, he must have had time to clean up by now. It must have been there for days... What was it, anyway? It didn't look like mid-season fruit...

A couple of bottles had been filled and sealed.

Margaret Ann reached across the wide table and picked up the nearest one. What she saw turned her cold. Whinberries. The valley people's favourite fruit; the rarest, because it grew only on the bare, remote mountain and had such a brief season. First week in July, regular as clockwork. . .she remembered her father taking her up the whinberry mountain, quite near here, on the first Saturday of July each year, to gather the precious fruit. By the second week, they were gone. Always take the first week in July for your whinberries. . .

But July ended day after tomorrow. You only preserved the freshest whinberries. So these bottles had been here nearly four weeks. . . That jar had spilled four weeks ago. The preserving pan had burned and then the fire had died four weeks ago.

Panic rose like bile in Margaret Ann's throat and she started yelling, 'Jenny – Jenny love, where are you?'

She searched every room in the house, even the sinister little apartment with its concealed trapdoor. Ghost stories paled to insignificance in the face of such real terror. There was no sign that Jenny or Harry had ever been here.

After a while, she forced herself to calm down. Someone had certainly been here much more recently than four weeks or more. The cat looked as contented as ever, and the cow – it may be uncomfortable now, but it would have been mad or dead if it hadn't been seen to for that long. Someone had been here. . .

Once she had a chance to think it through, it did not reassure her. If it was either Harry or Jenny, it must be Harry, because Evan had seen him only the other night. *Oh, Jenny*, she thought, *what have he done with you?* She started wandering aimlessly about in the garden, looking for a hint of what had happened.

Eventually she found something. Where the garden wall tailed off, over the precipitous drop into the

Gwyddon valley, there was the dim trace of an old
footpath. It must have been more substantial once,
but the end of the wall and, presumably, the footpath itself, appeared to have been washed out by
some long-ago storm. She had noticed it when Jenny
showed her around earlier that year. Then, it had been
quite overgrown. But someone – or something – had
careered down there quite recently. The tall weeds and
grasses had been smashed down by a hurried passage.
Did she dare follow?

Margaret Ann advanced timorously to the edge and
peered over. There was much more of a path than she
had expected. The steepest bit was near the top, and
below, it hairpinned in miniature echo of the farm
track, descending among summer wildflowers towards
the stream hundreds of feet below. She bunched up her
long skirt and petticoats, and set off in pursuit of the
unthinkable.

Half an hour later she was feeling foolish, and just as
perplexed as before. The path had been steep, all right,
but it had led to no mystery destination. It was the short
cut that sliced across the main track to take someone
in a hurry down to the point where the Trwyn farm
road forked from the upper Gwyddon valley track. The
valley track was only used by the couple from Trwyn
farm, and one of them had been that way recently. The
summer foliage was bruised here, too, as it had been
on the footpath. A patch of scarlet flared a few yards
along the road. She ran to it. It was a crumpled man's
handkerchief, red cotton spotted with white. Whoever
had come from the farm had hurried along this way. . .
Then the fear came back. She was getting her bearings,
now. This road only had one practical destination – the
sheep dip.

Margaret Ann was running again. She knew what she

would find and if she must confront it, she preferred to
do it headlong. The sheep dip – the dammed section of
stream where Harry Job's mad mother had drowned,
her foot trapped against the holding bars. Suicide, or
Pwka'r? Or Harry's father. . .or Harry? the thought
babbled on uncomfortably.

It was further to the dip than she had expected. By
the time she reached the point where rock buttresses
clinched the stream into a deep natural gorge, she was
gasping for air and there was a searing pain in her
right side. The old dip was so much a part of its surroundings that for a moment she failed to recognize
it as man-made. A couple of young broad-leafed trees
leaned over it, dappling the water and making it difficult to distinguish detail in the thundery half-light. Was
that a patch in the deeper water? Was that a woman's
skirt? Oh, *Duw*, no – no it wasn't – but just as bad. It
was the back of a man's jacket, ballooning up to the
surface with its trapped air pocket above the water,
making its half-submerged wearer look like a hunch-
back. . .Margaret Ann crouched to clamber beneath
the lower tree branches and get closer to the water.
Then she drew back with a scream. Twisting towards
her, bloated, bluish, grinning in his last desperate effort
to trap air, not water, in drowning lungs, was the face of
Harry Job.

She turned and was violently sick into the alders
behind her, then scrubbed at her mouth with her
handkerchief, unable to face rinsing away the vomit
even with water upstream of the corpse. Harry! Harry,
when she had expected Jenny. . . Then what had happened to Jenny? Had the Pwka'r really taken her? How
was Harry trapped like that, just beneath the surface?
It couldn't be the holding bars. He wasn't down the
weir end; he was upstream, towards the top of the dip,
apparently with nothing but clear amber-brown water
beneath him.

She must get him out. She bent and got her hands under his arms, tugging at the corpse, expecting the weightlessness of the water to help her. But he did not budge. Something was holding him. . .Margaret Ann stood aside and looked at the water where clear light hit it without the obstruction of the trees. Then she saw it. No wonder Harry was trapped below the surface. He had tied the upper half of the old stone corn mill from the farm yard to his ankle, then thrown it in. It must have pulled him after it, unless he had jumped with it. It was at least half the weight of a brawny man. He must have carried it all the way down, or, the macabre thought struck her, walked down with it already tied around his ankle, blundering through the flowers and grass, leaving a track wide enough for her to follow. Perhaps he had stopped, with the curious logic of the insane, to mop his sweaty brow with the red handkerchief, and then had remembered the finality of his task, thrown aside the handkerchief, picked up his burden again and headed for his last resting place. . .

Margaret Ann had stood enough. Weariness, misery and fear overcame her. She knew vaguely that Jenny could not be alive, but lacked the energy to speculate on her friend's fate. She sat on a rock beside the sheep dip and wept.

For all she knew it might have been minutes, hours or days before they found her. In fact, Evan and Alf Smith had arrived at the farm close behind her. When they heard Edith's story, they had taken Dai Ellis's delivery cart from the Commercial and driven up as quickly as they could, without even pausing to wash off the coal dust from their day's work. They had seen the recently-used path and had followed it just as Margaret Ann had done, and now they found her, crying beside the dead man in the stream.

Evan cradled her in his arms while Alf got into the dip and cut the rope from the millstone with his pocket knife. The corpse bobbed obscenely to the surface and floated, mercifully face down, the air pocket in the jacket maintaining its position.

'I'll just leave you a minute, girl, to help Alf, then we'll take you back up top,' Evan told her.

'N-no – not up there. . .never up there again!' Margaret Ann's teeth were chattering and she trembled violently from head to foot.

'All right, all right, easy, then. Nobody's making you do nothing, my lovely. You sit by there now a minute. Keep your eyes shut if you like.'

Evan pressed her back against the rock and turned to help Alf pull Harry Job out of the water. They laid him face down, then took off his sodden jacket to cover his head and shoulders before turning him over. Margaret Ann could not look away. She stared, fascinated, throughout the brief flurry of activity.

Then Evan was at her side again. 'Now we'll try and make it as easy as we can for you. I'll take you back along the track to where the farm road branches off. Alf will go up the footpath and get the horse and cart, then drive down and meet us. But we'm going to have to drive back up here and get old Harry.'

She whimpered. 'Have we got to go all the way down with him on the cart, Evan? Can't we send someone up to fetch him when we do get back to Abercarn?'

'Sorry, love. If we do leave him like this, the foxes or the crows will get him in next to no time. We can't do that to the poor bugger.'

She shook her head. 'No, you're right. Come on, then, let's get it over with.'

They were almost back in Abercarn, their sinister burden thumping soggily with every rut in the track, when Margaret Ann remembered to ask about Jenny. 'Not a trace, love. But don't get your hopes up. By the state of that kitchen, I shouldn't think the poor soul got very far. They'll find her soon enough.'

The storm broke as they got to the police station. Sheets of rain were smashing down across Gwyddon Road as two hefty constables unloaded Harry Job's body from the pub waggon. Evan and Alf made statements and they agreed to delay talking to Margaret Ann until next morning. Then, with Alf to guide them back to Trwyn Farm, the police set out in the dark with lanterns, picks and shovels, to look for the mortal remains of Jenny Job.

By the time they got back to Trwyn, the short summer night was almost over and the storm had spent itself. It seemed Harry Job had done more than disturb the upper millstone when he took it as his death-weight. He had also been digging beneath the lower one, and now the torrential rain had loosened the already-unstable soil, washing it away to a depth of six inches or more at the lower side of the remaining millstone. As the police poked about the site in the weak dawn light, one of them noticed a woman's hand exposed by the leached earth. The flesh was already beginning to rot around the wedding ring. Jenny Job had been down there for three and a half weeks. Her skull had been smashed – possibly by the millstone that Harry had used much later to drown himself.

In the front bedroom of their cottage in the Ranks, Margaret Ann lay wrapped tightly in Evan's arms, weeping until she had purged herself of some of the shock and pain. Then, as dawn broke, as the policemen exhumed Jenny Job's broken corpse five miles away, Evan took her with infinite tenderness and together they conceived their first daughter.

CHAPTER TWELVE

AFTER HER PREVIOUS, tragic labour, Margaret Ann's next confinement was easy. The baby was beautiful – one of those rare newborn infants who arrive without a red, wrinkled face and a bald head. The perfect, rounded skull was capped by soft moist curls of dark auburn. The wide, unfocused eyes were as blue as her mother's. Evan loved her instantly.

'Rose,' he said, almost reverently, as he sat gingerly on the bed holding his newest child. 'Here she is at last, our Rose of Sharon.'

Margaret Ann wanted to cry with gratitude. It was as if all her prayers were answered at once and the threat of Ellen Rourke wiped away beyond thought or caring. 'You remembered then, all these years?'

''Course I did, you soft thing! I could hardly call one of the boys Rose of Sharon, could I?'

'W-we won't put it on the birth certificate, though, will we? It'd look a bit. . .you know. . .funny. Just Rose, for outside – Rose of Sharon for you and me.'

He grinned, unable to resist a gentle taunt. 'Afraid they'll know you been reading the wicked bits of the Bible, are you?'

She was too happy to rise to his teasing, merely settling back to rejoice in the apparent return of her husband's undivided affection. Soon he got up and prepared to leave her resting. At the door he turned back. 'Don't forget, now, we got to try for our Lily of the Valleys, next – I s'pose you'll make me register her as plain old Lily an'all.'

'Give us a chance to wean this one before you start again!' she said, but beneath the token scolding she was overjoyed.

Margaret Ann always looked back on the years from Rose's birth in April 1897 to the end of the old century as the happiest of her married life. She had more work on her hands than she would ever have believed possible, and went through considerable financial hardship, but she bore it all with a light heart because of her new-found contentment.

She tried not to think of her husband's interlude of infidelity, and sometimes almost managed to believe it had never happened. After all, she would tell herself, he never said nothing about it. . . I never saw him with her. . .none of the neighbours said there was anything going on . . . But at that stage she invariably cut off her attempt at self-delusion. She did not need such obvious pointers. She could remember Edith Smith's knowing look when they discussed Ellen Rourke the night the travelling theatre arrived in Abercarn. Once again she saw Evan slipping past her, physically close but emotionally a world away, the evening he might have been at the pub but didn't smell of beer. Most painfully of all, she heard once more the longing, reaching, lust-laden timbre of their voices later that same night, as their cheap love song insinuated its devastating message to her in her virtuous cottage bedroom.

It would always hurt her like an old, crooked wound scar, but in a way it made her value Evan more than before. How he must love her to give up such a passion, so abruptly, and never to stray again! Yes, she would always remember lying alone in bed that terrible night, but equally vividly she remembered lying in his arms, only weeks later, letting the magic of his loving wash away the terrors of the appalling day at Trwyn Farm. That made up for everything. . .

So it was that she turned to him once again for love, far sooner than she had after any of her other children, and the next baby was born barely eleven months after Rose.

Lily was quite different from her sister. She roared into the world, red-faced, clench-fisted and screaming, a single lock of raven-dark hair curling absurdly over her wrinkled forehead. It was a couple of days before her eyes were open long enough for anyone to guess at the colour, but they seemed to be the shade of wet slate. Evan assured Margaret Ann with paternal pride that his own eyes had been like that in infancy, and his second girl was obviously going to grow up the living image of her father.

During the months that followed, Margaret Ann decided he was right. Early on, Lily's eyes started lightening until they achieved the uncanny silver brilliance of Evan's, contrasting with curly black lashes. Her hair thickened and grew straight, dark and luxuriant. Her ruddy complexion toned down and soon took on an almost alabaster clarity. Where Rose had always been small and round and typically baby-shaped, Lily's arms and legs grew long and slender, making her an ungainly, coltish infant who appeared set to become a tall girl later on.

Margaret Ann adored her. It was as if she had a tiny copy of Evan, completely in her power to shape for the future. The child showed little sign of sharing her father's temperament, beyond a certain waywardness when her appetites were not satisfied immediately. Margaret Ann settled down to lavish her heart on Lily, sometimes even forgetting herself sufficiently to call the baby girl Evan.

While his wife revelled in maternal bliss, Evan Walters gradually learned to live two lives at once. He was the last person who would tell Margaret Ann she was seeing only what she wanted to see. He had never given up Ellen Rourke: their reunion the night of the impromptu pub concert in May 1896 had convinced him he must never let her go again. But he had learned stealth, and he had realized that Margaret Ann was unable to manage without him. Anyway, he still loved Margaret Ann and found her physically desirable; it was just that one woman would never be enough for him. Once he came to terms with that, he found it almost easy to maintain a balance between wife and mistress.

Ellen was unlikely to give him trouble about his dual allegiance. She was thirty when he took up with her again and he knew as well as she did that there was no longer either a great theatrical career or a happy marriage ahead for her. She was philosophical about it. 'I know I chucked you away when I was too foolish to know what you was worth, but now I know, so I'll take you as you are and thank God I found you again,' she told him.

So she went on with her gypsy life and Evan crept away to see her when she was within reach of Abercarn. Sometimes, he reflected, a man got a run of really good luck. Look at him, with Margaret Ann for bread and Ellen for spice, and a nice living coming in. . .

But women were really little more than a diversion from the main business of life for men like Evan. In the end, he had only one driving force: coal. Coal had formed him, raised him, educated him so far as he had an education. Now, almost without warning, it reared up like an angry beast and seemed set to devour him.

For years the mining industry in South Wales had expanded on a brawling, chaotic floodtide and Evan Walters had prospered modestly with it. But times were changing in the 1890s, and finally Evan was forced to acknowledge that he would never make a fortune from coal.

He had struck out as an independent contractor at a time when the mine owners could not get enough skilled men to open up the new pits. In those days the population of the coalfield was growing as fast as that of the USA, as immigrants poured in from the Forest of Dean, the North-East of England, Ireland, Scotland, and even faraway Spain and Austria.

Anyone with a strong back and the experience to swing a mandril could earn a living; but the men who knew the coal and how to claim new seams were as valuable as diamonds. Evan was one of them, born to a family of miners and down the pit himself at eleven. In the 1880s the coal-owners had wanted skilled men to open up new headings, thrusting forward the front line of attack on the seams. When they could not employ enough colliers with the requisite skills, they went well over the odds and offered independents lump sums for opening up the headings. It was up to these free-lance gangers to strike a bargain with their men and then to drive them so that the work was completed within the deadline set by the owners. It often led to frightful accidents when they struck an unexpected change in the rock formations. The dust levels were so high that some members of every team were inevitably mortally sick with silicosis even after only two or three weeks driving a new heading. But they persisted, because they knew they could earn double or treble the weekly wage available on the coal face, and because their only masters were the contractors, men like Evan, who worked them to death but were prepared to grab a pick and punish themselves with the same hard labour.

At the beginning, he had seen it as the start of great things – perhaps even to accumulating enough capital to go into some real business venture of his own. But marriage and children had dissipated his nest egg. A weakness for gambling and a growing appetite for alcohol diminished it further. Then, almost before he knew it, the coalfield was losing its gold rush atmosphere and settling down as a mature industrial area. It made for greater stability but it also meant an end of opportunities for buccaneering gains by the likes of him.

The signs had become obvious by the time Margaret Ann was pregnant with Lily. Evan was never short of contract work: every colliery manager in Monmouthshire's Western Valleys knew the reputation of his evil rages as a stimulus for extra work from his gangs. But where he might have been one contractor among six only two years before, now there were seldom more than two gangs in a colliery, and often his was the only one. The Valleys had filled up with immigrants and they were waiting at the pithead to become permanent colliers. The owners had more control over such wage-earning labourers than over the freelance gangs, and once they were trained, they were cheaper, too. After a full month when his gang was the only contract operation working on headings at Risca, Evan called at the offices to collect his money in preparation to pay out on Saturday night.

'Manager do want to see you,' said the cashier, removing the canvas cash bag from the safe.

'Why? We'm finished before time, ent we? I'd a thought that would be worth a bit extra, not a choking off!'

'Who said anything about a choking off? Trouble with you, Evan, is that you always shout before you'm hurt.'

'You'll be shouting in a minute, But, and it won't be before you'm hurt, I can tell you. In his office, is he?'

The cashier nodded and went back to his ledgers. Evan Walters was too big to be lightly provoked.

Tom Gilchrist had been colliery manager at Risca for

five years. He was a beefy Yorkshireman, shorter in stature than Evan but as big across the shoulders, and able to match him curse for curse. Now he greeted the younger man expansively.

'Ah, sit down, Evan. Got something to say to you, lad – been meaning to have a chat for weeks.'

'Nothing wrong, is there?' There was no hint of anxiety in Walters's voice.

'No, of course not. Come on, sit down – I'll even give you a cigar if you fancy one.'

Evan was instantly wary. After twenty-five years in mining, this was the first time he had been invited to sit down in a manager's office. He accepted the seat and the cigar, then sat gazing steadily at Gilchrist, waiting impassively for him to speak.

'You're one of the best workers I've seen in all my years as a manager, Evan,' Gilchrist told him. 'More than that, you're one of the most intelligent, too. Not a common combination, I'm afraid. You're wasted where you are.'

'Oh, ta very much. I'll ask Mr Gladstone to move over for me tomorrow.'

'Don't be bloody cheeky – you know you're flattered by what I'm saying. Have you ever considered getting a job as an official?'

'I thought you come from Yorkshire, not China, Mr Gilchrist. Haven't you heard? They do ask for a certificate before you get on the staff.'

'Yes, and how d'you think most of the firemen and overmen in the Valleys got their certificate? A lot of them started as pitboys and worked up. They just had the sense to do some book-work as well and get their qualifications. It's about time you did.'

'How much d'you suppose they'm earning, with their fancy bits of paper? On a busy month, I bet I do take home a good bit more than any overman, and I don't have to take no shit from the managers, neither.'

'If you go on being so high and bloody mighty, you'll be taking plenty of shit from this manager, sonny Jim! Stop being clever and listen to me a minute. They've got a couple of decent evening classes in Abercarn Workmen's Institute. You a member?'

'Of course. Nowhere else I can get a good game of billiards, is there?'

'Don't play the lout with me, Evan. You've got a brain and it's about time you used it for more than barely keeping yourself out of trouble. Start working for your official's exams and I'll back you every step of the way. If you don't like the thought of classes at the Institute, I dare say I can find out about the right correspondence course and you can do it at home in your own time.'

Walters's booming laugh filled the cramped office. 'And in my own study, no doubt! Christ, Mr Gilchrist, have you got any idea how full a four-roomed house do get with six kids and a houseproud woman in it, well on the way to producing her seventh? I don't get no chance to read the paper, let alone books about pit safety and mining methods!'

'Then it has to be the Institute. Look, Evan, I'm not going to be put off. This industry needs men like you in management. You're bright, you're experienced, and you're Welsh – you even speak the language. There aren't enough like you about and you know they hate the guts of outsiders like me. Try it, and you'll go straight to the top.'

Evan drew on a lifetime's suspicion of bosses and demurred again. 'I'm thirty-seven, Mr Gilchrist. Bit old for book learning, now, don't you think?'

'And a hell of a lot too old to start again as a common collier. Take my word for it, three years from now there won't be an independent contractor on any heading in South Wales. You're a dying species, man. If you don't listen to me, you'll wind up back on the coal face as a hewer – and you outgrew that when you were barely twenty!'

'I'll think about it, Mr Gilchrist.' Evan was on his feet, towering over the manager, grateful but inhibited by distrust. Haltingly, he added, 'It-it was decent of you to think of me. . .oh, and thanks for the cigar. I better go now. 'Xpect I'll see you soon.'

Gilchrist shook his head, resigned to losing Evan. 'Not on the headings, Evan. I think you've just driven the last contracted ones in this pit. Good luck, though, anyway, and try to remember what I've said.'

When he got back to Abercarn, Margaret Ann was fussing around outside their front door, ineffectually bullying two muscular boys who were attempting to thrust a vast chest of drawers inside.

'Careful, now, don't rush at it, mun!' Her voice was querulous as she tried to prevent them damaging either the passage wallpaper or the wood of the chest in their hamfistedness.

'What the 'ell's going on?' Evan had endured enough turmoil in his conversation with Gilchrist. Now he just wanted a bath and his dinner.

'Oh, Evan, thank goodness you'm here! These two haven't got the first idea. . . It's Auntie Mattie's mahogany chest, come all the way from Cardiff.'

'I can see it's not her bloody coffin, can't I?'

'Don't talk like that, it ent nice. I never thought about it being a bit on the big side.'

'That thing'd be too big for Buckingham Palace. If they do get it inside, where are you going to put it?'

'In the boys' room, where the little pine chest is now. Edith Smith's having that. But it don't look as if this one'll go through the door.'

The prospect of dinner was fading rapidly. 'Soon see about that,' he growled. 'Right, Jimmy, come round

by here and tilt the thing. You hold steady, John,
and as it do tilt, tip it up an'over. It'll go by a
whisker.'

It did, too. 'Probably scared to death of Evan,' John
Smith whispered to his brother Jimmy.

But the front door was only the first obstacle. Disaster struck at the bottom of the stairs. Flushed with
success after negotiating the doorway, the Smith boys
rampaged along the narrow passage, clearing the walls
by a couple of inches on each side, until they reached
Margaret's pride and joy, her German wall clock.

Mahogany crashed into glass and clockwork. Mahogany won. Evan winced and closed his eyes as he
heard his wife scream. She might have been reacting to
the death of their firstborn. He hissed at John Smith, 'If
I was you, boyo, I'd shoot the chest up over them stairs
and then make yourself scarce. It ent going to be very
comfortable for you here in a minute.'

Guided by terror rather than skill, the boys turned
the chest and managed to get it upstairs without striking anything else. Evan shooshed them out of the back
door and they were gone before the full majesty of
Margaret Ann's wrath could descend on them.

But she was not angry; she was bereft. When he
returned to the dark passage, she had abandoned
the smashed ruin of the clock. He found her seated
in their glacially-neat little back parlour, tears rolling
unchecked down her cheeks, the hideous brass eagle
from the top of the clock clasped in her hand.

'Come on, love, it ent that bad, is it?' Evan was perplexed at the intensity of her reaction.

'Ent it? Not to you maybe. . .it never meant nothing
to you in the first place.'

'But it was only an old clock, Margaret Ann. Not as
if we could even see it proper out there in the passage
– there wasn't enough room or light.'

Now she was sobbing brokenly. 'You'll never under-

stand. . .it was – it was genteel, that's what. The only
one of its kind in the whole Ranks. There's only another
two in Abercarn. The Baptist minister have got one and
the other is in Dr Cann's surgery. It wasn't there to tell
the time. . . It made me feel we was going up in the
world, a bit better than this lot living down here.'

Evan strove to control both anger and mirth. Dear
God, was there no end to the girl's little snobberies?
No wonder they called her Lady Ranks. But he was not
completely insensitive and he knew that teasing would
not help her now.

'I'll find you another one, love, don't you worry. You
just wait an' see.'

Her voice was small and hopeless. She had stopped
crying but could not meet his eyes. 'Don't matter. It
wouldn't be the same, somehow. We'm not really going
up in the world, are we? It have passed us by.'

Suddenly he realized that their marriage had produced precious few of the things that Margaret Ann
valued. She was a pillar of her chapel, it was true, and
took in the best china and linen when she helped at
their social events. But all their symbols of respectability
were inherited from her mother, and the other chapel
women knew it. She had the children, and she loved
them, but she never had been a girl who looked at marriage as the route to a family. They were little more than
by-products. She had dreamed of a prosperous life as a
lady, maybe with her own house one day; certainly with
a husband who rose in the world. Instead she had Evan
Walters, because she had fallen for his shining eyes
and big muscular body. And now he had to prepare
her for the news that his source of independent work
was about to dry up. He was swamped by sorrow for
Margaret Ann. She could be a pest now and then, but
she was a good wife in the main, and she adored him.
What had he ever given her? For a moment, he almost
cried himself.

He felt the weight of the canvas bag against his leg. In it was the money for his contract gang's wages. With that, he could get her the best clock in Wales. Aye, he told himself, and then get beaten to a pulp when they come for their money and I haven't got it. He turned away from his wife, angry with himself for being helpless in the face of her distress. He knew this one lost possession had disproportionate importance for Margaret Ann. There must be some way. . .

He was still speculating about it when he arrived at the Commercial that evening. The temptation to subvert his gang's money was soon removed.

One by one, they arrived in the back bar of the Commercial and he paid them out, entering the sum for each man in a dog-eared notebook.

Evan was not fond of the back bar. It had a tightly-buttoned, respectable air which reminded him of his own back parlour and did not match his notion of a comfortable drinking place. It was more secure than the public or saloon bars for handling any large sum of money, so he used it as a pay-out point every Saturday night. Apart from that, he avoided it.

Now he folded the empty cash bag after tucking the notebook inside it, and passed it over the bar for Dai Ellis to put away until he was ready to leave. Company, a bit of cheerful talk – that was what he needed, and the public bar was offering it loud and clear. To reach the bigger bar, Evan walked across the little rear hallway of the pub. A staircase led up from it to the Ellises' living quarters. Normally the door at the stairhead was kept closed, and Evan had never ventured beyond it. But tonight it was open, and just inside it, majestically presiding over the staircase, stood the answer to Margaret Ann Walters's prayers.

It was a magnificent oak grandfather clock, over seven feet tall, the woodwork around the face adorned with more decorative curlicues of wood than Evan had

ever seen. The face itself was a masterpiece of vulgar-
ity, with wildly ornate Roman numerals, and the sun
and moon painted in vivid shades after the style in
which they were represented on old sea charts. The
theme was echoed at the corners of the face's square
outline by similar representations of the four winds.
If Margaret Ann once set eyes on this triumph of
ostentatious clockmaking, she would instantly forget
her drab German treasure. . . Then he awoke from
his reverie. It was impossible! For a start, there was
no reason for Dai Ellis to sell the thing. And then
there was the possible cost. Hell, he couldn't have
raised the money to buy a replacement for the clock
the Smith boys had broken, let alone a monster like
this one. Wait, though. . .Dai Ellis was as much of a
gambling man as Evan himself. . .perhaps a wager?

With this thought in mind, but no likely object for a
really rich bet, Evan went into the public bar to give the
matter his full consideration. Since his brawling bachelor days, on Saturday nights he had always handed
all his money over to Dai or Siân for safe-keeping. At
the end of the evening they took out the price of his
drinks and returned the rest to him. He trusted them
completely and they had never let him down.

Once or twice, before he started passing them his
cash, the likes of Billy Stout had picked his pockets
of a whole week's wages while he was too drunk to
notice. It cost him less to use the Ellises as bankers.
Even so, he frequently found himself going home in
the early hours of Sunday, far worse off than he had
intended. But he knew it was his own taste for beer and
cards, not a cheating landlord, that was responsible for
his financial state. Margaret Ann had never known how
much he earned, so she was none the wiser about what
he spent on drink. Now, automatically, he passed over
his money to Siân, ordered a quart of bitter to get him
started 'and a little nip o' whisky for yourself, if you

do fancy one,' then took his drink off to a corner table where a group of his cronies were already installed.

The pub was hardly the place for quiet contemplation. There were eighteen pumps ranged along the big bar and another ten in the saloon bar, where men in working clothes were barred from entry. On Fridays and Saturdays there were always between twenty and twenty-three staff serving drinks. As the hooter sounded to signal the end of Friday afternoon shift at the Prince of Wales and Celynen South collieries, they started pulling pints and quarts in the pub, which were ranged along the shelf below the counter so that as the first thirsty miners arrived, their beer was ready without need to draw a fresh glass. Twelve or fourteen pints were commonly consumed by one man before he went home for bath and dinner. He would be back later, clean and apparently sober, to drink a similar amount. His earlier consumption usually acted as a booster and now he got intoxicated quite swiftly. By Saturday night, a lot of them had been drunk for nearly twenty-four hours, and were in a fighting mood.

Evan had followed this pattern throughout his adult life, although his contractor's Saturday pay-out inhibited him on Fridays, as he was still waiting for his money. Dai Ellis knew him as a steady payer, though, and would usually let him get drunk on credit. This week he had not indulged. They had been expecting the chest Margaret Ann had inherited from Auntie Mattie to arrive last night, so Evan had stayed in, and there was never any drink in the house. Now, he wished he had a few Friday pints under his belt to dispel the sense of inadequacy he felt when he contemplated how little he had given his wife except a tribe of children. It was no fun, sitting here among the already-tipsy crush of his mates, wondering how Margaret Ann would take it on the day he came home to tell her he would be returning to the coal face as a wage slave. . .in fact, it called for a

large whisky, or perhaps two or three. That would clear
away the gloom. . .

At midnight, Dai Ellis ushered out all but his inner
circle of friends. Evan had stayed out of the evening's
good-natured arguments, remaining alone at his corner table long after the departure of the men he had
joined earlier. Now he felt the need of company.
Through a drunken blur, he heard Tom Sloman saying, 'Of course the old milestone's on the canal side, we
used to sit on it when we was kids and lob stones down
in the water. Couldn't have done that if it had been the
wood side, could we?'

'What're you getting so hot about?' said Evan. 'It do
sound like a lot of nonsense to me.'

'Nothing of the sort,' said Dai, who fancied himself
as a reliable source of obscure information. 'It's just
a matter of straightforward observation powers, that's
all. Tom do swear the Newbridge milestone's on the left
as you do go up.'

'Aye, well, so it is. I used to chuck stones in from there
an' all.'

'But that's where you'm wrong – your memory is
playing you tricks. The stone was the other side, and
there used to be a long narrow pond on the woodland
side, looked a bit like a river, but it wasn't. They must
have filled it in when you two was still little kids, and
now there ent no water that side so you do imagine it
must have been the canal side, that's all. Simple matter
of a good memory.'

Evan was rapidly losing interest. Christ, people
talked about some dull things near bedtime! 'All right,
Dai, anything you say. Just give me my money, all right?
I'm off home.'

Ellis was embarrassed. He turned away from the
other man and dropped his voice. 'I been trying to

tell you all night, Evan, every time you come for a refill. Nobody on your money can drink that much whisky on top of the beer and have a lot over. There's no more than a few shillings left.'

Evan was stunned. He knew better than to argue – Dai had never cheated him. Anyway, his spinning head and leaden feet were telling him he must have put away about a bottle of whisky as well as countless pints.

'Bloody hell,' he mumbled, 'wha'm I going to tell Margaret Ann? I don't think there's nothing in the house.'

'I'm sorry, Evan, but I did warn you. I know better than to refuse to serve you, you know that.'

The big man nodded. ''Course I do. My own damned fault. I better sit down a minute.' He staggered slightly and dropped into a chair close to the bar.

Tom Sloman, himself quite drunk, had not noticed the aside and was still maundering about the milestone. 'Always so sure of yourself, ent you, Dai? If I was a betting man, I'd make you put your money where your mouth is and have a little wager on which side that bloody stone really is.'

'Any time, Tommy boy. But it'd have to be big money, because I'm so certain I'm right, I'd want to teach you a lesson.'

Evan experienced one of those momentary flashes of clarity which pass for revelation in the profoundly drunk. 'A really big one, eh, Dai? How about double or quits on what you've took from me tonight and half my next week's money?'

Ellis looked pained. 'Come on, mun, you know I don't like to bet with my regulars when they'm tight.'

'Sober as I ever am on a Saturday, Dai. Come on, it'll get me out of a terrible spot with Margaret Ann.'

The publican sniffed. 'Rubbish – it'll make it worse. I tell you, I'm right.'

'And I do agree with Tom. That stone's on the canal

side. Look, tell you what – throw in that grandfather
clock of yours and I'll make it what I've spent tonight,
half next week's money and half the week after's. Can't
say fairer than that, can you?'

'That clock was our Mam's. I couldn't part with it,
she'd turn in her grave. Anyhow, I couldn't put you in
dock like that.' Ellis began to turn away.

'Of course you can, Dai. Evan is a grown man, not
a kid. He do know what he wants without you telling
him.' It was Siân Ellis. She had just finished clearing up
in the saloon and had come into the public bar in time
to hear the men's exchange.

'Knowing the soft spot you've got for Evan, I'd a
thought you'd be warning him off an' all,' said Dai,
sulkily.

'Well, I'm not. If you're right, it'll teach him a lesson
he'll never forget. Even Margaret Ann would be grateful for that.'

This drew hollow laughs from all three men, but
Dai finally shrugged and conceded the point. 'All right
then. It's your funeral, Evan, not mine. Just don't say I
didn't warn you, all right?'

'All right, Dai. How'm we going to do it?'

Siân chipped in again. 'Tom's impartial, as he ent
involved, so he can adjudicate. You can all take a stroll
up there in the morning. Your Margaret Ann will be
in chapel and I can open up here if Dai's not back in
time to do it. All you'll have to do is look at the stone,
won't you?'

They agreed to meet again in the morning, and Evan
turned unsteadily to find his way home. He had only
gone a few yards when Siân caught up with him. 'Hang
on a minute, mun – I got something to say,' she hissed
at him.

'What is it? Don't say we'm going up there now?'

'We'm not, no – but if I was you, I'd nip up there on
my own, a bit quick, like.'

He gazed at her owlishly. 'Why'd I want to do that, then?'

'To make sure you do win, you dull bugger!'

'How d'you mean, Siân?'

'Dear God, save me from drunks and innocents! Because you won't have a chance to do nothing about it if you do wait till the morning.'

'But what chance will I have if I do find I was wrong?'

'You'm going to make me cry in a minute. How d'you think they put milestones in place?'

'Hmm. . .bury 'em, I s'pose.'

'And what d'you do for a living?'

Even in his stupor, realization began to dawn on him. He turned and grabbed her in a great bear hug. 'Siân, you'm pure gold, my flower!' He swung her round and put her back on the kerb, puzzlement swiftly following elation. 'B-but why d'you want to make Dai lose the bet?'

'Well, it ent because you're my secret sweetheart, so you needn't worry about that. It's that bloody old clock. It have been the curse of my married life. You wouldn't know, but it do chime the quarters. . .three on the first; six on the second; nine on the third; twelve on the fourth – and then a single bloody stroke for each hour of the time! At noon and midnight it do strike twenty-four times. How would you like that outside your bedroom door all through your married life?'

Evan was fighting a desire to laugh. 'Couldn't you get rid of it?'

'Don't think I haven't tried. Every time it's been, "Ooh, Our Mam would turn in 'er grave. . ." If I had my way the old cow would be spinning non-stop! It'll be worth the money Dai do lose to you to get rid of that clock.'

'Siân, you'm one of the best.'

'Aye, well, don't spend too much time thinking about it – you got work to do. Best of luck, Evan – and don't you never tell no one about this.'

'Quiet as the grave, me. If Margaret Ann ever got to know she'd kill the two of us!'

Siân watched him fondly from the side doorway of the pub as he walked off up the road towards Newbridge.

Forty minutes later, Evan was almost sober, and furious. He was standing beside the old milestone, cursing steadily in acknowledgement that Dai Ellis had been right about its location. If only he'd thought, he could have saved himself a double trip. Now he'd have to go home for his tools.

Fortunately the outhouse where he kept his spare pick and shovel was to the rear of the house, away from the front bedroom. There was always someone mooching around late on Saturday night, and if Margaret Ann half-heard some muffled noises, she'd think it was a drunk or a cat. . . Sighing at the prospect of a second two-mile round trip that night, Evan got the tools and began trudging back towards Newbridge again.

By the time he was finished, it was after five o'clock. The stone had been buried deeper than he expected, and when he eventually prised it loose it left a sizeable hole. He blundered about in the dark wood beside the road for some time before he found a couple of rocks to fill in the gap. It was quicker than staggering back and forth across the road with the soil he had dug out of the new hole on the far side. Thank God there was no paving around the stone. If there had been, he'd never have got away with it. . . He tamped the last of the soil back around the stone in its new position on the canal side of the main road. Then he slid down the embankment near the canal lock gates, where he knew there would be plenty of moss. Nothing like a bit of moss to make stonework look as if it had been there for ever. . . Evan took out his pocket knife, cut a quantity of moss and returned to the stone. He rubbed

the underside over any surfaces he might have scored
with his pick, then packed the moss flat around the base
of the milestone.

By now, it was beginning to get light. He stood back
and looked across the road to the stone's original location. *Well I'm damned*, he thought – *I must have still been
drunk!* The original site was a good twenty feet further
north than the point he had chosen on the other side
of the road. He must have staggered a long way with
it. Well, unless the Government had it in mind to do a
survey, no one would notice they had a generous mile
one side and a mean one the other! Evan returned
briefly to the far side of the road and scuffed up the
dust and gravel around the rock, rubble and soil he
had used to fill the empty space. Then he shouldered
his tools and headed for home, for the second time
since midnight. This time, though, his step was jaunty
and he was whistling a popular music hall song.

'But Evan, you could never afford it!'

It was tea time on Sunday and Margaret Ann was
standing outside her front door, torn between ecstasy
and outrage at the sight of the Ellises' grandfather clock
on the path outside.

Evan shrugged modestly. 'Well, Dai said I could pay
him bit by bit. . . It'll be a bit of a strain, I know, but it's
worth it if you'm happy.'

'Oh, Evan – happy? I do love you so much!' And for
the first time in her married life, Margaret Ann flung
her arms around her husband's neck and kissed him
in public. Over her shoulder he caught the eye of Siân
Ellis, who had come along with the two potboys who
delivered the clock on a handcart. As he did so she gave
him a broad wink, and raised a finger to her lips.

There was only one spot in the house where the
ceiling was high enough to accommodate the clock –

at the top of the stairs, where the stairwell went up
to roof level, immediately outside Evan and Margaret
Ann's bedroom door. At midnight, as the chimes struck
twenty-four, Evan silently cursed all clockmakers. His
wife, half asleep, made a small chortling sound of
pure happiness, and twined her arms tighter around
his waist.

CHAPTER THIRTEEN

T OM GILCHRIST WAS right about the disappearance of contract work, but he had spoken prematurely. Risca colliery was using its own colliers on headings within weeks, but in Abercarn and Newbridge, Evan could generally keep his gang employed. Nevertheless, Gilchrist's warning worried him.

He was reprieved by luck. In April, spurred by their leader, Mabon, the South Wales miners came out on strike for a 10 per cent wage increase and abolition of the sliding pay scale which tied their earnings to the price of coal. The owners promptly turned strike into lock-out and the coal industry ground to a halt. As an independent, Evan was unaffected. His heading work was not technically coal extraction – he was only opening up routes to the coal. The men knew that eventually they would go back, and that they would need to get at the coal without delay when they did so. The strike pickets let him and his men pass and the threat of colliers taking over the contract work receded. But Evan was uncomfortable. All his life he had identified with the underdog and despised the master, yet here he was, doing the coal-owners' work while his friends and neighbours starved for a just cause. His discomfort grew more intense when he was approached to try a different type of work.

Once again, the proposal came from Tom Gilchrist. He sent for Evan at home one Sunday morning. Intrigued, Evan went along with the young boy who had come to fetch him from the Ranks, following him to a quiet spot along the main Valley road out of Abercarn. A modest rig waited beneath a tree. In it sat Gilchrist.

'Morning, Evan. Care to step up here with me and go for a drive?'

Evan eyed him dubiously. 'Why all the mystery? You ent up to anything illegal, are you?'

Gilchrist uttered a grim laugh. 'I don't need to be, these days. There's a strike on, or hadn't you noticed?'

'They'm calling it a lock-out up here.'

'Depends which side you're on, Evan, always depends which side you're on. I'd have thought that as an independent you'd have to stay above the whole thing.'

'Right – and there's some around here as wouldn't regard going driving with a boss as staying above it.'

'I wasn't thinking of anywhere too public – and I'm not going to propose anything shady: just honest work for honest money. How about it?'

'All right, then, but make it quick and keep it quiet.' He jumped lightly up into the trap and Gilchrist drove off at a brisk pace. Eventually he stopped, down the secluded old road that led to Chapel Farm. 'I take it you ignored my advice about training as an official,' he said.

Evan was impatient. 'Come on, mun, that's a dead duck. Told you, I'm too old to change. When the work do run out I'll go back on the coal, and that's all there is to it.'

'Maybe, maybe not. Ever thought of working as a sinker?'

That made Evan laugh. 'I can get killed soon enough on the coal without bloody committing suicide!'

'I know it's not the easiest job in the pits, but it's paying so well at present that you'd probably get enough capital together to invest in your own coal level if you were careful.'

'And how do I make my fortune so easy?'

'You know damned well it won't be easy. But you must have realized how many outside teams are in the coalfield right now, sinking new shafts. They're all over the place – and they don't stay long enough to merge with everybody else.'

'You're right there. The two gangs living around Abercarn have caused more fights in the last three months than I've had hot dinners.'

'Which is why I want to interest you in the trade. Have you ever worked with a sinking team?'

'Oh, aye, when I was a kid. But they was shallow shafts compared with these days, and even so it bloody terrified me. One fellow went straight down, head first. Slipped on a wet plank. Top of his spine was shoved straight up into his skull. I've never been too happy about heights since then.'

'But I bet you finished the job.'

''Course I did. My kind don't have no choice, or hadn't you thought about that?'

'No use coming the poor orphan with me, Evan, I started off from somewhere no better than the Ranks. Save the self-pity for the gentry. You finished the job because you were tough. What about the skills involved? They're a bit different from driving headings.'

He had caught Evan's interest now. The big man considered the question. 'Well, I do know what skilled men I'd need. Couple of brickies, for a start. I imagine you got engineer's drawings for the shafts.'

'Naturally. I'm not asking you to design the thing. There'll be a mining engineer supervising it most of the time, too.'

'You know I don't like working under nobody.'

That made Gilchrist laugh. 'The average mining

engineer would take one look at the width of your
shoulders and watch every word he said after that. I
don't think you'll have any trouble. They're not like
overmen, wanting to prove who's on top all the time.'

'In that case, I reckon I could do it with my present
gang, if I can find the brickies. They won't be scabs no
more than I would, because they'm not in the colliers'
unions. And they'll be short of work while the miners
is locked out. Should be easy. Aye – of course I could
do it. I'll just tell myself I'm doing my old job from a
different direction, that's all.'

Gilchrist considerately refrained from telling him
that a man could not fall a thousand feet along a
horizontal heading. In a mineshaft, it was perfectly
easy. There was a more obvious condition of the job
which he was anxious to broach. 'Of course, you'll have
to think about how it will affect you, being away from
home so much.'

'How d'you mean?'

'Evan, no pit needs more than two or three shafts,
and most of them already have one or two. That means
you might work here in Abercarn on one shaft, but
after that you'd be anywhere they were sinking –
Abertridwr, say, or Bargoed – they're both planning
new shafts soon.'

'But I couldn't get there and back – wouldn't be
worth it. I'd have to keep two places going, one for
me, one for the family.'

The manager chuckled. 'Oh, I think you'd find it
was worth it, Evan. The money the sinkers get is way
beyond anything you ever saw before.'

Walters was unimpressed. 'That's what some clever
dick told me when I went into heading contracts. Well,
they was right at first, but it looked more than it really
was. Never would have been worth moving around
for.'

'This is in a different class. Look – I shouldn't be

showing you this, but I brought it along in case you needed a bit of persuasion.'

It was a series of extracts from the South Wales Coal-owners' Association records, printed in pamphlet form as guidance for members who were investing in new shaft operations. The section Gilchrist showed to Evan was a table of expenses incurred in sinking a new shaft at John Nixon's Merthyr Vale colliery over five years, and it amounted to almost a quarter of a million pounds.

Evan studied the total with something akin to reverence for a few moments, then said, 'I don't think I've ever read a number with that many figures in it.'

'Exactly. More money than you knew existed. Now, look at the biggest single cost.' Gilchrist pointed at the first entry:'"Labour, £79,245." And that doesn't include the engineer – see, he's down under "Superintendence".'

'B-but, let's see, if that job took about five years, it do add up to nearly £16,000 a year!'

'Interested now? Even if you allow for a much bigger gang – up to two dozen, including the brickies, I think – you're averaging £600 a year per man. Needless to say, most of them get a lot less than that, but you get a lot more. You also get a cut out of the superintendence money. And you wouldn't have to worry about housing, either. They stick up cottages for the bigger work force they plan to recruit when you've finished, and put you and your men in them free of charge while you're sinking the shaft. Ten years as a sinker, Evan, and you could take your pick whether you wanted to be a coal-owner yourself in a small way, or get out of mining altogether and buy yourself a little business. Is that worth being away from home a lot?'

'It do sound too good to be true. Why me, Mr Gilchrist?'

The manager looked embarrassed. 'I was lucky,

Evan. I got my opportunity before I was twenty – somebody did me a good turn when they didn't need to, and I was off the coal face and studying for my papers. I'd never have done it if that favour hadn't come my way. I always promised myself I'd pass it on if I found someone who looked as if he deserved it – and you do. Maybe you'll do the same for somebody else in your turn.'

'That's fair enough. I'll try.'

'Mind you, I'm not doing you that much of a favour. It's a bastard of a job – but at least it gives you a chance to earn enough to get out.'

'It's all right, I know you don't get nothing for nothing!'

'Very well, is it a deal?'

'Aye, and thanks, Mr Gilchrist. What do I do now?'

'You come down to Risca to see me when your present heading contract ends, and I'll refer you to one of the owners who's been making enquiries. He'll take it on from there. I'll try to keep it fairly near home – no further west than the Rhondda, and perhaps only as far as the Rhymney Valley. How about that?'

'Fine. I could come back Saturdays and Sundays then, anyhow.'

'Good man; I thought you'd see sense this time. Let's shake hands on it.'

Evan walked back to the Ranks with a new spring in his step. What if he did have to leave home? Anything was better than walking past locked-out miners every morning and trying not to dwell on the probability that you'd be one of them within the year – and he could stop sucking mouthfuls of peppermints every time he'd been on the beer, too. . .

When he told Margaret Ann, she took it better than he had feared. Evan was almost disappointed. It wasn't as if sinking carried any cachet that might make his wife regard the new work as a step up the social ladder. With that in mind, he felt a distinct blow to his vanity. All right, so there was a prospect of money – a lot of money by their standards. But he thought she loved him so much she could not bear to be parted from him for twenty-four hours. Now here she was, calmly preparing to bid him farewell for the best part of every week of the foreseeable future. Evan was not a reflective man and it never occurred to him to consider how much his wife's attitude had changed since the birth of Lily.

Now, the day before he was due to depart for his first week's sinking, at Bargoed in the Rhymney Valley, Margaret Ann was bathing Lily in a big bowl on the kitchen table. The baby was chuckling at her mother and Margaret Ann's expression was dreamy, fulfilled in a way she had never been with him even after love-making.

'My Lily of the Valleys will look after me while you'm gone, won't you, my lovely?' she said.

Evan felt an unaccustomed pang of jealousy. Don't say he was going to have to play second fiddle to his own kids! 'Aye, keep you warm in bed o'nights, no doubt,' he growled.

'Hush, now, Evan. . .that's not nice!'

'How old d'you think she is, seventeen?' he said scornfully. 'Don't be bloody daft!'

'And you start as you mean to go on. I want this child to grow up respectable, like I did. No bad language, and no suggestive talk. It's never too early for that.'

'Christ, you'll be glad to see the back of me! No great big lout disturbing Lady Ranks's palace!'

Margaret Ann was conciliatory, but not abject, as Evan would have expected on his last evening.

'You know that isn't true. Of course I'll miss you – and that's a silly name they do call me, just 'cos I like things nice. Never mind that now, though. I – I been meaning to tell you something, but your news about this work made me put it off, in case it. . .held you back, like.'

Realization leaped in Evan, and with it the glowing pride he had felt every time before. 'Again? How long have you known. . .when?'

Margaret Ann was beaming, secure in his obvious pleasure. 'Oh, it's early yet. Not much over two months. I think it'll be a May baby this time.'

He became serious. 'Sure you can manage by yourself, girl? Just say the word and I'll stop here.' There was some bravado in his words, for he knew that with another child on the way, Margaret Ann would count security in the pounds he could earn. But part of him meant it.

'Go on with you! If I haven't got it right by now, I never will. I've had enough practice! Let's hope it's born on a Saturday or Sunday, while you'm here. There's always Edith Smith if you ent.'

Even Saturdays and Sundays at home were to be an event before very long. Evan's first shaft contract was at Bargoed, and the gang were housed in new coal company cottages adjoining the mine, as Tom Gilchrist had predicted. Working as a sinker was not physically harder than driving headings: that would have been impossible. But there was an extra element of tension which wore down the men faster than mere hard labour.

They were sinking the shaft to an expected depth of more than 1,800 feet, and the original contractor had been at work for a year before he abandoned the project. Evan's team of ten labourers and two bricklayers joined ten of the original gang employed on the shaft. It was a mess of slick mud and crumbling shale, the unstable shaft walls shored up with scaffolding and iron frames to await permanent brickwork. Through

the ooze ran a network of shaky planks, already coated
with slime and offering only hazardous access to the
excavation. The crews who worked in this threatening
environment looked more like lifeboat men than miners. Thick oilskin trousers with double flaps at every
opening protected their legs, topped by long oilskin
coats which reached below their calves. Sou'westers covered their heads, the back-flaps so long that they acted
as extra capes.

At first Evan was inclined to dismiss the need for such
garments. 'It'll cut our pace in half,' he said. 'Just lifting
that lot along with a mandril will stop us in our tracks.'

'I know it's hard,' said the supervising engineer, 'but
you'd find it impossible without those clothes. Just wait
and see what happens when we hit water.'

Within ten minutes one of the labourers did just
that. A jet of muddy brown fluid shot out of the shaft
side without warning, hitting the man in the chest with
such force that he fell. He tumbled from his plank –
fortunately, into a slippery hollow on the wall side of
the hole – and was engulfed in mud. The ooze was so
deep it took him five minutes to stand up and he was
coated with it when he finally got back to the plank.

The engineer jerked his head towards the casualty.
'See what I mean? We can just hose him down as he is,
but think what it'd be like if he was in ordinary working
clothes. He'd be finished for the day.'

Reluctantly, Evan accepted the necessity for protec-
tive clothing. He hated the weight of his oilskins, and
personal repugnance for such restriction was as responsible for his distaste as the more obvious drawbacks.

'Is it always like this?' he asked Panton, the engineer. 'If it is, I'm not surprised you get your gangers
dropping out.'

Panton was optimistic. 'This is a very bad one, I
admit,' he said. 'It usually depends on proximity to
the river and the nature of the surrounding soil. Some

shafts go down with scarcely a sign of moisture – but then you have to watch out for dust falls, of course.'

'Give me dust before water any time. You can't drown in earth,' said Evan.

'I'm afraid it's unlikely you'll have dust problems for a while, Walters. Most of the sinking around here is being done on wet ground. If you stay the course, I think these conditions will be typical.'

Evan sighed. 'I told Tom Gilchrist I knew I wouldn't get nothing for nothing, but this is ridiculous.'

It did not become easier. Evan was shattered by noon on Saturday, when work stopped for the week. Nevertheless, he cleaned himself up and caught a train back to Abercarn. By the time Margaret Ann served him a late dinner at four o'clock, he was too tired to eat. She fussed over him like a mother hen, chivvying him into having something, then almost leading him upstairs to bed. When he awoke it was broad daylight and he was alone. He had slept through until mid-morning on Sunday and Margaret Ann was already in chapel. *I could have died in my sleep and she wouldn't have missed chapel*, he thought, levering himself out of the deep feather mattress.

Down in the kitchen, his two eldest sons awaited him. John Daniel eyed him cautiously. He had always been wary of Evan, afraid his father's sudden rages might burn him up if he drew attention to himself. Finally he managed to speak.

'Our Mam let us off chapel to wait for you, Dad. She said we was to get you some food.'

Evan stretched and rubbed the sleep from his eyes. 'Aye, she's right, an' all, but you'm never going to get it, are you?'

The boy nodded, full of pride. 'Mam says I do fry bacon better than anybody in the Ranks. She've made us older ones learn to do it this week, in case we need to look after her when you ent here.'

Evan was touched. 'And you've learned to be the best
in the Ranks in a week?'

The boy dimpled shyly. 'Well, it was a bit hard at
first. Mam ate all the burned bits. She said everybody
do need a first chance, and I mustn't get discouraged.'

Evan could almost hear his wife saying the words,
and for a moment he was grateful that she found time
to be good with the children when there were so many
calls on her time. 'All right then, young man, let's see
what you can do,' he said, 'unless you'd rather catch her
up and go to chapel, of course.'

'Oh, no, Dad – I'm sick of Gentle Jesus. So's Billie.
He'll cut the bread.'

Evan fought an urge to laugh, then watched,
impressed, as his sons swept into action to prepare
his meal. Margaret Ann had missed her vocation.
She could have organized a battalion, he thought as
he watched.

Soon tea, bacon, eggs, fried bread and mushrooms
were placed in front of him. 'Mushrooms? We'm
celebrating my recent elevation a bit early, ent we?'

Now it was Billie's turn to speak. 'They was free. We
went all the way up Trwyn Woods Friday afternoon
and found them for you.'

'Trwyn, eh? I'm surprised your mam let you go up
there on your own.'

'She said we mustn't go any further up than Little
Trwyn, or we couldn't go again. Didn't matter, anyway.
There was plenty just up past the brewery.'

Evan nodded, pleased. 'D'you know, that's where I
used to find the best ones when I was your age. I didn't
think they'd still grow so close. Thought they'd have
been trampled in by now with all the people going up
around there.'

Billie took that as a personal compliment. 'You got to
know where to look, Dad. Not many people do bother
to get off the path, but I do. I know all the birds that do

nest up there, and some of the butterflies. It's lovely up there under the trees.'

'He's always there in the summer, Dad,' said John Daniel. 'Says he do want to work up there when he's old enough.'

That troubled Evan. Sunshine and fresh air were seldom the working conditions offered to pit boys.

'What do you think you'll do there, then, Billie?'

'Well, I been thinking. Some of the farmers must want labouring boys, mustn't they? Everybody do go down the pit because the money's good, but I wouldn't care about that if I could work outside.'

'That's just the half of it, boy,' said Evan. 'There ent no future in farming for the likes of us. You go and work like a slave for some bugger who can hardly feed himself on what he do make each year, and if you get sick, or want to change jobs, you do lose everything. At least down the pit you got the benefit club.'

Billie's face clouded. 'Aye. You do need it, and all, from what I've heard.'

'You ent tied, like on farms. And you can get on, improve things for yourself. If you start off as a farm labourer, you'll die as one – or in the workhouse, if you'm too sick to do your twelve hours when you'm seventy.'

Somehow this talk of the contrasting worlds of fresh air and dark confinement laid a blight on their morning fellowship. Evan resolutely turned the conversation in a new direction, telling them hair-raising stories of his adventures on the slimy planks over the vast abyss at Bargoed Colliery. This wasn't pit talk – this was excitement, more like the tales of a pirate captain than a miner. The boys listened, entranced, and when Margaret Ann got back from chapel she found them sitting awkwardly on the narrow arms of Evan's Windsor chair, agog for more stories.

It was a good day for Evan. Separation from his

family made their attractions more obvious. The
cosiness of his home and the standard of Margaret
Ann's housekeeping impressed him afresh now he had
spent a week in a coal company house cleaned and
victualled by a paid housekeeper. But if he was beginning to dream of returning to the Ranks, Margaret
Ann had other ideas. She sent the children out to
play, then made some tea before sitting down across
the table from him.

'We got to talk about all this travelling you'm planning to do, Evan,' she said.

'Don't say you think I can get there and back every
day!'

'Don't be daft! I was thinking the opposite. Look at
you, only at it for a week and you'm done in. All right,
so you feel better now, but that's after nearly sixteen
hours sleep and you'll have to start back in next to no
time. It's never worth it.'

He glowered at her. 'Well, how else can we manage?'

'You can come home every three weeks or so, that's
what. And after a few months, if you'm earning as
much as Mr Gilchrist said you would, maybe you could
take a week without pay and come back over here for
longer. I'd rather be here by myself, missing you, than
see you working yourself to an early grave just because
you felt I couldn't be left on my own.'

He tried to feel flattered by her considerate plan.
He told himself she was thinking only of him. But the
ease with which she could let him go tweaked his vanity
much as her enchantment with their baby daughter had
a short while ago. He grumbled and objected, turning
up endless obstacles to the proposal. But in the end
he had to acknowledge the truth of what she said. If
he tried to work the shaft and come back and forth
to Abercarn every week, he'd kill himself. Not from
overwork: he was too tough for that. But he knew how

careless tiredness could make a man, and those treacherous planks were no place to be tired.

Evan left the Ranks that evening feeling empty and curiously free. He had not been so detached for ten years or more. He still did not know whether he wanted such liberty, or even if he knew what to do with it.

Over the next couple of years, he learned quickly. It was surprising how easily the routines of a bachelor existence returned. He drank a lot; went for walks when the weather allowed it; read and played billiards at the workmen's institute. He would not have wanted such a life if there had been nothing else, but every few weeks he returned to a growing family who seemed to love him more intensely the less they saw of him.

Something with which he found it harder to come to terms was the scale of profit in sinking. Tom Gilchrist had been right about the expenditure he quoted from earlier excavations on the coalfield. But sinking, like heading work, was affected by the flood tide of immigrants entering South Wales. As more men became available for sinking shafts, so the going rate dropped. It was still very well-paid – good enough for Evan to keep his two households going and remain better off than ever before – but there was no mountain of spare money building up in preparation for his own business. Gradually he began to accept that he was tied to some form of hard labour attached to coal until he died or got too old to work.

Meanwhile, Margaret Ann seemed to flourish. She gave birth to another son, Elwyn, in 1899. In February 1901 there was another girl, a fairer version of Lily, whom they named Bethan. By now the house was so crowded that Evan wondered where they would put him if he ever came home permanently. There were nine children – three girls and six boys. The boys slept together, top-and-tail in two beds crammed into the second bedroom. When Evan was away, the girls slept with Margaret Ann. When he came home, he reclaimed wife and bed and their daughters slept on a mattress down in the parlour.

John Daniel was twelve years old in 1901 – old enough to earn a living. He had always been a happy, confident boy, apparently unworried by the club foot which made him walk with a pronounced limp. Somehow he managed to do most of the things that undamaged boys could do, and it never occurred to the family to regard him as an invalid. Everyone liked him for his generosity and sweet nature. It was unthinkable that he might object to a life down the mines, so of course he did not. On a June morning at quarter to five, he set off for his first shift in the Celynen colliery with Alf Smith, the Walters's next door neighbour.

Evan was home for a few days, taking an unpaid break while Bethan was teething. He felt a stronger sense of parenthood and responsibility for his daughters than for his sons, and he liked to be on hand to help Margaret Ann when they reached difficult phases. It was almost as if he hoped his presence would stop her resenting the children for being troublesome. Now, though, he found himself comforting his wife for the loss of a son. When John Daniel left for the colliery, she was tearful.

'I know he's a big boy for his age, Evan, but I always promised myself none of our sons would go down the pit. I wanted better for them.'

Not for the first time, Evan was swept by a sense of helplessness. 'How else would we manage, love?' he said. 'I know I could keep him for a good while yet, but what would he do when he got older? He've got to have a job, and he ent going to earn a decent wage as a grocer's boy, is he?'

'There must be other things – must be!'

'What, for instance? I can't see our John Dan sitting on a clerk's stool. You know what his writing's like. And if there's any other sorts of jobs around here for miners' sons, I'd like to know what.'

Margaret Ann silently conceded defeat with John Daniel, and began to move away from Evan. Then she stopped, apparently struck forcibly by a related idea, and turned back to him. 'Well, I'll tell you this for nothing. John Daniel may not have better prospects, but there'd better be some for our Billie!'

'In the name of faith, why? What's so special about Billie?'

'Everything. Don't you ever look at him or listen to him? He've got more imagination than the lot of this family put together. He's clever and quick – and the very idea of the pit do scare him silly.'

'Look, love, Billie's only ten yet – there's plenty of time.'

'Oh, is there? The last twelve years have slipped by quick enough, haven't they? Yes, he's only ten, and he can name you dozens of sorts of birds and butterflies, and he do love fishing and being in the open. You can't let him go down in the dark!'

'It's John Dan that's going down the pit! Let's get him sorted out first. Something will come up for our Billie, just wait and see.'

PART THREE
1903–1911

Set me as a seal upon thine heart. . .
for love is strong as death; jealousy is
cruel as the grave; the coals thereof
are coals of fire, which hath
a most vehement flame.

Song of Songs
Ch.VIII, v.6

CHAPTER FOURTEEN

B IRDS AND BUTTERFLIES were no more than a beautiful memory when twelve-year-old Billie Walters went down the pit for the first time on 27 December, 1903. It was icy cold and pitch dark and he was frightened. But his father had said it would be all right and he knew better than to doubt his father. Billie tried to whistle. The tune froze on his pursed lips. He tried turning his thoughts to his new clothes and that chilled his spirit as thoroughly as his whistling. These were not the sort of new clothes you wore to go out enjoying yourself. To Billie, they represented prison uniform.

The hobnailed boots were the most noticeable items of dress. Even after the heavy boots he had worn as a schoolboy (had that been only a week ago?) these great bruising symbols of manhood seemed like ton weights at the ends of his legs. The boots were built rather than sewn – cobbled together from the toughest leather with a seasoned, curving sole which raised the domed toecaps well above the ground. The hobnails in the soles produced a ringing click which announced the approach of a miner along a cobbled back street minutes before he arrived home. The boots were designed for hard wear and for protection – both from the hazards of falling rock and from attacking adversaries. They made excellent offensive weapons –

few assailants made a second attempt if they were once caught squarely in crotch or kidneys by the swinging toecap of a hobnailed boot. Billie tried to concentrate on the status they conveyed, but his humour did not improve.

He also wore sturdy duck trousers, tied under the knees with string. Beneath them was a suit of flannel underwear, with a flannel shirt providing another layer of insulation. The rough wool waistcoat and jacket of John Daniel's first suit had been made over for him, he wore a new cloth cap, and his rig-out was completed by a thick scarf knotted into the high neckline of the waistcoat. His food was packed neatly into a round-ended tin tommy-box, designed to fit inside a jacket pocket, and he carried a tin jack full of cold, heavily sweetened tea.

Evan Walters had been working for nearly two years on the new Brithdir shaft, and his company cottage was near the diggings. It was a two-mile walk from there to the steam coal workings at Bargoed Colliery. Billie and John Daniel had moved over and joined their father to make more room at home now that Margaret Ann was having yet another baby. At the thought of home, Billie's sigh was close to a sob. He would have exchanged his spacious bedroom at Brithdir without a moment's regret for the overcrowded corner he occupied in the Ranks.

It wasn't so bad for John Dan. . .at least it wasn't all new to him. He'd been working down the Celynen South for two years now. All he had to do was get used to a new pit. Billie had to adjust to a whole new world, a world he had never wanted to enter.

'Come on, then, I'm ready now.' John Daniel emerged from the cottage, slapping his tommy-box into a jacket pocket. 'Always hard to get back after the holiday, and this move do make it worse,' he said.

'You can say that again. Which way do we go?'

John Daniel gestured vaguely into the darkness. 'It

do look different than when our Dad showed us in the daytime, don't it? But we'll be all right if we go down the end of the street. There'll be plenty of others going and we'll just follow.'

He limped off ahead of Billie, who watched him, wistfully admiring the way the older boy managed to change a disability into a swagger. No one called John Daniel a cripple and got away with it.

Sure enough, there was a steady trickle of miners moving south towards Bargoed. It was not long after five in the morning, but the dark street was as busy as high noon. When they reached the pithead, these men would have to collect their lamps and get below ground in time to start work by six o'clock. This dark morning pilgrimage was commonplace to them. They had always risen half-way through the night and returned home again when day was almost gone.

John Daniel had given Billie one of his mandrils, a small one. 'Get used to the feel of it before you do try a bigger one,' he had said. Now Billie swung it in time with his crunching boot-steps, gradually building from an illusory to a real confidence and anticipation of a new world.

In the lamproom he was issued with a ball-and-cup oil lamp for his cap, and John Dan was given a Davey lamp as well as the cap light. Then he was jostled through a tangle of tram lines to the cages – two of them side by side at the top of a hole in the ground almost two thousand feet deep.

'Just think – our Dad sunk most of this,' murmured John Daniel in a thrilled voice. Billie suddenly got a vertiginous mental image of his father hanging in empty space, a giant silhouetted against flickering lamplight. For some reason it gave him an awful sense of the depths to which they were about to descend and he felt so faint he staggered against his elder brother. 'Steady, now, kidda,' said John Dan. 'It ent so bad as it do look.'

Billie gulped back a mouthful of vomit and smiled shakily. 'Ennit? I ent half glad of that!'

He felt the cage floor buck slightly under the weight of two dozen miners. There was a clash of sounds and suddenly they were sinking – sinking at a suicidal pace which Billie knew could never be stopped in time. Down, down, down into hell – and out the other side at this rate, he thought. It was black as pitch. The lamps were not lit yet. I'm going to die in the dark – at least they won't see how frightened I am, he thought. Then, halfway down, the engineman applied the brakes to check the momentum of the twin cages. Billie's stomach told him they were returning to the surface and he began to panic. Something was wrong – there'd been an accident down below... They'd never get out alive, just hang here for ever until the steel rope parted and they dropped again...dropped for good... Then John Daniel's fingers were curling through his, pressing reassurance into his sweaty palm. Again, the soft, reassuring voice carried to him, and no further.

'It's all right, Billie boy. We do all feel like that. It ent really happening, we'm still on the way down, just slowing a bit, that's all...' The voice went on, a soothing presence, pressing back the terrifying velvet blackness as they hurtled to the bottom of the world.

Evan Walters was well-known to plenty of the Bargoed colliers – some of them had worked as sinkers under him from time to time – and he had found men to sponsor his boys for their start on the coal face. John Daniel was already skilled, with eighteen months work at the Celynen behind him, but he was not yet regarded as fully trained. Billie was a complete beginner. Everything here was new to him.

It seemed he walked for hours in the blackness, the cap lamps around him only exaggerating the dark. They were heading along one of the haulage roads

to the stalls where their sponsors were working. As
they went, the roof grew lower, and they were soon
progressing in a crouched stance to accommodate it.
If Billie had thought about the pit bottom at all, he
had imagined it as a silent place, apart from the
miners' talk and the crunch of boots on coal dust.
But it was fiendishly noisy, with winding engines
rattling and banging, trams trundling down their
metal tracks, and, worst of all, the ominous creaks
and crashes as beams settled and rock fell in distant
workings.

The first time that happened, Billie thought there
had been an accident, and turned instinctively to flee.
Again, John Daniel saved his face, reaching out in the
dark to grab his arm.

'You'll get used to that,' he said. 'The pit's like a big
animal, see, never still. That's the noise it do make when
it turns over!'

Their workplace was almost a mile from the cages,
and it took them nearly half an hour to get there,
thanks to the uneven ground and roof. The boys'
sponsors were butties, and worked in adjoining stalls,
so the brothers were not really separated.

Billie's sponsor, Dai Pritchard, hunkered down
beside the boy and gave him an odd-looking scoop,
rather like a giant domestic dustpan with the handle
removed.

'You can put away that mandril for a while, Billie –
this'll be your working tool for a long time yet,' he said.
'Now look by here and see what we've got to do.'

He gestured at the limits of the section he was working – a piece about seven feet long, a yard high and
a yard deep. 'This is our stent. We got to leave it like
we found it, except for the coal I do cut, so the next
shift can carry on straight away. We do start off with
me cutting the coal. It'll fall in good big lumps with a
fair bit o' dust. You take that curling box I just give you

and scoop up the lumps. Try not to get small coal, they don't pay for that. Empty the scoop into that tram by there. I'll keep a steady pace going, and you'll learn to keep up with me without tiring yourself too much.'

Billie studied the tram. 'It do look ever so big for one man to fill,' he said.

'That's because it is, boyo – bloody big. You can get thirty hundredweight in there. Got to fill two or three of them each shift, and that's only the half of it.'

'What else have we got to do, then?'

'Told you – the stall have got to be left like we found it. So when I've cut the coal and you've loaded it, we got to take the gobs – that's the rubbish – and clear it away, then do all the timbering so the stall is workable again. We do stuff the gobs up behind the timbering, see? Like that behind you.'

'How d'you get it all done before we finish?'

'By working bloody hard and fast, and pretending you'm a man before your time. And by cutting out the chatter, an' all. Come on, let's get going. Oh – one other thing. Can you write?'

'Of course I can. Only left school last week, didn't I?'

'All right, then. Just remember, when I do fill that tram, chalk my name on the side good and big before they do take it up top. That's all I got to prove we been working.'

The rest of Billie's shift passed in a miserable swirl of effort, dust and scrambling about in the dark. His hands were soon bloody from scraping against the coal as he scooped the lumps from the ground. After a while, his back ached dully from constant bending. The curling box was hardly an ideal collecting vessel, but it was designed to preserve large lumps of coal, not to make the pitboy's life easier. A little after half past one, they stopped work. The stall was so neat it looked as though no one had worked there that day; but Dai had cut and Billie had loaded almost four tons of lump coal. The collier had showed him how the timbers were notched to prevent them rolling when the roof settled; how to stow the gob behind earlier timbering to pack it away out of the work area. Billie felt as if he had been imprisoned underground for centuries.

They made the return journey to the pit bottom much faster than the outward trip. 'Always the same,' said Dai when Billie asked about it. 'You get the smell of the fresh air up above and your feet do move faster, that's all. Come on, another day over. You'll do, Billie. You've done a good shift today.'

Billie wished he felt happier about it, but all he could think was that this was how he had to spend the rest of his life. The thought was insupportable.

It was two o'clock when they reached the surface, but their day was not finished yet. John Daniel and Billie checked in their lamps, then set off on the two-mile walk back to Brithdir. When they arrived at Evan's cottage it was after half past three.

Evan came in at four, radiating forced good cheer. 'And how's my great big boys, then – done a proper day's work, have you?'

John Daniel rushed in, eager to save Billie's face by cutting off any complaints. 'Dai Pritchard was ever so pleased about our Billie, Dad. Said he done a really good shift.'

'Grand, that's what I like to hear. And how about you?'

John Daniel shrugged dismissively. 'One pit's the same as another, ennit, Dad? Once we was down, I could have been back in the Celynen.'

'You'm a good boy, John Dan. Know how to settle in anywhere. Here, make up that fire a bit, and I'll boil the kettle. Mrs Parry will be round with some dinner soon.'

Then he turned to Billie. 'Come over here in the

light, boy, where I can get a good look at you. Come on, quick, they haven't worked you that hard, have they?'

Reluctantly, Billie moved across to him. Evan sat in front of the child, hands on his shoulders, and gazed deep into his face. 'You managed then, did you?'

All Billie could do was nod dumbly. They might think he had managed. He knew he had not. So did Evan. He looked at the boy and knew that this one would never adjust to mining. Despair flared inside him. What, in the name of God, could he do about it? The pits had served him well enough, hadn't they? He knew this boy was different, but he couldn't put him beyond the reach of coal. He shelved the problem, loosened his grip on Billie's shoulders and grabbed the boy's hands.

'*Iesu mawr*, they've given you an 'ammering! Rough floor, was it?' Billie nodded again, still unable to trust himself to speak. 'Come on,' said Evan. 'You have the first bath. Get them hands clean before they start giving you trouble.'

The fireplace in the house had one of the latest patent cast iron ranges, with a water boiler at the side, fitted with a tap. It made life much easier in households where they commonly needed water for four or five men to bathe each day. Evan got down the tin bath and set it before the fire, with a clothes horse hung with towels to intercept the draught from the front door. Billie knelt on another towel in front of the bath, stripped to the waist, and started lathering away the silky-smooth coal dust which insinuated itself into every pore of his body. When his top half was clean, Evan topped up the blackened, tepid liquid in the tub with a gallon of fresh hot water. Billie removed his trousers and underpants and stepped into the bath, sitting down with a sigh of pleasure as the warmer water swirled around his aching back. He leaned back as far as the little tin vessel permitted, closed his eyes and uttered a luxurious sigh.

'I never thought a drop of dirty water would be such a treat!' he said.

'That won't wear off, neither,' Evan told him. 'Every day it's the same. I've known really peaceful men hammer their wives for not heating the bath water enough. Now, let's have a look at them hands.'

While Billie sat in the bath, Evan gently cleaned the last coal dust out of the grazes on his fingers, then rubbed them with a sweet-smelling lotion he kept for small wounds. He scowled as he worked, and when he had finished, said, 'I got a pair of gloves should fit you. You'd better have them till your hands harden up. Won't do for you to get blood poisoning.'

'But what if someone do see them? They'll laugh.'

It was Evan who laughed, relieved to find an excuse for merriment. 'See you, down there? You could wear girl's drawers down the pit and no one would notice! You have the gloves.'

By the time they were all washed and changed, and the widow Evan had hired to clean, wash and cook had served their meal, Billie was half asleep. Evan stood up from the kitchen table and gently ruffled the boy's ginger-blond hair. 'I think it's an early night for you, kidda. Go on, up them stairs. Half past four will be here again before you can say Jack Robinson.'

'But it ent seven o'clock yet.'

'Believe me, Billie, for your first couple of weeks, you'll need every minute of sleep you can get. Ent that true, John Dan?'

The other boy nodded. 'Go on, Billie. Do you good. I'll be going to bed by nine o'clock, the way I do feel tonight.'

It was a matter of honour. Once he knew it was not childish to be exhausted, Billie was quite content to go to bed. Now he was relieved that he had a room to himself. As soon as he shut the door behind him, the tears came, not dramatically, but slow, steady and apparently

never-ending. They flowed while he undressed, got
into bed, turned out the lamp and composed himself
for sleep. Had exhaustion not intervened, he would
have cried all night. Billie Walters knew that if the
future held any happiness for him, it had nothing to
do with coal mines.

CHAPTER FIFTEEN

BILLIE HATED EVERY breath he took underground, but he was obstinate and proud and had no intention of letting down his brother or making his father ashamed of him. So he persisted at his detestable job, sometimes weeping silently in the darkness of the headings where he would not be seen. If he had to work in a colliery, he thought, better this one, far from home and family. If his mother came anywhere near him, she would know immediately that something was deeply wrong. As it was, the Saturday afternoon train journey home gave him time to compose himself, and when he arrived at the Ranks, his joy was such that it carried him through the week-end. Only when the train steamed out of Abercarn station each Sunday on the first leg of a zigzag progress through the valleys, did he begin to grieve again.

Mondays were worst, when home was still vivid in his memory and the whole barren week stretched ahead before he could be there again. Evan went back to Abercarn barely once in six weeks nowadays, and John Daniel only visited the rest of the family at fortnightly intervals, but Billie could never have survived without a weekly trip back to the Ranks. Even then, he felt he was becoming a stranger. Still a child himself when he went away, he watched in perplexity as the four youngest, Rose, Lily, Elwyn and Bethan, grew from babies to young children, scarcely seeming to be his brothers and sisters at all.

One Monday in April, he was walking back to Brithdir alone after his shift. John Daniel had stayed down to do two hours overtime with his butty to complete some new timbering. Billie turned into the mean street of coal company houses, shabby and worn-out looking although they had been built only eighteen months earlier.

He had been gazing down at the unpaved road directly ahead, unwilling to look up at these repulsive surroundings, but now something made him raise his eyes. Who was that at their front door? Not Mrs Parry, certainly. . .she could have given this one ten years in age and three stone in weight. The woman was tall, with long legs and a slim waist, but broad in hips and shoulders. She had a great mane of foxy-red hair which crowded around her fine-boned face in loose, undisciplined waves. To Billie, starved for beauty, she looked like a goddess. It was Ellen Rourke.

Her loveliness so stunned him that when he arrived at the front door he was at a loss for words, and stood dumbly in front of her with a half-witted smile on his face. The woman seemed accustomed to such reactions, for she merely smiled back and said, 'Does Evan Walters live here?'

'A-aye, he do,' Billie managed to stammer out. 'He won't be home for half an hour or so yet, though.' Then, remembering his manners, he added, 'If you'm a friend of his, p'raps you'd like to come in and have a cup of tea while you wait for him.'

Her eyes kindled with a merriment he did not understand, and she nodded. 'That's very civil of you, I will. And you'd be one of his boys, I expect?'

'That's right. I'm Billie. Our John Daniel won't be home till later.'

They went inside and Billie set the kettle to boil. The small task made him suddenly aware of his unwashed state and he blushed scarlet beneath the coaldust. 'Oh, *Duw,* you must think I'm awful, making tea in this state! But I do usually bath when I get in before I have a drink.'

'Oh, dear, and I've interrupted! I'm so sorry. Tell you what – I'll make the tea, then it won't matter. You just tell me where the things are.'

He watched her, bewitched, as she skimmed around the kitchen assembling cups, saucers, sugar and milk. In a few minutes they were sitting down drinking the hot, sweet brew, and it was as if Ellen Rourke had always been there.

When they had finished it, she entrenched herself still further. 'You won't want to be waiting around in your dirty working clothes, will you? If you'd like to get on with your bath, I can wait in the parlour. How would that be?'

He smiled gratefully. 'Would you? I do hate these clothes. Won't be long, I promise.'

He finished his bath in record time, stowed away his soiled working clothes and emptied the tub outside. Then he refilled the boiler for Evan's arrival, due any time now. The beautiful woman came back into the room and they talked again, though Billie could never remember the details of the conversation afterwards. He was content merely to look at her and take in the melodious rise and fall of her slightly accented voice, without bothering to analyse what she said.

His reverie ended abruptly when his father came in. Billie was sitting with his back to the door, and some children were shouting outside, drowning the sound of the latch being raised. Nevertheless he was aware someone had come in because of the effect on Ellen. She stiffened, and her latest words died on her lips, as she half rose from the high-backed armchair.

Time hung suspended before she finally spoke again. 'Evan, you've come home,' she said. There was another, lengthening pause. His father was as still as some big animal considering the hunter who confronts him.

Then he relaxed into surrender, and laughed. 'Well, well! P'raps I have an' all!' And Ellen was in his arms, laughing and crying at once, not attempting an explanation of her sudden arrival, oblivious of Billie's gaping presence.

Billie asked himself countless times in later years why he had felt no sense that his mother was betrayed. At the time, though, such a thought never crossed his mind. All he knew was joy that his father seemed immediately to find all he wanted in this lovely creature who had enslaved Billie himself at first sight. Evan apparently grasped that intuitively, for after the first long, passionate kiss, he looked over Ellen's shoulder at Billie and said, 'Like father, like son, by the look of it!' Then he kissed Ellen again, and laughed, and brought her back to the fireside and Billie.

It was more than a year since Evan had seen Ellen Rourke. She was still trailing around the coalfield with the Haggars, still singing, dancing and acting her head off to impress a handful of drunken miners and their wives outside a battered tent in some desolate showground or market square. Evan secretly admired her staying power, although it exasperated him more and more as time passed. Early in the spring of 1902, he had moved into the Brithdir house and asked her to join him. When she refused, he was so bitterly disappointed that he told her she was a middle-aged slut who had no idea when she should be grateful for a good man. Ellen lost her temper, flung his quart of bitter all over him and said she would share her bed with a pig rather than him. Since then they had been strangers.

But times were changing. Ellen was thirty-seven years old. She looked ten years younger, but both she and Evan knew the truth of it. Before long, there would be no room for her in any acting troupe where her value lay in her youthful appeal. Unless she settled down for good within the next few years, she would face old age homeless and destitute.

When Evan had calmed down after their last quarrel, he thought about that. He loved her, however deeply she exasperated him, and the following morning he left a note for her with Walter Haggar, who had taken over the travelling theatre from his father. Evan was no writer, but it said enough, 'When you want to find me, I'll be waiting.' Now, finally, it seemed she was here with her answer.

After the first rapturous shock of finding her, Evan had reservations about how his sons would react. He need not have worried. Almost subconsciously, they succumbed to the same magnetic appeal she had exercised on him. John Daniel started off more cautiously than Billie, but soon he, too, was singing her praises.

Evan found Mrs Parry another house to look after. He had just engaged three brothers on the sinking team and they had no one to keep house for them. Then Ellen was installed at Marine Terrace as though she were his wife. It was a rough area – new, brawling, used to seeing sights and living with situations that would have raised eyebrows in more settled communities. Half the neighbours knew Evan was already married with many children, but did not care. The rest neither knew nor cared. The boys compounded a conspiracy of silence. They loved their mother, but they loved their father just as much and were hypnotized by Ellen. Both of them were old enough to see that if they kept silence, no one would be hurt. If they talked, they would destroy their own family.

There was another year's work before the Brithdir

shaft was complete, and after that Evan had a contract up the valley at Penallta Colliery which promised
to keep him employed until the end of the decade.
Within months, it felt as though Ellen were his wife
and sometimes he even caught himself imagining that
John Daniel and Billie were their sons, not his and
Margaret Ann's. She certainly understood the boys,
and they loved her for it, Billie in particular.

Billie did not stop loathing his job underground.
Evan knew how he felt, but shrugged it off. Ellen took
it more seriously. She knew better than to embarrass
Billie by direct confrontation. Instead she talked to
John Daniel.

'I know he can't leave the pit, but surely there's something else he could do down there that wouldn't break
his heart?' she said.

John Daniel pondered for a while, then shook his
head. 'Can't say as there is. Our Billie do like outdoor
things – grass, and water, and animals. Nothing like
that for him down Bargoed, or any other mine I know
of.'

Then Ellen thought of something. 'But there is – you
use horses, don't you?'

John Daniel stared at her dumbly, then said, 'Yes,
'course we do, but our Billie's a collier.'

'Only because that's where your father started him
off. What if he changed? Do they pay hauliers any less
than hewers?'

Light began to dawn on Billie. 'I think it's about the
same. . . *Duw*, Ellen, why didn't I think of that? Give
our Billie a dumb animal worse off than himself and
he'll be as happy as a lark!'

'Now don't you go mentioning it to him yet. I'll need
to bring your father round. You know how stubborn he
can be – always likes to think his ideas are best. He may
take a bit of persuading.'

But Evan was still sufficiently besotted with his

mistress to fall in with her suggestion. He even knew one of the hauliers who might be willing to give Billie a try. 'Better still,' he said, 'p'raps there'll be a job up top with the blacksmith. I'll have a look.'

He couldn't quite manage that. Well-paid surface jobs were scarcer than gold and anyone who served an apprenticeship as blacksmith had a good future ahead, earning as much as a collier but without the hazards of the pit bottom. In the end, though, Evan succeeded in getting Billie a job in the stables.

John Daniel knew his brother well. Billie forgot his own miseries instantly when he had the horses to look after. Within a fortnight, he was transformed. He was eager to start work, and even talked about his day when he got home.

After one such evening, Evan rolled into bed beside Ellen, reached over and enveloped her in a bear-hug. 'Oh, you lovely, lovely girl,' he said, 'why wouldn't you come to me when you could have had all of me?'

Tears glinted in her eyes in the soft lamplight. 'I often ask meself that, Evan boy.' Then she shrugged. 'If I had, though, I don't think you'd ever have had that great regiment of children you've fathered.'

'I'd give them all up for a lifetime of you,' he said. 'I've never met a woman more like me, underneath.' He kissed her, long and passionately, and ran his rough hands over her body. 'So smooth. . .so soft. . .just like over Ynysddu – what? – twenty years ago, was it, that first time up the mountain with your dad bawling for you down by the Mynyddislwyn road?'

'D'you still remember that, then? I thought you'd have forgotten ages ago.'

'You was the first, Ellen, and the last, in a way.'

She could not stop herself. 'Well, what about Margaret Ann? You dropped me, once, for her.'

'Aye, I know. I could say it was wounded pride – it was, a lot of it. But there was something about her,

L.O.T.V.—9

too. Not enough to have took me from you if you'd
wanted me more than anything else. . .but something.
You got to understand. Even now, it ent just the kids
that takes me back to her. Sometimes I do get this
funny feeling, as if. . .as if you and she was different
parts of the same woman, and I'll only have the whole
one if I've got you both. Do that sound daft?'

She turned her face away with an angry little laugh.
'It sounds as if you've got us both just where you want
us, Evan Walters! Daft, no. We're the daft ones – me
and Margaret Ann. And John Daniel, and Billie, and
all the others, maybe.'

'I don't understand.'

Then she wanted to hurt him very badly. She turned
back to him with a smile. 'Well, we all worship you
because you're the big, strong man, tougher than everybody else – the one to live up to, the one who'll protect
us all against the world. But maybe you're none of those
things. Maybe you need all of us more than we need
you. . . For your sake, Evan, I hope Margaret Ann and
your children never realize it.'

She turned away again and put out the lamp, then
slipped out of his arms and moved to the far side of
the bed. Evan lay awake for hours, staring up into a
darkness that seemed as black as the pit bottom, and
feeling empty.

He got away with his double life for four years. After
a few scenes, Ellen settled contentedly into being not
quite his wife, and accepted his regular departures
for Abercarn. John Daniel and Billie continued to
keep their secret, and to participate in it. The Valleys
communities were well nigh self-sufficient, the miners
invariably living within walking distance of their pits
and seldom venturing to neighbouring valleys. Only
travelling work gangs like Evan's moved about much

within the manual labour force, and they were usually unmarried men with no family network with whom to gossip. Once the Brithdir shaft was finished and Evan started on the two new Penallta shafts, they moved to Hengoed to be closer to his work. The boys moved with them, and with their new neighbours they passed for a normal family. In Abercarn, Margaret Ann grew daily more complacent in her grass widowhood. In 1905 she even had another son, Edmund. She remained blissfully unaware of Evan's deceit until New Year's Day 1909.

Evan had spent Christmas back at Abercarn, taking John Daniel and Billie with him. In a fit of defiance, Ellen had told him she was taking up a Christmas engagement at Cardiff with the Haggars. She really did go to them, but to stay as a guest, not to work. She felt past that now, and anyway, William Haggar was off the road, working on his new passion, moving pictures. She was grateful enough to spend a wildly disorganized holiday with the family she had come to love like her own, listening to Haggar weave a spell of words about his new toy just as he had twenty years ago about the theatre. On Boxing Day she kissed them all goodbye and returned to Hengoed to greet Evan when he came back from Abercarn.

He had promised her a good New Year celebration to make up for Christmas, and at five minutes to twelve on New Year's Eve, they were embracing tipsily in the Six Bells Inn. The Penallta shafts were due for completion any time after mid-January, and everyone in the pub was in buoyant spirits at the prospect of hundreds of new jobs in the village. As the bells outside began to herald 1909, the landlord came over and dragged Evan to his feet.

'I think it's time we all drank a toast to the man who sunk the shafts,' he boomed. 'Come on, lads, fill his glass and toast – Evan Walters!'

A host of drunken well-wishers heaved Evan up on to the mahogany bar counter, where he stood, swaying happily, brandishing his beer glass at them all. Around his feet they set up dozens of glasses of everything from porter to whisky. 'Speech, speech!' they chanted. 'The sinker have got to make a speech!'

Abashed at this sudden wave of popular recognition, Evan cast around for a diversion and his eye fell on Ellen. 'Only got one thing to say,' he bawled out. 'I owe it all to my lovely Ellen – couldn't have run the course without her!' And in the next moment Ellen, too, had been hoisted on to the bar and was standing beside him, her arm round his waist.

He bent and placed a light kiss on her forehead and as he did, heard a familiar voice, long unheard, which extinguished all his good cheer. 'Happy New Year, Evan. I hope you do enjoy 1909 just as much!'

Evan looked over Ellen's head towards the door, knowing who he would see. There, doffing his hat in mocking farewell, was Billy Stout. As Evan leaped down to pursue him, Stout blew a kiss at Ellen and was gone.

By the time Evan had pushed through the crowd and emerged into the street, there was no sign of his old enemy. He had no idea where Stout would be now, but he knew where he would be in the morning. And he knew that his time with two women was at an end.

For Margaret Ann, it seemed an end to everything. She was returning from the corner shop mid-morning on 1 January, when Billy Stout bustled up alongside her and wrested the basket from her grasp. At first, astonishment made her passive, then she made an angry lunge at the basket and started berating him.

'And just what d'you think you're doing? I don't talk to men of your kind, let alone give them my shopping to carry home.'

'Aw, go on, Mrs Walters – let bygones be bygones. New Year, ennit? Time for good resolutions and Christian charity. As a chapel lady you can't deny that.'

She was still uneasy and distrustful, but curious about what he had in mind. 'What if I do let bygones be bygones?' she said eventually. 'How could you have anything to say that would interest me?'

'I can put your mind at rest straight away on that one – it's the most interesting news you'll hear this year, or ever again. And I'm the only one who'll ever tell you, so why don't you ask me back home for a cup of tea?'

Margaret Ann knew she should have refused out of hand, but now she was burning to know what he had to say. Her good sense warned her it would hurt her. This man had been her enemy ever since she had inadvertently unleashed Evan on him while still a young girl. Nevertheless, she had to know. After all, if it was bad, better she should know now than hear about it when he'd spread it through the whole of Abercarn.

'All right, you can have your cup of tea,' she said. 'But mind you do make it quick. Our Rose and Lily will be home from school by twelve, and I don't want you still here then.'

'Don't worry, girl. I'll be gone in twenty minutes. Just something I think you should know, see.' He was oozing bogus charm and she shuddered, realizing it must be something that would hurt her very much.

He told her as she was pouring the boiling water on the tea leaves in her second-best china pot. Later she wished she had flung the scalding stuff all over him.

After the first, unbelievable, terrible words – Evan and Ellen – she thought she must be deaf to the rest. But she was not. She was to learn that sons can tear apart a woman as effectively as husbands.

'. . .And of course, the shame of it is that them boys of yours have known about it all for four or five years, now, known, and lived with her and him, covering up, telling you lies, here on Sundays and then going back Mondays to share a house and a supper table with that fallen woman.' The cliché rolled off Stout's tongue with theatrical relish. His watery eyes gleamed as they fed on Margaret Ann's obvious pain. My God, this was worth coming all the way back to Abercarn for – put the stuck-up bitch in her place and no mistake! He licked his lips, relishing the prospect of her further anguish, and added, 'Them little houses over Hengoed are like chicken coops, an'all. I 'xpect your Billie and John Daniel could hear everything that went on between them two in bed all night – and by the look of them when I saw them, there's still plenty going on! Fancy, your own flesh and blood a party to that filth. . .'

That brought Margaret Ann back to her senses. She turned on him furiously, grabbing his shabby jacket in her hands and shaking him as she hustled him towards the door. 'Enough! Filth, you do say – well, you'm in a better position to judge it than most. You don't know nothing about my husband and sons, nothing! Now get out of here and don't you never come back, or I'll see Evan do kill you!'

Stout was not a big man, but Margaret Ann was tiny, and it was only his initial dismay at the fury of her onslaught that swept him to the back door so easily. When they got there, he decided there was still some malicious satisfaction to be wrung from the situation, stopped moving along with her and resumed his odious tale.

Outside the back door a wide square of paving stones led to the short flight of steps that connected the house with the back lane. There was no guard rail around it and Margaret Ann worried constantly that one of the children might stumble over the five-foot drop from beside the door. Now she gave one last despairing tug at Stout's sleeve, as though mutely begging him to be silent, then chose more decisive action. Abruptly she

shifted her weight and thrust towards him with all
her strength, catching him off-balance. He shot out
through the door, stumbled on the threshold and fell
sideways on to the rough ground below.

It was not a long drop, but he landed awkwardly
and Margaret Ann distinctly heard a snap as his leg
broke. It was the only satisfaction she knew that day,
and for many more. She wasted no more words on the
man, who was shouting his agony and outrage for all
to hear. She dusted her palms as though finishing a
long-overdue task, turned back into the house, then
closed and locked the door. It was more than ten minutes before the tears started.

Evan returned from Hengoed like a condemned man.
His wife had sent him a letter through the post for the
first time in their married life. It said little, only that
they must talk as soon as possible. But Evan had been
awaiting something like it throughout the week since
the encounter with Billy Stout. Throughout the tedi-
ous train journey across the valleys, he tried to antici-
pate the scene which lay ahead. What he actually found
was unlike anything he had imagined.

His wife was calm and quiet, although she looked
ghastly, and a quick call at the Commercial informed
Evan that the whole village was aware of Margaret
Ann's treatment of Stout. No one had seen her since.
She had sent the children out shopping and stayed
indoors, refusing to talk to even her closest neighbours. Evan walked into the kitchen, as usual feeling
awkwardly conscious of his great bulk as he bent to
dodge the low ceiling.

Noticing the gesture, Margaret Ann merely said,
'You'd better sit down. It'll take a while to sort this out.'
Nothing else, no recriminations, no tirade of abuse, but
something which promised a lot worse.

He sat in his Windsor chair opposite hers at the fire-side. Quite the old married couple, said a mocking voice inside his head. He banished the thought. 'What d'you want me to say?' he asked, even at this desperate hour unable to humble himself before her.

'Nothing. There *is* nothing to say. I know what have been happening. I've done something about it. Read this. If you agree to what it do say, we may be man and wife still. If you don't, it's all up for us both.'

Oh, God, he thought, not a love letter! How he despised this weakness women had for sitting down and writing sloppy thoughts on bits of paper. With Ellen it was scraps of poems she'd learned for the stage. Margaret Ann's amateur version would doubtless be as bad.

But this was no love letter. It was in a sealed envelope, addressed to Evan in a firm scholarly hand quite unlike his wife's. Puzzled, he opened it. It was from Gilchrist, manager of Risca Colliery in Evan's contracting days. It said:

Dear Evan

Your wife has explained how anxious you are to return to work closer to Abercarn, so that you might see more of your family. I have explained that without staff papers, I cannot offer you a job as deputy or overman, although I value your skills. I can, however, offer you a job on the coal face, and would be delighted to have you as part of my work force. The money is hardly in the league to which you will have become accustomed as head of a gang of sinkers, but that trade is as limited today as heading contracting was five years ago. I feel you could do much worse than accept the chance to return to work here at Celynen South.

Your friend
Tom Gilchrist

Evan read the note two or three times to get the full
sense of it, his face darkening as he did so. Then he
glared at Margaret Ann. 'What's this nonsense about
me wanting to come back and work in Abercarn? And
how the hell did Gilchrist get to know about it?'

Uncowed, she gazed steadily at him. 'Because I went
and told him. You knew he was managing the South
now – took over last year when Pegler retired, I told
you. Well, I went up to his house and waited until
he come home, then I explained about the trouble it
was causing, you working over the Rhymney Valley,
and how much you missed the children.' At this point
her look defied him to dispute the assertion. 'He was
very complimentary about you, and in the end he said
he'd manage something, even if it was just coal hewer.
They'm not taking anybody on up the South at present
and getting that was quite something, I can tell you.'
She injected a little triumph into her voice.

'Well, don't congratulate yourself too soon. I'm getting four times this much over Hengoed, and I went
up the Rhymney Valley in the first place so I wouldn't
have to go back on the coal face.'

'You may be getting four times what a collier brings
home, Evan. I've never seen a penny more than any
other collier's wife in this village, because it do all go
to another woman, don't it? It wouldn't make no difference to the way we live here if you was just earning
that much in the first place – and the children would
grow up knowing they had a father.'

'That haven't worried you before. You was almost
glad for me to go.'

'Don't think that haven't crossed my mind. There's
fault both sides. I was so bound up with the girls I just
let you go. If I'd made a fuss, you'd have stayed by me.
Instead of that, I saved all my best love for Lily, and
you went off. And I've never made a fuss all the years,

either, have I, never said or done nothing that would make you think I missed you? In a way, I s'pose I'm lucky you was coming back at all in the end, even every six weeks and Christmas time.'

Evan was bewildered. Margaret Ann had never taken the blame for anything before. This time he had expected tears, recriminations and demands for reform. Instead she was trying to make amends for some fault he had never really noticed in her. Certainly it paled to insignificance compared with his transgressions against her trust. He was sufficiently surprised not to notice that her terms still entailed giving up much of what he valued. That came later. Now he was moved by her willingness to understand both his needs and her failure to satisfy them. He sighed, already half-way to accepting the inevitable.

'What happens if I do come home?' he said.

'We'll be like we were before you went off on this sinking business, that's all. I told you, I never had big money, so I'll manage with ordinary collier's wages.'

That provoked a grim laugh from Evan. 'You tell me that after you've tried it for a bit, girl. It's easier said than done. I've never seen a collier's wife yet who do find it easy.'

She made a dismissive gesture. 'It will be worth it if we'm back as we was, without. . .without. . .' Then tears choked her and for the first time he saw the depths of her humiliation and misery.

'Ellen?' He finished for her, his tone gentle.

She nodded, not meeting his eyes, and whispered, 'Yes.'

Evan found small, helpless things tragic beyond bearing. It was one reason for his brutal toughness, which was the only defence he had found against suffering others' pain in his own imagination. Now he saw Margaret Ann's total vulnerability and it was too much for him. At that moment he would have done anything for her. And at that moment she looked up, met his eyes and said, 'If we are ever to start again, Evan, you must give her up for good – never see her again.'

He shrugged, trying to play down the turmoil he was experiencing, and said gruffly, 'So be it.'

She waited for more, but he remained silent, and Margaret Ann lacked the experience to understand that it was pain which moved him, not indifference to Ellen Rourke. At that point she began to recover, once again drawing strength from her own illusions about Evan's feelings. She smoothed down the long skirt of her woollen dress with small neat gestures, then ran her hands over her hair to ensure that it was in place. *Iesu mawr*, thought Evan, watching, *you'd think she was getting ready for a party, not seeing off her rival! She's stronger than you any day, boyo, and you remember it. . .*

But it was too late for such thoughts to do him any good. He knew that Margaret Ann's vulnerability was as real as her little signs of triumph and returning self-confidence. If he tried to evade defeat now, she would collapse again and he would be attacked once more by guilt.

'What do we do now?' he asked her.

'Do? I don't understand. I thought you was coming home and we'd start afresh.'

He sighed, trying to contain his exasperation. 'Margaret Ann, I know you don't like to think about it, but I'll have to wind things up over Hengoed. I can't walk out of a job and a house just like that, with no word to anybody. I must go back and sort it out.'

Panic flared in her eyes. 'No – I won't have you going back there. You don't know what might happen. . .'

Evan stood up. 'You've got me back, for all the good it will do you. But that don't mean I'm leaving the girl flat. Anyhow, there's our boys to think about, an' all. What d'you expect me to do about them? They'm working up Penallta Colliery, remember.'

For a moment her face was filled with hate. 'They can work on the moon, for all I care. One thing I do know, though – they'll never live under this roof again!'

He gasped at the intensity of her tone. 'You can't do that. They'm our flesh and blood. Why, our Billie'd pine away altogether if he couldn't come over here to his mam every other week. What're you talking about?'

'They should have thought of their mam when they betrayed her. It was different with you and her – even the Bible do recognize that sort of weakness. But they deceived their own mother, for the sake of some cheap fancy woman. Well, if they do love her so much, they can stay with her, or find lodgings somewhere. I'm not having them back here.'

That almost broke Evan's resolve to stay with Margaret Ann. But beneath his rekindled anger stirred another thought. Perhaps, if the boys could manage, it would be better like that. At least Ellen would have a chance of some support. She could keep house for them and in turn they could keep her. With him gone, she could even take in more lodgers and make a modest living from it. At her age, with no husband, there'd be little else for her. And as a collier, he'd certainly not have enough spare cash to help her. He turned his attention back to his wife.

'Tell you what,' he said. 'I'll go back over there tonight, talk it over with them and arrange it all. Then I'll stay until Monday morning, put in my notice at Penallta and see if Ted Parry can take over the gang for me. He've been my deputy for long enough to handle the whole thing if he do want to. To be honest, once I've settled it, I'd rather stay there till the end of next week. At least then I'd get another week's money. . .'

'No! I won't have that. I don't want you staying over there tonight with her, either. You'll – '

'I'll nothing, Margaret Ann. You don't own me, and you never will.'

It was his tone, more than what he said that stopped her. She had heard it before, but never directed against herself. She shivered involuntarily. The first time she had heard it, he was speaking to the Judas who started this business, Billy Stout, and she was an innocent seventeen-year-old seeing him as her knight in silver armour. Now she wondered if her triumph today had gone to her head too quickly and carried her over the abyss. She waited submissively for him to go on.

'I've told you that from now on I'll come back here and be a proper husband and father again. But I will not desert anybody without a word, on God Almighty's say-so, leave alone yours. I'm going back over Hengoed for the week, I'll tie things up, see the boys all right, then I'll be back for good. But don't try to make me go further than that or you'll be sorry.'

Inwardly she cursed herself for her corrosive jealousy. She knew she would have won him over totally if she had not behaved so badly about their sons, but she never wanted to see either of them again and felt strongly enough about it to endanger their own reconciliation. Now she conceded the point, though only with another of her silent nods.

Neither of them said anything for a long time. Then Evan rose, uttering a heavy sigh. 'Well then,' he said. 'After all that, I'm going down the Commercial for a couple of pints, then I'll get the train back. Sooner I do go, the sooner it's over and done with, Margaret Ann. A week from today, I'm yours for good.'

He did not kiss or embrace her and she, feeling the aura of coldness about him, did not rise to go with him to the door. As his footsteps faded down the street outside, she got up and went to the back door, and looked out wistfully at the children playing there. 'Lily!' she cried. 'Lily – come here, my lovely. Your mam do want to talk to you.'

The smallest girl detached herself reluctantly from

the boisterous game and came to the bottom of the back steps. 'What is it, Mam? I'm still playing.'

'Come on in here a minute, kidda.' The moment they were over the threshold, Margaret Ann slammed the door and dropped to her knees beside the puzzled child, burying her in a fervent embrace and resting her head on the small shoulder. 'Oh, Lily, my Lily – say you'll never leave your mam! Promise, now, if you love me!'

'Of course I promise. Mam. Don't cry, please. I'll always be with you, and even when you'm old, I'll still be ever so young.'

Margaret Ann smiled tearfully. 'So you will, my darling. Go on, then, back out to play. I didn't mean to spoil your game.'

CHAPTER SIXTEEN

July 1911

T HE THREE O'CLOCK hooter at the South Celynen pit-head marked the end of the Friday day shift. As its last echoes ceased, Siân Ellis began pulling pints behind the long main bar in the Commercial. Dai was still in the cellars, checking the barrels, but already fifteen staff were thronging the pub, ready to dispense a floodtide of bitter to the thirsty men who were about to descend on them. Soon the first arrivals were heralded by the ring of hobnails on cobblestones, and the mahogany swing doors flapped open to admit Evan Walters.

Siân sighed as she looked at him. Such a shame to see a fine man hell-bent for ruin! He still walked upright and proud, but there was a slackness around the formerly rock-hard jawline now, and the quicksilver eyes had lost their magnetism. Too often, they seemed fixed on some imaginary horizon where the cares of the world could not reach him... Siân shook herself crossly. *Silly old bitch as you are! You know damn' well he's just turning into a middle-aged drunk, but you've always been in love with him on the quiet and now you don't want to admit he's going down the same road as half the other miners in this valley. If the dust don't get him, the beer will before too long, so spare yourself the pain and stop dreaming about him now...* She slammed the door on her fantasies and gave him an everyday smile and a commonplace greeting. It did not make her feel better about Evan's visible deterioration.

Others said it was losing Ellen Rourke that had done for Evan Walters. Siân knew better. That Margaret Ann knew how to skin and bone a man and serve him up prime roast! Sending the other woman packing had been the least of it. Turning him into a wage slave and putting him back down the pit with another man as his master was what had really finished him. Nothing would convince Siân that Margaret Ann had not known that from the start.

She stared at him, trying to decide which way his mood would swing today. It was more than two years since he had given up his life as a sinker in the Rhymney Valley, and ever since he had returned to the coal face he had got drunk every pay day. Sometimes it was jolly, singing drunk. At others, mercifully less frequently, it was cold, vengeful and murderous. After a few moments, Siân decided today was reasonably merry. She wondered at her own relief. Evan's homicidal tempers were always directed at men, not women; with one exception – his wife.

'You never can tell, though,' she murmured to herself. 'One day he might mistake me or one of the girls for Margaret Ann, and then God knows what would happen!'

Evan had worked a reasonably good day. That meant he had not seen the overman, four years his junior and a lifetime behind him in mining expertise, who persecuted him mercilessly at every opportunity. Today the younger man had not run across him, so Evan felt at peace with the world. He swallowed his first quart of bitter in seconds, but Siân noticed that he only re-ordered a pint. Must be a special day. He'd never gone home on a Friday after so little. Margaret Ann would think she had the wrong day of the week when she saw him!

Evan was mellowing towards Margaret Ann. Since his
sacrifice and return to the Ranks, she had kept her side
of their bargain. Another son, Lewis, was born late in
1909. She had been a loving, hard-working wife, defer-
ring to him in everything but reconciliation with their
two eldest sons. She would never forgive John Daniel
and Billie for what she saw as their treachery, and could
barely tolerate Evan's monthly outings with them. He
had kept his word, too, and never went back to the
terrace in Hengoed where Ellen Rourke still kept house
for them, but Margaret Ann was powerless to prevent
him meeting his sons in Crosskeys or Pontllanfraith.

Her harsh attitude would probably have led to more
quarrels had it not been for their daughters. Evan
had discovered he had a weakness for them which
had never affected him with the boys. Rose, Lily and
now Bethan – lovely creatures, exquisitely pretty, soft
and loving; Margaret Ann without the bigotry and
snobbery. He adored all three of them, but Rose was
unique in his affections, possibly because she looked so
like Margaret Ann before life had made her shrewish,
and because Evan stood somewhere above God in her
picture of the world. Rose was the one who had saved
Margaret Ann from permanent injury from Evan's
fists.

When his terrible drunken rages started, he had
come home one Friday night and beaten Margaret
Ann until she was unconscious. Next day she had
trouble in walking and her cheek and eye socket
were badly bruised. For a week she had pretended
illness and stayed indoors, lest the neighbours should
see her humiliation. Rose, then twelve years old, had
run the house while she recovered. The next time
Evan came home with violence in his face, his eldest
daughter was waiting for him. It was inconceivable that
he would harm her, and she seemed to sense this. She
led him to the fireside, plied him with cup after cup of

strong sweet tea, and gradually calmed him. When he
was half asleep, she persuaded him into the parlour, to
sleep on the mattress she normally shared with Lily and
Bethan. They, she informed him sweetly, were keeping
Mam company upstairs tonight. Then she turned down
the bed for him, kissed him goodnight, and left him to
sober up safely remote from his wife.

Now it was a routine – one that reassured Evan as
much as his womenfolk. Sober, he had no wish to hurt
Margaret Ann. Drunk, and in the wrong mood, he was
powerless to stop himself. He did not understand how
Rose managed to control him – he was merely grateful that she could, and relied on her to be his moral
policeman.

Today he would need none of that, though. He felt
too good. Home, now, for a bath and a good dinner,
then he'd go back down the Commercial and enjoy
his drink instead of guzzling it. Might even be in bed
by midnight, at this rate... As he left the Commercial and headed for home, he chuckled ruefully at the
difference the overman's absence made to him.

Margaret Ann knew better than to express surprise
when he arrived home early and sober. They always
ate stew on Fridays, because he was so unpredictable,
and it was ready for him as soon as he had washed off
the coal dust and changed his clothes. They were alone
together. Rose and Lily were at the communal wash-
house which served the Ranks, working through the
great piles of laundry which Margaret Ann now took
in to add to their limited income. Evan had been right
about the difficulties of surviving on a collier's wage.
Bethan, though barely ten, had already begun to help,
but so far she did less than the older girls and now she
was playing outside.

Evan finished his second helping of stew, and pushed
his plate aside before lighting his pipe. He glanced
across at his wife, sitting at her embroidery by the fire.

Duw, but she was an attractive woman, though! Not many round here could have borne twelve children and still look like that. Some of them looked a damn' sight worse before they'd even started. He rose and moved across to her, stilling her busy hands by burying them in his great paw.

Bending, he brushed his lips across his hair, now mellowed to a softer, velvety auburn, and whispered, 'No need to have the girls in with you tonight, eh, love? I can keep you warmer than them.'

She glanced up, blushing as intensely as she had as a young bride, smiled and nodded her approval. Margaret Ann found it hard to talk of physical love, although her compact little body expressed it well enough.

'Think I'll go up an' have a bit of a lie down now,' Evan added. 'Don't want to be worn out, do I? Then I'll go back down the Commercial for an hour or two, and after that. . .' His grin emphasized his intentions for later on.

As he started up the stairs, Rose came in, face flushed with the steamy heat of the wash-house, her pretty red hair curling in moist tendrils against her cheeks. Her face lit up at the sight of her father. Suddenly gripped by boyish exuberance, Evan swept her up in his arms and swung her up to shoulder height. 'And how's my beautiful daughter today, then? Still showing the neighbours that Walterses have the best-looking women in the Western Valley?'

He dropped a smacking kiss on her cheek, planted her firmly back on the ground, and went upstairs for his rest. Rose gazed after him adoringly.

He was back in the Commercial, half-way through his first drink of the evening, when Billie found him. Siân Ellis saw the boy first, and let out an instinctive gasp of dismay, knowing that only trouble could have brought him back within his mother's home territory.

Seeing her expression, Evan swung round to confront the newcomer. 'Well I'm damned, if it ent our Billie!' His earlier happiness still swirled around him and it took his mind a moment to pick up the wrongness of the situation. A closer look at Billie was enough to tell him there was tragedy ahead.

His son's open, innocent-looking face was death-pale, eyes flicking from spot to spot, lips stiff as though fighting to control some terrible emotional reaction. 'Billie!' Evan's voice dropped to a whisper. 'Billie, boy, what is it? Something wrong with John Dan?'

'Who else do I live with?' Billie seemed to spit out the words, high and on the edge of hysteria. 'Remember the other one, our landlady – yours, an' all for long enough!'

Before he could go on, Siân Ellis was round the bar, herding both men ahead of her towards the back of the pub. 'Come on, boys,' she said, 'in the snug. Too many here as don't know how to mind their own business.'

In a moment she had them in the small dark bar which Evan had always disliked so much. At least it was private. Siân gestured through the counter hatch to one of the barmaids, and soon came across with an almost-full bottle of whisky and two large glasses. 'Compliments of the management,' she said. 'Give us a call if you do want any help.' Then she left them alone.

The moment he finished speaking, Billie had begun to cry. While Siân urged them out of the main bar, he had wept silently, tears coursing down his cheeks apparently unnoticed, his face blank. But as the door closed behind the landlady, he leaned forward, rested his head in his arms on the tabletop, and sobbed as though heartbroken. Evan watched him, his own face still as marble. After a while, he said, 'How did she die, Billie?'

That brought his son upright again. 'Ho-how did you know? It only just happened!'

Evan managed a bitter smile. 'Only one thing do have that effect on a man, But, and I've seen it often enough before. Tell me.'

'Cancer. Oh, Christ, Dad, it was terrible. . . I didn't know no one could suffer that much. It have been nearly a year now, and she made us swear we'd never tell you.'

Black rage was descending on Evan. 'What sort of promise would that be?' he raged. 'Nobody could expect you to keep to something like that. It – it's not human!'

Billie looked at him pityingly, calmer himself now that his father was losing control. 'We loved her, Dad, just like you, remember? She knew she could trust us. When she said promise, we did, and we kept to it. . .if we hadn't it would have been even worse for her.'

'But how – why? Surely it would have been better if I could have been there, helped her – helped you?'

The boy shook his head. 'No, Dad. At first, maybe, but not after. She said, when she was pretty sure what she had, that she couldn't bear you seeing her ugly, and she was going to get so ugly we wouldn't want to be anywhere near her. We understood that. You know how proud she always was about her looks, how we used to tease her about getting old and wrinkled. It'd have been even worse for her if you'd seen her near the end. We was hard pressed to make her let us in, the last few weeks.'

'Who looked after her, then?'

'Oh, an old midwife from up Penallta. Glad of the extra money. We had to get someone. There was lots of things she wouldn't let me or John Dan do for her, even quite early on.'

'What sort of things?'

'Please, Dad, don't make me go on. . . It was all

through her – she just rotted away. . . Bed had to be changed four or five times a day. . .the smell. . . And she knew how horrible it was right up to the end, nearly.' He began to cry again.

'What's happening about the funeral?'

Billie was collecting his wits once more. 'Don't even think about it, Dad. Me an' John Dan will say goodbye for you. It'll only make things worse for you and everybody else up home when Mam do hear – and you know she will in five minutes.'

Evan smashed his huge fist into the cupped palm of his other hand. 'Bugger Margaret Ann! Why did I ever listen? Why did I ever come back?'

'God knows, Dad. I don't. All I know is I've just lost a better mother than the one I've still got living.'

Now it was Evan's turn to weep. Great gulping sobs tore up from his lungs, and he sat with his massive head tilted upward as if preparing to curse God. After a while he started muttering between the cries. 'My fault, not Margaret Ann's. . .all me. . .she never knew what she was letting herself in for, marrying me. Ellen did, but it wasn't her fault either – Christ alone knows she've suffered enough to pay for any wrong she ever done!'

Helpless to ease his pain, Billie let him rant. He had seen colliers carry on like this after losing a butty in a roof fall. It seemed to relieve the pressure. He prayed that the calming effect on his father would start showing soon. When the storm of weeping showed no signs of abating, Billie resorted to Siân's whisky bottle. It was expensive stuff, of a better quality than either father or son had ever enjoyed, but now it might have been raw alcohol and tasted the same. Billie half-filled one of the tumblers and held it to Evan's lips. The big man choked on the first sip, but then took the glass from him and drained it. He poured himself another, and after that the bottle did not last long. Billie had one drink and then decided he preferred to face his pain now. He did not need to be told that his grief, though intense, was sweet in comparison to Evan's, because it was devoid of guilt. For the rest of his days, Evan would re-live Ellen's lonely sufferings during her last year, further tortured by knowing she had cared enough to spare him the sight of her as she died.

Some time during the evening, Siân came back into the snug and exchanged a few words with Billie, offering him a bed for the night at the pub. 'You can't leave Evan until he've finished here,' she said, 'and I know you can't go home to your mam.'

He accepted gratefully. 'It'll be rough on her when he do go home, but that ent my business no longer,' he told Siân.

'Oh, Billie, don't you think you should go up and see her now? No need to make it up – I know you'll never do that – but this could go really bad tonight.'

Billie shook his head. 'She've brought it on herself, Mrs Ellis. We haven't got nothing else to say to each other.'

Throughout the exchange, Evan had sat staring fixedly ahead of him, apparently unaware of their presence. Now he waved the empty whisky glass. 'Le's 'ave some more, then, Siân – not like you to be stingy, is it?' His voice was already almost incoherent.

Billie glanced up at her anxiously. 'Should you?' he asked.

Siân shook her head. 'Course not, but it's Evan who's my friend, not your mother. She'll have to look after herself. This stuff's medicine tonight and I seem to be the doctor.'

She went off to get more whisky. Evan finished that and started on beer afterwards. It was long after midnight when Billie and Dai Ellis took his limp form between them and started walking him home.

Once the night air hit him, he seemed to liven up,

but only physically. He was obliviously drunk – beyond memory of Ellen's death but fixed on an eternal enemy – Margaret Ann. By the time they had taken him within a few yards of his front door, he was muttering a stream of abuse against his wife. He broke off only long enough to mutter, 'Not the front – round the back. Don't want to warn her, do I?'

Alarmed, Dai Ellis flashed a questioning look at Billie, but the boy shook his head. ''S all right,' he said. 'When he's sober he've told me himself that our Rose can handle him when he's in this state and she won't let him near our Mam. Do as he says.'

Dai looked doubtfully at Evan, but complied. It didn't seem likely that little Rose Walters could keep this mad beast off anybody. Tonight was different from other nights.

At the back of the house, Dai sighed with relief. 'I've forgot how steep them steps is,' he said. 'He'll be knackered by the time he do get up there, even if he do make it. Come on, Billie boy. Time we wasn't here.' They propped Evan against the outside privy door and left him. Neither was prepared to confront Margaret Ann and supply explanations.

They were out of sight when Evan collected himself. He straightened convulsively from the slumped position in which they had left him, and took the steps as if they were nothing, wheeling at the top and throwing open the back door. Warm golden lamplight spilled out of the kitchen, and Evan blinked, mole-like, for a moment as he tried to focus on the figure who awaited him inside.

Eventually he murmured, 'Rose, my lovely little Rose of Sharon. . .' and moved unsteadily across to the table where she sat to caress her in unconscious echo of his early approach to Margaret Ann.

'Tea's brewed already, Dad,' said Rose in a somewhat

strained bright voice. She had never seen him this bad
before.

He shook his head as though trying to clear it. 'Don't
want no tea. Don't want nothing you can give me, kidda.
Just you go to bed, all right? Your mam's up there waiting for me.'

'No, Dad – Friday night, remember? Our Lily and
Bethan is up there with Mam and I'm on my way
up when you've had your tea. You'm in the parlour
tonight.'

'*Uffern dan*! Nobody do tell me where I'll sleep –
nobody, d'you hear? Now get them other two back
down here or there'll be real trouble. I've got things
to sort out with your mother.'

'Not tonight, Dada, please!' Her tone was still cheery
but she was white-faced and frightened. It was obvious
that her charm would not move him this time.

'Get 'em down here, I said – this minute, or I will.' He
turned towards the staircase. Rose, agile and sober, got
there before him and stood in his way.

'No, Dad, please – just sit down by there, have your
tea, go on. . .'

As she spoke he reached out to throw her aside.
Knowing that even drunk he was far stronger than
her, Rose skipped backwards up the stairs. 'I'm not
letting you up there, Dad – you'll have to go over me
if you'm going in. . . I mean it!'

She was at the top of the steep stairs now, and Evan,
four steps below her, was still at eye level with her.
His face contorted into an animal snarl. 'All right –
you asked for it!' and he reached up, grabbed her by
the waist, swung her away from him over the staircase,
then let go.

Rose crashed down the narrow boxed-in stairs to
the point where they turned sharply to the kitchen
entrance. He had thrown her with such force that she
rebounded off the wall, letting out one terrible shriek

as she did so. Then she must have lost consciousness, because total silence followed.

It lasted only seconds. Even was too drunk to be sobered by the incident, but it had slowed him down. As he stood, swaying, on the narrow landing, the main bedroom door slammed open and Margaret Ann was facing him. 'In the name of God, what have you done?' she cried.

The sound of her voice brought two of the boys out of the other bedroom. Normally they were under strict orders not to stir from the room when they heard him ranting, because Margaret Ann had always feared he might harm them more than he would her. Her intervention had freed them from their captivity, though, and now Elwyn and Gareth, the two eldest still at home, lunged out and instinctively grabbed at their father. But they need not have bothered. His violent attack on Rose had not been enough to stop Evan, but Margaret Ann's arrival had. At last he remembered why he was in this state; why there was no point in taking it out on Margaret Ann; and as he did so the black fury drained from him, not yet replaced by a grasp of what he had done to Rose.

That happened soon enough. The long moment when the boys, their mother and their father seemed frozen together at the stairhead was shattered by another dreadful cry from below. Then a series of almost animal screams was succeeded by desperate begging: 'Oh, dear God, help me, help me – it's hurting me so!'

The words were banal, but the timbre of Rose's cries left them in no doubt about the severity of her injury. Mother and sons left Evan where he stood and tumbled over one another down the stairs to get to the girl. As they moved, Lily and Bethan dashed out of the bedroom to join them. Evan, with a desolate groan, let his body slide down the flimsy wall until he sat on the

floor. Then he buried his face in his hands and began
to cry.

At the bottom of the stairs, Margaret Ann and Elwyn
bent to lift the girl, but as they tried to move her, she
began screaming even harder, and tightened into a little ball of agonized flesh.

'We'll have to move you, love – you can't stay like
that.' Margaret Ann was struggling to hold back the
tears.

With enormous effort, Rose managed to speak. Her
face already had the bluish-grey paleness of deep
shock, and her teeth were chattering. She muttered,
'I think it'll kill me if you do, Mam. I-it's down
by here. . .' – she managed to indicate her lower
abdomen '. . .it do feel as, if my back have caved
in through the front of me. . .' The words were cut
off as another spasm of pain swept through her.
Her whole body convulsed for a moment, then she
fainted.

'Quick, now,' said Margaret Ann. 'While she's out,
move her into the parlour and put her on the mattress.'

Elwyn was dubious. 'It's the first thing they do tell
us not to do underground, Mam. Leave them be till the
ambulance man have had a look. It's the most important rule.'

'Don't be daft! We'm not at the pit bottom – we'm
at the foot of our stairs and my daughter's not dying
here. There's no ambulance man and the doctor'll have
to move her when he examines her, won't he? We'll just
have to try and do it without straightening her out. Can
you try it, Elwyn? If we take her together, we'm bound
to pull her about.'

He nodded grimly. 'Just about manage, by the look
of it. Thank God she's so little. You go and get them

doors open to give us a clear run when I've lifted her, Mam, and see there ent no chairs or nothing in my way.'

Margaret Ann hurried to obey him, praying every second that Rose would not regain consciousness for a while. As she finished throwing back the covers on the parlour mattress, Elwyn arrived with Rose in his arms. Somehow he had managed to lift her from beneath, keeping her in the almost foetal position she had adopted to fend off the pain. Margaret Ann moved to his side and together they lowered the girl on to the makeshift bed, still keeping her curled up. Margaret Ann hurriedly pulled the covers over her, then called to her other children.

'Lily, find them hot water bottles, they'll be in the cootch. Fill two of them and bring them here as quick as you can. Bethan – you go and get Mrs Smith next door, and Elwyn can go for the doctor. At least Edith might help her while we'm waiting for him.'

One of the few advantages of Evan's job as a collier was family membership of the benefit club. Weekly contributions from his wages meant that the whole family were covered for medical treatment. Now it was all that saved Rose. Elwyn dressed hurriedly and headed for the doctor's house, a mile away. 'And if he won't turn out this time o' night, you tell him there'll be a girl's life on his conscience in the morning if he don't come now!' Margaret Ann called after him.

By the time Edith Smith came in, Rose was stirring uneasily, but had not regained consciousness. Even by lamplight, she looked terrible. Edith, veteran of a lifetime's difficult births and deathbed ministrations, felt the girl's forehead and looked at her inner eyelids. She shook her head.

'I've seen them like this time and time again when they have bad haemorrhages after childbirth,' she said. 'The fall must have done something like that to her. They always looks like this when they'm bleeding inside.'

'Isn't there any way for us to stop it?' Margaret Ann was frantic now.

'If there is, I've never found it out,' said Edith. 'We do make them lie completely still and hope it stops of its own accord. It often do, when it's after labour. But this must be some kind of rupture. Whatever started it is still there, doing the damage. Broken bone, I should think. Probably crushed her inside.'

'There must be something we can do before the doctor do come!'

'Well, we can get her clothes off her for a start – but we'll have to cut her out of them. I won't risk shifting her again.'

Margaret Ann found her big dressmaking shears and Edith cut roughly up the side seam of Rose's long skirt, through the waistband and up the bodice to the underarm seam. Then she made similar cuts from above and below on the other side of Rose's body, and stripped the ruined garments away like wrapping paper.

'And to think that outfit was new last month,' said Margaret Ann.

Edith, who was still bending over Rose, straightened slowly and gazed incredulously at her neighbour. 'If I was you, Margaret Ann, I'd get ready to thank your bloody Jehovah if this girl is ever well enough to wear anything again, not waste time grieving over a bit of sprigged cotton.'

Margaret Ann bit her lip, ashamed of her words, and held out her arms for the scraps of clothing. Edith turned back to cover Rose with the bedclothes, then let out a gasp of horror. 'My God, she is bleeding – if that do go on, she won't last till the doctor do come!'

Rose still had on her long white drawers and shift. At fifteen, she was not yet wearing stays. Now the dress was gone, they could see a huge bloodstain spreading across

the white cotton underwear. She was losing so much
blood that it had already seeped through the drawers
and started soaking into the linen sheet.

'It's beyond any doctor!' wailed Margaret Ann, and
fell to her knees beside the mattress. There, oblivious of Edith's disbelieving glare, she shut her eyes and
began reciting in a monotone, 'The Lord is my shep-
herd; I shall not want. He maketh me to lie down in
green pastures: he leadeth me beside the still waters.
He restoreth my soul: he leadeth me in the paths of
righteousness for his name's sake. Yea, though I walk
through the valley of the shadow of death, I will fear
no evil, for thou art with me; thy rod and thy staff
they comfort me. Thou preparest a table before me in
the presence of mine enemies: thou anointest my head
with oil. . .'

'I never saw prayer cure a dying patient yet, madam,
and I have no intention of waiting to see if it works this
time.'

The interruption shocked Margaret Ann to the core.
Even the cynical Edith Smith had refrained from
openly sneering at her supplication. This stranger
apparently had no such qualms. Nor did he seem
ready to listen to her views on the power of prayer.

'I can't examine the girl all the way down there,' he
said. 'She's obviously in a very bad way. I need her up
at a sensible height and I need every scrap of light in
the house.' He turned to Haydn and Tom, who had
arrived close behind him. 'You seem like a strong pair
of lads. Come on, it'll not take long.'

It began to dawn on Margaret Ann that this was the
doctor. She rose now, dazed at confronting a stranger
in such circumstances. 'B-but who are you? Where's
Dr Cann?'

The dark-haired young man turned back to her.
'Your son gave Dr Cann a very accurate description of
his sister's symptoms and Dr Cann decided she might

need surgery on the spot if she's to have a chance of survival. My name is Henderson. I'm the locum, staying until Dr Cann's new junior partner arrives, madam, and I've been working as a general surgeon in London for the past three years. Now, by your leave – we've more pressing matters to attend than my qualifications for being here.'

Briefly, he went outside with Tom and Haydn. Moments later they were back, with the door of the under-stairs cupboard, unscrewed from its hinges and covered with an old blanket to form a rough stretcher. 'Now,' said Henderson, 'we'll put the patient on this, then we can move her around at will without giving her unnecessary pain. I've had your daughter clear the kitchen table and we'll put her there for the moment.'

Although Rose was barely half-conscious, even the minimal movement required to slide her curled-up form on the door-stretcher made her groan and cry out. Henderson ignored the reaction, saying only, 'I'll have to straighten her out in a moment to see how bad the damage is.'

He directed the boys to raise Rose's stretcher on to the kitchen table, then sent them to collect every lamp they could find. Tom even went next door and brought back Edith's two biggest oil lamps. While they were doing so, Henderson positioned the existing light sources over Rose and gave her a thorough examination. Rose gave him no trouble. She was so severely hurt that the moment he straightened her body, she let out a long wail and lapsed again into a dead faint. Henderson dismissed everyone except Edith Smith and then, grim-faced, he sponged away the blood from Rose's thighs and slid his hand into her insensible body to explore the damage her father's violence had caused.

Edith watched him, apprehensive in case he should require help she did not know how to give, and frightened that he would confirm her fear that Rose would

die. He finished quickly, washed his hands and said,
'We'll never save her unless I operate on her here.
Woollaston House hospital is a good ten miles away
and she'll have bled to death long before we get her
there, even if she stands the pain. I could try moving
her down to the surgery, but I don't even know whether
she'd survive that. Are you willing to act as my nurse,
Mrs Smith?'

'What will I have to do?'

'You'll need a strong stomach and steady hands, for
a start – and the ability to follow my instructions to the
letter,' – he raised a hand to reassure her – 'No, they
won't be complicated instructions; but I need someone
with a clear head. I don't expect you've seen people
opened up before.'

'Oh, aye I have. Couple of the men as was brought
home from pit accidents when they should have gone to
the hospital mortuary. And two or three nasty suicides.
First lot had guts all over the place, two of the others
had cut their throats. They was all dead, of course, but
one lot of insides do look much the same as the next, I
should think.'

His smile was captivating. 'Then I'm a lucky man.
We'll have to move the girl out while the place is
scrubbed up, and bring her back in afterwards, all
right? I have everything we need in my other bag.' He
had brought in only a small medical bag. His instruments, chloroform and antiseptics were still outside in
the trap. Now he supervised the removal of Rose back
to the parlour, then set Lily and Bethan to scrubbing
down the already-spotless kitchen table. After that he
fetched the other bag, from which he produced a small
scrubbing brush and several bottles of perchloride of
mercury.

'Soak your hands in a bowl of this, Mrs Smith,' he said.
'Then, when the girls have finished, scrub down the
table again with some of it and finish off by giving your

hands another rinse in a fresh quantity of the solution. I'll prepare my instruments.'

Through the subdued bustle, Margaret Ann called timidly from the passage doorway. 'Doctor – what are you planning to do to Rose? What exactly is wrong?'

He frowned and went over to her. 'Too much for any hope of survival without surgery, Mrs Walters. Your son said she fell downstairs. Surely it was more than that? The injuries are more in line with her having been thrown. Her pelvis has been completely displaced and it's ruptured her uterus. No bones broken, but sometimes a dislocation can cause worse problems. I've got the pelvis back, after a fashion, but unless I perform a hysterectomy within the next couple of hours, nothing will save her. Even if I operate, I can give no guarantee.'

It was hard for Margaret Ann to digest what he had said. 'But that's h-her womb, isn't it? She's only fifteen. What about. . .about children?'

'Out of the question! Mrs Walters, stop worrying about your grandchildren. I'm trying to save the next generation, not insure the one after that. Now, if your husband is available, perhaps he'll be good enough to sign a consent.'

'No! No, he's – that is – he's not at home. Surely, if it's a matter of life and death, I could. . .?'

Henderson shrugged. 'Well, this is 1911, after all. I see no reason why a mother shouldn't have as much right as her husband to dictate a child's future. Very well, Mrs Walters. I'll find the form in a moment.'

Margaret Ann sighed with relief. If he saw Evan now, his suspicions about Rose's injuries would be confirmed immediately. Come to that, Evan was in a bad enough state to blurt it all out to the man. Better to keep that sort of thing inside these walls. . . Bad enough that Edith Smith had to know. . . She focused her attention on her kitchen, now a makeshift operating theatre, and recoiled at the sight of Henderson's array of instruments, which he was sterilizing. *What can I do*, she thought. *I can't leave our Rose, but if I stay I'll faint, I know I shall. . .*

The choice was taken from her. Rose abruptly regained consciousness and began screaming again. Margaret Ann rushed to her side, followed closely by Henderson. 'I think I'll knock her out in here,' he said, 'then we won't need to destroy the sterile table surface by putting that door on it again. Just pacify her a moment, Mrs Walters. . .' And he went back to get the chloroform pad.

Rose seized her mother's hand and pulled her down close. 'Is that man going to hurt me even more?' she asked through lips contorted with pain.

'No, my love, he's going to make you better. Lie easy now, there's a pet. It'll stop hurting soon, really it will.'

'Stay by me, Mam, please, whatever they do to me! I don't want to die on my own. Promise?' Her grip tightened.

'I promise. I'll still be there when you do wake up, don't worry now.'

At that, Rose even managed a small smile, before a new tide of pain swept over her. But within moments she was oblivious of everything. Dr Henderson rapidly sprinkled chloroform over a thick gauze pad, and held it to Rose's nose and mouth before she had a chance to question his purpose. Her body relaxed almost instantly, and Henderson called for the boys to carry her back to the kitchen.

Even now, propriety obsessed Margaret Ann. 'But Rose is naked under that sheet – they'll see her. . .'

Henderson sighed wearily. 'Mrs Walters, if you think I'm dressing a patient for two minutes, simply so that her brothers will not see she's a woman like any other, you're mistaken. If you can't be useful, please get out of my way.'

He strode back into the kitchen and submerged his hands in a fresh bowl of perchloride of mercury. He had already made Edith do the same. When he went over to the table, he checked Rose's pulse, then told Edith, 'She'll go through two distinct stages before we can start. She's in the first now – going down into the first deep slumber. Watch – if she doesn't react now, she's under.'

He put his hand over the girl's eyes and gently touched the lashes. There was no sign of movement. 'She's gone,' he said, satisfied. 'The next stage is unpleasant. She'll look as if she's coming round again, but she won't be. Symptoms are very like delirium. If she goes through that quickly, the next stage is a series of deepening sleeps. We have to wait until she has completed most of that stage before she is sleeping deeply enough for this operation.'

As he explained to Edith how Rose would react and what Edith must do to assist him, Margaret Ann joined them. She went to the head of the table, well away from the lower part of Rose's abdomen, where they were working, and stood with her hand resting lightly on Rose's shoulder. 'She made me promise to stay with her, Doctor. May I?'

Henderson was at a loss to know why Mrs Walters irritated him so much. She behaved no worse than any other patient's relative, and better than some. 'Only if you think you can stand up to it,' he snapped. 'We're hard-pressed enough without having to revive you when you faint.'

She shook her head and swallowed hard. 'I mustn't. I told you, I promised.'

'Very well, then. We're about to start.'

It was full daylight by the time he had finished. The miners on the Saturday day shift had tramped past hours before. Charles Henderson emerged from the reeking kitchen and gulped great lungfuls of morning air, for a few moments capable of nothing more than animal relief that he was alive and healthy. After a while his reverie was interrupted by a polite, frightened voice.

'Please sir, is my sister still alive?' It was Bethan Walters.

Only now did Henderson realize he was not alone. Tom and Haydn sat on the top step outside the back door, Lily and Bethan occupying the next step down. There were five other sons – Emrys, Elwyn, Gareth, Edmund and Lewis. Tom, Haydn and Emrys were lodgers three doors away, at a house where there was more room for them. Elwyn had gone to knock them up after fetching the doctor and they had joined the family vigil. But Emrys was on day shift and had left at five o'clock. Gareth was eight, Edmund barely six, and at two, Lewis was the baby of the family. After Elwyn had fetched the doctor, Haydn had ordered him to stay in the bedroom with his three younger brothers and the ensuing tumult had ensured the boy did so. During the night, Haydn had crept upstairs to see nothing was amiss. He had found the youngest three fast asleep and Elwyn guarding them like a sentry. Apparently Evan had moved from the landing to the other bedroom, for there was no sign of him and he had not left the house.

Now the four remaining young Walterses confronted the surgeon, anxiously awaiting news of Rose.

He managed a smile for them. 'The operation was successful,' he said, 'but that's only part of the story. She'll rest in the parlour for a day or two – I'm having a proper bed brought up from the surgery for her – and when she's a little stronger, we're sending her to the hospital in Newport. She'll have a better chance there. It will be a very long haul, though.'

The others digested the information in silence, but Bethan leaped to her feet and practically danced up the steps to him. 'Oh, thank you, Doctor, thank you so much!' She flung her arms round his neck and planted a kiss somewhere near his chin. 'Our Dad wouldn't never have forgiven himself if she'd died!'

Realization snapped into Henderson's eyes. 'What's it got to do with your father? Your mother said he was away. If I thought. . .'

He got no chance to complete the train of thought. The other Walters girl was at his side, oozing pretty persuasion. *My God, but they're a handsome family!* he thought. This one couldn't have been more than twelve or thirteen, but she had a woman's poise. 'Oh, our Bethan!' she said. 'All she ever thinks of is Dad. Of course he ent here. He's over the Rhymney Valley for the week – family funeral – but Bethan do know Rose is his favourite. What she means is, he'd never get over it if he lost her.'

Henderson looked deep into the silvery, dark-lashed eyes and was prepared to believe anything. He shook his head, trying to clear it of the tangle of exhaustion the night had brought on. When he spoke again, his tone was softer. 'Mrs Smith is cleaning up inside now,' he said. 'Your mother is trying to help, but I think last night was a bit too much for her. She bore it very bravely once the operation had started. I think you'd better see she gets to bed, Lily – er, that is, Miss Walters.'

The girl blushed becomingly. 'And when will you be coming back to see our Rose?' she asked.

'Oh, I shall be back by noon – earlier if any complications set in. Mrs Smith said she would get another of your neighbours to take turns with you at nursing the patient. I don't think your mother will be able to do it for a day or so. They'll keep me up to date whenever I call, and we'll move her to hospital the minute she's strong enough. Now, if you'll excuse me, I think I need a couple of hours sleep before I start my rounds.'

He went back inside to collect his bags and coat, then

drove away, followed by the adoring eyes of the Walters children.

Back at the surgery, he went upstairs to wash and change while the housekeeper prepared his breakfast. When he came back, she said, 'I'm sorry to disturb you again after such a night, Doctor, but there's a Mr Walters outside, says he must see you.'

Henderson's face was grim. 'I might have known that child was telling me a fairy story! Send him in, Mrs Jones, and let me have some coffee while we're talking.'

'But he's a workman, sir! Doctor don't allow miners in the house!'

'Mrs Jones, I can vouch for the man not stealing Dr Cann's silver. He's had a terrible night from what I can gather, and he certainly won't be up to talking outside by the door. Now cut along for that coffee – oh, and you'd better bring an extra cup and saucer.'

This last order deprived her of the power of speech and she flounced away to do his bidding.

Evan looked like a dried-up husk. He towered over Henderson, who nevertheless felt like a school headmaster confronting a repentant pupil. The doctor's first impulse had been to send the man packing as soon as possible, and only the housekeeper's freezing snobbery had stopped him. But now he sensed something in Evan's bearing which excited his pity. Henderson gestured him to a chair.

'I don't think it's part of my function to hear confessions, if that's why you came,' he said.

The man stared at him. It was like looking into Lily Walters's eyes again. 'Have I killed our Rose?' he said.

Henderson shook his head. 'I don't think so, Mr Walters. It was a near thing, though. You've certainly ended her chances of motherhood, and she'll probably be delicate for the rest of her life. I

don't know why I'm even giving you a hearing. You
beat her, didn't you?'

Then Evan was crying again. '*Iesu mawr*, no! I could
never beat our Rose. That's the thing I can't live
with. She knows I'll never hurt her, so when I'm
mad drunk and trying to hit her mother, Rose do
protect her. Only. . .only this time, it was so bad
I. . .forgot, like. . .forgot it was my Rose, even forgot
where I was for a bit. All I knew was I wanted my
vengeance on Margaret Ann. . . All I done was try to
shove Rose out of the way. Only I didn't just shove her,
did I, Doctor? The minute I threw her down the stairs,
I was sober. I knew what I'd done. . .too strong for my
own good, see. . .'

Mrs Jones arrived then with the coffee. Seeing Evan's
tears, she sniffed her disapproval and left them to it.

Intrigued, now, Henderson poured coffee for Evan,
then went and got brandy from the cupboard and
added a hefty shot to the cup. 'Drink that,' he said.
'It'll calm you down a bit. Then tell me something –
why did you want to avenge yourself on Mrs Walters?'

Perhaps it was because Henderson was a stranger.
Perhaps it was because he had saved Rose's life. Whatever the reason, Evan found he could tell this sharp-
eyed young man about the tragedy of his love for Ellen
Rourke, and her death the previous day. He had used
up all his tears on Rose, and now he told his story calmly, in a voice which sounded as if it, too, had died.

When he had finished, both men sat in silence for
a while. Then Charles Henderson rose, moved across
to Evan and put an arm round him. 'No one can ever
take away your guilt for what you did to Rose,' he said,
'but don't see yourself as a monster. You were under
intolerable strain.'

'Aye, I keep telling myself that,' said Evan, dully, 'but
when all's said and done, it wasn't no fault of Margaret
Ann's either, was it? I'm the one that made the mistakes

all those years ago, and I can't blame nobody else for what have happened now.'

'If all of us had to pay for every wrong we did, there'd be a lot more punishment about, Mr Walters. You can't change the past, but I think you've already paid more than most men.'

'Maybe. I'll never forget her, that's for sure. And now my boys are telling me I can't even go to the funeral – they say it'll cause too much trouble at home.'

'Will it make you feel better?'

'*Duw*, aye! At least I'd feel I'd given her a proper send-off. I can nearly hear her laughing at the idea – "Never thought this'd be the only way I'd get you in chapel with me, Evan!" – it would mean the world to me.'

'Then go. Your sons are going to need you there with them, anyway, whatever they try to tell you to the contrary. How old did you say they were – twenty-one and nineteen? That's no great age for a man to be coming to terms with death.'

For the first time, Evan managed a smile. 'D'you know, I think maybe I could live with it, after all, if I went. Well, well, what d'you think of that?'

Henderson patted him on the shoulder, then moved to escort him out. 'The Greeks called it catharsis, Mr Walters. It worked perfectly well for them. No reason why it shouldn't for you.'

At the front door, Evan turned and shook his hand. 'Thanks for listening to me,' he said. 'If I couldn't have told someone just then, I think they'd have found me in the canal before dinner time.'

Henderson regarded him sharply. 'No such thoughts still on your mind, I hope?'

The old Evan was returning fast. 'Never! I'll be there for my early shift Monday, same as ever.' He turned and started trudging back towards the village.

*

After the funeral at Hengoed, Evan and the boys discussed their futures. 'I think it's about time I put my foot down with your mam about you two not coming back home,' said Evan. 'It's not as if you'd be under her roof in the nights – you'd be lodging out like Emrys and Haydn. I can't let you just drift around over here with no family of your own, now Ellen's gone.'

'Don't you understand, Dad?' asked Billie. 'Mam could never be family for us again, after Ellen. Not the way Ellen loved us and looked after us. Anyway, we've made up our own minds. We ent going to be hanging round here on our own.'

'Yes, Dad, I s'pose you'd better be the first to know apart from our Billie,' chipped in John Daniel. 'Remember that Morfydd Lewis from Tredegar Street? We'm getting married next month. She said yes a fortnight ago. I've already asked about this house, and I can take it over as the tenant for the same rent as we paid when Ellen had it. So I'll have my own family, no need to worry about me.'

'And Billie? What about you, boy? You won't like hanging about here playing gooseberry to a couple of newlyweds, will you?'

'Don't be daft, Dad, of course not. This'll surprise you even more. I'm joining the Army.'

'You must be bloody mad!' Evan regarded military service as the last refuge of the desperate.

'No. I been bloody mad this last seven years, working down in the dark and the dirt. Can't be many jobs worse than that, as far as I can see. From next Saturday, I'm a private in the Royal Welch Fusiliers.'

Evan looked ineffably sad. 'I do remember Ellen saying that if she ever knew a boy with a poet's soul, Billie, it was you. What have happened to it?'

'The pit have happened to it, Dad, and the Ranks, too. All us kids jammed in that little house, more of us every year, and Mam taking in washing, and you doing all them back-breaking jobs to try to make us better. None of it worked. You'm still trapped in it. And there's no more room for poets there than there is in the Army.'

'That could have been Ellen talking, back in her wild days. Only with her, it was the theatre.'

'It *is* Ellen talking, Dad. If she ever taught me anything, it was that you got to look for your freedom, however hard it is, and when you'm lucky enough to find it, you mustn't grumble if you'm lonely. So, I'm going for mine. The Army's the only chance I'll ever get – no rich benefactor is going to send me off to Oxford University!'

'Come on, Dad,' said John Daniel. 'You'll get used to the idea soon enough. Bet our Billie'll never see a battlefield – he'll spend all his time snoozing in the Indian sun, guarding the Empire.'

'Aye,' said Evan. 'I do remember Charlie Beynon telling us that, an' all, when he joined up in '98 during the pit strike. Three years later he was shot by some Boer farmer in South Africa. Lot of good guarding the Empire done him.'

'If it's that or a roof fall, I'll take the bullet any time,' said Billie. 'Come on, Dad, let's part friends. We've just said goodbye to somebody we all love. She wouldn't have wanted us to quarrel.'

'No, you'm right. You go, then, with my blessing. And come home safe.'

Back in Abercarn, the house was slowly returning to normal after Rose's removal to hospital. She was expected to be there for at least six weeks, and there was some talk of convalescence by the sea if the benefit club cover extended to that.

Margaret Ann was acting as though it were merely

an unfortunate illness, and said nothing publicly or in private to suggest that Evan was responsible. At first Evan put it down to her all-conquering sense of propriety, but then he realized it was something more. She regarded Rose's tragedy as a bearable price for the final removal of Ellen Rourke from her life. At night, she welcomed Evan back to her bed without recrimination. By day, she relied more and more on Lily for companionship and amusement.

Only Rose's illness and her mother's unending fertility saved Lily from being bound to Margaret Ann for ever. Within three months of Ellen Rourke's death, Margaret Ann was pregnant again. The week after Dr Cann confirmed her condition, the seaside nursing home wrote to say that Rose was almost well enough to be discharged. The two events combined to transform the Walters family's life for the next few years.

Soon after they received the news about Rose, Dr Henderson, still working as Cann's locum, came to advise them on looking after the girl.

'She really must have a bed of her own, at the very least, Mrs Walters,' he told Margaret Ann, 'preferably in her own room. How would you be fixed to put your other sons out as lodgers?'

'No trouble with the older ones,' she said. 'They'm working, so there's enough to pay their keep. But Edmund and Lewis can't go for years yet – and what about Bethan and Lily? If Rose was to have a room of her own, I could really only keep two children here with the new baby on the way, and you can't expect me to choose between the girls and the boys – it ent natural.'

'But surely the girls will have to go to work some time? Lily must already be old enough, and if it was only Bethan still at home, I'm sure she could be fitted in on a separate mattress in Rose's room for a while.'

Margaret Ann's face was hostile. 'No girl of mine is

going into service, and that's the only kind of work for
girls away from home.'

Henderson was astonished. He had always assumed
that working-class girls automatically went into domestic service when they entered their teens. Then he
caught Evan's eye. His expression was saying, don't
pursue that line, my friend...Henderson bit his
tongue and waited for the other man to come up
with something.

'There's always our Rhys down Cardiff, love,' he said.
'He'd have Lily like a shot.'

'I'm not sending my daughters to a pub! I never
heard of such a thing!'

'Come on, he've got a girl of his own, same age
as Lily. If I do know Rhys, that place is straight as a
chapel. Other people's women is one thing. Family is
another... Anyway, if Rose is going to get better and
you'm going to manage her and another baby, what
choice have we got?'

Margaret Ann wavered. 'I'm not sending Lily by herself, even if he have got a daughter the same age. If it
do happen at all, our Bethan must go with her.'

'That would be even better, Mrs Walters,' Henderson
broke in. 'I told you, it will be best for Rose if she has a
room to herself.'

'Oh, all right, then. The parlour can be her room,
and the new baby can go in with Edmund and Lewis
after it do come out of our room.'

When she told Lily and Bethan, Margaret Ann
watched the older girl intently, trying to detect signs
of unhappiness. If she didn't want to leave her mam,
Margaret Ann thought, there'd be some way to keep
her home... But to her chagrin, Lily reacted as though
she were being offered a trip to fairyland.

'Cardiff! Oh, there's lovely! I've always wanted to go,
Mam! And we'll really live there, with Uncle Rhys, for
ever?'

Fighting down the hurt, Margaret Ann said, 'Well, not for ever, love. . .you wouldn't want to leave me for ever, would you?' And in case the answer was the wrong one, she hurried on, 'A year, p'raps. . .two at the most. It might take Rose that long to get better. That would be quite long enough, wouldn't it?'

Lily's expression suggested the contrary, but she was a good girl, and her desire not to hurt Margaret Ann produced flowery, if belated, expressions of regret. She managed to make sure, though, that her protestations were not strong enough to keep her in Abercarn at her mother's side.

Less than a week later, the sisters were waved off from Abercarn station by their father. Margaret Ann had to stay at home to look after Rose, who was exhausted by her trip back from the convalescent home.

Evan handed a small leather purse to Lily through the carriage window. 'There's five pound in there,' he said. 'Not pocket money, mind. Rhys will give you that, and I'll settle with him when I do see him. That's escape money. You mustn't use that unless there's no other way out of trouble, all right? Mind you keep it safe – and don't tell nobody about it.'

Lily took the money, wide-eyed, finally realizing that she was really leaving the nest. Evan kissed both girls. 'You tell our Rhys to look after you, mind!' Then he whispered, 'And next time you do see your mam, don't tell her about Lexie!'

The guard blew his whistle and waved his flag. The big steam engine puffed importantly and the train began to crawl away from the platform.

'Wait. . .hang on!' Lily cried inconsequentially. 'Dad, what d'you mean? Tell her what about Lexie? I don't understand!'

Smiling, Evan waved them off. 'You will, kidda – you will!' he murmured.

PART FOUR
1911–1921

By night in my bed I sought him
whom my soul loveth: I sought
him but I found him not.

Song of Songs
Ch.III, v.1

CHAPTER SEVENTEEN

LILY AND BETHAN huddled together, forlorn refugees, on the platform at Cardiff General station. Their train was a shrinking dot in the distance and the last of the billowing clouds of smutty steam had dispersed from under the glass canopy. 'You sure he said on the platform?' Bethan's piping voice skirted the edge of panic.

'I 'xpect he got delayed.' Lily hoped she sounded more confident than she felt.

'You must be cousin Lily.' Both girls turned to stare at the speaker, a tall, slender brown girl with brilliant dark eyes. She met their gaze and grinned, challenging them to comment on her exotic appearance.

'I'm Lily Walters, yes. But who are you?'

The girl laughed, showing a set of dauntingly perfect teeth. 'Lexie. Lexie Walters. Who was you expecting?'

The three girls faced each other in mounting perplexity. 'Y-you'm Lexie?' Lily stammered. 'But. . .'

Lexie laughed again. 'But they didn't tell you I was coloured. Our Dad said it would be a surprise. Come on, I've got a cab down below.' She started to walk away, realized they were still rooted to the spot, and turned back. 'It's all right – pubs is still open, so our Dad couldn't come yet. Too busy.' Bethan was still goggling

at her. 'Don't worry, flower, you gets used to the sun-
burn after a bit.'

Outside the station, Cardiff's unique, wonderful
smell hit them. Roasting hops and coffee beans mixed
with coal dust, horse dung, steam and overloaded
drains. 'Don't breathe too deep,' said Lexie, 'or you'll
be drunk before we gets to Butetown.'

They piled into a horse cab, Lily and Bethan round-
eyed and impressed at such opulence. The cabman
whipped up his horse and steered them through the
chaotic mass of traffic around Hayes Bridge. Lily
was conscious of her social obligations, but Bethan
relaxed and gaped openly at the throngs of people
who crammed the streets. This was where the town's
prosperous middle class and brawling dockland types
met head-on at the only point where their worlds converged.

'Sorry if I was rude,' Lily blurted out, 'but they didn't
say. . .'

'D'you think your mam would have let you come if
she'd known?'

Lily gasped. 'You mean she don't?'

'Of course not. Christ, I bet she's the sort that do go
on about a touch of the tar brush!'

'It don't seem to worry you, anyhow, Lexie.'

'No reason why it should, down here. Everyone else
is the same. Different up the Valleys, though, ennit?'

Lily nodded, still perplexed. 'But how could Mam not
have known all these years? Didn't she never see you or
your mother, or – or come to the wedding or anything?'

That really made Lexie laugh. 'Wedding? What wedding? Dad might like his bit of fancy, but he's not the
marrying kind.'

That was almost too much for Lily. 'So they still ent
married?'

'No. They'd have a bloody job, now, anyway. Our
Mam went off to Bristol ten years ago. Nobody've seen

her down the Bay since then, and there've been a lot of aunties in our place, too.'

Lily was torn between excitement and terror. What if her mother were to find out about this terrible, immoral world? She remembered her father's words about how straight and narrow Rhys Walters was with his womenfolk, and dismissed them after one glance at Lexie's clothes and manner. Mam would never forgive her for not turning round and bringing Bethan straight back home, trouble or no trouble. *But if she haven't found out yet, she probably never will*, a subversive voice told her. And it would be so exciting to stay. . .

She glanced at Bethan. The younger girl was gazing at Lexie in open adoration. There'd be no trouble with her. . . Lily sighed and began to relax. 'Why do they call you Lexie?' she asked.

'Oh, that's our Mam's fault, again. She always did have big ideas. Called me Alexandra, after the Queen – Princess of Wales as was then. They used to tease me something rotten down here, so I changed over to Lexie. They don't mind that. Lily's a pretty name. I do know another Lily – her full name's Lily May, though. I'll introduce you to her one day.'

But Lily was no longer paying attention. The panorama outside the cab had absorbed her as fully as Bethan now, and as they turned from Custom House Place into Bute Street, she gave a squeak of wonderment. 'Look – look there, Lexie – a real live Chinaman with a pigtail!'

Lexie, who had been momentarily interested in seeing what all the fuss was about, slumped back into her seat with a blasé expression. 'Christ, I thought it must be King George at least! Don't get worked up over one Chink, love – the Bay is crawling with them.'

'Ent you scared you'll be murdered in your bed?' Lily had heard of the activities of expatriate Chinese.

'Oh, aye, I never think of anything else! Don't be so bloody daft, girl – what'd they want to do that for?'

'Well. . .er. . .you know. . .'

'Yes, but I ent sure that *you* know. They'm all too busy working themselves to death or playing fantan to start letching after the girls. In Cardiff, Chinese is only interested in other Chinese, Lil. That do keep the buggers busy enough.'

'Don't your Dad mind you swearing?'

'Swearing, me? I been watching my language ever since I come to pick you up! 'Course he don't mind. God almighty, I'd have a job talking any different, with what you hear round our pub. Anyhow, if you'm going to settle down all right, you'll be the same before long. Girls have got to stand up for themselves around here.'

There was a teasing note in her voice which stopped Lily from feeling insulted. 'P'raps you wouldn't mind standing up for me while I'm learning, Lexie.'

'My pleasure, flower. . . Hang on, I do believe they've laid on a special performance for you this afternoon.'

Ahead of them, traffic had ground to a halt. The drivers and pedestrians who had urgent business were trying to filter off into side streets and skirt the blockage, but most people were eager to know what was going on. Lexie called up to the cabman, 'We'll get out here, but I want you to take the bags on home for us. Yes, that's right. . . Anglesey Hotel. If you turn off here, you can get to it quite easy lower down. Just tell the landlord his guests are here all right and we've gone sight-seeing. All right? He'll probably give you a bit extra if you makes sure you speaks to him in person. Name's Rhys Walters.'

She turned and began hustling the two sisters out of the cab. 'Come on, quick – don't want to miss nothing, do you?'

Lily was getting anxious. 'But what if he do go off with our things? That box is all I've got.'

'Don't be so soft, girl! Our Dad'll give him more for the fare and tip than both them boxes would fetch. Of course he'll go on down there. Time you grew up a bit!'

The mere suggestion of that taunt was enough to make Bethan want to prove her mettle. At ten, she heard it often enough from her brothers. 'Come on, Lily,' she said. 'Don't be such a spoilsport! It's like a carnival out there.'

'Bloody rum carnival if you ask me, but it's worth a look,' murmured Lexie, then shouldered Bethan aside to be first out into the street.

Some minutes after their arrival, Lily still had not worked out what was going on. 'Maybe I'll understand when that man up on the cart do start talking,' she told Lexie.

'Nothing complicated about it,' said Lexie. 'Your dad really picked his time to send you down here. The seamen have been out on strike for a month and the toff up there is their leader. That's Captain Tupper. He've been trying to get the dockers out in sympathy since it started, but Cardiff dockers have always been bosses' men and they still won't down tools. The Captain's always worth listening to, though – a real character.' And she started threading her way through the crowd to get a better position.

Following her, Lily was amazed that this gentleman was a trade unionist. The only ones she had ever seen at home wore working clothes like the other miners. This man did not resemble either a seaman or a docker. He looked more like a ship-owner.

Edward Tupper wore a well-cut frock coat and a tall silk hat, pushed rakishly to the back of his head. It was a sunny, dusty day and as he talked to one of his companions up on the cart, he mopped his forehead with a brightly-coloured silk handkerchief. Then one of the men said, 'There you are, Eddie – refreshment is on the way. The Lord will always provide, mind, courtesy of Bass!'

Lily glanced round in the direction they were looking. A big, dark, faintly familiar-looking man was shouldering his way through the crowd. His right hand, raised above shoulder height, balanced a metal tray of moisture-beaded glasses of beer and stout. He was grinning at people as he passed, obviously relishing the occasion. Lily stared at him, wondering why she felt she had seen him before.

'Trust our Dad to get in on the act!' said Lexie. 'The old bugger probably bribed the seamen to hold their meeting right outside his pub. The Captain have always done wonders for beer sales!'

Of course, thought Lily – he's just like our Dad in nicer clothes! Mystery solved, she watched the little drama unfolding before her. Rhys Walters arrived at the cart and handed over his tray of drinks. Edward Tupper took a glass of Bass in each hand, toasted the crowd and downed the first one in a single swallow. He took a sip from the second before putting it down on the makeshift table beside him, then removed his frock coat, gestured as if beckoning the onlookers to come closer, and began to speak.

'Brothers,' he said, 'I'm not here today to cover the big issues – you've heard me on that matter before. I'm here to expose the dirty tactics of the bosses who seek to divide us.

'This week's message is that the Chinese are your enemies. Well, I can tell you that the real enemy is standing among you, much harder to spot than a poor Chinaman. They're the toughs employed by the Shipping Federation to spy on you and beat you up. They're the employers' paid informers, who buy you a drink and trick you into saying something you'll regret later. They are the men you should hate and drive out, not the Chinese.

'You don't want to get smashing Chinese houses, boys. We've got the employers on their knees. You can get all you want without going on in that manner. Don't get excited and break the law, and above all, do not be guilty of any action that would warrant the soldiers coming out. If they wanted to rid themselves of the Chinese, the best method would be to starve them out, not pay them to do other men's jobs. They're deliberately using Chinese labour now to break the seamen, and I know many of you will be scared they'll do the same on the docks if you come out with us. Don't listen to their evil whispers – there aren't enough Chinese from here to Liverpool and back to take on all the work in these docks. Look at Butetown. The greatest concentration of Chinese immigrants here lies within ten houses on Bute Street. Even with fiendish overcrowding, does any one of you believe that adds up to enough blackleg labour to steal your jobs for ever?

'You all know my feelings about the enemy. You meet him half-way and you show him – physically – that you will not be cowed by his threats. Now, I can see a lot of men among you that I've seen at other meetings, on other streets, but they're not members of any working men's union. The only union they know is a bosses' union, where they're paid to take orders. I'm here today to challenge any one of those false unionists to come up here and fight me, in boxing gloves, and may the best man win!'

Excited at the mention of a fist fight, the crowd began shifting, with people eyeing their neighbours suspiciously. Was that fellow over there a bosses' spy? Or how about the one leaning against the shop front? He didn't look like a docker or a seaman. . .

The scattering of paid toughs were getting edgy. Butetown was small enough for most of the inhabitants to know each other by sight, at least, and now they were noticing there were strangers in their midst. One of these outsiders decided attack was the best form of defence, and stepped forward, raising his fist.

'Who says you can tell the working men what they must and mustn't do, Tupper?' he bawled. 'We know your kind won't be satisfied till the streets is full of blood – they've even said that about you in Parliament!' Pleased at his inside knowledge, he swaggered a little and turned to the crowd with a smug smile before continuing his harangue. 'If any of us is here as don't belong with your lot, it's because we'm paid to protect the property of law-abiding citizens. 'Tent just the Chinks who's afraid of what your seamen will do to 'em.'

'And whose sacred property are you protecting, Snell? Seems I remember you being a responsible citizen in Newport and Bristol not too long ago. Whose inalienable rights bring you to these parts?'

The man flushed, realizing too late that he should not have made himself conspicuous. 'No outsider. I'am local man. . .' he mumbled, beginning to back away into the crowd.

But they were unwilling to let him go. 'Tell us, then, chum – docker, is it, or maybe a homeward bounder with a good pay packet to guard?' The speaker was a big docker, who towered over the trouble-maker.

'Nothing to do with you. I'm a local man, though, right enough!'

'Want us to beat it out of him, Captain?' called up a deal-runner.

'No, boys, no need. I told the gentleman, I'm fully prepared to fight him, Queensberry Rules, to establish the truth.'

The spy looked Tupper over and thought better of his earlier belligerence. 'The bugger can fight his own battles,' he said. 'He've got enough money. It's Handcock, the tugboat owner. About six of us here's his men.'

The crowd was getting really ugly now. All of them

knew the dockland employers eavesdropped on politi-
cal activity and employed bullies to scare people back to
work, but they seldom had such tangible evidence.

Edward Tupper was ready to press home his advantage. 'Right, boys,' he said. 'Why talk to the monkey
when the organ grinder's here? Come on, we'll go and
issue my challenge to Mr Handcock in person.' He
turned to put on his coat again, then jumped lightly
down from the waggon and started off in the direction
of the Pier Head. The crowd fell in behind him, their
mood somewhere between festive and violent.

'Lexie, what are you doing?' Lily, panic-stricken,
grabbed her cousin's sleeve as the other girl started
off in the vanguard of the procession.

'Going to have a look, of course. Didn't think I'd leave
it here, did you?'

'But we might get hurt. . .'

'Oh, dear, Lily, I'm going to have to work on you, ent
I? That mam of yours haven't done you no good at all.
This'll be men hitting other men, if we'm lucky enough
to see it come to that. Nobody bothers with a bunch of
kids. Come on.'

'But what about Beth. . .' She broke off, realizing
Bethan had already joined in with the march on
Handcock's office, and fell in beside Lexie. Mam and
the Ranks seemed very far away.

One of Snell's cronies must have hurried ahead of the
mob to tip off Handcock's staff that trouble was on the
way. By the time they arrived at the building, the half-
glazed doors were locked and the blinds drawn. The
people turned mutinous now. They were after spectacle, and barred doors were inexcusably tame.

'Now, now, calm down. Nothing to be gained by losing our tempers,' shouted Tupper. 'Remember, I'm
here to issue a challenge.' He took a few paces towards

the offices, then raised his head and yelled up at the big windows on the first floor of the building, 'Handcock – I know you're there today – saw you this morning! I've come to issue a challenge. Are you man enough to answer me?'

The building remained silent. After a while, Tupper turned back to his audience. 'Looks as though the man can't find the stomach to associate himself publicly with his principles. Well, we've all met that kind, haven't we? Probably content to hide behind these mythical Chinese coolies who're going to steal our jobs. . .'

The upstairs window opened with a rattle and a furious red face thrust out. 'Tupper – get your mob away or I'll have the law on you! Of course I stand by my principles. There's not a man or boy here without reason to fear the Chinese will take his work if he walks off the job. And they will, mark my words!'

'Mark your words? I've come down here to make you eat 'em!' Tupper yelled back. 'Same challenge as I always give your men – Neptune Park, one to one, gloves or bare fists. Your principles strong enough for that?'

'I'm not an animal or a street brawler,' said Handcock with a sneer. 'Call your thugs off and let decent people get back to earning an honest living.'

'Ah, it's the money, is it?' Tupper made a large gesture. 'I wouldn't like to see you in the street for loss of an afternoon's work. . . Tell you what, accept my challenge and I'll throw in a £50 wager, an' all. That'll pay for your time and give you an extra incentive to win!'

'Oh, for God's sake, call off that guttersnipe army behind you and go about your business. I'm returning to mine now!' and Handcock slammed the window again.

On balance, Tupper was satisfied with his afternoon's work. He had pinpointed some of the hired toughs in the area and had ridiculed one of the employers before

a large audience. He turned to complete a successful day with a little more oratory. But for once he
had misjudged his followers. The seamen were disciplined and well-organized. When Tupper said no violence, they understood why and held back. Today's
crowd really were a mob – part dockers, part general
port workers, with a scattering of layabouts who had
drunk too much stout before noon and were becoming increasingly belligerent in the hot afternoon sunshine.

Now somebody drowned Tupper's message. 'Let's
drag the bugger out and make him fight!' he cried.
'We'll show him we don't put up with that sort of treatment!'

It was action – something to stop the afternoon ending in anti-climax. Tupper's protests went unheard as
a flurry of lump coal, stones and ordure started hitting the front of Handcock's offices. Within moments,
a bigger missile struck the plate glass ground-floor window, which seemed to hang suspended for a few seconds before it shattered into thousands of pieces. Now
Tupper's men were really worried. They struggled to
hold back the more violent agitators, while one of them
dashed to the empty window frame and shouted to the
staff inside to barricade the opening. But the moment
a couple of clerks stepped outside to try and place the
wooden shutters that went up at night, the troublemakers really got into their stride. Among the missiles
there now appeared a sprinkling of jack-knives, one of
which grazed a clerk's arm before embedding itself in
the shutter he was man-handling. He and his colleague
dropped their burden and fled back inside.

And then the police arrived. Tupper saw them coming and cursed himself for a fool. 'Christ, why didn't I
realize he'd have sent someone out through the back
door?' he murmured to the man at his side, then added,
'Let them take me, Joe. I'll be out in next to no time,

and God knows what this lot would do to those three coppers if we gave them an excuse.'

His deputy nodded, warily watching the ordinary people who had changed into a bloodthirsty mob.

A mounted policeman was forcing a path through the crowd. Behind him, on foot, were a sergeant and constable from the local station. They came to a halt in front of Tupper. 'Edward Jacob Tupper?' said the sergeant.

The Captain sighed. 'Oh, come on, Jack, of course I am! You've known me for twenty years by that name! Yes to all questions, and I'll come quietly. Let's get it over with before this lot really explode.'

The sergeant nodded with a half-smile. 'No handcuffs, I don't think, Eddie – might get them going, mightn't it?' he said under his breath.

'Nothing surer. Go on, you and your man come each side of me and we'll go through them quietly. I can beat the bosses without having a riot down here.' The small procession cut its way back through the crowd and Tupper was ushered into a motor-driven police van which waited at the kerb. As it pulled away, Tupper's lieutenant was already trying to dissuade the mob from causing further trouble.

Tupper's stoic behaviour defused their violent mood, if only temporarily. People began breaking away in ones and twos, but not heading home. It was clear they had a purpose in mind. This afternoon's disturbance had achieved more than any previous incident in rousing the dockers to down tools. Before Tupper and his escort had even arrived at City Hall, timber porters, coal trimmers and dockers were spreading the word that the port must be stopped, in support of the striking seamen and the hero of the hour, the Captain.

*

'Time for us to go, kids,' said Lexie. 'Nothing else is going to happen down here now. Old Handcock will have quite a bill for that plate glass, I bet!' She seemed to like the idea.

'What are we going to do now?' Lily was reluctant for the adventure to end. Having persuaded herself it was cowardly to hang back, she was now fully committed to a life of adventure.

'Going to introduce you two to our Dad, of course. He probably thinks we've been abducted by them Chinks you was so worried about earlier.' With a giggle, Lexie started leading them back up Bute Street. It was only a little less exciting to Lily than the near-riot she had just witnessed. Ahead of them, Bute Street stretched away out of sight, a long straight backbone supporting the whole dockland area. The left side comprised a terrace of three and four-storey buildings, the ground floors invariably shops, cafés and pubs, with living accommodation or small workshops above them.

Many buildings had first-floor balconies, often sporting parrot cages. 'Don't never listen to what them birds say, unless you want to learn to talk Tiger Bay in one lesson,' said Lexie. 'Most of them come here in the first place with some homeward bounder who spent half the voyage teaching them dirty language in a Cardiff accent.' Lily longed to get closer to them.

The right side of the street was bounded by a stone wall, punctuated with warehouses, behind which ran the railway line that brought in commuting clerks and book-keepers from more salubrious areas to work in the city's commercial heart.

Electric trams ran throughout Cardiff – great wooden vehicles with brass-trimmed interiors that gave a feel of being aboard ship as they creaked and swayed about the busy streets. Double metal tracks ran down either side of Bute Street's central reservation and there were always well-filled trams coming and

going along them. Between the sets of rails, elegant
lamp-posts were ranged, with double wrought-iron
light fixtures just below the overhead tramlines. Bute
Street was almost as bright by night as by day.

Lily, still an innocent when it came to shops, was
itching to look in some of the plate glass windows on
the left-hand side. The first few pleased her mightily.
They were largely food stores, but offering goods she
had never dreamed existed. Exotic vegetables and fruit
were piled in boxes outside the greengrocers', including damp sacks in which whole crops of bean sprouts
had been grown overnight for the Chinese community. The general grocers offered a range of spices that
made her mother's store for Christmas cake-making
look impoverished. At the fishmonger's, a tray of squid,
well past its best, made her recoil in distaste. But all the
while, Lily was dying to know more of it. Her narrow
life in the Valleys was fading faster with every minute
that passed.

Beyond the first rank of shops, they came to more
obscure premises. Lily flitted on, curiosity unabated.
A short, foxy-eyed man was lounging at the door of a
seedy café with a faded sign which said, 'Star of Asia'.
He brightened visibly when he saw Lily, straightened
up and raised a grimy finger, half-mockingly, to the
brim of his bowler hat.

'Well, well, well,' he said. 'What have we here? Nice
bit o' new talent, I'd say. . . Care to step inside for a little
light refreshment, my love?'

Lexie, who had been looking at some vividly-
coloured silk in a shop doorway, was at Lily's side
instantly. 'Sod off, Louis,' she said, never losing her
smile. 'This one's not for sale. She's family.'

'Oh, shit, don't tell Rhys, for God's sake,' said the
man, and hastily withdrew inside the café.

'Who was that?' said Lily, flattered rather than
scared.

'Now if there was ever a real white slaver down here, that'd be him,' said Lexie. 'Name's Louis Fenwick, and that's his café. 'Course, he's the only man in the Bay who do call it a café. . .'

'What d'you mean?'

'Take a look in the window. That's a fair sample of what's on the menu to eat.'

Lily peered through the grimy glass. Inside, beneath two filthy bell jars, languished a couple of piles of aged sandwiches, the mildewed bread curling away to reveal what might once have been cheese. 'Some people say he got 'em wholesale from the left-overs after Queen Victoria's funeral tea,' said Lexie. 'He ent in the food business. Never made a sandwich in his life.'

'How does he keep the café going, then?'

'There's lots of things more profitable than sandwiches – crumpet, for instance.'

'I still don't understand.'

Lexie stood back and looked at her. 'No, of course you don't. . . Well, look in as we go on past.'

They strolled on, slowly, and Lexie made much of bending down to refasten her boot as they drew level with the open door. Lily took a good look inside. The place was in semi-darkness, hardly surprising considering the cavernous size of the room and the filthy condition of the front window. There were no tables and chairs – no furniture of any kind, in fact. Just a long mahogany counter with a few bottles and glasses on it. To the rear of the room she could just make out a wide staircase. In the centre of the floor was an ancient iron contraption on wheels, which she realized was an old railway bogie. No other piece of industrial machinery ever bore such a cargo. Disposed around it were half a dozen girls and women of indeterminate age and assorted nationalities. They wore make-up, applied with sufficient brio to be visible even through the gloom, and they appeared to be dressed in skimpy evening gowns. Even Lily's innocence was not proof against such blatant advertisement.

Shocked and delighted at this evidence of wickedness, she turned back to Lexie. 'Are they what I think they are?'

'Now why else would they be tarted up like that at three o'clock in the afternoon?' said Lexie. 'Yeah, they'm Louis's dishes of the day. They don't vary a lot – that's why he perked up when he saw you. Get something as pretty as you in there and he'd triple his business in ten minutes. Now get a move on, or he'll think we'm interested in giving it a try!'

Lexie was beginning to wish she had packed her two charges aboard a tram, although the journey back to the Anglesey Hotel was little more than half a mile. At this rate it would be midnight before they got there. . . But Lily and Bethan had already crammed in more excitement in an afternoon than they had ever experienced before, and they were beginning to tire. After a few more rounds of questions and long glances at forbidden places, the two girls were willing to be herded back to their uncle's pub.

The Anglesey had a much-used look about it. A middle-sized pub, it catered for the odd clerk and messenger as well as dockers and seamen, so it was less rough than many similar establishments. The supporting wall beneath the bay window was clad in decorative panelling, and two ornately-carved columns pretended to support the doors and pediment.

The front window proclaimed the Anglesey's popularity with continentals. A succession of posters announced repetitively: 'LAGER BEER, THREE HA'-PENCE A PINT', and for those with more homely tastes, 'STRONG BEER, A PENNY A PINT' and 'BLACK BEER, THREE HA'PENCE'. Painted on the window itself were the words, 'WORTHINGTON'S PALE ALE IN BOTTLE', and on the plaster rendering between the first floor windows, 'HANCOCK'S ALES AND STOUT, IN CASK AND IN BOTTLE'.

'You seem to sell everything,' said Lily.

'Brewers pays us to put it up there,' Lexie told her.

There were two doors, one each side of the display window. 'Right-hand one,' said Lexie. 'Dad will still be in the bar. The other one do go up to our living quarters.'

Lily had expected to dislike the pub. Her mother's view of such establishments as dens of iniquity had been drummed into her from an early age. The Anglesey's interior was a pleasant surprise. At this time of day it was not crowded, so the smoke of hundreds of pipes and cigarettes had dispersed. Flagstone floors and thick walls ensured that the place remained cool, even on a hot afternoon like today, and the faint smell of beer was refreshing after the arid dryness outside. On balance, Lily decided she liked it better than chapel.

Then she saw Rhys Walters and again her heart lurched with almost-recognition, thanks to his resemblance to Evan. As she gazed at him, he glanced up, and her appearance seemed to have a similar effect on him.

'No need to ask whose daughter you are!' he said, grinning and coming round the bar counter to greet the girls. 'You'm the spitting image of our Evan – of our mother, too, come to that! Welcome to Tiger Bay.'

'Don't call it that, Dad, stick to Butetown – she's jumpy enough already!' said Lexie. 'She's thinking we have riots and arrests every day, with a little bit of murder thrown in for good measure.'

Rhys, who had been introducing himself to Bethan, turned back to his daughter at once. 'Oh, aye, I heard about the trouble down Handcock's. Serve the old bugger right – what he do pay wouldn't keep a flea alive.'

'Any news about Tupper yet?'

Rhys laughed. 'When have you ever known me not have the latest? They've served sixteen summonses on him, and he's up in front of the magistrate tomorrow morning. He'll be in his element. With his gift of the gab, they'll never stop him speaking his piece, and it'll all go in the paper.'

Lexie was getting slightly uneasy. 'Dad, it's ever so quiet out there. . . You know how they usually are after a bit of a go like that – all in the pubs, singing and carrying on as if they've just won a war.'

'Why? Ent they doing that now?'

'Look at this place. What d'you think?'

'Oh, stop getting nervous. You know we'm often this quiet at the tail end of the afternoon. It'll be the pubs down the bottom end as'll get the trade now, down closer to Handcock's.'

'No, Dad, they'm all as quiet as you. I noticed while we was walking back up. I don't know where they've all gone.'

Rhys shrugged dismissively. 'Nothing we can do about it, so let's wait and see. Now, what can I get you young ladies?. . . Wait, I know!' and he disappeared below the bar. 'A little something special to welcome the family!' he said, emerging with a bottle of champagne and four long-stemmed glasses.

'I-is that really champagne?' asked Lily. 'I only ever saw a picture of it once, in the paper, and Mam said that was wicked.'

'You do not amaze me, my dear!' said her uncle. 'Doubtless, your mam is a very worthy woman, but that don't mean she's right about everything. A little bit of this stuff raises the spirits and improves the digestion, and as we've got a good supper for you both tonight, you'd better get this down you now.'

The golden fluid frothed into the glasses and the girls drank to their own arrival with stars in their eyes. Even the cynical Lexie was slightly impressed. 'First time I ever saw you open a bottle of bubbly when someone else wasn't paying,' she told her father.

'First time I've had family here, ennit? Blood's thicker than champagne, Lex, even if it's a lot cheaper. Cheers, my flowers, and I hope you'll be very happy here.'

Looking around at the twinkling glass and brass, savouring the cool, intoxicating hoppy smell, Lily decided it was very likely she would be.

CHAPTER EIGHTEEN

By THE TIME they had finished their champagne, Bethan was nodding drowsily, although it was still quite early.

'I think you pair have had enough for today,' said Rhys, 'what with leaving home an' all. Better take 'em upstairs, Lex. Don't worry about the bar tonight. See the girls is all right... Oh, yes, I just remembered, you little madam! Their boxes is up in the living room. And next time I do give you enough to pay for the cab, p'raps you'll let the bugger have it and not send him round to me for more.'

His smile removed any sting from the remark and Lexie grinned back at him. 'All in a good cause, Dad – admit it, you'd have been disappointed in me if I had paid him.'

'Get on with you, before I take it back!'

Lexie shepherded her cousins back out into the street to the front door of the living quarters.

Upstairs, she explained their sleeping arrangements. 'There's plenty of room up here – used to be a proper hotel at one time – but Dad do still like to keep a couple of bedrooms in case an old mate turns up. I've given you a little room of your own, Bethan, and Lily can share with me.' She turned hastily to Lily: 'I thought Bethan would often be in bed before us so it would be better than you two sharing.'

'Yes, that's fine,' said Lily, delighted at the thought of a friend of her own age to gossip with and confide in – though what she would confide she could not imagine.

Once their meagre belongings had been stowed away and they had eaten an early supper, Bethan was ready for bed. Lily and Lexie sat talking afterwards in the big living room that overlooked Bute Street. Lily was beginning to think of bed herself, when she heard some sort of commotion outside. It faded, then swelled again, gradually drawing closer to the Anglesey.

'What on earth is that?' she asked Lexie.

'I got an awful feeling I know.' Lexie stood up and went over to the window, raising the sash and looking down into Bute Street. She sighed. 'Yeah, thought so. I knew that lot was set on more trouble this afternoon. Here comes Fred Karno's Army!'

Lily rushed over to look at what was happening. From the direction of the Pier Head, a ragged procession was approaching. It comprised a couple of hundred men, many carrying makeshift torches of pitch-coated wood, others armed with staves, blackjacks and nail-studded lengths of rope. 'Talk about Attila an' his Huns!' said Lexie, contempt dripping from her voice.

'What're they up to?' Lily was far more impressed.

'Give you three guesses. Anyway, we'll find out in a minute – look.' She gestured in the other direction, and for the first time, Lily noticed that the police sergeant she had seen at Handcock's that afternoon was standing in the road with three burly constables.

As the girls saw the police, the sergeant called out to the marchers, 'All right, lads, that's far enough! Time you was going about your business, ennit? And I don't mean up City Hall, neither.'

'Out the way, sarge!' bellowed a brutish-looking type at the front of the procession. 'We haven't got nothing against you, but we'm going to get the Captain out, and if we has to do it over you lot, we will.'

'Don't make me laugh, Evans! Tupper's leading a strike – a seamen's strike, remember? I know you – you've never done a day's work in your life and the closest you've been to the sea is to puke in the Alexandra Dock. Now, sling your hook and get off back to the pub, before I gets cross.'

But the marchers were in no mood to be intimidated. They made a threatening, low, collective sound, like a predatory animal stirring itself. The police sergeant seemed to settle himself more solidly into his boots, ready for the onslaught. Then a figure detached itself from the shadows below the Anglesey's living-room window, and moved across to the police line.

'Hmm, that's Tom Parry, one of the Captain's men. Bet he's telling Sergeant Paine that lot is nothing to do with him. . . Hope he do make Paine see sense. They'll mince him if he don't get out of the way.'

Whatever Parry said seemed to work. The sergeant shrugged and motioned his men out of the road. 'That's better,' said Lexie. 'They'm too few and too far from home to make any sort of stand against that bunch. There's enough bobbies up City Hall to send 'em all packing. Tell you what – if Tupper's on tomorrow, let's get a tram up there and see what's going on!'

Lily looked dubiously down at the wild men who were streaming past in the street below. 'Ent you scared of them, Lexie?'

'Yeah – scared enough to stay out of their way. We're going up to watch them, not join in. Come on, let's get off to bed now.'

Half Butetown turned out the following day to see what the magistrate would do to Edward Tupper. When Lexie and her cousins arrived, the marchers

of the previous night were ranged in front of the
crowd of spectators. But along with the rabble, Lexie
began pointing out substantial numbers of respectable
working men from the docks. 'If they don't let him go,
there's really going to be trouble,' she said.

At that point, a couple of men came out of the court's
public gallery. One of them waved his arms at the mob,
and yelled, 'They'm putting him away, men! Won't
even hear what he has to say for a week. He've been
taken back to the cells.'

Once again, Lily heard the low animal rumble that
had come from last night's crowd, but today it was
wilder and deeper. She caught sight of the union
official who had defused the confrontation between
police and demonstrators the previous evening. He
was talking to a small group, clearly workers or union
officers like himself. Within moments, he turned from
them towards a more disciplined-looking section of the
crowd.

'That's it, lads!' he called. 'We got it! The dockers
is coming out with us, as from now – God bless the
Captain!'

An uneven cheer from the true strikers was half-
swamped by the rising roar of the rabble. The trouble-
maker who had confronted Sergeant Paine outside the
Anglesey materialized in the front rank. 'God may bless
him, but he'll need us to get him out!' he cried. 'We'm
not leaving him locked up in there, are we, boys?'

Tom Parry tried to intervene. The last thing the
union wanted was a violent demonstration up here,
miles from the seat of the industrial dispute. 'No, wait!
Let the law take its course. Captain Tupper can handle
that without our help. He wants us. . .'

But his voice was drowned as the mob's low roar
became a full-throated bellow. Bludgeons, clubs with
knives and even open razor blades fixed in the ends,
broken bottles and scores of other makeshift weapons

appeared in hundreds of hands. The unionists had been in the process of turning to march on the docks. Now they moved back. Both groups converged as they swirled forward towards City Hall.

Parry and his colleagues were dashing about like madmen, trying to make the more disciplined unionists calm down. But the crowd's mood was too explosive. Police whistles sounded all around them and the constables on duty around the civic buildings formed a human barrier to prevent the rioters' passage. There would have been too few to stem the attack in any other location, but this was just yards from the city's main police station. Within seconds, two platoons of mounted police were counter-attacking the flanks of the mob, and all hell broke loose.

Once the pressure on the foot police was relieved, they set about the nearest rioters with their truncheons, and by the time they had made a few arrests the crowd's aggression had cooled considerably. Someone on the police side had the sense not to arrest Parry and his two stewards, and now they set to calming down the genuine strikers and turning them away from the law courts. It was all over only minutes after it had begun, but with a scattering of cloth caps, weapons, bloodstains and someone's front teeth at the foot of the City Hall steps as grisly mementoes.

Parry was starting to lead his members back to the docks to enforce the union's decision. 'God almighty, there'll be blood on the moon down there when the ship-owners get their bully-boys out,' whispered Lexie. 'Come on, Lil, back down the Bay – it's all over up here now.'

But Lily was rooted to the spot. 'Look at that man and girl over there, Lexie – what on earth are they doing?' she said.

'This ent no time to be gawping at the sights, girl – oh, hang on, I do know her! That's the other Lily I was mentioning, and I think that's her brother. God knows what they'm doing!'

The couple who had piqued Lily's curiosity were grappling with a handsome wooden box, which the girl seemed to be supporting while the man turned it round. He had been pointing it at the rioters throughout the disturbance, and now was apparently trying to turn it in the direction of the departing marchers.

'Lily May! What are you doing? What's that thing, some sort of gun in a box?'

The girl was about twenty, slim, pale-faced and boyish-looking, with a mass of wavy brown hair. 'Oh, hullo, Lexie. Me and Jim's trying to make a moving picture of the riot. . .can't stop. . .'

At that point the man made an impatient sound and stopped winding at the side of the box. 'It's no good,' he said. 'Too much movement spread too thin – don't think I've got anything worth showing. No point in doing any more now.' He propped the machine on a low wall and started pulling a padded leather case around it. Then he seemed to realize for the first time that his sister was in the middle of a conversation. He glanced at the girls, still more interested in his equipment than in them. When he saw Lexie, his manner changed completely.

'Jim,' said the girl, 'let me introduce you to my friend Lexie Walters and. . .?'

'And my cousins, Lily and Bethan Walters,' said Lexie. 'Lily, this is Lily May Haggar and her brother Jim. They make moving pictures.'

Lily was too impressed to think of anything to say, but Jim was ready to do all the talking. He was giving Lexie his undivided attention. 'Miss Walters,' he said, 'I've got a film drama in my mind which could use you to great effect – I need someone with your exotic looks. Would you be interested?'

Lexie shouted with laughter. 'This colour ent exotic

down the Bay, Mr Haggar – there's thousands of us down there!'

That did not put him off. 'I'm not a Cardiff man, myself,' he said, 'and I don't know Butetown at all. Take my word for it, where these pictures are shown, you'll be strikingly unusual!'

'I'll take your word for it, chum, but I think our Dad would have to give his permission first – I'm only fourteen, see. Tell us where you do live and I'll ask him – or you could drop him a line.'

'Very well, Miss Walters. Just a moment. . .'

He took down her address in a leather-bound notebook, then gave her his business card. Lexie glanced at it. 'Aberdare, eh? Come a long way to take pictures of a street fight, haven't you?'

'We weren't really expecting much, to tell the truth,' he said. 'We haven't done any news films for years, but our competitors are very keen on it, so I was getting in a little practice. Thought they might release Captain Tupper today, and I hoped just to film him coming out of court.'

'Well, there you are, you wasn't wasting your time, was you? What you got there's a lot more exciting than a man walking down some steps.'

'Yes, but sometimes exciting real life events come up looking terribly dull on the screen. We'll have to see. . . Now, we must be going. Got to put the film on a train. Hope to see you again, Miss Walters.'

A group of stragglers from the demonstration eddied towards them and they lost sight of the Haggars. Lily, impressed yet again by Lexie's knowledge of the world, said, 'How d'you know her, then?'

'Oh, accident, that's all. I went on the kids' Whitsun Treat to Barry Island in June and they was making a film down there. Not that brother, her father, that time. I went up the fair with her. She's a few years older than us, but she do love the rides and she didn't have anybody else to go on them with. Fancy bumping into her again!'

'But d'you really think they'll put you in the pictures, Lexie?'

The other girl laughed. 'It'd be lovely if they did, but they'll probably forget all about it by the time they get back to the station. Come on, let's go and see whether the fun have started down the Bay yet.'

But for then, it appeared to be all over. When they arrived back at the Anglesey Hotel, Rhys was waiting at the pub door, scowling blackly. 'Where the bloody hell have you been?' he demanded. 'What would I have told our Evan if something had happened to these two?'

Lexie gave him an injured look. 'Christ, Dad, it's only a little court case, nothing to get excited about!' she said.

'A little court case, with half the thugs in the Bay hanging round the outside in case the verdict went the wrong way? You've never been green before, Lexie. Stop pretending you are now. And get up them stairs – if you're watching the fun from now on, it'll be from a distance!'

He watched the trio troop sheepishly past him through the door to the living quarters, then slammed it behind them before returning to the bar. Upstairs, Lexie tiptoed over to the window and peered down. After a few moments, she said, 'Right, all clear. Four men have just gone in – he'll be too busy serving them for a while to look out. Come on, let's get going!'

Lily did not argue. By now she had forgotten her timidity in wanting to see what the mob were up to. They tiptoed back downstairs, and were just about to leave when Lexie noticed that Bethan was crying quietly. 'Hey, pet, what's the matter? Missing your mam?' she asked, genuinely concerned.

Bethan bowed her head and muttered, in a voice choked with shame, 'No-no, I'm frightened, Lexie. Have I got to go?'

'God love us, of course not! Just don't tell our Dad where we are if he do come up. Say. . .say we went out to get some sweets, just round the corner. Quick, shut the door, quiet like, behind us, then off you go back upstairs. You can see a fair bit out of the window if you want to.'

Moments later, the two girls were back out in Bute Street, heading south. This section was as ominously quiet as it had been the previous afternoon, but before long they began to see the results of Tupper's court appearance.

About half-way from the pub to the Pier Head, the windows of a Chinese laundry had been shattered. Shards of glass littered the pavement and the frightened proprietor was just emerging to try and board up the opening. Somewhere in the distance the mob was baying for blood. All around there were signs of hastily-closed businesses, as the small tradesmen of the dockland area rushed to protect their livelihoods. The trouble might start with victimization of the Chinese, but the older inhabitants remembered other riots where the desire for plunder quickly overtook any real grievances. Today they were taking no chances.

The union members were still attempting to mount an organized campaign, but they were heavily outnumbered. The port of Cardiff had never developed a united labour force and the men who worked there were invariably the losers in labour disputes. Now the dockers and general port workers knew they wanted redress, but could see no way to get it without smashing the property of those they regarded as enemies. First it was the turn of the Chinese, then the bosses. Edward Tupper had a talent for controlling such lawless outbreaks, but he was behind bars for a week.

Suddenly, close at hand, there was a loud crash and a cheer. Lily started violently. 'Where are they? It sounds as if they'm right by us, but I can't see a soul.'

'Over the wall,' said Lexie. 'They must be running riot along the dock – the warehouses along there are chock-a-block with booze. Bet they've broken in.' As if to verify her words, a column of oily smoke began to rise above the wall. The crashes and bangs continued, accompanied by tuneless singing now, rather than cheers. 'They'll have broke into the liquor stores, I bet,' said Lexie.

For the first time since they met, Lily saw her cousin looking frightened. She offered a method of escape without loss of face. 'D'you think, p'raps, we should go back – you know, in case your dad do find out we'm gone?'

Lexie managed a shaky smile. 'Yes, better had. Come on, then, let's run.'

She grabbed Lily's hand and began to sprint back in the direction they had come from. Moments later, Lily was panting. 'What's all the rush? I thought you was the one who wanted to see everything.'

'Not when they'm mad drunk. There's enough spirits the other side of that wall to send the whole docks crazy. Keep moving, for God's sake!'

They had covered a couple of hundred yards, but Bute Street seemed endless now. *At least it's still empty up here*, Lily told herself, clutching at straws. At that moment, a gate on the dock side of the street was pushed open and half a dozen men scampered out. Two of them were bruised about the face, and all seemed drunk. The leader was waving an open whisky bottle and spilling the contents all over the place. The others all seemed to have bottles either in their pockets or in their hands. For a moment they reeled about the street, getting their bearings after their headlong rush across the railway track. Then two of them saw Lexie and Lily.

'Wey-hey, lookathat – bits a skirt!' shouted one. 'Can't ask for the wrong thing today. . . Quick, Jack, don't lose 'em!' At that the whole gang began advancing towards the girls.

Lexie had stopped in her tracks the moment the men appeared. Now she stood in the middle of the road, still clutching Lily's hand. 'Don't let them separate us, Lil, and if they lays a finger on you, go for the eyes and the balls, all right?'

Lily glanced at her cousin and found her own panic draining away. Lexie might be frightened, but she was completely controlled, and prepared to fight to defend herself. Lily studied the way she was standing, relaxed, weight slightly forward on the balls of the feet, free hand outstretched. It was not the stance of a victim. She took a deep breath and tried to emulate Lexie. As she did so, there was a rush of heavy boots from the nearest side streets, followed by a clamour of voices, and the louts in front of them broke and ran. A contingent of policemen erupted from Patrick Street, followed almost as quickly by a dozen Chinese. Three constables pursued the looters back into the dockyard, while the sergeant came over to the terrified girls.

Lexie, always reluctant to show fear, gave him a bright smile and said, 'I've heard of police protection, but *Chinese* police protection? Must be the latest thing, I s'pose!'

'Lexie Walters, I might have known you'd be out where you shouldn't be! Your father must be weak in the head leaving you on the streets at a time like this!'

Abruptly the smile left her face. 'Don't let on, Sergeant Gray – he'll kill me if he do find out – and my cousin, too.'

'Oh, so you sneaked away, did you? Won't you never listen when you'm told to do something? There's been somebody killed this afternoon, and God knows how many injured. Have you ever seen Bute Street so empty? And even so, you'm prepared to go out sightseeing.

Your father should strap you within an inch of your life.'

'He just might if you do tell him how you found us. Oh, please don't, sergeant! I've learned my lesson, honest.'

The big policeman finally grinned at her. 'You'll never learn your lesson if you live to be a hundred,' he said. 'You'm too cheeky by half. Now look, we've got to take these Chinks back home safe, and it's down the other way, so I can only spare two constables to go up with you. If I promise not to tell your father, will you promise me that you'll stay indoors till all this nonsense is over?'

Lexie nodded. 'Tell you the truth, once I'm back inside today, you wouldn't get me out again with a tin-opener!' she said. Then, overcome by curiosity, she added, 'Why was those Chinamen running after you when you come to save us? I'd a thought they'd have run away.'

'You daft little devil, we'm not arresting them, we'm protecting them. A gang of coal trimmers had them locked in one of the sweatshops round Hannah Street and they was threatening to burn it down. They know when they'm well off – which is more than I can say for you two. Now – home!'

He gestured to two of the biggest policemen, who fell into step on either side of the girls and marched them back up to the Anglesey. When they got within a hundred yards of the pub, Lexie began trying to persuade the men to leave them. 'Honest, we'll be quite safe now,' she said. 'We can see our front door from here, look!'

One of the constables smiled at her. 'If we didn't see you in, our lives wouldn't be worth tuppence with the sergeant. You get delivered to your door.'

'But our Dad will see – and Sergeant Gray promised he wouldn't tell. . .'

'And he won't, neither, but we'm not leaving you here

just because you'm frightened of your dad. That's your business.'

In any case, her pleas were in vain. Knowing his daughter's propensity for mischief, Rhys had gone upstairs only minutes earlier to check on the girls, and had discovered Bethan, alone, weeping distractedly at the sight of the huge cloud of black smoke which was now pouring out of the two warehouses that had been set on fire. He was just taking a last look around the street before sending someone to find a policeman.

Seeing him there, Lily closed her eyes, feeling sick. If that were Evan instead of Rhys, no one in the family would escape unscathed. . .

But it was not Evan. Catching sight of his daughter, Rhys shouted, 'Oh, thank God!' and hurried to meet them. He flung his arms around Lexie, hugging and kissing her as if she had just been saved from a ship-wreck. 'You silly little bitch!' he murmured as he held her, 'don't never do nothing like that again, all right?'

Lexie was crying now. 'Promise, Dad. I'm ever so sorry. . .didn't think it'd turn so nasty.' Then she brightened. 'Bet you never thought to see a Walters coming home on the right side of the law, though!' She winked at the handsomer of the two constables, and made her escape inside while her father was still feeling too relieved to punish her.

Trailing along behind her, Lily heard the other policeman say, 'You'll have to watch that one in a year or two, Rhys – she's pure jail bait.'

'Year or two, hell,' said Rhys. 'I been having to watch her since her tenth birthday!' And with that, the door slammed on the most exciting day Lily had ever known.

CHAPTER NINETEEN

T HROUGHOUT THAT NIGHT the riots rumbled on, mercifully remote from the Anglesey. Next morning, Rhys still refused to let them out, so Lexie fretted about in the upstairs living room. Eventually, about noon, her father came to tell them the worst was over. Edward Tupper had been released on bail. On his way out of City Hall, he was already saying the magistrates knew he was the only man who could control the mob.

Apparently he was right. Sporadic outbreaks of violence continued in Cardiff, with bands of port workers besieging a local brewery and a sweet factory until the workers there agreed to a sympathy strike. Meanwhile other trades, from brewers' draymen to the Cardiff Jewish Amalgamated Society of Tailors, were coming out voluntarily. The dispute appeared set for a long run. Tupper moved on to strengthen the cause in Newport and Bristol. Without his charismatic leadership, the unions were not strong enough to hold the strike in Cardiff. The ship-owners and railway companies refused to talk, and the strikers gave in and returned to work. When the dispute ended, Cardiff was the worst-paid port on the Bristol Channel.

Lily and Bethan were still young enough to adjust to almost anything, and the violent events of 18 July were over so quickly that they soon became less important to the girls than their complete change of surroundings. Tiger Bay had a marked effect on both of them.

For the first time in her life, Lily was learning to breathe freely. Until now, her mother had been at her elbow every moment, telling her to see she was a good girl and did nothing to offend God or mankind. With minimal effort, Margaret Ann had managed to imply that life was to be endured, and that exhilaration, pleasure and excitement were sinful. Enforced attendance at chapel services twice every Sunday and religious youth clubs during the week reinforced her mother's austere teaching. Long ago, Lily had decided she must be a creature of irremediable wickedness, for in spite of them all she was often excited and exhilarated. Now she had been dropped into a family where comfort and pleasure were all that mattered, where affection was demonstrated by flaring rows and passionate embraces, where insults were returned tenfold and then forgotten in a rush of amusement, and she found it suited her far better. Church was never mentioned, except when Rhys took a disparaging swipe at the people he called God-botherers. He swore like a trooper and never seemed to notice that Lexie's language was as colourful as his own. No subject seemed taboo, and sometimes he made remarks to Lexie about her precocious behaviour with men that made Lily blush to the roots of her hair.

Nevertheless, she enjoyed every minute. Lexie was her idol – a fact which did not escape the other girl and which pleased her mightily. They became fast friends, lying awake in their shared double bed late into the night, while Lexie told stories of Butetown, or recounted her fantasies and ambitions. By day, with money wheedled from the ever-indulgent Rhys, they set about transforming Lily's tiny and childish wardrobe into something akin to Lexie's – an unlikely mixture of Champs-Élysées and Cardiff waterfront.

Lily was a good basic seamstress – no daughter of Margaret Ann's could be anything else – and Lexie was a stylist of near genius. Her own clothes somehow contrived to be within the limits of what a young girl could wear – but only just. She stuck to the conventional skirt length for under-sixteens, a couple of inches above the ankle, but that was because it suited her. She had lovely legs and the glimpse of slender ankles below a flurry of petticoats was riveting to any man who saw her. She looked wonderful in white, a popular colour for girls in their early teens, but she also wore brilliant yellow and pale green, both of which showed off her flawless coffee-coloured skin and black hair to perfection.

'I do love that sunshine yellow. D'you think I could have something in it?' asked Lily.

'Can if you like, but it'd be like sour milk on you, love. With your skin and hair, you want something deeper – a nice vivid marine blue, p'raps.'

Lily sighed. 'Oh, I wish I had your colouring! It looks so wonderful in them light frocks. . .'

For the first time ever, Lexie turned on her. 'Don't you never say that to me again, Lily! You could have every yellow dress in my cupboard if I could have your skin. You don't know what you're talking about!'

Seeing angry tears in her eyes, Lily was bewildered. 'What have I said wrong? You do always joke about it – and you know you'm beautiful, far prettier than me or Bethan'll ever be.'

Lexie stifled a sob. 'Yeah, but the joking's all show. I'll never amount to nothing outside the Bay. I'm coloured, Lily, and nobody's ever going to let me forget it, unless I spend my whole life down here barmaiding in my old man's pub. I want more than that.'

'I never realized. . . I told you, I'd never seen any coloured people before we come here.'

'No, that's the trouble. If I do go somewhere like the Valleys, they'll all stare at me like a freak, and if I go

up the town, or over the posh parts of Bristol, where
they've seen plenty of my kind, they'll call me names,
and worse. . .'

'You wasn't like this a few weeks ago. What have happened?'

Lexie shrugged irritably. 'Oh, I don't know; just getting older and wiser, I 'xpect. . .no, dammit, I do know. I
went up St Mary Street, shopping, on my own the other
day, remember, when Dad took you and Bethan round
to the school? I felt great. I was wearing that yellow
frock you like so much, and people was looking at me,
admiring, like. And then a bloody great toff, reeking of
cigars and whisky, staggered across and caught me by
the arm. "Hullo, Blackie," he says. "Coming with me,
then? I fancies a drop of hot chocolate today!" I shook
him off – he was too tipsy to be any real trouble – but
oh, Lily, the shame of it!' She was crying openly now.
'In front of all them smart people, me thinking I was
one of them, ready to take on the world, and that – that
ape, could just put me back in the jungle with his dirty
mouth! I'll never get up into that world, never!'

She buried her head on her cousin's shoulder and
sobbed as if her heart would break. After a while,
when she was calmer, she said, 'I'm so glad you'm
here. I can't tell our Dad. He'd blame himself. . .and
he'd start thumping anybody who so much as looked
at me the wrong way. At least you do listen, even if you
can't understand how I feel.'

'Oh, but I do, Lexie. It's not just your skin as stops
you fitting in. Being poor is just as bad.'

Lexie was sceptical. 'People can't see if you'm poor.'

'That's where you're wrong. Them two cotton frocks
and the one pair of good boots I brought with me is
all I've got fit to wear. When I was home, our Mam
would keep them packed away for fear they'd wear out
and I wouldn't have nothing good for Sunday school.
I used to go round in one of our Gareth's old knitted

jumpers, all darned at the elbows, and a cut-down skirt of Mam's, and. . .and a pair of boy's hobnail boots. It was awful, Lex.'

The other girl forgot her own problems, horrified at the picture Lily was painting. 'But I thought you was so respectable!'

'Oh, we are. It's not like the Bay, with only the real slum kids down Rat Island dressed like that. None of the big families have got two ha'pennies to rub together, and some of the youngest ones don't have any boots at all till they'm school age. They're all ever so respectable, though, and respectful, too! If the doctor's wife or the minister's mother do come round and pat us on the head, we've got to be grateful for their kids' hand-me-downs. Mind you, they're usually nicer than our new stuff, but if I had a choice I'd go naked rather than wear the things!' Her voice rang with scorn.

As she talked, Lily began realizing how much she despised attitudes which until now she had accepted as normal. 'I'm finished with it all!' she announced. 'And if people outside the Bay do sneer at you for your colour and me for my boy's boots, bugger 'em. We'll stop here for good!'

All trace of Lexie's tears had vanished now. She was laughing. 'Lily Walters, welcome to Tiger Bay. You've just said your first swear word. My mam would be proud of you – but yours wouldn't.'

Lily gasped and clapped her hand to her lips, then she started giggling, too. 'I'll just have to watch out that she never hears me doing it, won't I?'

Bethan, too young to be inside the magic circle, watched from the edge, entranced, as Lexie coached her sister to join the exotic adult world which seethed around them. She was somewhat isolated at present, but the following month both she and Lily were to start attending the local school. Lily would only be there for a year, but Bethan was likely to be a pupil long enough to make plenty of friends.

'You'm only a few months older than me, Lexie,' said Lily. 'How come you'm not in school next year?'

'Let's say they was as glad to lose me as I was to get lost!' said her cousin. 'I wasn't learning nothing, and Dad was making a real pig's breakfast of keeping the house tidy. He had one woman after another walk out on him and in the end I said I'd had enough aunties to last me a lifetime, so we made a bargain. I left school early to look after the place, on condition he kept his love life away from the Anglesey. It have worked a real treat for six months.'

'You know, I'm still amazed that our Mam let me and Bethan come down here. You'd think she'd know some o' this, at least.'

'I know, I asked Dad about that. Uncle Evan told him that ever since he first knew your mam, she said she preferred him to keep this side of the family a closed book. . .something about the pub, and her parents being Temperance. He used to come down and see Dad regular – this was before I was born, mind – so he always kept in touch. But he and your mam never talked about his bad Butetown brother!

'When he was working over the Rhymney Valley all those years, he used to come down more often – but from what I do hear, he and your mam wasn't talking much about anything in them days. Anyhow, I saw him now and again all the time I was growing up. Dad was always telling him that he or any of you could come down if there was ever any trouble, and now here you are.'

Lily was intrigued about this hitherto unknown life of her father's. 'Did our John Dan and Billie ever come with him?' she asked.

'Oh, aye, and on their own, after – well, you know –
after he went back to Abercarn. Billie have promised
he'll come here when he do get leave from the Army,
so you'll see him again.'

'It's funny to have brothers you hardly know,' said
Lily. 'I was only five when he went to work in Brithdir,
so really I only ever saw him when he come home on
Saturdays. And I saw even less of John Dan.'

'Now he's getting married, and you'm down here,
p'raps we can go up and see him some time in the
autumn.'

'Lexie, I been meaning to ask you. Where d'you get
the money to do all this gadding about, and have nice
clothes an' all? You'm like millionaires compared with
us.'

'Pretty poor millionaires! But you're right, I s'pose,
we do live well. First, this is a good pub, and Dad's
a sharp landlord. Second, there's only me and him –
no tribe of brothers and sisters like your lot. On top
of that, Dad would gamble on two flies crawling up
a wall – and nine times out of ten he'd know which
one had been nobbled beforehand! He'd die rich if he
was careful, but I'm happy to say he don't know the
meaning of the word.' She lowered her voice. 'Truth
to tell, he's a bit of a villain, and I wouldn't have him
any other way.'

Lily swiftly grew fond of her Uncle Rhys. She had
always adored her father, but was rather frightened
of his violent temper and wary of the moodiness he
showed to all his children with the exception of Rose.
Rhys was like her father with none of the complications. He had remained free, had travelled the world
as a seaman, and had come ashore with enough saved
to take this pub. Now he could afford to be everyone's
friend and a perfect uncle.

*

The seamen's strike ended and gradually Butetown set-tled back to its normal boisterous life.

'Now we've got your clothes fixed, we'll see what's going on outside,' said Lexie, towards the end of August. 'Things'll warm up a bit, with everything back to normal. You don't want your life to be just school and pub, after all.'

Lily considered the aspects of Butetown life she had seen so far. 'I can't imagine there's anything we can go to,' she said, nervously.

'Don't worry, flower, I won't take you down the House of Blazes!' This was the local name for the Rothesay Castle, a pub notorious for the potency of its rough cider and the vicious fights that frequently broke out among women drinkers. 'There's a good social life in these parts for respectable young ladies with charitable natures. Our Dad'll have to come with us, mind. . .'

That reassured Lily rather than putting her off. 'Where are we going then?'

'Dancing with sailors, girl – there's nothing like it!'

For once, Lexie was not letting them in for trouble. There was an officers' social club, strictly Temperance, attached to the seamen's mission in the docks, and twice a month the organizers put on a dance where the men got a chance to talk to and dance with pretty girls. There were plenty of part-time philanthropists around to see that was all they did, and enough of the locals, like Rhys Walters, were sufficiently relaxed to let their daughters act as dancing partners. Rhys himself took the evening off when Lexie went to the dances, accompanied her and spent the evening picking up gossip among the other volunteers and visiting ships' officers.

So it was that in the late summer and autumn of 1911, Lily Walters acquired a lifelong addiction to dancing. Lexie drilled her to perfection in all the steps she would need – 'No use relying on your partner, he often haven't got his land legs back yet for walking, leave alone dancing,' she said.

She did the seamen an injustice. Some of them were clumsy and inexpert, but many enjoyed dancing as much as the girls, and they knew before going to the club that they would be given no opportunity for more libertine activity. Soon Lily was dancing well enough to be an asset to any ballroom.

In September, Lily was jolted out of this artificially-adult world and back into the classroom, when she and Bethan finally started their studies at South Church Street school.

'It'll be a bit beneath you, really, Lil,' said Lexie. 'The bright ones goes off to high school at eleven or twelve, and what's left over is mainly dimwits or troublemakers like me. But put up with it this year and then you can forget it for good.'

Lily refrained from telling her cousin that the standard was quite high enough for her. Margaret Ann had never seen much advantage in sending girls to school when they only went and got married as soon as they grew up, so although Lily had officially attended the local elementary school full time, she seldom completed a full week. There was always a pile of laundry to be done for a few coppers, or errands to be run for her mother while Margaret Ann was attending some worthy gathering of chapel women. This summer there had been the added disincentive of Margaret Ann's shame at any of her family appearing in public while the gossip was still going the rounds about Rose and her frightful injuries. Lily had always been an avid reader, and her brother Gareth willingly brought books for her when he went to the workmen's institute. She loved light novels and anything historical, so she was relatively well-informed and was good at writing and spelling. But her mathematical knowledge had never progressed much from reciting tables and mastering the basics of mental arithmetic.

Now, she found a tough school with dedicated teachers, who managed to drum into her an understanding and enthusiasm for geography, and to improve her maths and general knowledge. She was grateful to them for their efforts, but knew that no one would ever turn her into a genius.

It was different with Bethan. Within a few weeks of her starting in the scholarship class, her form teacher called to see Rhys. When he introduced himself, Rhys grinned wickedly and said, 'Know you already, remember? You was the one who begged me to stop my daughter shouting out, "Hey my handsome, give us a kiss" every time you stood up to read the lesson in assembly. Don't time fly?'

Edgar Roberts blushed and looked away. He had hoped Rhys would not remember the incident, which was graven on his soul. Doggedly, he returned to the reason for his visit. 'It's about your niece, Mr Walters – Bethan. I think we need to discuss her future.'

'Oh, Christ, don't say she've been shouting, "Hey handsome, give us a kiss!" They do start younger every year, don't they?'

'No, Mr Walters. Bethan's behaviour is exemplary. It's quite another matter. She is also a child of exceptional intelligence. Until now, I gather her schooling has been somewhat patchy, but in less than a month she has caught up with the general class level and now she seems to be pulling ahead. She's bright, very bright. She should get a scholarship to the High School without too much trouble.'

'Well, fancy that then! Always did say the girls in our family had more brains than the boys! Wonderful. Why d'you need to ask me about it?'

'I – er – understand that her stay with you might not be permanent. If it is not, there's little purpose in us preparing and entering her for the examination. If she gets a place and then leaves without taking it up, it might deprive one of her classmates of a similar chance.'

Rhys's face had darkened as the schoolmaster spoke. That morning he had received a letter from Evan. Judging by its tone, there was little chance of either of his nieces returning to Abercarn in the foreseeable future. 'Don't worry,' he said, 'she'll be here for a couple of years at least. Is that all that was bothering you?'

'Ah – no, not entirely. It's a little. . .er. . .delicate. Are you temporarily responsible for her. . .er. . .*in loco parentis?*'

'Come on, mun, talk English. If you're saying am I her guardian till she goes home, yes. Why?'

'You might not be aware that there are several levels of scholarship to grammar schools. We always aim for the full fees and books awards, naturally, but many able children win a fees-paid place only.'

'That'd be good enough for our Bethan, I'm sure.'

'Unfortunately, Mr Walters, that entails someone paying for the books – no small expenditure over five or more years – then there's uniform and any extras which arise. It can be terribly expensive, and you may not wish. . .that is, her parents may be unable to afford. . .' Abashed, he tailed off, seeming to shrink under Rhys's belligerent gaze.

Rhys let him stew for a moment, then presented his most villainous grin. 'And wicked publicans down Bute Street ent known for their respect for the world of knowledge, is that it, Mr Roberts?'

'N-no, no, sir – you misunderstand me! I simply thought that as the child is only your niece, you can scarcely be expected to fund her in such a case. . .'

'Just try me! It's about time someone on our Evan's

side got a leg up in life, and if it's going to be Bethan, good luck to her! Put her in for the scholarship, and if she do just gèt the place paid, I'll find the rest. Ent going to be like Eton, is it?'

'Hardly, Mr Walters. Perhaps ten pounds a year.'

'Good God, mun, I spent twice that at the races last week! Stop blathering. Whatever it is, she can have it!'

Ruminating on the extravagance of the betting classes, Edgar Roberts returned to South Church Street School.

Bethan slipped into her class as easily as a fish in deep water. A natural mimic, she quickly dropped her distinctive Valleys accent and adopted the broad, distorted vowels common to Cardiff and the nearby port of Newport. After that, she stood out only for her quick intelligence, and there were plenty of others who shared that.

She grew away from Lily naturally, now, drawn closer to children of her own age and interests. Lily coped easily with school, but her real life was outside, exploring the Bay with Lexie. It was Lexie who introduced her to fantan, the universally popular Chinese gambling game. The one Lexie favoured was run from the back of a house in Bute Street. She led Lily down the filthy back lane to a wooden hatch in the wall. When she knocked, it crashed open and a rail-thin Chinese glared out at them. 'What you want?' he yelled.

'Oh, God, Lexie, let's go – he's cross with us!' said Lily.

'Don't be daft, it's just the way he talks English! He's a businessman, same as Dad.' She held out a shilling. 'Come on, Lil, where's yours? Nothing risked, nothing won!'

Lily's shilling had been a casual gift from Rhys, and he gave the girls his small change often enough, but she still remembered it was more money than she had seen in a month at home, and hated to see it flung away. She could not lose face with Lexie, though, and reluctantly took the money from her pocket. The man nodded brusquely, snatched the coins and disappeared. Lily gawped into the smoke-filled room beyond the partition, particularly interested in an elderly, fine-boned man who sat at a table, writing beautifully with ink and brushes. Moments later the fantan man was back with two cards, each bearing Chinese characters. He handed them over, then shut the partition in their faces.

'Pretty expensive piece of card, ennit?' said Lily. 'What do we do now?'

'Just wait, and come back later to see if the numbers came up. I think they play the game with them, and if the winning number's the one you bought, you get some money. It's not bad winnings, sometimes, but Dad doesn't like it because he says no gamble should be left completely to chance!'

Miraculously, Lily won – and won a small fortune by her standards. She got two pounds when they returned.

'Pity about that, really,' said Lexie. 'You should always lose first time, you don't catch the bug then.'

She need not have worried about Lily. The girl was so impressed at the sight of so much money belonging only to her that she never went near the fantan house again.

A less expensive and endlessly absorbing entertainment was the penny slot piano in the fish and chip shop in James Street. During the day, the girls had to pay for each tune like anyone else, but on fine nights, after the shop had closed, two of the owner's children would bring the piano out into the street, unlock it and play it for hours on one penny, retrieving it after each tune.

Further along James Street was a wholesale butcher's shop which victualled the ships calling at Cardiff. Lily could never pass it without shuddering at the bulk of the vast beef carcases hanging outside, much as a small leg of lamb would in front of a family butcher's shop.

On Mondays, they peered into Mr Zussen's pawn

shop, to see who had been hocking the bedlinen and Sunday suits in order to survive until next pay day. 'I've known Dad come down here on the quiet and redeem something if he do know the chap who pawned it's in real trouble,' Lexie explained. 'I always have a quick look in case I see something I think he should know about.'

Butetown was a dangerous place, but only to strangers. Sailors were regarded as fair game, and frequently got rolled and beaten for their pay packets. Fights broke out within the small criminal fraternity, but seldom spilled outside it. The dockland families went about their business unmolested, leaving their doors unlocked, and life was lived as much in the street as inside the houses.

It had started off as a grand residential area, and elegant buildings still survived, particularly in Mount Stuart Square and Loudoun Square, the two great Victorian dockland developments. Mount Stuart Square had kept its grandeur because the Coal Exchange, the big banks and the industrialists' clubs were still located there. But Loudoun Square had always been residential. Now the ships' captains and rich docksmen had fled to more salubrious areas of the city, leaving the stately façades to crumble as the houses behind them turned into tenements. The businessmen who flocked in every morning by train were no more part of the community than the sailors who passed through the port, and were probably even less conscious of the grinding poverty which oppressed so many of the families who lived so close to the greatest source of commercial wealth in Wales.

Lexie liked to watch them, caught half-way between contempt and longing, and once said, 'D'you reckon it would be all right to be married to one of them – live in a stone mansion out Lisvane or Gabalfa, and go shopping in a carriage?'

Lily pondered it for a while. 'I s'pose it would be all right if you didn't want to do no more than have pretty gowns and go out driving, but what d'you think they do the rest of the time?'

'Well, in them novels of yours, they'm always yearning after some handsome young fellow Who Is For Ever Forbidden To Them.' Somehow Lexie managed to convey that such young fellows were always described in capital letters.

Lily regarded the passing businessmen sceptically. 'I can't imagine any of them even knowing somebody that interesting, so if you was one of their wives, where would you meet him?'

'Aw, I'd find a way. . .' Lexie turned and started walking dreamily away from Mount Stuart Square. 'Maybe I'd come back down here in my carriage, pretending I'd come to see if my dearest wanted to drive home with me. Then I'd sneak off down the Pier Head and see what I could pick up. There, see? Where there's a will, there's a way! And talking of the Pier Head. . .'

That was usually the prelude to Lexie spending a happy half hour strolling around making eyes at men even her father would have regarded as unsuitable, for as long as Lily could stand the embarrassment. Then they would wander home along Bute Street, endlessly absorbed by the smells, sounds and images of five continents which comprised the world of Tiger Bay.

CHAPTER TWENTY

May 1915

REMEMBERING ABERCARN, LILY sometimes wondered whether the child in the shabby boy's sweater and heavy boots was anything to do with her. Her initial two years in Cardiff had expanded imperceptibly to four, and now the graceful creature who faced her each morning in the bedroom mirror bore only the most fleeting resemblance to the unformed girl of those long-lost days.

'Anyone would change if they swapped our Mam for Lexie!' she said, smiling at the thought. Her cousin was her best friend, much closer than any of her own sisters, and although they were almost the same age, it was only now that Lily was beginning to shake off the feeling that the other girl was generations ahead of her in experience and wisdom.

Apart from their natural compatibility, the cousins enjoyed the stir they caused when they went about together. They were like story-book illustrations chosen to show opposite, but equally pleasing, aspects of beauty. They were both tall, but there any physical similarity ended. Lily had shed all signs of childishness long ago. Dockland street life swiftly turned girls into women. She was tall, with black hair and pearly-pale skin complemented by light, quicksilver eyes which held the same mesmeric quality as her father's. A straight nose and finely-chiselled lips gave her face an

almost classic beauty, humanized by a small, rounded
chin. She was five feet eight inches tall, with broad
shoulders, deep, well-formed breasts and long legs.

Lexie's hair and eyes were as black as ebony, the
hair a dead-straight jet waterfall. Fine features and
pale coffee-coloured skin, along with the straight hair,
gave her less of a conventionally African than a Latin or
South American look. She was boyishly slender without
being skinny, and moved so gracefully that she always
seemed to be dancing. She exploited her own fashion
sense and Lily's skill as a seamstress to create clothes
which would have made them stand out in any crowd.
In Butetown, where poorer women were often seen in
men's flat caps and sacking aprons, they stood out like
stars in a dark sky.

The contrast between herself and Lexie and the girls
and women of the industrial valleys was equally strong,
and much on Lily's mind today: her mother had just
written to ask if she would come home for a visit.
These days she felt so much a stranger in Abercarn
that the prospect was daunting. She had been home
only a handful of times since 1911, initially because
there was insufficient space to accommodate her and
Bethan for more than a couple of days; later because it
was obvious that longer or more frequent visits strained
the family finances too much.

Rose was still a semi-invalid, Edmund and Lewis
were schoolboys, and Margaret Ann had borne another
baby, Angharad, in 1912. The older boys, all working
at the Celynen South and Cwmcarn collieries, had
taken over the house next door to the Walters home,
when it became vacant a year or two earlier, divided
the rent between them and treated both buildings as a
single dwelling. Even so, conditions were still crowded.
Evan and Margaret Ann and the new baby had one
bedroom in the first house, with the younger boys
sharing the other. Next door, Haydn and Tom shared

one upstairs room, Emrys and Gareth the other. Rose
was in the ground floor parlour, now permanently
converted into a bedroom. She managed to get the
older boys' breakfasts each morning, and to prepare
the food they took to work, but after that her small
strength was exhausted, and Margaret Ann acted as
housekeeper for both houses.

Lily's last trip back to the village had been the
previous Christmas. It had been more than a little
disturbing. She was then a few months short of her
seventeenth birthday, but by Valleys standards looked
and behaved as if she were twenty. She sensed that the
only thing preventing her mother from delivering long
lectures was the impermanence of her stay. Had she
been home for good, it would have been a different
matter. The atmosphere had grown particularly tense
when it was time to go to chapel.

There was no problem over the Christmas services.
Lily loved the New Testament stories of the nativity
and enjoyed singing carols in her rich contralto voice.
But she never attended a place of worship in Cardiff,
and so far had not missed it. That year, Christmas Day
fell on a Friday, so two days later she was expected
to turn out for services again. When Margaret Ann
came into the kitchen at ten to eleven on Sunday,
dressed in her best coat and hat, she found Lily sitting with her brothers at the table, wearing an ordinary blouse and skirt protected by a full-length pina-
fore.

'Lily, you'll be late, girl! What have got into you?'

Her daughter looked up, suspiciously innocent.
'Late, Mam, what for? You said it'd help if I did the
dinner today. I'm half-way through it. One o'clock all
right, like we used to have it?'

Margaret Ann ignored the last bit. 'I thought you
meant you'd get it on before we went to chapel and
finish it off when we come back, like I always do,' she

said. 'You know I never missed a morning sermon just
for the sake of food.'

'Nobody's asking you to now, Mam. Go on, or you'll
be late.'

'And what about you, may I ask?'

'The boys don't go, do they? I ent, neither.'

'Oh, no, you don't, my lady! The boys is your father's
business. You are mine. Now in that parlour, quick,
and get into your best clothes. I'll go on up. If you'm
quick, you'll only miss the first hymn.' She was already
turning to leave, muttering, 'The very idea. . .' when
she realized that Lily had not moved.

The girl smiled at her gently, but remained seated
at the table. 'Mam, I said I'm not going, and I ent. I
enjoyed the Christmas service, but that's enough for a
bit. Now let's leave it there, shall we?'

'No we will not, my lady! I always knew you'd go
wrong if I let you go off down Cardiff. . .and where's
our Bethan? I s'pose she've gone the same way?'

'Here I am, Mam. Ready to go, are we?' Bethan had
been changing in the parlour, which she and Lily were
using as a makeshift bedroom. She had not heard the
disagreement, only her mother asking where she was.

'Oh, at least one of you do still try to keep up appearances. That's something, I s'pose. Lily – for the last
time, are you coming or not?'

'I've already told you I'm not, Mam, so why make a
meal of it? You might as well get used to it now as later.
Now, will you want roast potatoes, or just white?'

'Like a lot of Gadarene swine, just thinking of their
stomachs!' declaimed Margaret Ann with a look that
bracketed Haydn and Tom with Lily in her condem-
nation.

The door slammed behind her and Bethan, and
Lily turned, wide-eyed, to Haydn: 'I didn't know the
Gadarene swine was that interested in food, did you?'
she said.

Haydn chuckled and hid his head in his hands in mock despair. 'If you don't start toeing the line, either you or Mam is going to be six foot under ground before this holiday's over,' he told her.

Abruptly, Lily became serious. 'Well, it ent going to me,' she said. 'Mam had her own way with me when I was little, but it's different now, and she's going to have to get used to it.'

Somehow, that Sunday morning had set the tone for the rest of their visit. By the time Lily and Bethan returned to Cardiff on New Year's Eve, mother and daughter were scarcely on speaking terms.

Their day-to-day contact had been patchy for the whole of Lily's stay in Butetown. Margaret Ann was no great writer, and it was too expensive for her to make the train trip to Cardiff very often, even had she been inclined to hob-nob with the brother-in-law of whom she disapproved so strongly. Deep in her heart, Margaret Ann found it hard to forgive herself for consigning her two daughters to Rhys's care, and she lived with her guilt by ignoring the whole situation as much as possible.

Evan came to visit Rhys at irregular intervals, but both girls had always been in awe of their father, although they adored him. They found their uncle far less intimidating, and therefore grew closer to him.

Rhys Walters often reflected that it was fortunate his sister-in-law did not enquire too closely about the girls. Not that there was any problem with Bethan: she was doing very well at Cathays High School and would remain there until she had taken her School Certificate at sixteen. With Lily, it was different. Lily had taken to the pub as though she had been born and bred there. Lexie was already helping out behind the bar at busy times when Lily arrived in Butetown in 1911. Within months, she, too, had joined in. After she left school in 1912, it seemed the most natural

thing in the world for her to work full time at the
Anglesey.

It fascinated Rhys that two girls could turn out as
differently as Lexie and Lily and yet both remain
at home in dockland. Lexie was sexually precocious,
had an outrageous tongue and was quite capable of
physical violence if she felt she was being insulted.
No one was indifferent to her; she was either loved
or hated – fortunately for her, more the former than
the latter. Lily was quieter, apparently more tranquil;
superficially more of a lady; but if she was provoked
sufficiently she displayed a temper that put Lexie's in
the shade. Her narrow Valleys upbringing had been
strongly overlaid with Butetown ways and she was now
a unique mixture of two completely divergent cultures.
Rhys often wondered if people would ever know how
to handle her. He did, instinctively, but then, he had
only ever met one human being who did not respond
positively to him – Margaret Ann.

The thought of Margaret Ann brought her letter
to mind. Rhys had a feeling this was his sister-in-
law's attempt to get Lily back to her side permanently.
There was something too ingratiating about its tone to
be wasted on a short visit. If Margaret Ann was prepared to be that humble, she wanted more than a few
days with her favourite daughter. That would be the
War... So far, it hadn't made that much difference
down here, except that the coal was moving through
faster and making more money for the mine owners.
But the talk was that the docks, always little better than
Sodom and Gomorrah to Valleys folk, were about to
turn into an even more unspeakable den of vice, with
foreigners streaming in to take the jobs of men gone to
enlist, and innocent girls white-slaved to the broth-
els which served their ungovernable passions. That
picture always cheered Rhys – tell it vividly enough
and it would keep the busybodies out for good –

but now it looked set fair to deprive him of lovely
Lily.

He sighed. He'd be sorry to lose the girl. . . She was
more like his daughter than his niece, now. Still, it
might be better for her in the long run. He had never
tried to prevent the sexual adventures he knew Lexie
had indulged in for years now. He had too many sins
of his own to condemn others, even as a parent. But
somehow Lexie seemed to have the right take-it-or-
leave-it attitude to such peccadilloes. Lily was different.
Too much old Welsh religion crammed into that pretty
head when she was too young to do much about it. . .
It might not stop her going her own way, now, but
if she followed the same path as Lexie, it would give
her terrible conscience pangs later on. Rhys had seen
plenty of the regulars down in his bar gaze longingly
at Lily, and not a few of them attempting to kindle
her interest. So far, they had failed, but it couldn't go
on for ever. The other day, he had come out of the
restaurant in the basement of Cardiff Coal Exchange,
to catch sight of Lily blushing prettily as she talked to
one of the young blades who came to Mount Stuart
Square daily on business. Now if she got tangled up
with one of them, it could really end in tears. . . One
way and another, it might be just as well if she had a
few months back with her mam.

Rhys laughed ruefully, and said aloud, 'At least it'll
make her realize how well off she is down here!'

Getting off the train at Abercarn on Saturday afternoon, Lily experienced an odd feeling of having done
all this before. There was her father, waving to her on
the platform. Here was she, wondering what lay ahead
of her, plunging again into the unknown. . . But of
course it wasn't the same. He was meeting her, not
seeing her off. She was coming back to a familiar place,

to familiar people. The train rumbled to a halt and she was out of the door, into Evan's arms, laughing with delight to see him again.

Why was he so different when they were on their own, she wondered, so free, so affectionate. . .and the minute Mam arrived, he would go all quiet and act as if she were a bit of furniture. . .

It was the same today. Evan took her luggage and swung it lightly as if it weighed nothing, as he swaggered along beside her on the walk from the station to the Ranks. 'How long are you home for this time, kidda?' he asked. 'Flying visit, or for good?'

'You tell me, Dad. I got this letter from Mam last week – didn't you see it? – saying she wished we had more chance to be together and she knew Bethan couldn't break off school, but maybe I could come back. Then instead of saying any more about how long or anything, she started writing about our Billie being home. I didn't know what to think, so I thought I'd better come and see. Uncle Rhys do think she wants me back for good.'

Evan stopped and put down her bag for a while, as he made much of filling and lighting his pipe. 'Aye, I think Rhys is right – though she never showed me the letter, just told me you was coming. The thing about Billie is a bit of a smoke screen, I think. You know how your mam do hate to have to ask someone direct for anything. She'd make a rotten beggar – too bloody proud by half!'

'But Billie? Dad, I've seen him once or twice myself since he've been in the Army. I didn't think I'd ever see the day he'd stay under the same roof as Mam again.'

Evan shrugged, and bent to pick up her bag. 'The War might change a lot of things, Lil. It haven't so much changed Billie, as made him even more what he was before, if you know what I mean. . .and the gentle bit of him have decided it's time to let bygones be bygones with Margaret Ann.'

'I'm surprised she's willing!'

'Oh, the War is making a big difference to women with a lot of sons, girl. There's plenty of mothers up the Valleys asking themselves how long their boys'll stay alive, and your mam is one of them.'

Yes, she would be, thought Lily. A couple of chapel sermons about the horror of war and she'd be terrified one of them would die without making peace with her. . .always was a terrible one for tying up loose ends. . .

Evan was talking again. 'Of course, it do help that Billie's in the other house with Haydn and the boys. I don't know if they'd rub along so well if they was under one roof together. Like this, Billie boy can pretend he haven't really gone back on his promise that he'd never cross Margaret Ann's threshold again.'

Lily shook her head. 'What a family we are. Scattered half-way round South Wales, one lot quarrelling with another. No mixing with Uncle Rhys 'cos he's common. No contact with John Daniel because – well, because. . .'

'Go on, might as well finish it. Because of me and Ellen Rourke.'

She blushed and looked away. 'That ent none of my business.'

'Yes it is. You must often have wondered how I could have all you kids back here and another woman somewhere else. Must have thought I was a real Judas from time to time.'

'Never!' Her tone was fierce. 'I love you, Dad. All I ever wanted was for you to be happy. But all the time I was little, you looked miserable. I never knew why, then, but when I got older, I found out soon enough – that's the advantage of having lots of big brothers – they can never keep a secret.'

'I wondered how old you was when you found out.'

'I knew before I went down Uncle Rhys's. Just as

well, an' all, because he and Lexie knew, and they'd
have thought I was a proper idiot if I hadn't.'

'Didn't they try to keep it quiet?'

'What for? Uncle Rhys said you loved her, and as you
did, she deserved respect. You can thank him for me
accepting it.' She was silent for a moment, then, taking
her courage in both hands, she said, 'D'you still wish
you'd married her instead of Mam?'

'Oh, Lily, what a bloody question! How do I know,
now, what I'd want if I could have it all again? If I'd
married Ellen, I wouldn't have had any of you children, for a start.'

'Would that have been such a bad thing?'

'D'you know, kidda, you'm the first one as have ever
thought of that? I don't really know. . .but if I hadn't
had you lot, what other memorial would I have?'

'Memorial! You ent going to die – why're you talking
like that?'

His laugh was devoid of humour. 'Don't know how
much longer you expect me to live. I'm nearly fifty-
five. You don't make old bones working on a coal face
above that age.'

'You're as strong as an ox, Dad – you'll see me off.'

'Aye, that's what they do tell them old fools they have
sitting up in bed, half blind and with no teeth and
eighty-five years old. Christ, love, if that's the price,
I'd rather go now!'

That seemed to dispose of the topic, and he went on
to less weighty matters. But it set Lily looking at him in
a way she never had before. To her he had always been
Our Dad, huge, monolithic, ageless. Was he, though?
She glanced sidelong at him as they walked. His back
was as straight as ever, and his skin fair and clear, but
deep lines cut furrows from his nose to the outer corners of his mouth, and there were dark shadows under
his eyes. Was it just the strong pipe tobacco that made
the breath whistle so, in and out of his lungs, or was

dust getting a stronger grip on him? Involuntarily, she glanced down at his hands, an infallible sign of how far coal dust had seeped into a miner's body. The big veins, corded on the backs of his hands and standing out on his partly-exposed forearms, were midnight blue. Just as if they were carrying pure coal dust, not blood, she mused. Always a sign their days are numbered, echoed back the old wives' tale from her childhood.

She shook off the unpleasant prospect and slipped her arm through his. 'Oh, Dad, I'm so glad to be home with you again,' she said.

He looked down on her, pleasure suffusing his face. 'You do really mean that, don't you?' he said wonderingly.

''Course I do! I can't pretend Uncle Rhys is you for ever, can I? Come on, let's go and keep the peace between Mam and Billie!'

CHAPTER TWENTY-ONE

'BILLIE BOY! THERE'S lovely to see you!' Lily had got to know her brother when he came to visit Rhys in Butetown on his infrequent leaves, and now he seemed more a friend than a kinsman.

He looked her over appreciatively. 'Damn me, Lil, if the blokes in my company could see you, I'd be the most popular sergeant in the British army! You'm a real picture.'

'Ooh, sergeant now, is it? Since when have that happened?'

Billie laughed ruefully. 'It ent a sign of my military genius, don't worry. It's just that things are moving fast now, and any regular worth his salt who saw action before this lot is getting promoted fast. It's a mixed blessing.'

Outside, Evan was getting restless. 'Hey, come on, now, Lily. Your Mam's next door and she've been bobbing about like a flea in a frying pan all the morning waiting to see you. Come back and have a natter with Billie when you've said hullo to her.'

'That'll be the day!' said Billie. 'Once our Mam do get hold of Lily, none of us will see any more of her today. So, before you go, Lil, better meet another new member of the family.' He turned away from her momentarily and called, 'George — come on in and meet my beautiful sister!'

The passage door opened. Lily looked at the young man who came through it and her world stood on its head. Colour surged to her cheeks and she felt an overpowering need to sit down. The young man smiled shyly and held out his hand. She took it, and never wanted to let go.

'Lily, this is George Griffiths, our Dad's new butty. George, at long last, this is our Lily of the Valleys.'

The others all laughed at the family joke her name had become, and Lily was thankful for the boisterous noise. It served to cover her confusion. Why on earth did she feel like this? He was good looking, certainly, but not spectacularly so... She knew nothing about him, save that he was a miner and worked with her father. How could he be tying her in such knots?

She had no time to speculate further. Evan, understanding at a glance, said, 'That's enough, now, you can talk to George later – he's lodging here with the boys. Come on, I told you – your Mam's waiting.' And he hurried her back out into the street.

Outside, he turned a sympathetic smile on her. 'Oh, Lil – a miner? Haven't you learned from your mam's terrible example?'

She blushed furiously again. 'I-I don't know what you mean, Dad.'

'Oh, I think you do... I've had that feeling, an' all. Useless to ignore it, I can tell you that for nothing. I think he's just as struck, if it's any consolation. If anything do come of it, for Christ's sake don't tell your mother for a bit, that's all.'

She managed a forced laugh. 'There's nothing to tell, but why?'

Evan shook his head and laughed. 'Your mother have got it into her head that all you girls is going to "marry well" as she do put it. Now, I've looked up and down this valley and all I can see is miners and tinplate workers – and soldiers, now, of course. Unless we'm invaded by an army of unmarried German barons with a thing about Welsh girls, I got a feeling she'll be disappointed... Anyhow, now you know why you shouldn't show any keenness on George.'

With that, he opened the back door, led Lily into Margaret Ann's kitchen and left her there to be monopolized by her mother for an hour or so.

It did not take long for Margaret Ann's domineering nature to push through her real joy at Lily's return. 'Don't you think that costume's a bit old for you, Lily?' she asked, critically fingering the sleeve of her daughter's jacket.

'I'm seventeen, Mam. What did you expect me to be wearing, a white muslin smock?'

'Now, now – no need to be cheeky. It's just that up here, that sort of outfit is more for married women than young girls. Look at Rose...she's a year older than you and she still dresses the way I'd expect.'

'That's up to Rose, Mam. I like dressing like this – and before you do ask, yes, all the things I've got with me are like this. It's what smart young ladies do wear in Cardiff.'

Margaret Ann sniffed. 'I suppose you'll be telling me next that our Bethan is dressing like that!'

Lily laughed. 'Oh, Mam, she's not fifteen yet, and still in school! Of course she's not. You'd be proud of her.'

That set Margaret Ann off at a tangent. 'And what's all that school going to do for her, that's what I'd like to know? Fancy a girl doing school certificate! Young men don't like a girl to be too clever!'

'I thought you wanted us to better ourselves.'

'Of course I do. I don't want none of my daughters ending up in the Ranks, like me.'

'Well then, ent it better for us to be independent and be able to make a decent living?'

'Don't talk daft! The best thing you can do is find a

man with good prospects and marry him. No decent woman can make her way on her own.'

Lily's eyes sparkled mischievously. 'Well, there you are, then, Bethan's doing just what you'd want. All she can talk about is training to be a nurse. Think of all those handsome young doctors and rich male patients she'll meet. You'll have her off your hands in no time, Mam!'

The conversation was making Margaret Ann uncomfortable. She was unused to being challenged. Rose had an obstinate streak, but she was quiet and when she disagreed with her mother, tended to keep her opinion to herself. Angharad was still scarcely more than a baby, so any trouble from her lay far in the future. Evan had given up long ago. When his wife's opinions clashed with his own, these days he simply went out.

Margaret Ann changed the subject. 'Now I got you home again, I was thinking, you could join some of the young ladies' things that the Garn do organize. There's ever such a lot going on now, what with voluntary work for the War Effort and all.'

'Perhaps – if I've got time. But the first thing I got to do is find a job.'

'A job? Talk sense! Walters girls don't go out to work.'

Lily was growing impatient. 'No, they'm at home, scrubbing somebody else's sheets for pennies from the time they'm seven years old! I can tell you now, Mam, I ent washing anybody's dirty linen to keep body and soul together, so you'd better get used to the idea now.'

After that, there seemed little more to be said between them. Margaret Ann sulked and Lily decided to go and see her brothers. But by Sunday, the inhabitants of both houses were mixing freely and the sheer weight of numbers lessened the friction between Margaret Ann and Lily. On Sunday Margaret Ann managed her regular conjuring trick of spending the crucial hour between eleven and twelve in chapel and still producing a perfect meal of roast beef, Yorkshire pudding and a vast choice of vegetables for one o'clock dinner.

Lily, looking at the meal spread out on the kitchen table, said, 'You'd never know there was a war on! How d'you do it, Mam?'

Margaret Ann sighed. 'This'll be one of the last times, according to Claude Parfitt,' she said. 'When I went up there to get the meat yesterday, he said the Army's taking everything. He's getting less and less choice and this year he don't even think everybody'll get Christmas poultry.'

'Tut tut,' said Evan. 'There you are, Billie, see what you lot of brutal and licentious soldiery is doing to the poor working man and his family?'

'It's all very well for you to joke about it, Evan. You'm not the one as has to wheedle away at the shopkeepers all the time.'

'No, but you've spent enough of my money with them over the years to expect a bit of special treatment when things do start getting short.' His jovial tone was fading, and Haydn rushed in with a flurry of inconsequential chatter to stop the good humour vanishing altogether from their meal. All of them had sufficient experience of family quarrels to know they did not want one today.

The good, plentiful food and the novelty of Lily and Billie both being home was enough to restore everyone's good spirits. Afterwards the girls washed up and Margaret Ann went upstairs for a sleep so that she could attend evening services fully refreshed. Once everything was put away, Rose got started again – this time at laying the tea.

'Good God, girl, what is this, a factory canteen?' said Billie. 'Why not sit down and relax?'

Rose eyed him disapprovingly. 'Mam do like everything ready, so we can just make the tea and cut the
bread and butter later on,' she told him. 'If it do irritate
you, why don't you go out somewhere?'

'Aye. Think I just might. How about you, Lily? Fancy
a walk with your big brother?'

Why must I always blush, she thought, failing dismally in an attempt at nonchalance. 'Thanks, Billie, but
I-I've already said I'll go out this afternoon. How about
tomorrow?'

Billie studied her high colour for a moment then
smiled. 'I don't need to ask who with, do I? Girls don't
blush like that over their brothers.'

Evan came back inside after talking to a neighbour
and caught his last words. 'Leave the girl alone, mun.
Don't you remember what love was like at seventeen?'

Billie's face hardened and his playful attitude dissolved. 'Hardly,' he said. 'I was spending every minute
of every hour trying to work out a way of getting away
from the pit.' He slipped past his father and went out
into the street.

The exchange saddened Lily. 'What was that about?'
she asked Evan. 'It wasn't your fault he had to go
underground.'

Evan sighed. He looked tired and defeated. 'Funny
thing, ennit?' he said. 'Billie boy will never really love
his mam again after all the trouble there was between
them. And yet he do still believe the tales she told him
when he was a little boy about how she'd been trying to
save him from the pit and I was the one as made him
go. Honest to God, love, I didn't. . .it was just there was
nowhere else for him. It was all very well for her to give
him fancy ideas about farm work and such, but there
was none to be had.'

'He must realize that now.'

'I don't think so – not really. Truth is, I done it all
badly. Ellen worked it out in a minute, and got him a

job with horses. It was still underground, but at least
it give him a little bit of what he wanted. I 'xpect he
thinks I should have thought of it, not left it to her.'
He shrugged. 'It's all water under the bridge now, any
road. He's about as far away from mining as he can be.'

Lily needed to get away, and she was glad she had
agreed this morning to meet George and go for a walk
after dinner. By half past two, she had shaken off the
tensions of the two terraced houses and was strolling
with George up the unsurfaced lane which led to the
distillery pond and beyond that to the Gwyddon valley.

Throughout dinner she had wondered nervously
what she would say to him. Now it was childishly
easy. All she had to say was, 'Tell me how you come
to be living with us and working with Dad.' He did
the rest.

George Griffiths was a miner's son from Cilfynydd.
His father and elder brother had worked at Senghenydd colliery, where an explosion in 1913 had killed
more men than any mining disaster in history. The
two other Griffiths men were among the casualties.
His mother had been ill for years with an obscure
chest complaint for which they had never been able
to afford proper treatment. Now, with only George's
apprentice wage of less than a pound a week to live on,
she developed tuberculosis and was dead barely a year
after her husband.

No one took much notice of George. The Valleys
were full of boys whose parents had been casualties
of poverty, mining or both. For months George had
drifted about, doing labouring jobs here and there,
putting off the evil day of his return to the coal face
which he now loathed and feared. He had run into
Evan in the Commercial one night, when he had been
drinking himself into a stupor on the money he had

earned in a three-week stint with a Cwmcarn black-smith. By now he was little more than a vagrant.

'Your dad told me after, it was just like the way he met your mam,' said George. He laughed. 'Said if I didn't watch out, he'd be proposing to me!'

George had been half asleep in a dark corner of the Commercial's rough cellar bar. A small, shifty man universally known as Jack the Rat was playing cards at the same table, along with a fat, older man in a battered brown bowler hat. The ratlike man had won a hand. As he reached forward to take the pool of small change, the man in the bowler jumped up, cursing, grabbed the winner and manhandled him outside, yelling accusations that he had cheated. George, who hated such violence, automatically felt sympathy for the smaller man, and staggered outside behind them. There he found the bowler hatted man straddling the other's puny chest and gouging at his eyes, still yelling abuse at him.

In spite of his drunken state, George had intervened, and the fat man, seeing how feeble he was, set about him instead. At that stage, Evan Walters had arrived.

'I couldn't make out what was happening at the time,' said George, 'but all of a sudden this giant sort of chucked the fat man off me as if he was a fly or something. I was gasping for air, trying to stay conscious, but then I heard your dad say "I been waiting ever such a long time for this, Stout".

'By the time I could sit up, he'd smashed the bugger all over the place. Stout was lying down, trying to wrap his arms round his ribs and protect his crotch at the same time. I remember, he kept squealing like a stuck pig and in between, he was saying, "Hang on, Evan, your Missis have already done for my leg, remember!" as if that made it quits.'

'What did Dad do then?' asked Lily.

'He smiled, the sort of way the Devil would smile

when he really had you, and he said, "Aye, Billy, but
I do still owe you a couple for Ellen". And then he
kicked the shit out of him – begging your pardon, Lily,
but there ent any other way to describe it.'

'And then?'

'Well, two of Evan's butties come and dragged Stout
away – said they didn't want to see Evan in prison – and
he turned round to me and said, "*Iesu Mawr*, what's the
world coming to? It used to be just girls who got themselves in that state." Then he took me in the saloon bar
and he and Siân patched me up. After that he took me
round to the house where your brothers do stay, and
Haydn said I could bunk in with them. I been there
ever since.'

'He must have said why he was doing it. He ent in the
habit of coming home with strangers.'

'Well, yes, but I'm still not sure I do really understand. He said some man had give him a chance once,
a chance he'd thrown away, and the condition was that
he helped somebody out in his turn. He reckoned I was
it. Next thing I know, he've got me a job working as his
butty, and I'm respectable again. I even got a family.'
He ended with a nervous laugh.

'You don't sound as if it's what you want.'

He gazed deep into her eyes. 'I don't know why I
should tell you this, seeing as you'm Evan's daughter,
but – well, the only reason I go down that pit every day
is him. When our Dad and Ken died over Senghenydd,
I made myself a promise I'd never see another pit bottom again. Now here I am, regular day shift, set for
life.'

'Why are you sticking it? It must be awful.'

'It's bloody terrible. I stick it because I admire Evan
so much, and I can't throw all he've done for me back
in his face.' He seemed to reflect on what he had said,
then added, 'Christ, why'm I saying all this to you? You
don't want to have my troubles on your shoulders.'

'I'll listen to you for ever if it will help you.'

They had been sitting on a grassy bank high above the Gwyddon stream. They were only a few inches apart, facing each other. George could feel and smell her sweet breath on his cheek. In a moment he was kissing her, and along with a deep-rooted desire for her, he experienced a profound sense of peace. Involuntarily, he said, 'Oh, Lily, don't ever leave me. . .'

She laughed and drew back a little. 'Don't you think this is all a bit sudden? We only met yesterday.'

He shook his head, reaching for her again. 'Oh no – you felt it, an' all, I saw it hit you. You'm just as bad as me. . . It's a miracle we met, and I'm afraid you'll disappear if I let you out of my sight.'

Lily took his hand. 'Yes, it is the same for me, don't ask me why 'cos I don't know, but let's enjoy it while we can.' She came back to his arms and they lay back against the sweet grass of the bank, kissing, touching and exchanging unimportant confidences, for the rest of the afternoon.

Margaret Ann would have been blind if she had not noticed her daughter's preoccupation with George Griffiths. After a few days she went to Evan and started fulminating about outsiders taking advantage, and dishonourable intentions. Evan took it all in his stride. Over the past couple of years he had become resigned to Margaret Ann's provocative tongue, and found it easiest to handle if he ignored most of what she said. Today, though, that approach was doomed. She was ready to go on until midnight if necessary.

Eventually, Evan said, 'What if there is something going on? She's the age you was when you met me; she've seen a bit more of the wide world than you had at her age, and if she've found what she's looking for so soon, I ent going to be the one to stop her.'

'Not with a miner – not my Lily. I want something better than the Ranks for her. . .'

'Oh, God, Margaret Ann, have a bit of sense for once! Unless she do move away from here altogether, it's going to be a miner or a tinplate worker, ennit? And when she did move away, you was the one as brought her back. If you keep trying to find her a good catch she'll end up an old maid, and then see if she'll thank you for it!'

'Better an old maid than a house full of brats in a coal company terrace!'

'Ent that nice. . .who could you be referring to, I wonder. . . Sometimes, my dearest, I do think you'm trying to tell me something. . .you know, subtle like.' He dropped the exaggeratedly bantering tone as abruptly as he had assumed it. 'Well, you fought like a wildcat to get me in the first place, and to hold on to me when you thought you was losing me, so don't give me no rubbish about better an old maid.'

He flung aside the evening newspaper and stood up. 'I'm going down the Commercial for an hour. I just got one more thing to say to you. Leave our Lily to make her own mistakes. You'm her mother, not her wife!' Then he left.

Like her father, Lily was a great one for instincts. This felt right, and she had no intention of questioning it. She surrendered herself to romantic love and found it every bit as entrancing as the storybooks said. But although her relationship with George seemed perfect, little else about his present life seemed to suit him. He loathed and feared mining, and constantly worried away, trying to find a means of escape. Before too many days had passed he found one – through Billie.

Billie was home for a couple of weeks because he had been given embarkation leave before his departure for

France. It was unlikely he would get back to Britain again until hostilities ended, and the length of the break reflected that. Lily often wished afterwards that she had prevented Billie and George going out drinking together, thus avoiding the inevitable, but in her heart she knew it would have happened anyway.

Until the end of his first week home, Billie had seen little of George, because he was always out somewhere with Lily. But when Friday came, Lily had private business. She told George to amuse himself for a few hours, and went off alone, refusing to tell the family where she was going.

Redmond's Brewery, beyond the distillery pond, was a small family concern that employed a couple of dozen workers, all men except the chairman's secretary. That had changed radically by early 1915. Miners and steelworkers were not actively encouraged to enlist – it was already recognized that their jobs were vital to the war effort. That put greater pressure on men in less essential jobs, and soon male shopworkers, railway porters and service workers were all being bombarded with challenges to join Kitchener's army.

The boys at the brewery had been among the first to go, and so the brewer had become one of the first Valleys employers to start recruiting women to fill men's jobs. It was slow going at first. Only the bolder female souls were prepared to brave the disapproval and mockery of such a conservative community, to don trousers and caps and start taking on men's work. As a result, Redmond's vacancy sign had been displayed all over the village for months, and when Lily came home in May there were still half a dozen jobs going begging. Today she was going to apply for one of them.

It took her barely half an hour to tour the little brewery with the master brewer, go through a desultory interview and accept an offer of a job at wages beyond her wildest dreams. She would start in ten days time,

the day Billie's leave ended. As she was leaving, the
brewmaster said, 'Oh, Miss Walters – I don't suppose
you'd be interested in learning to drive, by any chance?
We'm losing our last drayman the day you start, and I'll
have to train a bright girl to take it on.'

Willing? thought Lily. *I'd pay you if I could afford it*!

Aloud, she merely said, 'Of course, Mr Williams. I'll
even come in next week for a few lessons before I start,
if you like.'

When she arrived home, she went looking for
George, to tell him her news, but could not find
him. There was still no sign of him a couple of hours
later, when Evan and the boys came home from the
day shift. 'Well, he ent in the pub,' said Evan, 'because
me and Emrys called in for a quick one before we come
home. Our Billie have took him off somewhere, I'll be
bound.'

Lily was white-faced, already suspecting the worst.
'That's what I'm afraid of, Dad.'

They finally got home at seven that night, slightly
drunk, Billie more than slightly shamefaced. 'Meet Private George Griffiths, of the Royal Welch Fusiliers!' he
shouted with forced joviality. 'Took the King's Shilling
this afternoon down Newport recruiting office, and
he've got to report for duty along with me on Monday.
Make you feel proud, don' it, Lil?. . . Lily? Christ, what
have got into the girl?' Lily, stifling a sob, had rushed
from the room.

She was inconsolable that evening. Margaret Ann,
now all in favour of George because he would be safely
out of reach within days, was her main comforter. She
sat on the bed, cradling her daughter in her arms and
making small reassuring noises. 'It'll all come out all
right in the end, love, don't you worry. . .everything
will be all right. . .' like some religious talisman.

By the next morning, Lily had got herself under control, but she was still downcast and reluctant to speak to

George. Eventually, he persuaded her to go for a walk with him and discuss it.

The moment they were out of the village, she turned on him. 'Why did you do it, George, just like that, on the spur of the moment? Don't you care for me at all?'

'Of course I do, Lily! I've told you how much I do hate the pit. . .I just couldn't think of any other way out.'

'But they'm killing people over there, every day!'

'Aye, and they'm killing people over here every day an' all, down the pit. What about Dad and our Ken? Believe me, I do feel safer going over there than staying on at the Celynen South. At least they won't stick me in a cage five o'clock every morning and send me down to the centre of the earth!'

She knew then that she could never find an answer for him. She sighed, wiped away her tears, and took his hand. 'What'll you do when it's over. . .if you do live through it, that is?' You'll have to go back to the pit then.'

'I'll live through it all right, Lily – nobody's going to kill me up in the fresh air! I don't know. . .I got this feeling I'll be able to strike out for something different after that. They say it do make a man of you!'

'But you was man enough for me already. . . Oh, George, what am I going to do, losing you straight after I've found you?'

'You ent losing me, Lily. When I come back – when it's all over – I want us to get married. Will you?'

She gazed longingly at him for a while. 'Yes, all right. If you do come back.'

'I'll come back – that's a promise!'

On the Saturday, he went to Newport and spent every penny he had on an engagement ring. When Margaret Ann saw it, she said, 'Oh, there's lovely – I always did like opals. It's such a pity they'm supposed to be unlucky, really, ennit?'

Lily refused to rise to the bait, telling herself that as long as her mother was behaving like this, she would not be refusing to countenance the match. 'Let her pray the Huns will get him,' she whispered fiercely to herself, 'I'll just pray they don't, and cancel it out!'

Meanwhile, there was the matter of her new job. Evan was delighted. 'Well, well, doing your bit for the country, eh?' he said, for Margaret Ann's benefit, adding so low that only Lily could hear, 'And for the thirsty miner, an' all! Well done, kidda.'

Margaret Ann was furious, but with Evan and her sons extolling Lily's patriotism in volunteering to release valuable fighting men for the Front, she was forced to keep her rage to herself. The army, after a bad start with Valleys people, was enjoying an improved image as increasing numbers of preachers delivered patriotic Sunday sermons and sent mothers home to push their sons off to war. Margaret Ann was more resigned to the propriety of Lily working for the cause than to seeing more of her boys march off to the Front. At least it was only her unforgiven Billie who was in danger in that direction. . .

Lily refused to go to Abercarn station on Sunday evening to see Billie and George off. 'I'll say my goodbyes here,' she said in a tear-choked voice. 'And you two mind you do bloody look after each other, d'you hear me?' Then she rushed off and shut herself in Rose's parlour-bedroom, where she cried for an hour. For the rest of her life, she would find herself unable to face waving off trainttt'zs carrying those she loved.

At first her suffering was intense, but she was young, she was starting her first job, and very soon she had been apart from George longer than she had known him. She remained certain of her feelings, but gradually she accepted her new circumstances and settled

down to wait out the war. She and George wrote
to each other as often as they could, and she was
delighted to discover that she found him as pleasing
on better acquaintance through his letters as she had
during their fleeting courtship. He seemed to lead
a charmed life, suffering nothing worse than a few
minor cuts when his arm was torn by shrapnel. As
the months spun out and their first year apart drew
to its close, she began to feel a glimmer of hope that
he might survive.

After a while, Margaret Ann was secretly glad she
had not openly disapproved of Lily's work. When the
shortages inevitably started to bite, it was very handy
to have the girl's large extra wage packet to swell the
family budget. And, to her intense surprise, her daughter's new skill brought prestige among the neighbours.

The whole thing started almost accidentally. Lily
proved to be a natural driver, and within a few weeks
all thoughts of using her to do anything else at the
brewery had faded. She became a familiar sight, driving the chocolate-brown delivery lorry back and forth
between the Western Valley villages. She had been
doing the job for more than a year when she encountered someone she had never expected to meet again.
She got out of the van to collect a prescription for Rose
from the village chemist. As she opened the door, a
vaguely familiar male figure was coming out – a tall
man with thick black hair and an intense stare. Lily
was momentarily at a loss. Surely she knew no one
like that? Certainly she knew no army officers, and this
man's uniform said he was one. The stout walking stick
and the stiffness in his left leg also said he had been
wounded.

Her perplexity about having seen him somewhere
made her stare at him, and he returned her gaze with a
ferocious look. Then it dissolved into a smile. 'Well I'm
damned, it's the baby vamp! Lily – Lily Walters, isn't it?'

Now Lily was completely bewildered. 'Yes. . .but what d'you mean, baby vamp? I don't know you, do I?'

'Oh, but you do! I'm Charles Henderson – I operated on your sister Rose, ooh, it must be five years ago, now, surely? Don't you remember?'

Her face lit up. 'Of course, Doctor! You must think I'm so rude. . .but the uniform, and – and. . .'

'And the limp? I've been growing accustomed to it for four months, now. It'll improve, but I'll spend the rest of my life with steel pins and plates holding my ankle together. So here I am, back where I once served as a humble locum. . .I'm Dr Cann's new partner. The other chap bought it in the Middle East three months ago, and since the Army wouldn't have me back after this, here I am. My civilian suits are being delivered from my old home in a couple of days. What are you doing with yourself? I never thought I'd see a respectable Valleys girl in trousers!'

Lily had stopped blushing at such remarks months before, but something in his smile and voice made her cheeks redden now. She hastily turned to her job to hide her confusion. 'I'm driving for King and Country – and Redmond's Brewery!' she said. 'Best driver north of Newport, so I'm told.'

He put aside his walking stick and seized her by the shoulders. 'By God, you've been sent by my guardian angel! Are you really an experienced driver?'

'Yes, of course! That's my van. They wouldn't let me in it if I wasn't, would they?'

'In that case, I'm poaching you! What time d'you finish?'

'About half past three, usually. I do start early, see.'

'Fine. Have time to settle it before evening surgery. . . Can you call down at the Swan at about four?'

'I suppose so, Doctor, but why?'

'Tell you then. Surprise. Until later. . .' He retrieved his stick and limped away.

Lily, still mystified, presented herself at the surgery near the Swan public house at four o'clock. Henderson was waiting impatiently outside the front door. 'Ah, my ministering angel, at last!' he said. 'Come with me, I've something to show you.' He led her off to the side of the building, and got her to help him open the coach house doors.

Inside were two large, gleaming motor cars. He gestured widely at them. 'Two chariots, with but one charioteer,' he said, 'and between you and me, that charioteer is getting more irritable every day!'

'I don't understand.'

'You will, shortly. My injury prevents me from driving for at least two years, maybe for ever. If I waggle my foot around on those pedals too soon, it will undo all the good work of a very expensive orthopaedic surgeon. So, I cannot drive. And my senior partner, who accepted the situation without demur when I first joined him, is finding it more irksome every day. You see, he has to do all the house calls, while I spend my time in the consulting room. He is exhausted; I am bored. Therefore, the practice needs a driver, but the war has ensured we cannot find one – until now, that is!'

'B-but I already have a job!' She did not say it with any great enthusiasm.

'Mmm. . .I had cause to telephone Mr Redmond at the brewery this afternoon. On consideration of the vast amount of medical attention required by his aged mother, he was forced to agree that it was his patriotic duty to see the doctor had a driver. I fear that unless you come to me, you are now unemployed.'

She gaped at him, the seeds of indignation beginning to sprout in her mind. 'You didn't seem a bit like this when you saw to our Rose,' she said. 'What have happened to you?'

He roared with laughter. 'My dear girl, an emergency operation after some sort of violent family incident hardly forms a suitable backdrop for assessing a man's true character, does it? Not to mention the fact that you were a child at the time. . .'

'Or the fact that now I can be bloody useful to you if you do just take the trouble to charm me out of the trees? I'm going. The brewmaster will talk old Redmond into giving me my job back – he do know they'll never get another driver as good as me. . .'

Henderson let out a little yelp of surprise and hobbled after her as she started to leave. 'Wait, Lily. . .Miss Walters! Please don't be offended! I thought. . .that is. . .'

'You thought you only had to turn on the charm and I'd fall for it like a ton of bricks, didn't you?' As she spoke she turned and glared at him, hands on hips. 'Well, Dr-bloody-high-and-mighty. . .you were right!'

Now it was her turn to laugh. 'Of course I'll come and work for you. But I couldn't resist giving you a taste of your own medicine first. Who d'you think you are, ordering people around, losing them their jobs, just because you think they can't say no to you?'

'Touché, Miss Walters – oh, it's no use. You can only come and work for me if I can call you Lily. Is it agreed?'

'Agreed.' They shook hands on it, both grinning broadly. Then she said, 'Oh, one thing, though – you'd have to match my wages up the brewery.'

'I think we might even do a little better than that, Lily, so don't worry your head on that matter. Now, I suggest that we take a short spin in the car to ensure it's entirely to your satisfaction. . .maybe take it up to see whether your mother approves.'

That really made Lily laugh. '*Iesu mawr* – she'll think I've come home with the rich husband she've always wanted me to find!'

'Well, you never can tell.'

'Oh, but I can. I been spoken for a year or more. It's just that she'll never accept it as long as there's breath in her body. Come on, let's try her out.' He was never sure whether she meant the car or her mother.

Charles Henderson transformed Lily's life. Her mother almost grovelled when she arrived home with him to explain her planned job change, and by the time the doctor left, Margaret Ann was already becoming jittery in her desire to escape and tell the neighbours about it. But that was only the beginning. Shortly before Lily started working for the practice, Henderson came to see her mother again.

'I thought I should come in person, Mrs Walters, because I understand it might be a delicate matter. In order to perform her duties properly, Lily must be on call at all times, so of course it will be necessary for her to live in. I realized after I had left the other day that I had failed to raise the matter.'

Margaret Ann was so shocked she was barely beginning to marshall her protests before he went on. 'Naturally, we shall take care that everything is quite proper. You know Mrs Jones, our housekeeper. She has her own quarters within the house, but there will be no need for that with Lily. There is a small apartment over the coach house which would have had to be modernized eventually, so we've decided to do it now, and Lily will live there – rent free, of course. It will be an extra on top of her wages. She'll have her own small bathroom and kitchen, and a sizeable bed-sitting room. Her quarters will be completely separate from the house.'

He gave Margaret Ann his most winning smile. 'Perhaps you'd care to come and inspect it as soon as the builder has finished. He shouldn't be too long.'

Lily, eavesdropping out in the passage, was hugging

herself with delight. She had no need to see her mother
to know the scale of the conflict being waged in her
mind. She wanted Lily tied to her always, but she also
wanted her to have status and respect. She wanted to
police the girl's morals, but she was too much in awe
of Dr Henderson to dare suggest that his proposal
was anything but proper. Henderson emerged from
the kitchen, only a couple of steps ahead of Margaret
Ann, and Lily jumped up guiltily from her seat at
the bottom of the stairs, striving to keep a straight
face.

'Oh, there you are,' said Margaret Ann, still flustered
from her summary defeat. 'The doctor have come to
offer you accommodation with the job, but I said I
didn't know if you'd think it was right. . .'

'I'll have to live in, Mam. What would he do if there
was an emergency call?' She had the good sense to cut
off the other half of her remark – in the middle of the
night – suspecting that it would have pushed Margaret
Ann a little too far.

With a vast inner sigh of relief, Lily left the family
home three weeks later and moved into the old coach-
man's flat above what was now the motor house. She
had quickly tired of sharing Rose's parlour-bedroom,
and Rose was not sorry to see her go. Both of them
had become accustomed to privacy after a lifetime of
overcrowding, and neither now relished the prospect
of losing it.

Lily loved her new job, and it expanded to suit her
own developing talents. Cann and Henderson had discovered they needed someone to keep the surgery records and handle the increasing amount of paperwork
that war and bureaucracy were wishing on them. They
seldom needed clerical help and a driver at the same
time, so Lily began taking on the office work. It was

straightforward enough, and she found herself enjoying it. Imperceptibly at first, the cultivated atmosphere of the practice started rubbing off on her. It took less than a year for the wilder twists of Valleys patois to fade from her speech. Soon 'ent' was replaced by 'isn't', and she started recognizing the grammatical difference between 'has' and 'have'. Her Welsh accent was as strong as ever, but the elimination of the commoner blunders from her speech made her sound as if she had never been near the Ranks in her life.

Fortunately for her, she had not been home long enough before she took the driving job for the neighbours to realize she had not brought the new accent back from Cardiff. It was more acceptable that she should have grown up speaking thus; had they realized it was a new, though accidental, acquisition, she would have been accused of snobbery. Margaret Ann adored it; Evan teased her but on the whole approved, and her brothers good-naturedly mocked her at every opportunity. Lily herself, still convinced she sounded as she always had, could not understand what all the fuss was about.

In mid-1917, George got his first home leave – ten days away from the Front, his only leave yet outside France. By now there was sufficient news of wounded and shocked soldiers to make Lily nervous about the nature of the man she would meet. For the first time, a one-week courtship two years before seemed a pathetically insubstantial basis for life-long commitment.

But when he arrived, her doubts were swept away. There was something fresh and eternally young about George Griffiths which not even two years in the trenches could expunge. And whatever the conflict might do to the hearts and minds of others, he appeared to thrive on it.

After the initial excitement over his arrival, the

family tactfully found other things to occupy them and
left him with Lily in the parlour. Lily giggled nervously
and looked round at the chilly, buttoned-up little room.
'I always hated this place,' she said. 'Unless you're too
tired, shall we go for a walk?'

He smiled. 'I thought you'd never ask. It's a bit
like the railway compartment between Paddington and
Newport in here.'

Hand in hand, they strolled back to their old
courting ground alongside the Gwyddon stream, and
sat beneath the same trees to exchange lovers' confidences and, inevitably, to talk about the war.

'It's strange, George,' said Lily. 'I expected the war to
have marked you, but it hasn't. You look happier now
than before you enlisted.'

'I am. If the fighting went on for ever, I think I
could put up with it. Anything's better than what I
come from.'

Lily was powerless to prevent herself from shuddering. She tried to remember that coal had destroyed
George's whole family, but still it seemed unnatural to
enjoy the life he had now. Somehow this was not the
way she had expected her perfect knight to feel. With
an effort, she redirected her attention to what he was
saying. Now he was chattering happily about the pleasure the men felt when they received parcels or letters
from home.

'You do never realize how exciting a parcel is until
you open it in the trenches, sharing it with your mates,'
he said. 'Knowing someone back home is caring about
you. . .it's like all the best Christmases rolled into one.
I bet you never thought Oxo cubes was exciting! *Duw*,
I don't think I'll ever see one after the war without it
cheering me up!'

He ran on from impression to impression, and Lily's
unease faded as she was caught up in his vivid descriptions. He was certainly brighter since she had last seen

him. Perhaps it was true; perhaps, for some, the real threat was the pit, and even the war to end all wars paled by comparison. After all, he was not the first man to flee the coalfield. Her brother Billie was another. . .

'Billie. . .' she interrupted. 'Do you ever see Billie these days?'

''Course I do – I'm in his company, en' I? We'm still good butties.'

'How is he, George? He must be dying for a bit of leave himself.'

'To tell the truth, love, I wish he could have had this one instead of me. God knows he do look overdue for it. Funny, he was fine in the beginning, but since he've been off sharpshooting, he's a changed man.'

'Sharpshooting? Billie was doing that?'

'Aye.' George laughed, aware of the irony of gentle Billie cold-bloodedly lining up men in a rifle sight and shooting them one by one. 'It was sheer accident he ever got stuck with it. Seems he did a fair bit of target practice when he was on quiet postings before the war. Real expert marksman by the time we started bashing the Huns. So they put him in a sharpshooting detachment.'

'And he was all right?'

'Fine, great. Never got scratched, always bright and chirpy. I asked him about it once, and all he'd say was, "George, they ent really men – they'm cardboard targets at the fair, running across the front of the shooting booth and getting put up again when we shoots 'em down. Long as I keep telling myself that, I'm all right." He was, an' all.'

'On the surface, maybe. But Billie's not stupid. He couldn't blot it out like that for ever.'

'Aye, that's what the company commander said when he took him off it. Of course, he had reasons of his own. The army don't never do nothing except to suit its own convenience. They wanted miners, see.'

'Miners! Dear God, don't say they set Billie to mining!'

George nodded. 'Me, too. We was in the same party. Didn't bother me, but it played havoc with your Billie.'

'I'm not surprised. I *am* surprised at you not minding, though. What about all your feelings about the pits?'

He shrugged. 'Don't really understand it myself. When they put us on the detail, I thought, oh, no, that's me gone. But it wasn't like that at all. You see, Lil, all the time I'm in one o' them tunnels, I do know the fresh air is only fifteen or twenty feet above my head.'

'But there's still enough rock and soil overhead to smother you or crush you if it falls.'

'I know that, an' all. You'll just have to take my word for it. The only thing that do seem to frighten me about mining is doing it down a coal pit. Get me away from there and I'm happy as a sandboy.'

'Billie wasn't, though.'

'Hell, not him! He's a brave lad and he don't make a fuss, but I've seen his face when we'm listening for the krauts digging the other way, and he do always look as if he's dead already. I don't know how much longer he'll be able to bear it, Lil.'

She found it hard to go on discussing Billie. It was much more straightforward for her to understand his trouble than George's lack of it, and she longed to be able to ease Billie's terror.

Eventually George saw how upset she was, and turned the talk to other things. She was half-way through a deliberately dramatized account of her doings as a driver, when he stopped her by putting his fingers against her lips.

'Sorry to interrupt you, my darling, but I had to do that. You got the loveliest mouth I've ever seen. When Billie introduced us that day, it was all I saw – that beautiful, smiling mouth. . .' He leaned forward and kissed her, gently at first, then with mounting excitement.

His embrace released two years of tension in Lily, and she relaxed against him, swept by the desire she had dimly sensed in that long-ago week with him, fuelled, now, by her growing maturity.

As his hands began to explore her body, she heard a dog bark close by and sprang away from him. 'Not here, George! Half the village do come up here rabbiting now meat's so short. . .' She saw and understood his frustration, and reached out to stroke his cheek. 'That – that doesn't mean, not anywhere. . .I've got a place of my own, now, remember.'

He stared at her, disgesting the implication of what she was saying. A girl didn't issue that sort of invitation if she was going to stop at a quick kiss and cuddle. 'What about your boss, or the housekeeper? They'd tell your mam if they was to see me, and then you'd be for it.'

'Why do they have to see you? They sleep at night, same as anyone else. You've just got to be careful, that's all. Come down late – after midnight – and go back before daylight. Only the boys'll know you're gone, and even they might be too fast asleep to see. Anyhow, they wouldn't tell on us.'

They walked back to the village together, but without touching, both of them intensely aware of the gravity of what they planned. Lily had to be on duty for evening surgery, and now George walked down to the Swan with her to see precisely where the entrance to her flat was.

He kissed her chastely on the cheek before they parted, and whispered, 'See you later, then. I'll be counting every second.'

'And me. Oh, George, I do love you!'

As she turned in through her front door and hurried up the stairs to the flat, she wondered whether that was true. Impatience swept over her. Whether it was or not, she had realized this afternoon that she wanted him physically, and she was sure now that unless she had him, she would never be certain of the depth of her love.

It was almost one in the morning when she saw him hurrying down Commercial Road. She slipped downstairs and opened her front door silently as he arrived there. Once she had closed it behind them, she went to his arms at once, breathless as much at her own daring as with passion. Her long, smooth arms twined round his neck and he bent to kiss her, feeling as if he were drowning in her lips.

Lily led him upstairs. A heavily-shaded lamp burned at the bedside. The curtains were tightly drawn. Just inside the door, she stood away from him and unbuttoned her dressing gown, slipping it from her shoulders and letting it fall. George uttered a long sigh and stood, gazing at her.

After a moment of complete stillness, Lily murmured, 'You'll have to show me, George. I've never done anything like this before.'

'Oh, Lily, my beautiful, wonderful Lily! Come to bed!'

A couple of hours later she lay in the crook of his arm, watching his profile as he slept, and stifled an impulse to giggle. Not that it had been her first reaction. At the beginning, he had excited her unbelievably, raising her to such a pitch of arousal that she thought she would faint. As he moved both hands down between her thighs and spread them, to enter her without hurting her too much, she felt her whole body surge out to meet him, and there was no pain at all. But then, for her at least, nothing further happened. George was obviously enjoying himself, he was moaning and heaving against her, calling her name occasionally in a low, choking voice. But Lily seemed to be suspended on a threshold somewhere between excitement and fulfilment, and nothing he did took her any closer to one or the other. Eventually, he made one huge final thrust against her and was still for a while before he started stroking her hair and kissing her again.

Was that really the great moment the books hinted at? If only Lexie were here to tell her whether it was or not. . . That was when she had to stifle the giggle. Oh, well, George seemed happy enough. Maybe it would be more impressive the next time, or the time after that. . .

And maybe, said a disagreeable voice in her heart, *maybe he's not right for you after all. . .*

He came back at night twice during the rest of his leave. By now, Lily was nervous. It was impossible to have grown up in Bute Street and not to know what happened to girls who did what she had done this week. Perhaps she would be lucky, but her parents' fertility gave her no great confidence of that. It wouldn't have been so bad if it had been the best thing that ever happened to her, but really, she felt she had been more excited the first time she drove the brewery truck on her own.

After a while she decided her best course was to concentrate on her work and hope she was all right. It would be at least three weeks before she would know. She also decided she would not let George come to her flat again before he returned to the Front. It made her feel ungenerous and guilty to deny him after encouraging him, but on reflection, she decided it would not have taken a great deal of thought on his part to avoid giving her the worry she was going through now. Lily dismissed George from her mind and went to start up the car for Charles Henderson's morning round.

As he climbed into the front passenger seat beside her, Henderson said, 'Lily, don't drive off for a moment. There's something I must say to you.'

She turned to face him, and alarm jolted her when she saw his sombre expression.

'I saw your young man leaving this morning; and yesterday.' Horrified, she began to babble excuses at him, but he silenced her with a gesture. 'Stop. Hear me out. I'm not going to criticize you or tell anyone what you've been up to. I'm worried about you, that's all.'

Lily took a deep breath and leaned back in the driving seat. Henderson went on, 'He could be killed next week, Lily. I don't want to upset you, but it's all too true. Then where would you be? This community has unforgiving attitudes. Your own mother is one of the worst. She would disown you and they'd run you out of the village.'

At last she found a voice. 'H-how did you find out?'

'Thank you for not assuming I'd spied on you. I confess that thought had worried me. I still don't get much sleep, thanks to this leg of mine. It gets particularly bad when I've lain in one spot half the night, and I often get up in the small hours and go for a short walk. I've done so twice this week. . .at about four in the morning. Each time, I've seen George Griffiths leaving the motor house.'

Lily closed her eyes and took another deep breath. She felt faint. After a moment, without opening her eyes, she said, 'What if I'm pregnant?'

'There are several answers to that. The most obvious one is that you can marry the boy earlier than you intended. Unfortunately, his absence at the Front militates against that. . .er, there is another solution, of course.'

He said no more, and after a while Lily opened
her eyes again and stared at him. 'What? Tell me,
please.'

'I could help – help you not to have the baby.'

'B-but that's against the law!'

'I know, and it happens every day. Lily, I don't want
you to throw yourself away, and if you are pregnant
as a result of a few nights' youthful foolishness, that's
what you'll be doing.'

'Even if George and I marry in the end?'

'Especially then. What a dreadful start for a marriage! Anyway, I'm getting a distinct impression that
you're less than completely enamoured with our
Mr Griffiths.'

She felt herself blushing furiously. 'Why would you
think something so silly?'

'Because you have different concerns from those
normally shown by a girl in the grip of full-blooded
passion. Lily, I'll say it again – don't throw yourself
away. Let me help you if necessary.'

'I'll think about it. Can't say more than that, can I?
There may be no need.'

'Let's hope not. Now, it's time we did the round, I
think.'

The fortnight that followed seemed interminable.
Lily scarcely noticed George's departure for France,
although he positively wallowed in devotion to her
and said he hardly knew how he would last without
her until his next leave. To Lily, nothing seemed real
except the possibility that she was pregnant and would
be disgraced.

On 3 July, Charles Henderson was in his consulting
room early, reading a medical journal article which
covered research findings that interested him. The
door burst open and a radiant Lily rushed in.

'It's all right,' she said, 'oh Dr Henderson, it's all right!'

She was so lovely, and Henderson felt so relieved, that before he knew it, he had crossed the room and taken her in his arms. He managed to regain control before he actually kissed her, but it was a near run thing. Instead he gave her a little shake, which he hoped was fatherly, then held her at arm's length.

'Now, Lily, you promise you'll be sensible in future?'

'I swear I will – really I do! I never went through such a terrible time in all my life!'

'Go on then, back to work. Just remember, if you're ever in trouble again, you know where to come.'

Outside his consulting room, Lily was fussing with medical records she could not even see clearly. Her hand still burned where he had held it, and she felt his physical presence like an electric shock. '*Iesu mawr!*' she murmured. 'Maybe that's what it should have been like with George!'

CHAPTER TWENTY-TWO

T HE WALTERS FAMILY turned out in force for Christmas services at the Garn chapel in 1918. Billie and George were back from France, and whole, even if Billie had trouble with his nerves. On Christmas morning, Evan himself went with them, and his big basso voice sang out as enthusiastically as his women's contraltos and sopranos in thanksgiving that the two had been spared.

It was George's first week out of the army, and all the sweeter for that. Lily clung to him at every opportunity, touching him and smiling at him as if she found it hard to believe he was really home and safe. George was merry and talkative, and the mud and blood of Flanders seemed to him to have existed in another universe.

Billie was not home yet. He was suffering from a condition the army described as battle fatigue, or alternatively, shellshock, and had recently been transferred from a specialist centre in rural England to the county mental hospital near Abergavenny.

George was forced to confront hard reality early on the morning of 27 December, when he and Evan descended together in the Celynen South cage for George's first underground shift since 1915. The alternative jobs he had envisioned back in 1917 had not materialized, and now he was back at the work he hated more than anything else.

As they stepped out at the pit bottom, he muttered to Evan, 'I'm trembling, and my teeth's chattering, Evan. Even Ypres didn't feel as bad as this.'

Evan gave him a sympathetic punch in the arm. 'Told you the real heroes stayed home, mun! Come on, it ent that bad – you do just forget the dark and the smell, that's all.' They moved off into inky blackness, punctuated only by the fitful glimmer of cap lamps.

They were working as butties, on a narrow seam which could only be attacked from the side. As they got down, George said, 'Evan, I ent a man for premonitions, but I'm shit-scared. If I do feel like this every morning when I come on shift, I ent going to last a fortnight.'

The older man gave a grunting laugh. 'Funny how much easier it do get when there ent no alternative.'

'I don't understand.'

''Course you don't – you've never had to, have you? When it felt wrong for you, you could bugger off into the army. There wasn't no war like that when I was twenty – nor no other job, neither, just an old granny to support and a black hole in the ground. So I went down, for the five or six hundredth time – I'd started when I was eleven, see, but I still wasn't used to it. My teeth was chattering, and all, even after all them goddamned shifts, and I was sweating, although it was bloody cold down there. We still used candles in them days, and they was flaring and bobbing and you kept telling yourself you wasn't deep enough for bad firedamp. . .and not believing yourself. I don't mind you shivering and shaking, But. Just don't kid yourself it's because you'm special. I could have told you this was worse than Ypres and the Somme put together, and I've never been away from it. What could be worse than this? There had to be an end to the War, but this do go on for ever.'

Around them, water dripped and small runnels of

coal dust occasionally poured down harmlessly from
overhead. Distant engines clattered, and the irregular clang of metal against metal told them where the
nearest journey of trams was moving. A constant hot
breeze swept over them, keeping fresh air circulating
through the pit. They settled into their stint, and after a
while George realized Evan was right: anyone with half
the sense he was born with was terrified every time he
went underground to start a shift. He was not unique
because he felt it.

Somehow, the thought comforted him. His fear and
his sense of doom had quite vanished when they
stopped half-way through the shift for their meal
break. That was when the roof came down.

The rumbling started a long way off, like a vast belch
in the belly of a sleeping giant. It surged along the
headings, taking its time, testing the pit props, shaking one here, snapping one there. But it waited until
it got to Evan and George before it really showed what
it could do.

Evan was just about to start eating when he sensed
something was wrong – at first, only a suspicion of
another noise over the multitude of noises that made
up his working world. Then it rippled closer, and
he was sure. Hurling aside his bread and cheese, he
yelled at George, 'Into the stall, mun – roof's coming
down!' and jumped for shelter, dragging his startled
butty with him.

As they moved, Tommy Pearce, working a few yards
further back, started running towards them, his lamp
bobbing erratically as he came. 'Fall, it's a fall –
back th. . .' Then his light went out, there was a
soft 'Crump!', a lot of dust, and they were sealed
in blackness.

The first thing George was aware of was a swaying
beam of dim light against broken coal and rock very
close to his face. He was not uncomfortable, but he

could not free himself. After a while, he realized the bobbing light was his own cap lamp.

'Y-you all right, are you, George?' The voice, hoarse and choking, was Evan's.

'I think so. . .your light gone, have it?'

'Aye, and the Davey lamp. Think it's just you and me, George. The fall took Tommy. . .I think I can just about reach my jack, if a drop of cold tea will help.'

'Can't think of nothing I'd like better, Evan. Pass it over, will you?'

'Don't think I can, mun. Only my fingers seems to be working. . .the other. . .other arm's gone altogether. . .I can grip the jack, but – not – lift. . .'

George managed to twist the upper part of his body and feel down along Evan's arm towards the jack. They seemed to be lying close together in a space that had been virtually filled with rocks, coal dust and bigger lumps. 'Pity you ent a girl, Georgie,' Evan gasped. 'This might be quite amusing then. . .' His words were cut off by a low cry, and for the first time, George managed to turn himself and his lamp to illumine the area around the older man.

'Oh, Christ! Evan – can you breathe?'

It seemed impossible that he could, for two twisted timber roof supports had crashed down across his chest, and were still pinned there by a boulder. His left arm had vanished altogether under what appeared to be solid rock. Evan managed a rattling laugh. 'Not so's you'd notice, But. I don't think I want a drink, anyhow. . .you have that.'

George's fingers touched Evan's on the tea jack, and he managed to move it up where he could unscrew the top. As he drank, the other man started coughing. George put aside the jack and focused the lamp on him. Blood was trickling blackly out of the corner of his mouth. He gripped Evan's hand again, and felt the other's fingers close convulsively on his own.

'Told you it was worse than the fucking Somme,' said Evan. He was silent then for a long time, apart from the terrible rattling cough. Some time later – hours or days, George did not know – the coughing stopped, and Evan said in a voice free of pain, 'Sorry, love. I really am sorry.' Then there was a rush of blood and coughing and he was still.

They lay together, living and dead, in a strangely comforting embrace. George passed into a light-headed state, part of his brain reassuring him he was all right, because he could still wonder whether it was shock or lack of oxygen. Eventually, beyond all hope, he heard faint tapping from beyond the fall. He mustered every ounce of will he possessed, and yelled at the top of his voice, 'Here – I'm here! Dig, you buggers!' Then he fainted.

The rescue team had already taken out three corpses and two badly injured men. Everyone was accounted for now except Evan Walters and George Griffiths. Dai Williams, who was leading the rescue team, said, 'This do look bad – mainly loose dust. They'll be lucky not to have suffocated.'

They started working carefully into the mountain of small coal, then the lead collier encountered a pair of legs protruding through the dust. He started scooping it aside, and was faced by a barrier of heavy rock and broken timber which pinioned the man to the ground. As he moved back to get better purchase for moving the load and freeing the casualty, a voice started shouting to them to dig him out.

It took over an hour to lever Evan Walters's body from beneath the roof fall. He had taken the main brunt of the roof fall on his shoulder and torso, had been crushed from midriff to knees and had been dead for hours. They never found his left arm. As they pulled him free, there was another long, threatening rumble, but ahead of them this time. Moments later,

George Griffiths, still trapped by his crushed legs, was killed as the remaining section of roof collapsed over his workplace.

Haydn broke the news to Margaret Ann. She already knew there had been a roof fall: such news travelled fast in mining communities. She was in the kitchen, brewing the latest in an endless succession of pots of tea for when Evan would come home. There was no soft way of telling her.

'The two of them, Mam. George and our Dad. Same roof fall.'

Margaret Ann uttered an animal howl and sank to her knees on the jute mat by the fire. 'No!' she shrieked. 'God, no! Take everything, but not him – not him, please, not yet!' And she bundled herself into a tiny ball of misery, stooped over the piece of matting.

Haydn stood frozen for long moments, then he moved across to her. 'Mam? Come on, love, let's get you into a chair. . . Sorry I come straight out with it. . .no other way, see. . . Come on, now, have some tea, ennit?' But he might not have been there. His mother had wrapped herself so tightly that he could not straighten her. She remained thus for over an hour, mumbling, sobbing and occasionally crying out.

Finally, when Haydn had given up and Gareth had gone to fetch the doctor, she relaxed, uncurled her small body and dragged herself upright with the support of Evan's Windsor chair. She slumped into it, then turned to her son.

'They'm a long time bringing him back, ent they?'

Haydn went over to her and grasped her shoulders, pressing her small, frail body against his own. 'They won't be bringing him back, Mam. He was hurt too bad. Tom Gilchrist have arranged it all – they've been

taken up Ellis Williams's chapel of rest. Ellis will see to
him and then you can go up and say goodbye.'

'No. I want him here. I'm going to lay him out.'

'You can't, Mam, I told you. . .it was too bad. Please
wait till Ellis is ready!'

But he was wasting words. She was incoherent again.
At that point, Dr Cann arrived and gave her a massive
sedative. After that, they made sure she was half asleep
until the funeral, and she accepted that she could not
see her dead husband until the undertaker had made
his appearance bearable.

Lily did not get even this comfort. At least Evan's
skull and face had been left intact. George Griffiths
had taken the full impact of the final fall on his head
and shoulders, and there was nothing left for the
undertaker to improve upon. His battered remains
were cleaned up, wrapped in a shroud and sealed
without any question of an open coffin.

The day of the funeral was cold and brilliantly sunny.
The family had let Margaret Ann surface gently to
reality in order to pay her last respects to Evan. Now
she waited, dressed in black from head to foot, to be
taken to the Garn for the funeral service. From there,
two horse-drawn hearses would take the remains of
Evan and George to the cemetery at the Chapel of Ease.

Everyone had come home for the funeral, even John
Daniel, whom his mother had not seen for ten years.
Bethan, now in her first year as a probationer nurse
at Cardiff Royal Infirmary, arrived by train the day
before the burial. Rhys travelled up in his new motor
car on the day, largely to save Margaret Ann the
embarrassment of dealing with him for too long. Only
two members of the family who had known Evan were
absent – Lexie and Lily.

It did not occur to Margaret Ann to ask about Rhys's

daughter. She had never acknowledged the girl's existence and saw no reason why she should start now. Lily's
absence was different.

Lily had risen very early that morning and had gone
off up the Gwyddon valley alone, retracing the walk
which she and George had taken so often in their few
short days together. Now she sat, looking down at the
distillery pond, and wondering about the nature of her
own feelings. Where there should have been grief for
the man she had planned to marry, there was only
an aching void. The pain she felt at the loss of her
father was unspeakable, but her guilt at feeling only
emptiness for George eclipsed it for the time being.
She did not know what to do. She wanted to go to the
chapel and pay her last respects to Evan, but despised
the tacit lie she would tell by apparently being there as
chief mourner for George Griffiths.

Too late, she understood she had loved a will-o-the-
wisp. She had seen a tall, well-made young man who
had led a hard life, and she had fallen in love with
her own picture of him. It had no substance, and his
death had released her rather than blighting her life.
She found it impossible to come to terms with such a
brutal reality.

Lily sighed, stood up and brushed the winter grass
from her skirt, then started along the path back down
to the pond bridge. She still wavered in her intention
to attend the funeral. At the bridge, she stopped again,
and stared gloomily into the water. Nothing offered
her an answer. Perhaps she should simply stay here
and brood, and let the funeral take care of itself. . .

'Come along, Lily, you won't find any solace there. If
you're staring deep into liquid, a glass of whisky will do
you more good!'

Startled, she glanced up. Charles Henderson stood a
few feet from her, at the village side of the bridge, his
hand extended to bring her back across.

'H-how did you find me?'

'I followed you, my dear. I didn't want another corpse decorating the place tomorrow.'

She managed a tired laugh. 'I'm not the sort who commits suicide.'

'No? If anything could make you, perhaps guilt would. Nothing else, though, I think.' He came across the bridge. 'Lily, you have nothing about which to feel guilty.'

'He's dead, and he died thinking he was the love of my life. . .and oh, Dr Henderson – he wasn't! Perhaps I'll never have one!' For the first time since the accident, she shed tears. 'That poor boy, going to his grave with no one really to love him. That's terrible, isn't it?'

'Perhaps. It's also a state common to a vast proportion of the human race. We are all common clay in the end, Lily, as I'm sure you'll find out if you listen to the admirable sermon the minister will doubtless have prepared. May I take you back? Your mother needs you.'

'No, she doesn't. She thinks she needs me, because she thinks I'm suffering the way she is. Well, you know I'm not – it's sham! So how can I shame my father's memory by pretending to grieve for a sweetheart in the same way as Mam is grieving for him?'

'I think it's time you stopped this self-indulgent nonsense and started helping your family with some of your strength.'

'Me, strong? Don't be silly. I'm nothing.'

'Lily, listen carefully to me. You have just lost the two dearest people in your world. You are strong, very strong, so you are surviving by denigrating your own grief, pretending it's unworthy. That might make you feel better, but it will devastate your mother. She needs you now, at least. Go to her. Stay by her until this terrible time is over. Then go away for a while and recover yourself. But don't injure yourself for ever by making this ridiculous pretence of unworthiness.'

She looked at him sharply. 'You mean that, don't you?'

'I never meant anything more sincerely in all my life.'

'But you know better than anybody that I don't really love George! I think you're the one person who realized it as soon as I did.'

'Possibly sooner.'

'Then you should see why I feel guilty.'

'I see why someone else might feel guilty, but I think you have more intelligence. There's more than this waiting for you, Lily. You're not twenty-one yet. Say goodbye to your past, bury your dead. Then get away for a while and make peace with yourself. After that you can begin to live properly.'

'For what? Everything's gone.'

He laughed. 'Now that really is self-indulgence! Go off and live your life, for God's sake – or the Devil's!'

'But there isn't anyone waiting for me – just me – anywhere in the world.'

'I might.'

Silence spread like a wide ripple from his last remark, and throughout it he regarded her steadily. Lily was the first to look away.

'I never thought of that.'

'You're dissembling again, Lily.'

'I don't even know what dissembling means.'

'I think you do. However, let's not split hairs. I shall rephrase what I said. When you are ready to return to Abercarn, please feel free to regard me as a friend. I'll find a way of keeping your job open for a few months – I don't think you'll need longer – and when you've worked out all your misery, you can come and confide in me on any terms you like. There – does that suit you better?'

She was eyeing him warily now. 'Have you ever lost an argument?'

'Several, my dear. I have some very private scars to

prove it. But I have a feeling I shan't lose this one. Now, are you coming? If we don't go soon, it will be too late.'

She stretched out her hand to him. 'All right, then; on one condition. After the fuss has died down, you'll get in touch with Uncle Rhys for me and ask if it's all right for me to go back to Cardiff with him and Lexie.'

'By all means, but why do you want me to do it?'

'Because if I do, I'll feel as if I'm letting Mam down. She'll expect me to stay with her for good now, but I'll go mad if I do that. With you getting hold of Rhys, I can say it's doctor's orders, and p'raps she won't take it quite so hard then. All right?'

'All right. Come, now. We still have time to get back to the house before they leave for the Garn.'

CHAPTER TWENTY-THREE

T HE SMELL, SHE thought — *I'd forgotten how wonderful the smell was! All this time, I could only remember the scent of the smart end of town, because you get it coming out of the station. But this is my home smell, the Bay!*

Coming into Cardiff by open car, they avoided the station area and she was able to appreciate Butetown's aroma to the full. Rhys had insisted on driving up to fetch her from Abercarn, and Lily was grateful for his considerate act. He was a perfect companion, cheerful and affectionate without showing false sentimentality. Occasionally he talked about Evan, and did not apologize for his memories. He referred to George only once.

'I 'xpect you'll want to have a cry on our Lexie's shoulder about that boy of yours,' he said. 'But she haven't had a hard knock like that herself yet, so remember, if you want someone who've lived through it, you can come to me.'

Momentarily, emotion choked her. She shook her head and reached over to touch his hand. 'Thanks, Uncle Rhys,' she said eventually. 'I think I might.'

'Good girl. You'll feel a lot better once you've talked it out — and cried it out, an' all. Anyway, here we are, back home, so you can put the grieving off until you'm ready for it, all right?'

'I'll cry now if you go on like that, Uncle Rhys.'

'Why? Thought it would cheer you up to be back.'

'It does. I feel tons better already. But when you say
I'm back home, it – it makes me feel I belong somewhere.'

He was perplexed. 'I'd have thought you were up to
your eyes in belonging places. You got one home up
Abercarn, and another here.'

Lily shook her head. 'No. I thought so at one time,
but I haven't, I can see that now. Mam was always all
over me, but that was just because I reminded her of
Dad except I was easier to manage. You were just the
two when you were boys, weren't you?'

'Yes, but what's that got to do with it?'

'You've got no idea of what it's like being one of a
family big enough to make up a football team, that's
all. In a big family you're always part of a crowd, and
nobody ever really notices you. That isn't home. . .
Look at the way our John Dan and Billie went off. It
wasn't just Mam turning against them that kept them
away. There was nothing worth coming back for. But
when I'm with you and Lexie and Bethan, it's all different. You care about me, and you're always glad to see
me, and you don't just think of me as another pair of
hands to do the washing or get the coal. It's about time
I said thank you for that.'

Rhys laughed, although there was a catch in his
voice. 'Well, well – so much for the joys of a houseful
of brothers and sisters! And I've spent years wondering
how we could make up to you for not having them with
you!'

'Make up to me? I should have been paying you!. . .
Oh, dear, that was a terrible thing to say about them,
really. Don't take any notice of me. I'll get over it soon.
It's just been a bit too much for me, that's all.'

'Lexie wanted to come with me to really give your
mam something to grizzle about, but I said if she did,

you probably wouldn't be allowed back to Abercarn if
you ever wanted to go.'

'Oh, Christ, Uncle Rhys! Poor Lex must feel rotten!'

'Not Lexie. She don't mind being teased by people
who are on her side. It's when they'm enemies she do
get in a state.'

As they talked, he had been driving along the drab
streets behind Cardiff Prison. The bewitching smell
was getting stronger every moment now, as they
approached Hayes Bridge. The bad drains and coal
dust were still there, but there was no trace of the hops
and coffee of the better end of town. A stiff breeze
straight off the East Dock carried the salt-sweet aroma
of tainted sea water, with an undertow of rich oriental
spices, garlic and curry sauce. And underneath that was
the faint whiff of opium and cheap scent.

Rhys wrinkled his nose appreciatively. 'Tide must be
down,' he said. 'You never get that marvellous pong of
gone-off plum cake unless the mudbanks is exposed.
Lovely, ennit?'

The *Anglesey* was looking smarter than when she had
left. 'Spent a bit of my war profits tarting the old place
up,' said Rhys. 'We tycoons have to put something back
into Society, you know.' He moved away to talk to a
regular by the bar.

'War profits? What's he on about?' Lily whispered to
Lexie.

Her cousin gestured at her to drop the matter. 'Don't
ask him, flower. All I know is there was a lot of little
bags of white powder coming through here regular as
clockwork. An awful lot o' the dealers got mopped up
and put in the forces during the war, and the matlows
bringing the stuff in was looking for new distributors.
Who better than good old Rhys Walters, friend of the
rich?'

Lily was fascinated rather than shocked. Butetown quickly leached away moral outrage in all but the most narrow-minded. 'Thought the Chinese wouldn't let anybody else have a look-in,' she said.

Lexie sighed with exasperation. 'Not opium, you daft thing – who uses it except the Chinks, anyway? No, this is snow.'

'What are you on about now?'

'Snow, Lily – sniff the powder and see the pretty picture – cocaine! Christ, you have been gone a long time!'

'I've never even heard of it.'

'No reason why you should have. Seems the rich is going crazy over it. Beats the shit out of whisky and soda and doesn't give them no hangover. Now, leave it alone. I don't like messing with it – there's some pretty awful types tangled up in the trade and I think it's nasty even if it ent dangerous. Fancy being stinking rich and taking stuff to escape from a life that most of us would give our eye teeth for. I wish he'd go back to fencing. There was something respectable about that, somehow.'

Lily found a laugh unexpectedly bubbling to the surface. 'Only down the Bay. . .' she said. 'You wouldn't hear a remark like that anywhere else. Oh, Lex, I am glad to be back!'

Lexie came and put her arms around her, and soon Lily's laughter turned to weeping as she finally began to let out the grief for her father and her lover.

Lily really was happy to be back in Butetown, but soon she noticed that a subtle change had come over her relationship with Lexie. When they had been growing up here together, Lexie invariably led and she followed. Somehow, now, their roles were reversed. Lexie sensed her cousin had been through a harrowing experience which had matured her in all sorts of ways,

and that now, emotionally at least, she was the follower
and Lily the leader.

Rhys noticed it, too. 'Do her good,' he told Lily. 'She's
getting flightier every day, and you know she was bad
enough before you went back to Abercarn. If she don't
slow down soon, she's going to land in real trouble.'

Looking around the pub, Lily decided that Lexie
might not be the only one. It was a different place
from the one she had known until 1915. In those days
it was rough enough – though not by the standards
of places like the House of Blazes or the Packet –
but it had been the roughness of hard-working men
let loose with their pay packets. Now there was a
more sinister atmosphere. Strangers slipped in and
out of the cubby hole at the rear of the main bar
which Rhys used as an office. They certainly had no
connection with the brewery, so there was no obvious
reason why they should be there. The little bags of
white powder insinuated themselves back into Lily's
mind, and she wished Lexie had never mentioned
them to her. At the time, she had assumed it was
something Rhys had stopped when things returned
to normal in 1918. If the number of men slipping
in and out was any indicator, he was only just getting
started.

Nothing was said about Bethan, either. At first, Lily
assumed her sister was simply on a concentrated spell
of hospital duty. But when there was no sign of a visit
after she had been back a week, she asked Lexie about
it.

For once, Lexie was evasive. 'Oh. . .er. . .she've been
a bit funny since she come back after the funeral, Lil.
You know how she worshipped her father. And she've
always been one to keep it to herself. She come back
here as usual, after it was over, but then she said she
was going to be busy for a couple of months, making
up the extra time off she'd taken to go up Abercarn,

and she said she'd better just stay up the nurses' home permanent for a while.'

'But she's been living in ever since she started training, Lexie. It didn't stop her coming down here on the tram every time she got a week-end off – or just an evening, come to that.'

'N-no, I know. But like I said, she really took it hard about your father, and I think she's working herself into the ground until she can get used to it. We didn't like to interfere. . .you know you and me was always much closer to each other than we was to Bethan.'

'How long is it since she came down last, then?'

Again, Lexie avoided looking directly at her. 'Oh, don't know, really. . .hard to tell, with so much going on.'

'Come on, you must have some idea, at least of how many times she's been down since she got back from the funeral.'

'Well, just the once. . . She stayed, mind you, but when she went back on duty, she packed her bags and said she'd move all her stuff in the nurses' home, as half of it was there already.'

'That doesn't sound like Bethan. She always loved being here.'

'Oh, hell, I'm not lying to you, Lily – we'm too close. She got wind of Dad and his. . .his bit o' business. They had a row.'

'I don't believe it! Bethan wouldn't say boo to a goose, let alone Uncle Rhys. As far as she's concerned, he's our Dad's deputy!'

'People change their minds when they start seeing the world, Lil. She went on casualty when she come back first, and a girl our age was brought in, in a bad way. They tried to revive her but they couldn't. . .she'd had too much snow at a party. Chap who dumped her in casualty up the infirmary was in here the next night, through the back office with Dad.'

'And Bethan saw him?'

'Yes. She went mad. Said Dad was no better than a murderer. He said he wasn't taking that, even from his own flesh and blood, and after that it just got worse and worse. In the end she said it was up to him if he wanted responsibility for killing young kids who hadn't had a chance to live yet, but she wasn't spending another minute under the same roof with him.'

'Oh, God, there's awful! Did she have a go at you an' all?'

'No.' Lexie laughed bitterly. 'As a matter of fact, she assumed I didn't know what he was up to. She told me, and asked if I'd like to go with her. If it hadn't been so tragic, I don't think I could have kept a straight face!'

'I don't follow. . .why not?'

'Well, even if I hadn't known, can you imagine me getting by anywhere but down here? I'd hardly fit in up the infirmary, or working in one of the stores along St Mary Street, would I? Up there they think all blacks is good for is a bit of nooky or housework – and I ent earning my crust doing either!'

'Oh, Lex, I am sorry! I didn't know you still felt so strong about it. But what're you going to do? You can't just hide away down here for the rest of your days – you've got your whole life in front of you.'

'Don't worry about me – I got plans, and they don't involve getting old as Dad's housekeeper, neither! But it'll take a bit longer yet. . . I'll tell you about it when things is more settled.'

And with that, Lily had to be content. She was still grieving too much to seek out Bethan and attempt a reconciliation – she needed time, too. In any case, having thought things over and seen the people Rhys ran with now, she was not at all sure she could defend her beloved uncle with much conviction.

*

Spring in Butetown was always an uneasy time. The quickening of plant and animal life which happened even in the industrialized valleys was completely absent here, although the lengthening days and lighter breezes brought restlessness to the inhabitants. The dirty streets seemed shabbier than ever when the first sunbeams showed up the dust and cracked paint. The soaring gulls hinted at a better sea coast than the battered Windsor Esplanade. If ever there was a bad time to see the Bay, it was this, thought Lily. Never was much cop in the sunshine. . .but a voice in her mind said that was not all. She could not decide whether the area or she herself had changed beyond recall in four years, but settling in was far from the easy passage she had expected.

Towards the end of May, she and Lexie spent a sunny afternoon well away from dockland, strolling in the luxuriant greenery of Roath Park. The picture-book tea room, the island lighthouse on the boating lake, the glowing flowerbeds, all conspired to make Butetown seem even more run-down than it was.

As they lingered over a second pot of tea on the terrace outside the little café, Lily said, 'Why doesn't it seem comfortable down there, Lex? Have I changed that much in four years? I don't feel as if I have.'

Lexie shook her head and kicked out moodily at a piece of tree bark. 'Not you – it's the place,' she said. 'I don't like it, neither.'

'But the buildings are the same as ever – I don't think anywhere but the Anglesey has even been painted since 1916! What's gone wrong?'

'Well, it was the War as started it, shifted people around. . .' She adopted an exaggerated Cardiff bully-boy accent: 'Give them bloody blacks an' wogs an' dagos ideas above their station and stopped honest men earning their rightful living.'

'What? Who says that?'

'That's what every white bugger down the Bay is saying these days. If it ent ship the Chinks back where
they belong, it's niggers back to Africa. A couple of
them have said it to me and they know I'm Bay born
and bred.'

'But there's always been people from everywhere
down Butetown. Why now?'

'Told you, the War. We was all colours, before, it's
true, but if you lined everybody up and ignored some
of the light brown 'uns, there was always more whites
than others. It don't look like that any more, though.
They put all the pimps in the army, see – one day they
was all here, next they was in a hole on the Somme. A
lot of 'em never got over it. And to make things worse,
they didn't call up the blacks!'

'What! That must be the first time it's ever been an
advantage.'

'Telling me! The pimps thought the same. See, most
of the coloureds down here may be locals to you and
me, but a lot of them was born in other countries. And
if they wasn't British, they didn't get conscripted. Then
there was so much work going spare down here that
every time a ship full of Arabs or Lascars arrived, half
of them stayed. Human nature being what it is, the gay
girls didn't lose much time moving in with them, and
by the time Our Boys come back from the front, their
berths was permanently taken over.'

Lily was fascinated. 'But surely the girls all rallied
round and gave them a hero's welcome?'

'Not a chance! There can't be many lower forms of
life than a Tiger Bay pimp. They take every penny off
their girls, beat 'em senseless every time they get tanked
up, and sling 'em out on the street the minute they gets
too old or sick to turn over enough money. Half them
girls had never known what it was to be treated right by
a bloke – and most of the blacks and Arabs had been at
sea so long that a double bed with a nice well-padded

tart was the next best thing to heaven. They treated the
girls well, and you can work out the rest for yourself.
When Johnny come marching home again, the front
door was locked.'

'There must have been a lot of trouble.'

'What d'you mean, must have been? It's still brewing.
Haven't nearly come to the boil yet.'

'But the War finished more than six months ago!'

'Aye, and it's taking them months to demob the
troops. Every week we gets another batch coming home
with their German souvenirs and their tall tales, only
they end up sleeping on Poverty Corner instead of in
their old places. There've been flare-ups with a couple of gangs, but it's small beer compared with what's
coming. Mark my words, the top'll blow off the Bay
this summer. You'm uncomfortable because you can
feel it.'

Lily shuddered. 'All these years without trouble
between the races, and now this! Are you sure they'll
turn on each other?'

Lexie shrugged. 'If it was just Bay people, I'd say no.
They'd squabble a bit and break bottles over a couple
of heads, but that would be the end of it. I've heard
rumours, though. People are saying there's outsiders
getting interested in stirring it up. If that do happen,
it could set the whole Docks alight.'

'It makes me feel helpless. You can't ask anybody to
do anything to stop that sort of thing happening, can
you?'

'No, you can't. Think how bad I do feel. I'm black –
well, brown, anyhow. They'm not going to stop and ask
if both my parents was coloured. Lil, for the first time
in my life I'm getting scared of going down the street
after dark.'

That killed Lily's pleasure in the fine afternoon.
Apart from the night after Captain Tupper's arrest
in the 1911 dock strike, she could not remember a

time when any Butetown woman had to worry about
walking unmolested along Bute Street. If it frightened
hard-boiled Lexie, clearly there was cause for anxiety
now.

Throughout May and into June, the pressure mounted, as more soldiers were demobbed and the pre-
war dockland male population came home to find
themselves displaced. The usurpers affected not to
notice the tension. Many of them had lived all their
lives under such pressure. White and coloured ideas
of relaxed multi-racial communities were often poles
apart. The new lords of Tiger Bay were quite prepared
to take on a few fist or bottle fights to retain their king-
dom, and so far it looked as if that would be the worst
of it.

But it could not go on for ever. The home-coming
troops from north of the railway tracks returned to
their old ways. Those from Butetown might find new
homes, but there was no obvious way for them to earn
a living. The port workers had to confront new foreign
labourers, employed at a fraction of their old wages,
whom the employers consequently favoured. The others were ex-pimps, and the girls, their raw material,
were now lost to them.

Just after nine o'clock on the morning of 11 June,
Lily was walking south along Bute Street to buy fish
at a James Street fishmonger's. Glancing along Lower
Bute Street, she saw an unusual flurry of activity for
such an early hour. Outside the Packet, a wonderfully
brash collection of tarts and pimps had gathered, and
two spanking-new horse brakes were drawn up at the
kerb. A barman from the Packet was loading crates of
beer and cases of spirits aboard the vehicles. She even
saw a few bottles of champagne.

Full of curiosity, she scanned the crowd, seeking

someone she knew. After a moment she spied Black
Bet O'Donnell. Black Bet derived her nickname from
her ostentatiously dyed hair and her provocative lace-
trimmed corsets, the top of which were invariably visible nestling in the vertiginous depths of her cleavage.
Bet was a regular at the Anglesey. According to Lexie
she was a former mistress of Rhys. At first she had
frightened Lily, but eventually she got to know her as
a tough, vulgar, noisy, good companion, always ready
to buy drinks for her friends and food for any down-
and-out who asked her.

Today she wore an eye-catching ensemble of black
lace over pale pink silk, a calf-length dress and a
vast hat trimmed with blue-black feathers. Her black
kid high-heeled shoes were fastened with ribbons that
criss-crossed on the instep before twining seductively
up her silk-stockinged legs. It was impossible to ignore
her.

'You look very smart today, Bet,' said Lily. 'Off somewhere nice, then, are you?'

Bet grinned. 'Be seeing us in the *Tatler* next, kid.
Talk about classy! We'm off for a day-trip. The boys
have arranged summat with their mates in Newport.
We'm meeting up with a party from there and going
down St Bride's lighthouse for the afternoon.'

'What's the celebration?'

The woman winked lewdly. 'Better conditions for
working girls, that's what! Most of us here this morning is better off than we ever was before the War. If it
do get any better, I'll be sending the old Kaiser food
parcels as a thank-you for starting it! Anyhow, we'm
off, now. Might see you up the Anglesey tonight, 'cos
we'll be back in time to go to work this evening.'

Lily almost wished she was going with them. They
looked happy, prosperous and exotic – infinitely
removed from day-to-day chores like shopping for
fish. She stood and waved them off as the horse brakes

clattered away, many of the women gesturing with the newly-fashionable Japanese sunshades they carried.

Although there could have been no more than forty on the trip, Butetown seemed strangely deserted for much of that day. Once the businessmen had closed their offices and caught their trains away from dockland, an odd silence descended on the streets.

Lexie was up in town, on some errand of her own about which she was being secretive. Lily knew it had something to do with her plans for self-improvement, but beyond that she could find out nothing. Rhys was out too, and Lily was running the pub in his absence; not that there was any trade to speak of.

It was a hot, brilliantly sunny day and when Lexie arrived home at about six o'clock, she collapsed on a chair in the empty bar and said, 'Quick, give us a cider before I do die of thirst. It's like the bloody Sahara out there!' Then, glancing around her, she added, 'And it's like the *Marie Celeste* in here! Where is everybody?'

Lily told her about the outing. Lexie said, 'But that's only a handful. Where's the rest of 'em? I don't like this. . . Remind you of anything, do it?'

Remembering her thoughts of 1911 a few weeks ago when Lexie had talked of her fears about being out at night, Lily nodded. 'The strike,' she said, barely above a whisper. 'Just like this, wasn't it?'

Lexie nodded, her eyes sombre. 'Saw something ever so funny on the way home,' she said. 'I walked back down East Canal Wharf, because I wanted to see if that man had got our Indian silk in yet. There was a bobby on point duty there. I been going along there all my life, and that's the first time I ever seen a copper there. There ent enough traffic to need point duty. And then I got to thinking. . .I ent never seen uniformed soldiers around them parts, neither. But there was two of them a bit further up, just before I passed the bobby. They wasn't carrying rifles or nothing. Just, sort of, lurking around. Didn't even look as if they was supposed to be there.'

Before Lily had time to respond, the back door opened and Rhys came in. He had just put away his car in the old stable building behind the pub. Without any greeting, he started forward down the room.

'Seen Joe anywhere?' he asked. Joe was the cellar-man, and was due to start his evening's work any time now. Both girls shook their heads. 'I'll need one of you two to help me, then. Come on, let's get the shutters up. Lily, you'm not dressed up in your best, you come and lend a hand. I want you by the door, Lex, ready to lock up the minute we've finished out there.'

Lexie stared at him. 'What the hell's going on?' she asked. 'I know we ent bristling with customers yet, but it's only ten past six! You'd think the Germans was coming.'

'This could be worse – now get moving. When we'm locked up, I want you out through the back and upstairs. There's going to be a lot of trouble tonight.'

'What sort of trouble?' Lexie was still not convinced, in spite of her own unease.

'I just come from Rumney in the car. Drove back round Splott and down Adam Street. From the jail down, there's little groups of thugs standing about. That's just not the sort of place where they get together – specially as I recognized half of them as bruisers from down here.'

'If they're up there, I can't see why you'm worried. Maybe there's going to be trouble up Splott.'

'Grow up, Lex, it's dead as a doornail up there! No, they can't be waiting for someone coming out of the prison. They don't let people out this time of day. But they just might be waiting for somebody on their way back here from Newport. . .'

Lily gave a gasp of dismay. 'Oh, God, the outing! They'll be coming back along there!'

Suspicion flared in Rhys's eyes. 'What outing?'

She told him about Bet and her cronies in their two
horse brakes. Before she could finish what she was saying, he broke in. 'Jesus Christ almighty – the bastards
are going to move in and cut 'em up, then take their
old patch back!' He remembered the shutters, which
he had neglected while he talked to the girls. 'Come
on, get moving. The whole of Bute Street will go up
like a powder keg once it do start.'

Within twenty minutes the breakable stock was
stowed in the cellar and the pub was securely locked.
Joe had arrived while they were working and Rhys had
promptly sent him away again. 'And if I was you I'd stay
indoors till the morning, Joe,' was his parting shot.

'I think somebody up City Hall do know about it,
Dad,' Lexie said after a while. She told him about the
unnecessary policeman on East Canal Wharf.

'Hmm. . .it do certainly sound like it. Not that it'll do
Bet and her crowd any good. Nobody'll have told them.
They'll drive right into it.'

They thought that over in silence for a while, then
Lexie said, 'She's a friend of ours, Dad. We probably
know most of the rest of 'em, an' all. You know she'd
warn us if we was in a scrape like this.'

'Yeah, I know. . .I been thinking that. I wouldn't
know how to face her if they got hurt.'

'If half what you've said about that mob is true, you
probably won't have to face her – she'll be in the cemetery!'

He stood up. 'You're right, flower. I should have
gone the minute Lily said what was up. I'll get the
car out and go back the way I come, see if I can get
to them before they comes into the city. Better go up
St Mary Street and Queen Street in case any of the
gangs recognize me as I go by.'

'No – you might miss them,' said Lily. 'Last thing Bet
said was that she'd see me later because they had to be

back for this evening. They must have been planning to get back any time from now. . . They'll probably be in Jail Lane or Moira Street already.'

'Oh, Christ, I better risk that back way then,' said Rhys. 'Look, just in case – bugger it, why did I send Joe home? – just in case I don't turn up again, leave it an hour after I've gone and then if it's still this quiet, go down Bute Street police station and tell the desk sergeant what have happened. After that, don't stir from there unless he gives you a copper to bring you back. And I want the two of you to go down together, not one alone, all right?'

He was ready to go, now, but seemed loath to leave them. An awkward silence fell on the trio, then Lexie said, 'Dad – why don't you take us with you? I don't want you going by yourself, and you don't like us being here by ourselves. . .'

'No! If they do see you and manage to get hold of you, I don't even want to think about what they'll do. They'm not going to be stopping tonight to ask if coloureds was born in the Bay.'

'You know they ent after girls, Dad, black or white. It's the fellas they'll go for.'

He sighed heavily. 'I wish I could believe that, love, but I've seen enough of this in the past. When they'm running in a mob like that, once they gets the taste of blood they'll go after anybody. I can't take the risk. . .I'm not even happy about the pair of you staying here on your own, and you're a bloody sight safer locked in here than you would be out on the streets. Now, do as you'm told. I'm off.'

Lexie's pleas seemed to give him the initiative to make a move. He bent to kiss each of them in turn, then left. Moments later, they heard the car moving out of the stable yard. After that, the eerie silence outside was unbroken.

*

By half past seven, Lexie was frantic. 'It's no good, Lil, I can't wait no longer. He could have got to St Mellons and back by now. Something must have gone wrong.'

Lily was equally apprehensive. 'Come on, then,' she said. 'Change into something a bit less noticeable than that frock, just in case.'

Lexie was over-wrought and flared up immediately. 'Afraid somebody'll notice me more 'cos I'm a black all dressed up like a rich white girl?'

Lily refused to rise to the bait. Instead she put her arms round Lexie, giving her a little shake as she did so. 'Don't be so bloody soft! You know better than that. I expect I'd be just as bad, if I'd had to put up with what have been going on lately. Come on, change into an everyday dress like mine. You know very well what I mean.'

Lexie laughed shakily. 'Aye, I'm sorry. Oh, Lil, I never thought I'd live to see the day I'd be ashamed to be coloured, but they'm making me get like that.'

Furious, Lily said, 'Well, now's the time for us to stop them in their tracks, ennit? Come on, let's go and tell the bobbies about Uncle Rhys.'

Fifteen minutes later, dressed in their dowdiest clothes, they were in Bute Street police station, explaining what had happened. The minute they walked in they realized the police already knew something was about to happen. There were twice as many uniformed men in evidence as were normally here at this time. Fortunately for them, the desk sergeant was Gray, the man whose detachment had saved them from the rioting dockers eight years previously.

Now he grinned wryly at them. 'We do only seem to meet up when there's trouble down here. Don't you girls ever know when to keep out of the way?'

'Please, sarge, do something about Dad!' said Lexie.

'He's bull-headed enough to join in if he finds the out-ing and the gangs have got 'em cornered. He won't stand a dog's chance. . .'

The sergeant was pessimistic. 'What can we do, love? We already knew what was up. You can't have missed how tense things have been down here lately. . .might have had plenty of fights anyhow. But this is a lot worse. One of our big men in City Hall have had a tip there's outsiders involved, stirring things up all over the country to try and kick out the foreigners. It do sound as if they'm going to use Cardiff as the rehearsal for a lot more of it, if it do work tonight.'

'But our Dad will be in the middle of it!'

'So will lots of other innocent people, Lexie. Now look, we're just sending out a squad of mounted police to patrol all up as far as Caroline Street and the western end of Bute Terrace. If your dad have got that far, he'll be all right, don't you worry.'

'And if he haven't?'

'Lexie, I can't spare the men. We'll be pushed to the limit keeping the lid on the Bay tonight, without straying outside. I can't even give you anybody to take you back home. You'll be safer staying in here.'

Lily had been silent so far, letting Lexie do the talk-ing. Now she waded in too, eyes blazing. 'Sergeant Gray, Rhys Walters is my second father. I've just lost my real father and I ent seeing this one go without a fight. Now, if you already knew what was up, you'll have a fair idea of where they'm going to make their stand. If you'll be so good as to tell us, we won't waste no more of your time.'

Gray laughed mirthlessly. 'If you do think I'm letting two girls out there unescorted, you can think again.'

'All right then, we'll follow your constables. They won't all be going on horseback.'

He started to come out from behind the desk to

restrain her. Lily backed away from him. It was the
first time Lexie had ever seen anyone backing away
threateningly. 'Touch me and I'll scream the bloody
place down,' Lily warned him. 'And if you think a
drunken Bay tart have got a bell on every tooth, you
wait till I do get going. Now get out the way!'

Gray hesitated, then broke into a resigned laugh. 'All
right, all right,' he said. 'I did my best, anyhow. If any
of them toughs manages to get the better of you two,
I'll be bloody amazed. Get on with you – but please try
not to go too far from one of my men, eh girls?'

They turned to leave, but his parting remark stopped
them: 'P'raps I should tell you. We've been tipped
they'll be coming down East Canal Wharf, not Bute
Street. If anything's going to happen, that's where it'll
be. I got mounted police all up around the monument.
Mind you go careful.'

It was 8.30 by the time they reached the monument, moving unobtrusively behind a pair of mounted
policemen. As they turned from the side street on
to the wharf, Lexie put a restraining hand on Lily's
arm. 'That's far enough, flower,' she whispered. 'Look
across there.'

Around the monument and ranged about in apparently haphazard groups were at least two dozen men.
Lily knew about half of them by sight from the old days
when they had hung around outside the more disrepu-
table dockland pubs. The others were strangers. One
or two of them were wearing soldiers' uniforms, presumably because they had just received their discharge.

'The ones in uniform ent local – don't recognize
none of them,' said Lexie. 'What's the betting they'm
hanging on to them uniforms to come the old soldier
when they'm stirring up trouble. I can just hear them
going on about making this a land fit for heroes!'

After a hasty reconnaissance, the girls found a doorway a few yards back along the street, where they could

hide themselves reasonably well and peep out occasionally to see what was going on. 'Can't see as this'll do our Dad a bit of good,' muttered Lexie. 'But at least we ent back home doing nothing.'

They hung about in the doorway for about fifteen minutes. Butetown was as silent as if it had been evacuated. Then, somewhere far off, a clock struck nine. As the echo of the last chime faded, they heard hoofbeats and the clatter of wheels on the wharf cobbles.

'It must be them!' hissed Lexie. 'And the rate they'm coming, they know what to expect. Either Dad managed to warn 'em or they've been attacked already.'

The two girls stepped out into the street and as they did so, the first horse brake clattered full pelt into the area by the canal bridge. Black Bet was up in the driving seat beside a big muscular Nigerian who was controlling the frightened horses with some difficulty.

'Christ, man, am I glad to see you!' he said to the mounted policeman. 'Get them bastards across the other side of the canal or we're in for trouble!'

As he spoke, the loosely-grouped white men along the wharf began closing ranks and advancing on the waggons. 'Bet, get them girls off the other side,' the Nigerian said. 'Hurry up – no time to do nothing else.'

Bet eyed the gang who advanced on the waggon. 'Fuck that!' she said. 'I ent never run from scum and I'm not starting now. How about you, girls?'

A full-throated roar greeted her from the horse brake, as the women began sliding out of their seats and on to the wharf. Whatever was on their minds, flight seemed to have nothing to do with it.

By now, Lily and Lexie had abandoned their doorway, far too interested in what was happening to consider their own safety. As they emerged from the side street, a braying klaxon sounded from a few yards up the wharf.

'Dad – it's our Dad, he's all right!' screamed Lexie,

and flung herself forward through the crush of people
to find Rhys.

'Lex, for Christ's sake come back!' Lily was beside
herself. She knew as well as Lexie that Rhys was on
the other side of the day trippers, but the gang of
pimps was between them, too, and now Lexie was in
their midst.

'Oh, Lex, what have you done?' she sobbed, stum-
bling towards the eddying mass of bodies, praying her
cousin was unhurt.

At the edge of the crowd she ran into Rhys. Ashen-
faced, trembling, he grabbed Lily's arm and yelled,
'She's in that lot, ent she?'

Lily could only nod. Rhys looked at the tangle of people and turned back to her. 'Don't even think of going
into it,' he said. 'Over there, by that copper – quick!' He
waited until he was sure she was obeying him. As she
reached the policeman, who pushed her behind him
into another shop doorway, she looked back at her
uncle. From his coat pocket he took a set of spiked brass
knuckledusters. He slid them on to his right hand as
though putting on a kid glove, then turned and hurled
himself on the nearest check-coated back he could see
heaving away around the leading horse brake.

By now the policemen had all drawn their truncheons and were yelling to the trippers on the first
horse brake to get back. But half of them had already
dismounted and started fighting with the white pimps.
Then the second waggon arrived and it became clear
that it had stopped somewhere to prepare for the
trouble ahead. The men who got down from it were
well-armed, with iron bars, stout sticks, half bricks and
even a few open razors. One of the uniformed whites
let out an awful scream as a blade sunk deep into his
cheek.

After the first attack, the women had the sense to
move back, taking shelter behind some of the mounted

police. But a pitched battle was in full swing now by the monument, and somewhere at its heart were Rhys and Lexie. Lily, trapped behind her police guard, kept jumping up and down to try and get a look over his shoulder, but she could see nothing. The violence went on unabated for at least ten minutes, and Lily found herself wondering how fictional fights could go on so long. Already, this one seemed to have lasted hours, and there were plenty of people already hurt beyond retaliation, sitting or lying at the fringe of the struggle. The surrounding streets, so silent moments before, had erupted into bedlam, with partisans for both sides either yelling encouragement or joining in the mayhem. As time passed and her family still did not emerge, Lily grew frantic with worry.

Until now, the uproar had been caused by human voices, neighing horses and the clatter of wheels on cobblestones. One sharp, discordant sound cut through all others and temporarily silenced them. Someone fired a revolver. The sound shocked the mob into momentary inaction, and as they froze there was a mighty clatter of breaking glass. The bullet had shattered the window of the York Hotel.

Into the silence, a man's voice cried hoarsely, 'After me, lads! They've fired a house in Millicent Street,' and before the shock of the gunshot had worn off, the white gang streamed away northwards, under the East Canal Bridge towards the splinter of Butetown which protruded above the railway line and behind St Mary Street.

The brawl was over as quickly as it had boiled up. A thick-set man in a bowler hat leaned, groaning, against a bollard on the wharf. A deep razor slash ran down his right cheek and blood poured from it. A couple of people lay unconscious around the monument. The Nigerian pimp and a Sicilian man friend of Bet's were leading away the frightened horses. Already, the tarts

were forgetting their earlier fear and beginning to
compare notes about who had done what to whom.
Lily dodged out from behind her police protector and
came face to face with Rhys.

She gasped and pressed her hand to her mouth to
stop herself crying out, for in his arms he held Lexie,
and she was not moving.

But before she could react further, Rhys grinned
broadly at her. 'I had the bugger as knocked her
down,' he said, 'and when he do wake up he'll need
stitches. She'll be all right, don't worry. He give her a
clip on the jaw – had to, she`was clawing his eyes out –
and she went out like a light.' He paused to redistribute
his daughter's weight. 'She'll have a terrible headache
when she wakes up, but apart from that, I think she's
okay. Christ knows what have happened to the car,
though.'

They found it eventually, completely undamaged.
Rhys had used it as a battering ram to scatter the
white gang when he drove on to the wharf, but
once they started moving they had gone on and concentrated the fight around the horse brake, leaving his
car untouched. He laid Lexie gently across the back
seat and gestured Lily in at the front.

'Sooner we get home the better,' he said. 'Fighting
may be over for us, but it'll go on for days unless something drastic happens to stop it.'

Already, East Canal Wharf was empty. The fighters
from both sides had streamed away down the warren of
back lanes, pursued by police whose main concern was
to drive them off rather than force another confrontation. Now an uneasy peace was settling over Butetown,
but Lily did not need Rhys to tell her it was only temporary.

CHAPTER TWENTY-FOUR

T HIS TIME THERE was no hero locked in the City Hall cells who could emerge and defuse the riots. The rabble-rousers remained anonymous and free and the trouble surged on through Butetown for four days. By then, several houses had been burned to the ground and – previously unknown in dockland troubles – there had been numerous deaths. After the first shock attacks, the coloured population retaliated by arming itself and fighting back ferociously. The police watched helplessly each time as the trouble surged back only minutes after they had cleared the latest outbreaks of violence.

The two bridges at the top end of Butetown were the crucial strategic points. They separated the rough end of Cardiff from the more genteel sections, and there was a tacit conspiracy to spare the city's residential areas from troubles the authorities saw as belonging solely to dockland. By the fourth day, James Fraser, the police inspector in charge of the operation, split a detachment of mounted officers between Bute Street Bridge and East Canal Bridge. Below them, throughout Butetown, the main thoroughfares were in chaos, with people thronging the streets to find out what was going on, and individual quarrels flaring in seconds into full-blown physical violence. The gangs of agitators who had started the unrest mingled with the residents, egging them on to indulge pent-up resentments. The coloured population kept its head, relying on police protection whenever possible but well-armed and ready for confrontation when trouble broke out in isolated pockets.

After setting up his mounted detachment, Fraser dispatched foot patrols to warn people that if they were in the streets when violence broke out, they would be mown down indiscriminately. At first, few bothered to listen. Over the years they had come to see the dockland force as part of the community, not as a disciplinary body which could dictate their behaviour, and they were sceptical now about their chances of being hurt.

Shortly before noon, separate fights on Canal Street and Bute Street grew spontaneously to riotous proportions. One of the few shop windows left unshuttered on Bute Street was smashed by a half-brick intended for an antagonist's head. On Canal Street, the minor incident erupted into something worse when a Senegalese was thrown into the oily water by three white pimps.

At that moment, Tiger Bay was introduced to a different police force than the one it had known before. Whistles blew, there were two shouted commands, and the mounted detachments, hooves and night sticks flying, descended on hundreds of people, bent on driving them off the streets. The crowds of idlers who had been there merely as spectators were gone in seconds. The hardened rioters took longer to clear, but once a few ringleaders had been cut out and arrested, they, too, broke and ran. By one o'clock an uneasy peace had descended again.

But it was short-lived. By late afternoon, the arrested gang leaders were replaced by others. Yet another house was fired in Hannah Street. Then the inspector received news that two black people unconnected with Butetown had been attacked by another white gang as they got off a train at the General station. It put an end to Fraser's patience. He called in the army, and within the hour his mounted detachment was replaced by a pair of machine gun patrols, with one gun mounted on each of the two bridges, pointing down the main dockland streets. Soldiers patrolled the top end of Bute Street and East Canal Wharf. There was something far more believable about the retaliatory power of a rifle or bayonet than that of a police truncheon.

After that the end was in sight. Even the most violent agitators recognized they had no chance against machine guns. Gradually the Bay drifted back towards normality, with only the shells of burnt-out buildings and a scattering of incurable personal resentments to indicate anything had happened.

It made a permanent difference to Lexie Walters. Her only physical injury on the night of the first riots had been a bruised jaw, but the spiritual hurt went far deeper. The new Lexie was morose and listless, drifting about the upstairs living quarters over the Anglesey but seldom bothering to go out, or even downstairs. Lily hoped the girl would recover her old liveliness and concentrated on filling in for her in the bar until such time as she might feel better.

About a week after the riots petered out, Lily went upstairs to eat her mid-day meal after a morning's work, and found Lexie transformed. For a moment, Lily's spirits leaped. Then she realized what her cousin was doing. She was dressed in her newest, most flamboyant outfit and she was packing her bags.

'Lexie, what's happening? I didn't know you were going anywhere.'

Lexie looked sheepish. 'I – I didn't seem to be able to tell you,' she said. 'It's no good, Lil, I can't stay here any longer. I was getting edgy before, you know that, but after this. . .'

'But where will you go? What will you do?'

Lexie laughed and waved a hand dismissively. 'Don't worry your head about that, love! It's all fixed up. That's what I been waiting for. I was up town seeing somebody about that the day all this rotten business started. . .meant to tell you about it that evening, but everything got on top of us, didn't it?'

Lily nodded. 'What about Uncle Rhys? You haven't told him – he could never have kept it to himself. He'll go mad when you do.'

'I know. I been really scared about that. . . Oh, Lily, I love him more than anybody else, even more than you, but he must see there ent nothing for me here, mustn't he?'

'He might understand it, Lex, but he won't want to let you go. And what are you going to? That's what'll really make the difference.'

Her dismissive attitude returned. 'Oh, I don't s'pose you remember the Haggars, do you? They was that boy and girl we met, trying to film the crowds at City Hall that time.'

'Of course I remember. I often wondered why you'd never tried to see them again.'

Lexie grinned. 'I did. It took me years, mind, but in the end I plucked up a bit of courage and wrote. They hadn't come on to me again because they've got out of the picture-making business, ages ago. They do run a chain of cinemas now. Their dad's called William Haggar. He was the one as started the film shows. He's retired now, lives in Aberdare, but he've still got lots of friends in the movie business, and some of them want to use me!'

Innate good sense warned Lily that such instant demand was highly unlikely. 'As what?' she asked.

Lexie was almost euphoric now. 'Meet Dolores Herero, the Latin spitfire!' she declaimed.

'The what? But you're not Spanish!'

Her cousin glared at her. 'And the films ent taking on pretty little black girls, neither, except as nigger slaves in plantation movies. From now on, I'm Spanish, all right?'

'It's your life, Lex, but if Uncle Rhys do let you out through that front door on the strength of that, I'll be surprised.'

'Sorry to disappoint you, Lily, but somehow I don't think I've got any choice – have I, Lex?'

Neither of them had noticed Rhys standing at the living-room door. Now Lexie uttered a squeak of alarm and turned to him, aghast. 'Oh, Dad – I didn't see you there. . . I didn't want you to find out like this!'

'If you could have done it any other way, I don't think you'd have wanted me to find out at all, kidda.' Rhys looked weary. He seemed to have aged years since Lily had seen him downstairs only half an hour ago. Now both girls held their breath, awaiting the tidal wave of his wrath.

It never came. Rhys merely sighed and came into the room, closing the door behind him. 'Stop looking so bloody scared, girl. Anyone'd think I'd taken a strap to you every time you did something I didn't like. . . I ent going to make no fuss. Your life's your own. Just go careful, that's all. I never heard of them paying a kid from Tiger Bay to act Spanish.'

'It'll just be little parts at first, Dad. Everyone have got to start somewhere. . .but d'you really mean you won't make a fuss?'

'You'm a silly little bitch at times, Lex. 'Course I won't. You and Lily's the only two people I care very much about, and I'm not daft enough to think I'll make either of you care any more about me if I try to hang on to you too long. Go with my blessing – and a bit of my money till you get on your feet. Just promise me one thing.'

Lexie's eyes were shining as the full realization hit

her that he would not make things difficult. 'Anything you like, Dad.'

'If it don't work out, no false pride. Come back here to me. It's still your home, even if you've gone off it a bit now. There'll always be something else you can do.'

Lexie laughed, optimism taking over. 'Oh, I'll promise you that all right, Dad, but I ent going to fail. A couple of years from now I'll be making movies in America, you just watch!' She glanced at the clock on the mantelpiece. 'Hell, look at the time! I told these people I'd be ready to catch the two o'clock train.'

'These people, Lex, or this man?' Rhys did not sound angry, only wary.

She blushed. 'Yeah, all right. . .this man. . .but it ent what it do sound!'

Rhys smiled at her, attempting to look reassured. ''Course it ent, Lexie – not yet, anyhow. Just remember I was never too strong on best behaviour. There's nothing you need to hide from me. All right?'

'Right, Dad. In that case, how would you like to take me up to the station?'

He crossed the room and buried her in a bear hug. 'Oh, Christ, flower, I'm going to miss you – but I'd never try and keep you where you wasn't happy. We'll both come up the station with you.'

'N-no, that's all right,' said Lily, unable to account for her own reluctance. 'I'm terrible at saying goodbye to people going on trains. Rather do it here. You two go together and have a few minutes in private. I'll see to the bar till you come back, Uncle Rhys.'

'All right, Lily. Thanks. I'll go back down now till you'm ready, Lex. You got plenty of time.' He left the girls together.

Once he was gone, Lily turned awkwardly to Lexie. 'Was it really true, what you said to him about this man, just – just being business?'

Lexie's old flirtatious smile curved her pretty mouth. 'Well, yes and no. . .it is now, but he've got a lovely pair of shoulders on him, and he dresses ever so smart. Depends on his approach on the way to London, don't it?'

Lily laughed, powerless to disapprove of her cousin. 'Oh, Lex, you'll come to a bad end one day, but I bet you'll enjoy yourself on your way to it!'

She helped Lexie to finish her packing, then embraced and kissed her tearfully at the door. 'You promise you'll send your address as soon as you've settled in? I don't want you losing touch, mind.'

'Promise. I'd give it you now if I knew myself. But Bertie – that's this agent, Bertie Shaw – Bertie do say he'll book me into these theatrical digs he knows as soon as we get there. Haven't made up my mind if I believe him yet!' And with a last flurry of giggles and kisses, she was gone.

It was strange, lying alone that night in the big bed she had always shared with Lexie. Where would Lexie be tonight, curled up in some cramped little bedroom in theatrical digs? *Silly bitch as you are, of course not!* It might have been Lexie saying the words inside her head. No, if she knew her cousin, the girl would be installed somewhere comfortable and expensive – and she wouldn't be sleeping on her own, either. The night wore on and sleep continued to elude Lily. In the end she stopped seeking it, put the light on and went to make herself a cup of tea. Rhys was already in the kitchen.

'Uncle Rhys! It's nearly three o'clock! What're you doing up at this hour?'

'Same as you, love, I 'xpect. There's a hell of a draught without Lexie about, ent there?'

'Yes. I couldn't sleep. I was going to make some tea. . .'

'Help yourself. Fresh pot just made. And there's a bottle of whisky open by the side of it. You look as if you need it as much as I do.'

She added a shot of whisky to the tea, then went to sit opposite him at the table. She made much of straightening her cup and saucer precisely in front of her, avoiding his intent gaze apparently by accident. As the short silence grew longer, Rhys said, 'It's all right, no need to worry. I know you'm going, too.'

She glanced up, to find him smiling quizzically at her. 'Didn't know yourself till you come out here, did you? I did. . .knew you'd be going home before I realized our Lexie was off.'

'But how? I don't think I've even considered it until tonight. I admit I've been lying in there for hours, realizing how much I miss Abercarn, but I hadn't really been thinking of going back there. . .'

'Truth to tell, love, I don't think you really left there, this time round. You needed to get away for a bit, but that's where your roots are now, even if you did spend five years down the Bay when you was a kid.'

'It's funny, Uncle Rhys, all the time I was in Abercarn, after George was killed, I kept thinking, this place isn't for me, it do destroy everything. All I wanted was to be back with you and Lex, and work behind the bar, and forget the Valleys and the pits and all that misery. But then when I did come back, I started seeing for the first time that you and Lex belonged down here and I didn't.'

'Lexie don't seem to think she belongs down here any more.'

'Oh, you know as well as I do that'll pass! Fathers like you aren't easy to come by. When her dream doesn't work out, she'll come home – and what's more, I think she'll be happy down here, once she's been out in the world for a while.'

'Aye, maybe you're right. It's going to be a bit of a

rough wait for me while she's sowing her wild oats, though, ennit?'

'Nobody can help you there, you'll just have to sweat it out. But d'you think I've got any chance at all of settling down if I go back to Abercarn? I'm beginning to wonder if I'll ever fit in anywhere.'

Rhys reached out and took her hand. 'Why have you been thinking it may help you to go?'

'Mam, for a start. I've been thinking about her a lot, lately, thinking about the rotten time she must have had. We all thought our Dad was such a hero, we never really considered her feelings at all. Nothing was ever said, but I think we all assumed she'd, sort of, driven him to all the bad things he did.'

'And now you don't think she did?'

'Maybe – but have you ever thought that p'raps he'd have been a lot worse without her? There's two sides to every story. She never got much out of it, did she? A lifetime of having babies and scrubbing other people's dirty sheets, and then knowing he was off up the Rhymney Valley with his bit of spare and two of her own sons all those years.'

Rhys bridled at that. 'I'd hardly call Ellen Rourke a bit of spare, Lil. She was more than that – a lot more.'

'P'raps she was, but not from Mam's point of view. No, Mam can be a bit of a bully when she gets going, but she's never had much chance of happiness. Maybe, if I go back now, I can make it better for us both.'

'Careful, Lil, you'm too pretty by far to end up as the spinster daughter looking after her old widow mother until she's too dried up for anything else. If that's your only reason for going back, it's a bad one.'

She blushed and looked down at her hands. 'I-it's not that on its own, no. There's ever such a nice man – not that he shows any real interest in me beyond friendship, mind – said he hoped I'd come home soon, because he missed me. . .'

'Is there, now?' Rhys gave a heavy sigh. 'I got a feeling I'll think this is just as bad as going back for your mam. He's a collier, I s'pose?'

'Oh, no! No, he's the village doctor.'

Rhys brightened perceptibly. 'Now that, our kid, is more like it. Let's get a bit of real class in the family. God knows, it's about time. If that's the way the wind is blowing, I'll get the old motor out at the end of the week, and take you back home myself. How about that?'

She raised his hand from the table top and kissed it. 'Thanks anyway, but no. You know how scratchy Mam gets when you go anywhere near her. . .she can't help it. For her it must be like seeing Dad the way he'd have been if he'd got away from her. Must be maddening! No, I'll write to her tomorrow, ask if she wants me back. If she does, I'll catch the train home Saturday afternoon, unless that's bad for you.'

'Any time you go will be bad for me, Lily,' he said sombrely. 'But one time's no worse than another. Don't you worry about me. I'll be fixed up with a cuddly little housekeeper before you can turn round. Now that'd really give Margaret Ann food for thought, wouldn't it?'

Lily finished her tea and stood up to go back to bed. 'D'you think I'll fit in back there, Uncle Rhys?'

''Course you will,' he said. 'But I wouldn't half like to be a fly on the wall when you do lose your temper and start using Bay language, or see the faces on your mam's chapel sisterhood crowd when you lace your tea with whisky. Thing about you now, Lil, is you look just like a lady, but there's something else there as well, something special.'

Flattered, she fished for the rest of the compliment. 'What can that be?'

He grinned wickedly. 'There's a gorgeous Tiger Bay tart inside, fighting to get out. God help Abercarn if she do ever escape!'

After dinner on Saturday afternoon, the boys went out to play rugby. Angharad was off somewhere with her friends. Margaret Ann went into the parlour and took the great leather-bound family Bible from its shelf. Back in the kitchen, she opened it and looked at the special family register pages before the text, laid out with fancy borders for photographs and blank lines for details of date of birth, name and marriage details of each generation. She had filled in all the information in her best handwriting, but the picture borders had remained empty. When the time came, there had never been enough money to have photographs taken of the children. The snapshots that had been taken since reflected a reality too far from Margaret Ann's girlhood dreams of how her family would look. They showed children with darned clothes and dirty faces, scuffed boots and grazed knees. No, better to leave the frames unfilled, and daydream about them on the basis of the written details instead.

She patted the smooth page, as if caressing an old friend. 'Well, you are my friend really,' she said aloud. 'Never had another one, not since poor old Jenny Job. You'm always there, ent you?' And she began turning the familiar, well-worn pages.

Apparently by accident, the heavy paper slipped through her hands and stopped, treacherously, at the second chapter of the Song of Songs. The words leaped from the page at her and she was blinded by tears. But she did not need to be able to see the text. She had known the words by heart for thirty years, ever since Evan had said them to her on their wedding night:

Behold, thou art fair, my love, behold thou art fair; thou hast doves' eyes. . .

Pain and pleasure mingled in her memory and weeks of broken sleep caught up with her. She slipped down in her high-backed chair as drowsiness took her.

Momentarily, she tried to hang on to wakefulness, but was too sleepy now to remember why she should. The warm depths took her and the wonderful words of the ancient poem rolled on through her dreams.

Thy lips, oh my spouse, drop as the honeycomb: honey and milk are under thy tongue. . .

There were tears in that. She stirred, starting to get uneasy now; something there, something sad. . .not the loss. . .that had to come some time, no. . .in the Song. . .

Take us the foxes, the little foxes, that spoil the grapes: for our vines have tender grapes. . .

. . . Yes, that was it. . .foxes, robbing the vineyard. . .her vineyard, so carefully tended. . .laying it waste. . .

She was twisting in her chair now, still asleep, exhausted from so many months of grieving. The tears were flowing from beneath her closed eyelids. So painful. . .why did love hurt so. . .why were the good things spoiled. . .no, not always. . . There was more than that. What about those earlier parts, his favourites?

I am the Rose of Sharon, the Lily of the Valleys. . .

Lily. . .yes Lily, that was it. Lily was worth all the pain. . .but she wasn't here, oh God, where was she?

Down, down further into sleep, but someone was stopping her, pulling her back. . .the foxes, the little foxes. . .

But there were no foxes. It was Lily. Lily standing over her, concern all over her face, touching her gently to try and waken her. . . Margaret Ann started surfacing from her slumber, a final fleeting impression in her mind that it was Evan, alive, young and vigorous again, standing in front of her, loving her. . . She awoke, the final words of her reverie trickling contentedly from her lips:

Rise up, my love, my fair one, and come away. For lo, the winter is past, the rain is over and gone. . .

'Lily, my darling Lily, you've come back!' She was smiling like a child on Christmas morning.

'Of course I have, Mam! You knew I was coming on the three o'clock train. Are you all right?'

'I'll be all right now. Everything will be all right now. You're not going back to Cardiff, are you?'

'No, Mam. I'm home to stay. You rest there a minute and I'll make us some tea. Then maybe we'll go for a little walk. It's a beautiful afternoon. How would you like that?'

'I'd like that better than anything, Lily.' She touched the lovely face, so familiar, so like Evan's in his beautiful, careless youth. '. . . Better than anything, my love.'

MUMMY'S BOY

William Paul

'He held the phial in a cupped palm and tossed it a few inches in the air. His mother's laughter echoed in his ears. He had no need to be frightened, she told him. Not her only son.'

Moments later, the first steps were taken on a bizarre odyssey of revenge: a peaceful pub was transformed into a hecatomb. Innocent, unsuspecting people died a filthy degrading death. Clive Quinn was erecting a monument to his mother.

He himself had killed her. It was no tragedy – she was in great pain and already close to death. But his sense of guilt was only added to the debt the world must pay. And over a horrifying ten days he extracted that payment in an orgy of mayhem and destruction, the more terrifying for its apparent randomness. Governments trembled, powerful men went in fear, the very fabric of society was at risk.

And still Clive was not satisfied. There was more – much more – to come before his mother could rest in peace . . .

'A strong psychological tale, vividly written, depressingly believable in its horrific details' *The Times*

'Well plotted . . . very entertaining . . . moves at breath-taking pace' *Independent*

Also from Futura

SEASONS OF REVENGE

FUTURA PUBLICATIONS
FICTION/THRILLER
0 7088 3668 2

SUMMER HARVEST

Madge Swindells

'a spellbinding read' Sarah Harrison

Set between 1938 and 1968 in a land where gruelling poverty rubs shoulders with remarkable opulence, and moving from the Cape to London and the West Coast of America, SUMMER HARVEST is a family saga in the finest tradition.

At the heart of the story is Anna, a woman as strong and passionate as she is ambitious, who fights her way up from near destitution to become one of the Cape's most prominent and powerful businesswomen. Only love eludes her. For Simon – a poor farmer when they marry – has too much masculine pride to stand on the sidelines while Anna plunders her way to a success that threatens tragedy and loss.

'Anna van Achtenburgh mirrors the strengths and the weaknesses of her beautiful, harsh country; the toughness, the dazzling material success, the moral dilemmas, the tragedy. I was gripped from start to finish.'
Kate Alexander, author of *Fields of Battle*

FUTURA PULICATIONS
FICTION
0 7088 2528 1

THE LADY

'The irresistible saga' *She*

Alan Stratton
bestselling author of THE EMPIRE BUILDERS

THE LADY is Gina Rossi: warm, spirited and beautiful – but her young life is blighted by tragedy. A refugee from fascist Italy, struggling to protect her young brother and sister among the teeming millions of New York in the slump, she nurtures two burning ambitions. One will make her; the other could destroy her.

THE LADY is the dream Gina shared with her father: the most fashionable restaurant in New York, her passport to wealth, fame and security. But within her burns a lust – for revenge. And that lust could lose her everything: her love, her dreams and all she holds dear.

THE LADY
a magnificent rags-to-riches saga of love, ambition and revenge, sweeping from Rome to New York, from war-torn London to the birth of Las Vegas, and starring an unforgettable heroine.

'Splendid' *Annabel*

Also by Alan Stratton in Futura
**THE EMPIRE BUILDERS
THE HUNTERS
THE PEDDLERS**

FUTURA PUBLICATIONS
FICTION
0 7088 3158 3

BELINDA

Anne Rice
writing as Anne Rampling

A Lolita for the Eighties by the author of
EXIT TO EDEN

Jeremy Walker is 44, handsome, refined and world famous for his lavishly illustrated children's books. His life is ordered, comfortable – until he is seduced by a beautiful and precocious 16-year-old runaway. Belinda: innocent yet passionate, she becomes his elegant muse and lover. His portraits of her, shocking and erotic, are the finest work he has ever done – yet to reveal them could destroy his career for ever.

As his passion for her deepens, so does his obsession with the past she will not talk about. Terrified of losing her, he is unable to live with her silence; and as he probes for the truth, he finds himself swept up in the world Belinda has fled from, a world of Hollywood money, lust and dark family secrets.

BELINDA

A dazzling, erotic story, racing from the stylish world of San Francisco to the luxurious mansions of Beverly Hills and the sun-drenched beaches of a Greek island paradise.

FUTURA PUBLICATIONS
FICTION
0 7088 3580 5

THE HEAVEN TREE

Edith Pargeter

England in the reign of King John – a time of beauty and squalor, of swift treachery and unswerving loyalty. Against this violent, exciting background the story of Harry Talvace, master mason, unfolds.

Harry and his foster-brother Adam tasted injustice young and together fled to Paris, where Harry's genius for carving drew him into friendship with the enigmatic Ralf Isambard, Lord of Parfois, and the incomparably beautiful Madonna Benedetta, a Venetian courtesan. In their company he returned to his native Shropshire to build a church for Isambard beside Parfois Castle. Soaring heavenwards, the tree of stone became an arrow of light: but as it flowered, darkening shadows presaged jealous, pitiless revenge – and death.

'If you do not appreciate this superb novel, I despair of you' *Illustrated London News*

'The glamour and adventure of medieval life is there, the colour and squalor, the songs of the students and the groans of the oppressed, but at the centre of the story is this man, the work of whose hands will stand for centuries as a monument to the idealist who could be banished, tortured and destroyed but never defeated . . . Beside this dramatic and intense book almost any other historical novel would appear banal.'
Rosaleen Whatley, *Liverpool Daily Post*

'a rattling good story' *Tribune*

FUTURA PUBLICATIONS
FICTION
0 7088 3056 0

THE WHITE EARTH

Norman Sharam

1949. The world is on the move, a fact hardly noticed in Ridstone, nestling among the chalk downs of the West Country, under the benign gaze of the neolithic White Dog.

Until John Ridd makes them see it. He's young, ambitious, sexy; his past is murky, his future as an entrepreneur is bright. Cars and the squire's daughter are the ambitions that drive him. A hard man in a soft society, there seems no reason why he shouldn't achieve both – and enjoy his aristocratic mistress on the side.

But the old order, though dying, is not yet dead, and even a soft society will fight viciously in self-defence . . .

THE WHITE EARTH

the masterly epic of a new social order, a new brand of business, a new taste in loving – and of a new kind of man, big enough to encompass it all.

FUTURA PUBLICATIONS
FICTION
0 7088 3280 6

AN INDECENT OBSESSION

Colleen McCullough

THE THORN BIRDS was an international bestseller on a greater scale than any other novel of the last ten years. Now, in AN INDECENT OBSESSION, Colleen McCullough repeats that success with the moving story of a young woman caught up in the tearing conflict of love and duty.

The dutiful and disciplined Sister Honour Langtry has sole charge of Ward X of a military hospital in the Pacific, where she cares for soldiers who have gone 'troppo' and are battle fatigued. War with Japan has only been over a few days when into this intense, confined world comes a new patient, Sergeant Michael Wilson. Immediately, his arrival transforms Ward X into a pressure cooker of emotion leading inexorably to tragedy for Sister Honour Langtry as she is torn between her obligation to all her patients and her love for one of them.

FUTURA PUBLICATIONS
FICTION
0 7088 2124 3

All Futura Books are available at your bookshop or
newsagent, or can be ordered from the following address:
Futura Books, Cash Sales Department,
P.O. Box 11, Falmouth, Cornwall TR10 9EN.

Please send cheque or postal order (no currency), and
allow 60p for postage and packing for the first book
plus 25p for the second book and 15p for each additional
book ordered up to a maximum charge of £1.90 in U.K.

B.F.P.O. customers please allow 60p for
the first book, 25p for the second book plus 15p per
copy for the next 7 books, thereafter 9p per book

Overseas customers, including Eire, please allow £1.25
for postage and packing for the first book, 75p for the
second book and 28p for each subsequent title ordered.